"Trust me. We're perfect together. I'll give you everything you could ever want." At that moment he truly meant what he said, but then his understanding of her potential desires was more limited than he could possibly have guessed. He envisioned dazzling her with his lovemaking, swathing her in furs and adorning her with jewels. She would live surrounded by wealth and power, wanting for nothing. What more could any woman possibly ask?

"Say yes," he demanded as his hands wandered down her back to encounter the swell of her bustle and train. His lips caressed the swell of her breasts.

Liquid fire darted through Elizabeth. Instinctively she arched closer to Drake. What had always before been a shadowy reality safely enfolded in some future time was suddenly vividly immediate. For the first time she was forced to explicitly think of what it would mean to lie with a man, this man. To be possessed was a frightening prospect, yet it beckoned irresistibly to a primitive part of herself that would not be denied.

"Through her rare ability to create 'living history,' Maura Seger exquisitely illuminates the present with the heart and soul of the past."
—*Romantic Times*

SCOTT CORNER
12 SCOTT ADAM ROAD
COCKEYSVILLE, MD 21030

Elizabeth

MAURA SEGER

WORLDWIDE®

TORONTO • NEW YORK • LONDON • PARIS
AMSTERDAM • STOCKHOLM • HAMBURG
ATHENS • MILAN • TOKYO • SYDNEY

ELIZABETH

A Worldwide Library Book/December 1987

ISBN 0-373-97048-X

Copyright © 1987 by Maura Seger. All rights reserved.
Philippine copyright 1987. Australian copyright 1987.
Except for use in any review, the reproduction or utilization of
this work in whole or in part in any form by any electronic,
mechanical or other means, now known or hereafter invented,
including xerography, photocopying and recording, or in any
information storage or retrieval system, is forbidden without
the permission of the publisher, Worldwide Library,
225 Duncan Mill Road, Don Mills, Ontario, Canada M3B 3K9.

All the characters in this book have no existence outside the
imagination of the author and have no relation whatsoever to
anyone bearing the same name or names. They are not even
distantly inspired by any individual known or unknown to the
author, and all incidents are pure invention.

® are Trademarks registered in the United States Patent and
Trademark Office and in other countries.

Printed in U.S.A.

For Mappy Tavara.
In appreciation of her endless
kindness and patience.

_____ *Child*

ELIZABETH CALVERT'S earliest memory was of a tall, thin man in a tattered gray uniform coming to the door of the kitchen and asking her mother if she could spare something to eat. He said little as he wolfed down a plate of stew. Afterward he and her mother talked, and the man offered to stay awhile to help with the chores.

Elizabeth could never remember if he had stayed or not. She only knew that in that summer of her third year there was a seemingly endless stream of exhausted, hungry men, who found their way up the long gravel drive to Calvert Oaks and knocked at the kitchen door. No matter how many came, her mother managed to find a smile and a plate of food for them, though often, as Sarah Calvert watched them make their weary way back down the road, her daughter saw tears in her eyes.

"Don't cry, Momma," she would say then, lifting her chubby arms so that her mother would bend down and she could put them around her shoulders. "Please don't cry."

"It's just dust in my eye, poppet," Sarah would say. "That's all. Such a dry and dusty summer we're having."

Later, after all the work in the kitchen was done, the laundry washed and the big house cleaned, they would sit on the veranda and wait for Elizabeth's father to come home from the fields. That was Elizabeth's favorite time, sitting on her mother's lap in the rattan rocking chair, listening to her croon lullabies and waiting for her father to come up the road. When he did, she would run to him, and no matter how tired he was, he would swing her up in his one good arm and make her squeal with pleasure.

Her father was the handsomest man in the world, just as her mother was the prettiest lady. Once they had gone to wonderful parties, worn beautiful clothes and laughed a lot with all the other people who had lived in the big houses along the James River. Then something called the War had come and the parties had stopped. Now many of the houses were no more than burned-out shells, and many of the people were mere names on gravestones.

"The Yankees killed them," her half brother, William, told her. He was eight years older than Elizabeth, and she could not remember a time when she hadn't idolized him.

"Does that mean the Yankees are bad?" she asked. It was another year, another memory. She must have been about five, because her Great-aunt Louise had died not long before, and Elizabeth still missed her badly. She and William were sitting on the picket fence near a pasture where a few horses grazed. The scene stuck in her mind, because William's answer was very important to her. She knew that her mother had come from the North and that they still had family there, including her Uncle Nathan, who had come to visit and brought Elizabeth a doll with blond hair and blue porcelain eyes, which she cherished.

"No," William said finally, after giving the matter some thought. "Least, not all Yankees. It was a war, you see, and in a war people get killed."

"But not Momma or Poppa." That was self-evident, since they were both very much alive, but she needed the reassurance of hearing William say that they had always been safe.

Instead, William's old/young face, next in handsomeness to her father's, darkened. "Poppa almost got killed, at a place called Antietam. That's where he lost his arm."

So the Yankees had tried to kill her father but had only gotten his arm instead. That was bad enough. Maybe she should hate the Yankees, as so many people seemed to, except that whenever she thought of that she would remember Uncle Nathan and someone named Mari, whom her mother spoke of with fondness, and the impulse to hate would erode in confusion.

When Elizabeth was eight, her grandfather in the North was taken ill. A rider came to the door with a telegram from the same Mari of fond memory, who it turned out was Grandfather Mackenzie's second wife. Elizabeth's mother cried when she read the news. Her father put his arms around her, and together they went up the stairs to the bedroom they shared. It was several hours before they came down again.

Over supper that night, Philip Calvert said to his wife, "I think you should go."

Sarah demurred. "It's too expensive. Besides, there's so much to be done here."

"You could take Bethie with you. It's time she saw something of the North."

Across the table, they exchanged a glance, that Elizabeth already knew meant more than words. Her mother and father could communicate with a touch, a look, a smile. For a long time, she had thought all married people could do that. It had come as a shock to discover that was not the case.

Sarah shook her head. "The money..."

"We'll find it," Philip assured her. "Now that the mill is operating again, things are easier."

"Speaking of the mill," Sarah said, "I wonder what Father intends."

"You'll find out in Boston."

So it was settled. They would leave Calvert Oaks and go north, to where the Yankees were. Elizabeth was both excited and filled with dread. The farthest she had ever been from home was Richmond, and she had only gone there once. Of the wider world beyond, she knew nothing except what was in the books over which she struggled several hours each day.

"I wish you were coming with us," she said to William the next morning, when preparations for their departure were already under way. Mammy Augusta was upstairs helping her mother pack, while old Uncle Rameses was in the stables, spiffying up the carriage that would take them as far as the railroad station.

"Ain't goin' in no wagon," he had said as he went off about his self-imposed task. "Goin' in style, lahk in de old days."

"I wish I was, too," William said. "But Father needs me here."

That was true enough. At sixteen, William was as tall and broad-shouldered as many men. Accustomed to responsibility from an early age, he had a maturity about him that made him seem older than his years. Once Elizabeth had heard her father say to her mother that he worried William was growing up too fast because the War had robbed him of his childhood.

The War was always finding its way into conversations. Her parents talked about it far less than most, but even they seemed to mark time from its beginning and its end, as though whatever there had been before had vanished so completely that it could barely be remembered. She wondered if people up north spoke of it the same way.

Early the next morning, as the eastern sky was turning red with the first hints of the hot day to come, they set out for the station. Sarah wore a gray silk dress her daughter had never seen before, with a high-necked collar trimmed with lace, and a wide skirt. Her chestnut hair was put up in a neat chignon beneath a straw bonnet decorated with dried flowers and a satin ribbon. There was white lace at her wrists, and she wore a pair of white cotton gloves. An ivory cameo broach nestled at her throat, and there were small pearl earrings peeking from beneath the curve of her hair.

She looked as elegant as any of the pictures Elizabeth had seen in the old fashion magazines stored up in the attic. She fervently wished that she might have a dress like that instead of the sensible navy-blue skirt and white blouse that were the proper attire for girls her age. She wished her hair had the rich gleam of her mother's, instead of being what she persisted in thinking of as a dirty blond. Most of all, she wished that she didn't always feel so clumsy and awkward, cursed by long legs that made her taller than every boy her age.

By contrast, her mother was everything Elizabeth imagined a woman should be, yet as impressed as she was by her mother's appearance, she almost burst with pride when she looked at her father. She was used to seeing him in plain cotton shirts and broadcloth trousers, which by the end of each day were streaked with dust and sweat. That morning he was dressed in a fawn-colored jacket, matching trousers and a cream-hued silk shirt. His boots were polished to a high gloss, and his blond hair shone in the sun like beaten gold.

Elizabeth and her mother rode in the carriage, while Rameses sat up in front, the reins in his gnarled black hands. Philip and William rode alongside, the boy on a fine roan that would have attracted attention by itself had his father not been mounted on the legendary King's Ransom, the pride of Calvert Oaks's once renowned stud farm and, it was hoped, the means of reviving it.

They arrived in the city early enough to leave their bags at the depot and stop at the Richmond Hotel for breakfast. The liveried gentleman who escorted them to their table recognized Philip. He called him "Captain" and made a fuss about seeing that everything was done properly for them.

Elizabeth could barely eat for drinking in every detail of the high-ceilinged room, and of the men and women who filled it. She basked in a profusion of wealth and luxury unlike anything she had ever experienced before. She loved the snowy linen tablecloths, the gleaming crystal and china, the black waiters in white jackets who offered warm cinnamon rolls from silver mesh baskets.

It was all so different from home, where there was a pervasive sense of harsh struggle beneath the superficial serenity. Not that she blamed her parents. How much harder it must be for them when they so clearly belonged among the privileged company that seemed to not have a care in the world. How terrible for them to have lost all that, and how brave the fight to regain it.

"Augusta knows what needs to be done while I'm away," Sarah was saying. "I'm sure she'll do her best, but . . ."

"But she's not as young as she thinks," Philip finished for her. "I understand that. Don't worry, we'll manage."

"Of course we will," William agreed. "And look at it this way, when you get home, we'll appreciate you all the more."

Sarah gave her stepson a smile, but the worry did not fade from her eyes. Instead it sharpened, as a man approached their table, inclined his head in greeting and spoke to Philip.

"I'm a bit surprised to see you here, Calvert. I thought you never left those fields of yours."

The man's derisive tone would have been enough to make Elizabeth dislike him instantly, but his appearance also weighed against him. He was tall and slender, younger than her father but older than William, and flashily dressed in a way that, even with her limited experience, she recognized as ostentatious. In addition to a meticulously tailored frock coat and trousers so snug as to make her wonder how he could move, he wore an elaborately embroidered waistcoat, a gold stickpin with a large stone that looked like a sapphire, and a matching ring on the little finger of his left hand. An aroma of too much bay rum clung to his smooth cheeks, and his black hair was slicked down with an excess of pomade.

"Durand," her father said shortly, his failure to rise eloquently expressing his disapproval of the other man. Durand, however, either ignored the silent reprimand or was unaware of it, for he smiled again, even more unctuously, at Sarah. "Miz Calvert, nice to see you, too."

Sarah inclined her head but said nothing. William scowled, but also held his tongue. Slowly it dawned on Durand that he was being snubbed. His sharp features tightened, and a dangerous light came into his small eyes.

"You'd do well to listen to what I have to say, Calvert."

Philip's attention appeared concentrated on a corn muffin he had split in half and was buttering. "I don't think so."

"I've offered you a fair price. Better than that, a damned good one."

Philip placed his napkin carefully on the table and rose. He faced the man with a complete lack of expression, as though he were not worth the effort of anger. "That is not appropriate language around ladies, Durand. Your company is not welcome here."

"Why you..." Durand's fists clenched at his sides, but he was wise enough not to raise them. Philip was oblivious to the nervous glances of the waiters and the other patrons. He stood his ground with a simple confidence of a man who accepts his own superiority not as a subject for pride, but as an innate fact of life. In stark contrast, Durand's arrogance unraveled swiftly. His breathing grew labored, and a sheen of sweat broke out above his narrow lips.

William had not moved, but Elizabeth sensed his instant readiness to move to his father's assistance, though that seemed unlikely to be called for. One-armed, Philip Calvert might be, but there was a hint of leashed violence about him that dared any man to consider him disadvantaged.

Sarah's eyes were downcast. There was a slight flush to her cheeks, but otherwise she seemed unaware of the scene being played out in front of her. Elizabeth could not match her mother's aloofness. She was fascinated by what was happening and did not want to miss a moment of it. When Durand, after a muttered curse, turned his back and marched stiffly out of the restaurant, she was almost disappointed.

Several moments passed before the normal rhythms of the gracious room were restored. As though abruptly unfrozen, waiters moved to refill coffee cups, a couple that had been standing by the door waiting to be seated was escorted to a table, and the string quartet seated in a corner lifted their bows and began to play again. Conversation resumed, a shade more loudly than before, as though all were anxious to forget what they had just witnessed.

Elizabeth, on the contrary, wanted to know far more. Who was Durand, why had he approached her father, what had he meant about offering a fair price? Surely he didn't mean for land, because everyone knew that Calverts did not sell land. Not to pay taxes, or put food on the table, or spare themselves the most backbreaking toil. To avoid parting with a single acre of Calvert Oaks, her father would work sixteen hours a day in the fields—"lahk some darkie," Uncle Rameses had said once, when he didn't know she was listening—her mother would spend every waking moment contriving to make do, and her brother would leap from childhood to manhood without knowing the joys of youth.

Moreover, they would do it without ever for a moment feeling sorry for themselves, or forgetting who they were and why their heritage meant so much.

Elizabeth straightened in her chair. She withdrew her gaze from the crowded restaurant and turned it inward, as she had seen her mother do. Consciously, she strove to achieve the same sense of serene self-possession.

The meal concluded without further interruption. Philip paid the check, and the family proceeded the short distance to the train station. In the last few minutes before the train arrived, conversation was difficult. The reality of their parting had struck Elizabeth, and she stood tongue-tied, fighting the impulse to cry.

"It'll be all right, sport," William said. "You'll like it up there, and besides, you'll be home before you know it."

"I wish we weren't going," Elizabeth murmured. She hid her head against his broad chest for a moment as he gave her a quick hug.

A plume of smoke rose from around the curve of the track. They could hear the long, mournful whistle as the train approached. There was a stirring on the platform as people gathered their cases and bundles, and prepared to depart.

Philip raised his wife's hand to his lips and pressed a gentle kiss on it. "Write to us," he said.

She nodded, but did not try to speak. They stared at each other for a moment before, heedless of the surrounding crowd, they embraced. The iron wheels of the train screeched to a halt. Smoke billowed into the air as steam hissed. There was a clamor of voices—farewells, last-minute admonitions and reminders, jokes and promises. Porters surged forward to hoist the luggage on board.

Philip assisted Sarah up the steps to the train, then turned to Elizabeth. "Be good, sweetheart," he said, bending to kiss her gently. "Do everything your mother tells you."

"I will," she promised. Then she, too, was up the steps into the train. Whistles were blowing, the wheels screeched again, the train lurched forward and slowly, slowly, began to pick up speed.

Elizabeth took Sarah's hand, and together they found their way to their seats, but did not take them. Instead they stood together, leaning out the window and waving until the two tall figures standing on the platform grew blurred and indistinct, whether from tears or distance they did not care to tell.

THE JOURNEY TO BOSTON took three days. They would have liked to break the trip in New York or elsewhere, but Grandfather Mackenzie's condition did not allow for delay. Because they were making the trip without pause, Philip had insisted on spending the additional money to get them berths in the ladies' compartment.

Since the war, increasing numbers of women had taken to traveling alone, something that Sarah told her daughter had been unheard of even a few years before. The more enlightened train lines had responded to this by setting aside part or all of a car for unaccompanied ladies and children. There they were protected from the presumably uncouth behavior of strange men, though beyond that the amenities were few.

Elizabeth didn't mind. She had grown up free of the dependence on luxuries that could rob new experiences of their fascination. The hard mattress of her bunk, the dusty hangings that closed it off from the corridor, the lack of hot water and the primitive sanitary arrangements, made no difference to her. She was enthralled by the view of flat fields slumbering in the sun, interrupted by the occasional crossroads that flashed by. A boy in a wagon waved to her. A barge on the river they crossed on a trestle bridge tooted its whistle. Old men dozing on the platforms of way stations opened their rheumy eyes as the train paused for a few moments, carrying a whiff of the great world beyond.

The rhythm of the mighty coal-fired engines seeped inside Elizabeth. They sang her to sleep at night and woke her each morning. They shaped the cadence of conversation and of life itself. Within the confines of the train, a separate world sprang into being, destined to exist only for the span of a few days. Tentative acquaintances were struck up among the women traveling alone. Mothers shared rueful smiles at the antics of their children. Names and the purposes of their journeys were exchanged. News of other places was given and received.

Elizabeth heard of loss and sadness, spoken of without pity. Of husbands and fathers dead, of homes burned and lands lost, of dreams shattered. She listened to women who had grown up in a world of protection and privilege, and who were forced out on their own to seek new lives for themselves and their children. She heard fear beneath the matter-of-factly told stories, but she also heard courage.

Many of the women were going north in the hope of finding work. They had held on as long as they could in the ravaged South, and still would not have left if their situations hadn't been desperate. Few had been trained for employment, and fewer still knew how to go about securing it. They dreaded being without a place, without value, without hope.

Some spoke of the West. It was an enticing mystery to Elizabeth, the subject she most enjoyed reading about in her schoolbooks, and she longed to learn more about it. But the women seemed to know little, only that there were Indians and drought, unimaginable distances and vast emptiness. Who could make a life in such a place? Yet many were trying, and many more were beginning to look in that direction.

Rather than dwell on the grimness of the choices facing these women alone, Elizabeth preferred to think about Boston. She bombarded her mother with questions, wanting to know every detail of the city before they had even arrived there. Sarah had to remind her that she herself hadn't lived in Boston in more than a decade, not since her marriage in 1859. She presumed that less had changed in the North than in the South, but she also did not expect to find the city of her memories still intact.

Yet that appeared to be largely the case. Accustomed as they both were to the sight of the burned-out ruins and desolate fields, the impact on them of the vital, bustling metropolis could not be exaggerated. Barely had the train entered the outer reaches of Boston than they were struck by the constant movement of people and vehicles streaming toward the center of the city, as though drawn there by an irresistible compulsion. Even the great ships along the Charles River, standing yardarm to yardarm with their sails gleaming white in the summer sun, all seemed to have the city center as their goal.

Unlike Richmond, where so much had perished by fire, Boston was graced with stately buildings that bore the patina of age. Beside them were newer ironwork structures, some as many as five stories high, that fairly took the breath away. Over all were the church steeples, their carillons competing to ring out the noon hour.

The same sense of intense activity and urgency permeated the train station. Sarah and Elizabeth felt fortunate to secure the services of a porter, who would gladly have ignored two females alone had not Sarah placed herself directly in his path and made her requirements clear. Grudgingly he seized their small trunks, one under each burly arm, and thrust his way through the milling crowd of travelers, dragging them in tow.

Her mother looked around anxiously as they reached the gate that separated the platforms from the main station, until she spied the slender figure of her brother making his way toward them. At twenty-nine, five years his sister's junior, Nathan looked even younger. His narrow face and gray eyes held an expression of sweetness that belied the cruelties he had seen while fighting with the Union army. The clerical collar around his neck further emphasized an innate aura of otherworldliness.

"My dears," he said as he embraced them both, "I was becoming concerned that you might not be on the train."

At the sight of the man meeting them, a minister no less, and, despite his clerical garb, obviously prosperous, the porter became rather more accommodating. He readily agreed to take their trunks as far as the curb where, Nathan informed him, a carriage waited.

Suddenly feeling much better about everything, Elizabeth was further delighted when her uncle offered her his arm, the other going to her mother. Doing her best to appear grown-up, she tried hard not to gawk at the immense marble dome covering the waiting room, or at the line of gleaming carriages waiting immediately beyond.

"How is Father?" Sarah murmured as her brother helped her into the brougham drawn by a stately pair of chestnut geldings. A groom hurried to secure the trunks on top.

"Slipping away," Nathan said. He was not one to imagine there was kindness in deception. "I believe he's held on this long only because he knew you were coming."

"I almost didn't. It was Philip who insisted."

"I trust he is well?"

Sarah nodded. Under her brother's gentle urgings, she told him of events at Calvert Oaks, how many fields had been replanted, how many colts born. "The new dairy barn was completed last month. If all goes well, Philip hopes to begin buying stock soon."

"And the mill?" Nathan asked. "How is that?"

"Fully operational again, thanks to Father sending the funds to replace the damaged parts."

Elizabeth listened to them, thinking of the day the great mill wheels had begun to turn again. She knew the Yankees had tried to destroy it when they came through Calvert Oaks at the end of the War, for no better reason than because it had produced material for the uniforms of an army that was already vanquished. They had placed explosives beneath vital gear shafts. Only a sudden change of wind and a providential rainstorm had prevented the resultant fire from burning the structure down.

"As I recall," Nathan said dryly, "he insisted in return that his ownership of the mill be increased from fifty to seventy-five percent."

"True," Sarah admitted. "But then, he was always one to drive a hard bargain." She did not add that even with the

Calverts' share reduced to a mere quarter, the mill's earnings were still absolutely essential to the recovery of Calvert Oaks. Surely her father would have realized that?

"He's certain to have made appropriate provisions," Nathan said.

Sarah met his gaze directly. "I sincerely hope so."

Her brother's smile was gentle and understanding. "Father has mellowed. Surely you know that. Since he and Mari married..."

"I want to believe you're right, but..."

"But old grudges die hard?"

"You make it sound so childish," she said.

"Why not? The most important events in our lives happen when we are children. Certainly they have the most long-lasting effect."

There was silence for a moment. "It is very disconcerting," Sarah said with a touch of humor, "to discover that one's younger brother has turned out to be wiser than oneself."

"Hardly that. It's only that I can look at the situation from a different perspective. I'm well aware of how you protected me, and not only from Father."

A shadow passed over Sarah's face. "I suppose Gideon is here."

"He rarely leaves Father's side."

"Such devotion." Sarah turned away to look out the window, leaving her daughter to wonder at why she seemed to be angry.

THE HOUSE ON Commonwealth Avenue looked dark and forbidding. Its stone facade was heavily ornamented with elaborate scrollwork and medallions. The parlor floor's tall windows were closed despite the summer warmth, and the curtains were drawn. The pale, gaunt manservant dressed in black who opened the door might have been inviting them to enter a mortuary.

No longer ashamed of appearing childish, Elizabeth clung to her mother's hand. Sarah's skin through the thin cotton glove was cold, as though she had been plunged into the depths of a winter more chill than her daughter had ever known. The slight color that had returned to her cheeks during the carriage ride had disappeared.

"I imagine," said Nathan, giving her a concerned glance, "that you would like to get settled in your rooms first."

Sarah shook her head. "If one of the maids could take care of Elizabeth, I'd rather go up to him now."

"As you wish."

Elizabeth did not want to go with the girl in the black-and-white maid's uniform who appeared in answer to Nathan's summons. She looked nice enough, but she was one more unknown element in a place that was already baffling enough. Yet a look at her mother's drawn face made Elizabeth realize that to object would be to inflict further tension where it did not belong.

Without protest, she allowed herself to be led away up the curving marble staircase and down a long carpeted corridor to a room that proved surprisingly cheerful.

"Mrs. Calvert will be right through here," the girl said with a soft Irish burr as she indicated a connecting door. "And this is the bath you'll share."

Elizabeth peered into the room hesitantly. The last thing she wanted to do was display her ignorance, but she had never seen anything of the like. At Calvert Oaks, bathing was done in a big tin tub laboriously filled by hand. Once an army of slaves had been available to carry the water upstairs, but now that they were gone, the tub resided in the kitchen, near the cast-iron stove where the water was heated. In pleasant weather, the river was handy, and there was always the spring-fed pond behind the dairy barn.

As to certain bodily functions, she thought no more of using an outhouse than she did of pumping water from the well, although she had to admit that emptying chamber pots was not her favorite chore.

But here in Boston, everything was apparently quite different. Bridie, the maid, sensing her discomfort, matter-of-factly showed her how to turn on the water in the tub and basin, and how to pull the chain that flushed the commode.

There were further wonders in her bedroom itself. Lavender-scented sheets without patches, plump down-filled pillows, a rug that even through her shoes felt thick and soft. There was even a frosted carafe of cool water with ice shavings beside the bed.

"If you're hungry," Bridie said, "I can bring you a tray. Supper will be at seven."

"Oh, no." Elizabeth was unaccustomed to being waited on and could not imagine ever becoming used to it. Besides, in her excitement, she felt it would be impossible to eat anything.

"Well, if there's nothing else..." Bridie said.

Sensing that the maid was hesitant about leaving her alone, but also anxious to get back to her duties, Elizabeth said, "I think I'll lie down for a while."

Relieved, Bridie took her leave, with a backward reminder that should anything be needed, it was only necessary to pull the cord beside the bed.

Elizabeth did rest for a few minutes, after carefully folding back the satin counterpane and removing her shoes. But she was far too alert to sleep, and only so much diversion could be gotten from watching the shadows on the ceiling and listening to the sounds of traffic beyond the windows.

What she really wanted was to discover more about the place where she found herself, but she was uncertain of the etiquette of wandering through a strange house. Natural curiosity nonetheless asserted itself, and she stole from her room, after carefully glancing up and down the corridor to make sure no one was about.

It was gloomy in the hallway. Dust motes danced in the thin slivers of light that seeped through the drawn curtains at either end. The air smelled of old, well-cared-for wool and wood, as did her own home. But here there was a damp mustiness, in contrast to the dryness baked in by years of hot Southern sun. She heard the murmur of voices and paused, holding her breath, but no one came, and after a moment she went on.

At the opposite end of the corridor from her own and her mother's rooms, a door stood partly ajar. Peering through it, she could make out the shapes of people gathered around a high, wide bed. They were whispering, but even so she could hear that they were agitated, even angry.

"You have no right to be here," a tall, thin man with dark hair and gleaming black eyes hissed. "Not after all these years of keeping your distance. And you," he went on, turning his head so that Elizabeth could see him in profile, "you overstepped yourself inviting her."

The small, blond woman he addressed so coldly appeared unfazed by his condemnation. "This is my home, Gideon. I will invite whomever I please. As to that, Sarah is your sister, Josiah's daughter. She has every bit as much right to be here as you do."

Elizabeth's eyes swiveled to her mother, who held out a hand to the blond woman. "Please, Mari, don't concern yourself. What Gideon wishes or does not wish is immaterial to me."

"Damn you," the dark man murmured with such vitriol that Elizabeth flinched. "You always were a stubborn bitch."

"That's enough," Nathan snapped. He stood beside the bed, holding the wrist of the man who lay there. The hand that dangled from it was long and pale, the flesh spotted by age and hanging loosely, as though without substance. "It's almost over. The least you can do is behave decently until then."

"Don't preach to me, brother," the dark man sneered. "I've never been able to stomach your holier-than-thouness."

Nathan started to speak again, but the blond woman caught his eye and shook her head. She moved gracefully to the side of the bed. Elizabeth could no longer see her face, but in the stalwart strength of her narrow back and the erect carriage of her shoulders beneath black silk, she sensed pain and grief.

So did her mother, for she was clearly touched by it. She went to stand beside Mari, lending what support she could. "Didn't the doctor say he feels nothing now?"

"Yes, and I want to believe him. He was in pain for so long."

"You didn't tell me."

"He didn't want anyone to know. To the end, he kept his pride."

Elizabeth had avoided doing so until now, but finally she forced herself to look at the man who was the object of such conflicting attentions. He appeared very old, ancient even, with his almost white hair and beard, and ashen skin. Yet the harsh lines on his face looked unnatural when she compared them to the markings on the face of old Rameses, on whom time had carved its passage. Her grandfather was marked not simply by the passing of years but by disease that was perhaps more than physical. He bore the ravages of a suffering that had slowly eaten away all hope and vigor.

Yet there were still remnants to be seen of what had once been. Shrunken as he was, she guessed that he had once been quite tall and robust, a man who could dominate any gathering. The attitudes of the people around the bed seemed to confirm that. Only Mari was genuinely engulfed in sorrow. The others, whatever their varying degrees of regret, were wary, as though half expecting him to rise up suddenly and demand to know what they thought they were doing there.

The impression was so vivid that she stared in fascination, almost waiting for it to happen.

Minutes ticked by, marked by the captain's clock on the marble mantelpiece. A wagon went by outside, the horse's hooves resounding on the cobblestones. Nathan's head was bowed; he prayed silently. Tears trickled down Mari's pale cheeks. Sarah bit her lower lip and drew in a deep, unsteady breath. Only Gideon remained unchanged, scowling at the others. Yet Elizabeth thought she caught a hint of fear in the furtive gaze he fastened on the dying man.

"He's gone," Nathan said at last. He lowered his father's hand gently onto the covers, clasped his own hands and prayed. "Heavenly Father, receive into Your keeping the soul of Your servant, Josiah Mackenzie. Forgive him his sins and allow him to dwell with You in everlasting light, we humbly beseech You. Amen."

In the silence that followed, Gideon turned without warning and strode from the room, pushing the door open so abruptly that Elizabeth fell back against the opposite wall. She slumped there, staring at him numbly.

"What the hell . . . ?"

Regaining herself quickly, she jumped up and nervously smoothed her skirt. "I'm sorry. . . ."

"Who in damnation are you?"

"Elizabeth Calvert."

His eyelids dropped as his gaze wandered over her in a way she had never before experienced but that made her feel somehow unclean. "Sarah's brat. I might have known."

He took a step toward her, a faint smile twisting his thin mouth. She wanted to dart around him, but was strangely frozen in place. When his hand dropped heavily on her shoulder, she trembled with the force of something she did not understand.

"You look like your mother."

Elizabeth's eyes widened. Her mother was beautiful; she was anything but. "No, I don't."

He ignored her disclaimer. "She was the same at your age." Long, cold fingers cupped her chin, forcing her to look at him. "I'm your Uncle Gideon."

He seemed to expect her to say something, but Elizabeth had no idea what it might be. She had never heard her mother speak of him, had not known until that moment that she even had an uncle other than Nathan. How improbable that two such different men should be brothers. They were light and dark, goodness and evil, love and hate.

Her frightened gaze moved past him to the open door. A sigh of relief escaped her as she saw her mother standing there.

"Elizabeth, come here," Sarah said in a voice her daughter had never heard before. Angry, insistent, with the briefest flicker of . . . fear?

To obey, it was necessary to disengage herself from Gideon. He proved reluctant to let her go, but after a moment, with another slight smile, he released her. Elizabeth hurried to her mother's side, resisting with difficulty the impulse to cling to her.

Sarah put an arm around her. "You were leaving, Gideon. I think that's wise."

Her brother laughed, a malicious sound. Over his shoulder, he said, "But I'll be back."

JOSIAH MACKENZIE WAS BURIED two days later next to his first wife, Catherine, dead now some twenty-two years. She had been thirty-five when she died; Josiah was sixty-two. Elizabeth found herself wondering if they would remember each other should their paths cross in Heaven. Would Catherine Mackenzie recognize her husband when he appeared before her as an old man, or would he be miraculously restored to youth in the hereafter? And if they did meet again, what would happen when Josiah's second wife, Mari, joined them?

It was all very puzzling, particularly since she knew that her own father had been a widower when he met and married her mother. In the Calvert family cemetery, set some distance from the house on a gentle rise overlooking the river, there was a gravestone for William's mother, Daphne. She had been barely twenty when she died, like Catherine Mackenzie, in childbed.

Such thoughts kept Elizabeth safely distracted during the funeral and the burial service that followed. There was a very large turnout from both Boston and farther afield in Lowell, whose textile mills were the roots of Josiah's fortunes.

In the days between her grandfather's death and interment, Elizabeth slowly became aware that there were concerns about what would happen to his wealth. No one spoke of it directly—not her mother or Mari or Nathan—but oblique references to the absent Gideon suggested that they had cause to worry.

"Gideon was rarely away from his father's side in the past few years," Mari said the evening after the death, when they were sitting in the parlor. "As Josiah's illness worsened, he virtually took over running the businesses."

Seated beside her mother on a plush velvet sofa stuffed with horsehair that scratched her legs through her skirt, Elizabeth held herself very still. She didn't want to do anything that might cause her presence to be noticed and result in her being sent off to bed. Not that she wasn't tired. The events since leaving Richmond had drained her. Her thin shoulders slumped slightly, and it was an effort to keep her eyes open. Yet she was driven to learn everything she could about the bewildering adult currents swirling around her.

"Josiah didn't always welcome his help," Mari continued, "yet as his illness progressed, there was little he could do to stop him."

Her comment made Elizabeth wonder if Mari didn't wish her grandfather's other children hadn't taken a more active part in the last years of his life, but there was not the slightest hint of that in her manner. She even smiled gently as her fingers worried a white lace handkerchief.

Elizabeth watched her covertly. She was puzzled by how a woman little older than her own mother could have been her grandfather's wife. She and Sarah might have been sisters, except that they looked nothing at all alike. Whereas her mother was tall and slender, with a carriage Elizabeth thought of as regal and features that expressed both courage and intelligence, Mari looked like a pretty blond princess who had stepped from the pages of a book of fairy tales. There was a delicacy about her that made even Elizabeth want to protect her. Yet beneath the porcelain perfection were glimmers of something more, like light gleaming off deep, still waters.

"Father kept a close eye on things, didn't he?" Nathan asked.

"Always," Mari said. "There was never any possibility of him fully trusting Gideon."

"Then we shouldn't have anything to be worried about," Sarah said.

Mari nodded. "At least not from Josiah."

The day following the funeral, two short round men in black suits with high, starched collars came to the house. The elder of the two was introduced as Mr. Peckinpah, the younger—by perhaps a year—as Mr. Rummler. To Elizabeth, they were interchangeable. She quickly dubbed them Tweedledum and Tweedledee.

Mr. Peckinpah carried a large black briefcase. With due solemnity, he laid it on top of the desk that had belonged to Josiah, undid the straps holding it closed and removed a thick document written on long sheets of paper bordered by red lines, as though to stress the importance of what lay within them.

From her vantage point on the balcony that overlooked the library, Elizabeth observed the scene. Her mother and Aunt Mari—as she had been asked to call her—were both dressed in mourning black and seated on a settee facing the desk. Nathan stood beside them, in his full clerical garb, which had the added advantage of being suitable to the occasion.

Mr. Rummler took out his pocket watch and glanced at it with a frown. They were waiting for Gideon—Elizabeth could not bring herself to think of him as uncle. The clock in the entry hall chimed once. Minutes passed, five, then ten. The elder of the two lawyers cleared his throat.

"Uh…perhaps Mr. Gideon did not understand when we would be here?"

"He understood," Mari said quietly. "If he is not here in five minutes, we will proceed."

The two white-haired men looked at each other with such surprise that Elizabeth had to stifle a giggle. Clearly they were not accustomed to receiving such firm instructions from a lady. But then, she was already learning that Aunt Mari was what Mammy Augusta would call a steel butterfly.

The seconds dragged by. In unison, so that they looked almost like mirror images of each other, the lawyers withdrew handkerchiefs from their pockets and patted their brows. Nathan eased a finger beneath his collar and tugged at it surreptitiously. Sarah turned her head slightly, as though the muscles in her neck had begun to hurt and she was trying to ease them. Only Mari remained motionless, with every outward sign of complete calm.

The doorbell chimed. A servant, poised nearby, hurried to answer it. There was the quick, decisive sound of footsteps, then Gideon entered the room.

Alone among those gathered there, he was not dressed in black. A mourning band on the left sleeve of his tan cutaway was his sole concession to the circumstances. It was more than offset by the jaunty plaid vest he wore beneath, as though to directly contradict any thought that he might be grieving.

Sarah's mouth tightened when she saw him. Nathan looked on the verge of saying something, but apparently thought better of it. Mari ignored him altogether.

The elder of the lawyers, having recovered from his shock at so unseemly an appearance, coughed discreetly. "If we might begin..."

"Certainly," Gideon said with a broad smile. "I'm sure we're all quite eager to hear how we've made out."

He took the chair beside the settee, stretching out his long legs in front of him and looking for all the world as though he were enjoying himself immensely.

"Uh...yes..." the hapless lawyer murmured. "As you say. Well, now..." He peered at the document before him, repositioned his pince-nez, and said ponderously, "We are here to learn the last will and testament of the late Josiah Mackenzie."

"We already know that," Gideon interrupted. "Get on with it."

"Take your time, Mr. Peckinpah," Mari corrected. "We have no wish to rush you."

"Speak for yourself, dear stepmother," Gideon said. "The sooner this nonsense is done with, the better."

Mari gave him a long, steady glance, but said nothing. She merely inclined her head to Mr. Peckinpah, who, thus encouraged managed to continue.

I, Josiah Mackenzie, being of sound body and mind, do declare this to be my last will and testament.

"There is then a series of relatively small bequests to longtime servants, charities and the like. If you prefer, we can save them for later."

Gideon waved a hand impatiently, but the lawyer kept his gaze averted from him and waited instead until Mari gave her approval.

"Very well, then we shall proceed to the meat—as it were—of the document." He paused and took a sip of water from the glass near his hand, cleared his throat again and, having been assured of everyone's rapt attention, went on.

To my beloved son Nathan, I leave the sum of fifty thousand dollars to be disposed of as he sees fit, but with the hope that he will use some of it for the creature comforts his calling to the ministry has so often denied him.

The recipient of this largesse gasped softly. "I had no idea," he murmured. "Father was too generous."

Mari placed a hand over his and smiled gently. "He loved you very much."

Mr. Peckinpah gave them all a moment to recover, then went on. "To continue . . .

> To my beloved daughter, Sarah Calvert and her husband, Philip, I leave my shares in the mill at Calvert Oaks, as well as the sum of fifty thousand dollars, which I hope will be devoted in large part to the rebuilding of their plantation.

Elizabeth inhaled sharply, barely able to contain her excitement. Such a sum was all but inconceivable. She had been happy enough for her Uncle Nathan, but now her joy was far more personal. In a flash, she saw in her mind the difference her grandfather's legacy would make. Her father could afford to hire field hands; her mother could have servants. More fields could be put to seed, perhaps even— the most exciting possibility of all—more land purchased. The possibilities were boundless, and she was so caught up in considering them that she almost missed the next item the lawyer read.

> To my beloved son Gideon, I leave the sum of one hundred thousand dollars in recognition of his service to the many Mackenzie enterprises over the years.

One hundred thousand dollars. That was a veritable fortune. Surely even Gideon would be overjoyed.

Except that he looked anything but. His narrow features had turned suddenly dark, and his eyes glittered ferally. "What the hell are you talking about, Peckinpah?" he demanded harshly. "That's not how the old man's will reads."

"I assure you, sir," the lawyer said stiffly, "it most certainly does."

Gideon's hands had tightened on the arms of the chair. He was leaning forward, all pretense of calm gone. "I saw the will," he said. "I know what it says."

"I have no idea what you saw," Lawyer Peckinpah said. "But this—" he gestured to the papers before him "—is Josiah's last will and testament. Of that, I am quite sure."

Gideon rose. His teeth were bared, and his nostrils trembled. To Elizabeth, he looked for all the world like a weasel she had seen once about to attack a hen's nest.

"Go on," Gideon demanded. "I want to hear the rest of it." As he spoke, his dangerously bright eyes were fixed on his stepmother, who gazed serenely ahead, refusing to acknowledge his anger.

Mr. Peckinpah was not so unaffected. His voice rang with a particular note of vehemence as he continued.

To my beloved wife, Mari, who has been my comfort and joy these happy years, I leave the house on Commonwealth Avenue with all its contents. In addition, she is to inherit full control of all the Mackenzie businesses, including but not limited to the Lowell mills, the Nantucket shipping yard, the Pennsylvania coal mines, and the real estate holdings in downtown Boston and New York. I also bequeath to her all stocks, bonds, bank certificates and other funds in any form. It is my hope that my dear wife will choose to take an active role in the management of my many businesses and through her intelligence and sensitivity guide them to even greater prosperity.

Nathan and Sarah both looked surprised, but very pleased. But their pleasure was more than compensated for by Gideon's rage.

"You won't get away with this," he hissed. "The old man must have been mad to think he could leave that kind of wealth to a goddamn strumpet who happened to warm his bed for a few years."

"Sir!" Mr. Peckinpah exclaimed, rising in indignation.

"That's enough," Nathan said. He was also on his feet, having stepped protectively in front of Mari. "Whatever you think, Gideon, you have no right to speak to our stepmother in such a fashion. No one could have been a more honorable or loving wife. Father was extremely fortunate, and he had the wisdom to know it."

"It's all right," Mari said softly, placing a hand on his arm. "I wish that Gideon could accept this and be glad of the generosity Josiah showed him. But," she added, looking directly at Gideon, "it will make no difference if he cannot."

"Don't be so sure of that," Gideon snarled. "I'll fight this with everything I've got. You'll end up out on the street, where you belong."

Before any of the others could comment, he stormed from the room. A moment later the front door shut with a crash behind him.

In the silence that followed, Mr. Peckinpah gathered up his papers, mopped his brow and patted a stray strand of thin white hair back into place. "Perhaps," he said at length, "I should explain why Mr. Gideon was so surprised."

"Clearly," Nathan said, "he presumed he was father's major heir."

"And at one time he was," the lawyer confirmed. "But after Mr. Mackenzie's remarriage, he began to have second thoughts about the way he had disposed of his wealth. He also, quite frankly, had doubts about Mr. Gideon and his worthiness to carry on so great an enterprise. About five years ago, he came to us with the intention of rewriting his will. The results are as you have heard."

"Did you know?" Sarah asked softly, turning to Mari.

"I suspected. When he realized how ill he was, Josiah began insisting that I learn about the businesses. I thought it was because he wanted me to be able to keep an eye on Gideon after he was gone, but now I can see that he had much more in mind."

"What will you do now?" Nathan inquired.

"Carry on as Josiah would have wished." She smiled sadly. "I can't say that I relish the task. To be honest, the mere thought all but overwhelms me. But your father was always vividly aware of his responsibility to the hundreds of people who worked for him. He cared far more for their well-being than Gideon ever could. I must do what I can for their sakes, and," she added softly, "out of respect for my husband's memory."

She stood up and nodded to each of them. "But now, if you will excuse me, I am going to lie down for a little while."

Elizabeth expelled her breath slowly. Her lungs ached, but she was hardly aware of it. All her attention was caught by the scene she had just witnessed. Though she knew that she didn't understand all its implications, she was enthralled by the courage and determination shown by Aunt Mari. With the example of her mother before her, she had always known that women could accomplish a great deal. But that had been in the sphere of home and family.

Where Mari was about to venture was very different. She would have to prove herself in the world of men, that mysterious place in which commerce took place, money was made or lost and no quarter was ever asked or given. Elizabeth trembled with excitement at the thought. Frightening it might be, but how thrilling to suddenly see the confines of one's world exploded and to reach so far beyond them.

Silently, she crept from the balcony and made her way back to her room. Her mother would undoubtedly come looking for her there before much longer. She longed to be able to ask her about what had happened, but of course it wouldn't do to reveal that she had been eavesdropping. She was taken aback by her own behavior and vowed it wouldn't happen again.

But even as she did so, she sensed that deep inside she was beginning to question at least some of the rules by which she had been taught to live. There was a streak of rebellion in her that seemed to be growing with each passing year. When she thought of Mari, and tried to feel sorry for her having lost her husband and been thrown into conflict with Gideon, all she could really see were the glorious possibilities that suddenly lay before her aunt. In comparison, the limitations of her own life chaffed unbearably.

_____ *Girl*

_____ *Chapter Three*

THE FIFTY THOUSAND DOLLARS that Josiah Mackenzie had left to his daughter and son-in-law did make the difference at Calvert Oaks that Elizabeth had foreseen. Her father still worked as many hours each day, if not more. But he had to do less of the backbreaking physical labor himself and was able to spend more time planning and supervising all that needed to be done, which was a considerable amount.

In the year before Josiah's death, barely a quarter of the plantation's fields had been put to seed, and that only at tremendous effort. The year after, the total was up to half, and by 1875 Calvert Oaks was operating above its prewar levels. To achieve that, Philip spent many of his days in Richmond and elsewhere, negotiating directly for the sale of their crops instead of going through middlemen. He was so effective in this that inevitably a number of other planters, those who had managed to hold on, asked him to place their own crops as well. He accepted on condition that they agree to raise only what he knew could be sold.

During his increasingly frequent absences, more and more responsibility fell on William. He rose to the challenge, indeed, relished it. Before he reached his early twenties, he was a man in every sense of the word, a fact that did not escape the admiring notice of the young women in the neighborhood.

Elizabeth watched with envy as a social life of sorts began to revive, not anywhere as glittering as it had once been, but still exciting to those who weren't old enough to have known anything else. At thirteen, she was still too young to do more than observe from the sidelines, a position she found more frustrating than amusing.

"I don't understand why we can't dance," she said to her cousin, Melinda Hudson, as they stood off to the side of the ballroom, watching the couples waltz by. The occasion was her parents' sixteenth wedding anniversary, for which Philip had returned just in time after a month-long trip to meet with the men whose crops he sold.

Her father appeared tired but undeniably happy as he guided her mother across the dance floor. The two seemed locked in a private world of their own, where nothing mattered except the love they shared.

"It must be wonderful," Melinda said, sighing as she watched them, "to be like that. My parents aren't at all romantic, but yours . . ." Her voice trailed off, her eyes wide and glowing.

Elizabeth had always taken it for granted that her parents loved each other. Only recently, as the changes in her body alerted her to nuances she hadn't noticed before, had she realized that they shared something special.

"Your parents are very nice," she said loyally.

Melinda wrinkled her turned-up nose. "Nice isn't very exciting."

It was true that Aunt Kitty and Uncle Jeremy did not exactly strike sparks off each other. Elizabeth had seen a portrait of her aunt done when Kitty was sixteen, which showed she had once been a lovely, blond-haired belle, much as Melinda was shaping up to be. Jeremy had never, strictly speaking, been handsome, but the miniature of him that Kitty wore showed a strong, sturdy young man who looked eager to tackle life.

The years, many of them hard and sorrowful, had left their mark. Kitty had borne seven children, of whom five had lived. No amount of corseting could disguise her thick waist or fallen breasts. Her hair was dry and streaked with gray, and her once magnolia-smooth complexion bore a web of fine lines etched by worry.

The same worry that wore down Jeremy. Elizabeth and Melinda did not speak of it, but both knew that the Hudson plantation was in dire straits. Jeremy worked hard, but he had neither Philip's tenacity nor his luck. Several of the decisions he had made, in opposition to his brother-in-law's advice, had turned out badly. Several parcels of land had had to be sold off in order to pay the taxes on the rest. There were rumors that more was to follow.

"Charles Durand came to see Father yesterday," Melinda said suddenly. She was still watching the dancers, but her expression was no longer pleasant. "They talked in the library for about an hour. When he left, Father looked very upset."

"I wish he didn't live near here," Elizabeth said, speaking of Durand. "No one likes him, but he has to be included in everything just to be polite."

"He isn't here tonight," Melinda pointed out.

"No..." Elizabeth wished she could take back the words. Her father was one of the few men who dared to disdain the carpetbagger. But then, he could afford to do what almost no one else could.

"Everyone was really shocked when he bought the old Devereaux place," Melinda said. "And at what he's done to it." She rolled her eyes expressively.

"That was his wife's doing. She's awful."

They spent a pleasant ten minutes repeating everything they had overheard their elders say about Isabelle Durand—Madame Durand, as she insisted on being called. Theories as to her origins were hardly complimentary; a friend of Sarah's mother had gone so far as to say that if she hadn't "crawled out of a cathouse, she certainly should crawl into one." Neither of the girls was absolutely certain what a cathouse was, but it was certain that no lady would be caught in one.

"And what about that girl of his, if she is a girl?" Melinda said. "Why, she's our age, and she goes around dressed like a boy, a ragged one at that."

"She has a strange sort of name," Elizabeth said. "Sunbird. It's different, but pretty."

Melinda leaned forward, in the attitude of one about to disclose a juicy bit of scandal. "Surely you know why she's called that? She's half Indian."

Elizabeth's eyes widened. "But Madame Durand isn't…"

"Isn't her mother. There was somebody else, a squaw Monsieur Durand never married. So not only is she a half-breed, but she's also a bastard." She grinned maliciously.

Elizabeth was still attempting to digest this when Melinda's elder brother, Davey, joined them, putting an abrupt end to the girlish talk.

"What's so funny?" he asked, looking as though he would enjoy a good joke. Davey was a slender boy of fifteen who had recently shot up in height, with the result that he looked rather gawky and self-conscious. His light brown hair tended to fall into his hazel eyes, and he blushed more easily than anyone Elizabeth had ever seen.

"Nothing," Melinda said hurriedly. "Why aren't you dancing? Sally Watson's been making cow eyes at you all evening."

"Cut it out," her brother muttered, "or I'll invite you to dance, and then you'll be sorry."

"He has two left feet," Melinda advised Elizabeth. "Don't ever let him get you out on the dance floor, or you'll be crippled for life."

Davey turned beet-red. He mumbled something about sisters being a plague and turned away. "Maybe I shouldn't have teased him like that," Melinda said when he was gone.

"He does seem a little uncomfortable," Elizabeth agreed. "But then, all fifteen-year-old boys are like that."

"I'll bet William never was." Banishing Davey from her thoughts, Melinda smiled dreamily. "You know, all the girls are wild for him, but especially Nancy Haddrick. She's determined to have him."

"She can scheme all she wants," Elizabeth said, frowning as she thought of the beautiful redhead with whom William had already danced twice that evening. "But I don't think William will ever marry her."

"Why not?" Melinda asked.

Elizabeth hesitated. She really was trying to learn to be discreet, but the temptation to share such a tasty morsel of gossip was too much for her. "I heard William and Father talking about her. William said all that red hair could warm up the coldest set of sheets, but he needed more than that in a woman."

Blushing apparently ran in the Hudson family. Certainly Melinda turned a most satisfying shade of crimson. "He didn't really? To his father? Oh, how bad of him." Her delighted squeal made it clear that his daring was more than forgiven.

"I'm not absolutely sure what he meant," Elizabeth admitted. "But it seems to have something to do with men and women."

"Yes, and with beds," Melinda added solemnly, though Elizabeth thought that was rather self-evident. "And it has to do with being married. In fact, you can't do it until then... whatever *it* is."

"Are you sure?"

"Why... of course, didn't you know that?"

"I thought... well, it just seemed to me that men do it without being married. And since they must do it with someone, then some women have to be doing it, too."

"Why, Elizabeth Calvert, you're as bad as your brother."

"It just stands to reason, that's all."

"Maybe so," Melinda sniffed. "But I don't think a lady should admit it."

It was very hard to be a lady at thirteen. In fact, from what Elizabeth could see, it wasn't easy at any age. Having slipped away from the ballroom, and Melinda, she drifted along the rim of the garden, noticing that several couples had sought the shadows of the yew hedges. There seemed to be a great deal of giggling, accompanied by low, persuasive male voices. Once she even heard a resounding slap, followed by "Brad, you scoundrel!" followed by more giggling.

She supposed they were kissing, as she had seen her mother and father do. Not the formal kisses that occurred on the front porch when he returned from the business trip, or the playful kisses beneath the Christmas mistletoe, but truly passionate kisses that gave Elizabeth strange feelings in the pit of her stomach.

The year before, when certain changes had begun to occur in her body, her mother had gently explained what they meant and prepared her for the monthly flow that started shortly thereafter. She didn't think much about it, since she experienced little discomfort, but she did wonder from time to time why such a thing should happen to women and not to men. Apparently it had something to do with having babies, though the direct connection eluded her.

The night was warm and starlit, with a rising moon over the river. She made her way to a favorite place beside an old stone wall. There was a slight breeze redolent of the roses her long-dead grandmother had planted when she came as a bride to Calvert Oaks.

Elizabeth wiggled into a more comfortable position. Away from the ballroom, she could relax. Since infancy, she had been accustomed to her own company, living as she did in a place where there were few children. Once, she knew, the quarters behind the big house had been filled with slaves, including many little boys and girls. But they had gone away, and only recently had their places begun to be taken by the hands her father hired to work the fields. She had heard him say to her mother that ironically many of them were former slaves. Freedom, it seemed, had not turned out to be all they had imagined.

She swung her legs absently as she looked out in the direction of the river. Earlier in the day, she had watched a heavily loaded barge move slowly downstream, carrying goods toward the coast. She had wondered exactly where it was going and what the people on board would find when they got there.

The trip to Boston at the time of her grandfather's death had whetted her appetite for travel. There were nights when she could not sleep for thinking about the wide world beyond Calvert Oaks. Then she would rise from her bed and tiptoe to the windows, seeing not the familiar gardens and fields, but the vast stretches of other lands beckoning to her.

Someday she would have to leave. Not even because she desired it, but because that was simply the way of things. No one had to explain it to her. William, as a male and the eldest child, would inherit Calvert Oaks. She, as a female and the younger, would marry some other man and go to live in his house. It would not do to form too strong an attachment to what could never be hers.

Yet there were times, such as now, when the peace and security of her home wrapped themselves around her like the most loving arms, and she wondered how she would ever be able to go. Only a very special man could make the leaving worthwhile. A man who would love her as her father loved her mother. Who would be handsome and strong, and—as Melinda had said—romantic.

She closed her eyes, trying to imagine what such a man would look like, and when she opened them again, she found Davey watching her.

"I'm sorry," he said when she jumped slightly. "I didn't mean to startle you."

"It's all right. I didn't realize anyone else was here."

He hesitated before coming closer, as though half expecting her to order him away. When she did not, he sat down gingerly beside her on the wall. "I saw you leave the ballroom and wondered if you were all right."

"I'm fine. I just wanted to be outside for a while." Courteously, she didn't add, *alone*. To her surprise, she didn't really mind Davey's company. He wasn't loud and arrogant like a lot of the other boys, nor did he alternately ignore or tease her. Instead he was a steady, even soothing, presence that she could accept without regret.

"I don't much like parties," he admitted. "I guess I never quite see the point of them."

Elizabeth laughed softly. She had wondered about that herself. "My mother says it's so the ladies can get all dressed up and give the gentlemen the chance to tell them how lovely they look."

"Seems like a lot of bother to go to," Davey observed.

"You mustn't be a spoilsport."

"I'm not. Oh, I know that's what people think, but really, I like to have a good time as much as the next person. It's only parties that don't appeal to me."

"What *do* you like, then?" she asked.

He gave her a quick, cautious glance. "I like to read."

"Oh, so do I. Have you read *The Lady of the Lake*?"

"By Walter Scott? He's my favorite. *Ivanhoe* is the best book I ever read."

"I haven't read that one yet."

"Perhaps . . . you'd like to borrow it?"

Their eyes met, shyly at first, then with a shared smile. Until they remembered the passage of time.

"I suppose we should be getting back," Davey said. He jumped down from the wall and offered Elizabeth his hand. Though she had clambered up and down that perch more times than she could remember, she accepted his help. His fingers curled around hers were warm and dry. They felt reassuringly strong. When she stood beside him, she couldn't help but notice that unlike so many other boys, he was slightly taller than she was.

She was oddly disappointed when he let go of her hand. They walked back through the garden, listening to the music floating from the ballroom. Through the French doors they could see couples drifting by, talking and laughing. An ineffable sense of longing filled Elizabeth. She yearned to be suddenly far more grown-up, safely on the other side of the great changes stirring within her. She wanted to be one of the lovely women secure in the arms of a handsome man, instead of a still gawky child/woman who could not be sure which side of herself she would encounter from moment to moment.

"Davey... can you truly not dance?"

"Not very well," he admitted. "I'm... clumsy."

"So am I."

"You? No, you're very... graceful."

The compliment startled her. She looked at him warily, not quite sure that he wasn't mocking her. The candid admiration in his eyes was a further surprise. She had never inspired anything of that sort before, and could hardly credit that she had done so then. Yet that didn't prevent her from basking in its warmth.

With wiles she had not known she possessed, she said, "I feel self-conscious dancing in front of other people."

"Me, too. Yet there are times when I think it must be fun."

"I'm sure it is, in the proper setting." Purposefully, she glanced around the garden.

Davey had a sudden inspiration he blissfully credited as his own. "We could... uh... dance here."

Her eyes widened with surprised delight. "Oh, could we? Really?"

He straightened his shoulders manfully. "Of course. There's nothing wrong with that." Actually, he thought it rather daring, which added to the pleasure.

The first notes of a waltz reached them. Tentatively, he held out a hand, and when she took it, he placed the other

with great care on her waist. With the proper eighteen inches
of space between them, they began to dance.

Davey stepped on her toes twice, mumbling apologies
each time. Elizabeth stumbled once. They both had to concentrate intently, counting the measures under their breath.
But halfway through, the dance became easier, and they
both relaxed a little. Davey actually smiled, and she managed a soft laugh.

When it was over, they regarded each other gravely.
"That was very nice," Elizabeth said.

He inclined his head. "Thank you for the pleasure."

Still they did not move apart. For the space of several
heartbeats they stared at each other. Then Davey bent his
head slightly, and slowly, with the caution of one approaching a precipice, he touched his lips to hers.

The sensation was odd, but not displeasing. Elizabeth felt
a small tingle of surprise down her back and stiffened
slightly. She had a moment to savor the softness of his
mouth, and his gentleness, before he withdrew.

"I'm sorry," he said instantly.

"Why?"

"I was too forward...wasn't I?" He looked at her
doubtfully.

A flush of warmth stained her cheeks. If he had been too
forward, what had she been? "Well, if that's how you
feel..." She picked up her skirt and ran down the gravel
path, heedless of him calling her name on the cool night air.

LIFE GOT BETTER after that, or at least more interesting.
Elizabeth no longer felt quite so much like an observer of
adult life but more like a participant. Davey found numerous excuses to visit Calvert Oaks, and when he came, he invariably brought her something: a flower still moist with
dew; a crisp, juicy apple; a handkerchief trimmed with lace;
and once, on her fourteenth birthday, a fat, wiggly puppy
she promptly christened Happenstance.

She and Davey exchanged books and talked about them. On fine summer days they went fishing together, and Davey took pride in the fact that Elizabeth would bait her own hook and remove her own fish, though she drew the line at cleaning it. They played as children might amid the ancient oak trees and rolling lawns, but between them there was an awareness of something children did not feel, begun on the night of the ball and beckoning from no more than a comfortable distance beyond their reach.

Time passed, and the sea change awaiting them grew closer, like a tide surging beneath a waxing moon. Elizabeth stopped growing taller, to her intense relief, and began to grow in other ways. Her dresses had to be let out and finally replaced altogether. She left the short skirts of girlhood behind and began, in her fifteenth year, to dress as a woman. Her breasts were small but rounded, her waist slender, and her hips, though barely perceptible beneath her wide skirts, were, when she was naked, gracefully defined.

Her hair remained, to her, a dissatisfying shade midway between brown and blond. But Davey likened it to the color of spun honey, and that made her feel a great deal better. He was becoming a handsome young man, still a bit too slender for his height and inclined to occasional awkwardness, but attractive nonetheless. Elizabeth privately thought that his best feature was his smile, which turned an otherwise somber countenance into a sweet beam of light. But she knew that Davey took pride in his slowly broadening chest and shoulders, and she took what opportunities she could to let him show off his strength for her.

It did not occur to her that by his faithful attentions Davey effectively prevented other young men in the neighborhood from paying her court. They tended to be more aggressive and self-assured than he, which made her uncomfortable, and at any rate, she was more than content with his company. She began, as young girls do, to think of the future in more specific terms. To marry Davey and move only as far away as the Hudson plantation would not be a very bad thing.

It was William who finally burst the shimmering bubble of her dream the year she was to turn sixteen. He did it as gently as he could, but with an implacable firmness born of love. They were walking back from the paddock, where she had gone to watch him training a lovely little chestnut mare destined to be hers. The horse was dainty and instinctively well behaved. William treated her with none of the fierce strength he displayed with the stallions, but with a gentleness that quickly won her over.

"She'll do well," he said after he had turned the horse over to one of the grooms. "In another week or so, you'll be riding her."

"I can't wait," Elizabeth said. She had been riding since childhood, but never so fine a horse as the thoroughbred mare. Since the chestnut would not be bred for several years yet, her purchase was a luxury, one more indication of Calvert Oaks's rapidly recovering prosperity, as was the gown she wore, a mauve silk trimmed with embroidered rosebuds. The overskirt was scooped up in back to allow for a modest bustle and display a gored underskirt of flowered organdy. In her hand, she carried a straw bonnet trimmed with ribbons, conveniently forgetting that it was supposed to be on her head. Her hair had been left unbound and flowed midway down her back.

To William, brother that he was, she looked delightfully lovely and feminine. And unexpectedly grown-up. Which brought him to think of Davey. He frowned as he considered that young man. Not that he didn't like their cousin; on the contrary, he thought he showed a great deal of promise. Which was fortunate, considering the challenges he would face.

"Father is at Quail Run today," he said as he closed the paddock gate behind him and strolled with her across the lawn toward the house.

"Oh, I wish I'd known. I'd have gone with him." She visited the Hudson plantation whenever she could, loving the old house, with its ramshackle air, and the gardens that were more often than not overrun with weeds. Everywhere she looked, she saw the possibility of what could be, and she itched to begin bringing it to fruition. But lately, now that she thought of it, her father had seemed oddly unwilling to take her with him on his frequent visits.

"He wants Uncle Jeremy to plant less cotton and more tobacco," William said. "That's the way the market is moving."

"I'm sure Uncle Jeremy will be glad of his advice."

William stopped, causing her to do the same. He hesitated a moment, then said, "It's more than advice, Bethie. Father owns part of Quail Run."

"Really? I didn't know." She cast him a sidelong glance as they began walking again. "But Father has a great many investments. I suppose it stands to reason that he'd put a little money into Quail Run."

"It was more than a little," William said. "He bought more than half of it, which means that he has the final say about everything that happens there."

Elizabeth tensed. She stopped again, her feet digging into the soft earth. "But why...why would Uncle Jeremy give up so much?"

"Because he was desperate for money."

Such bluntness made her flinch. She met her brother's eyes and found in them concern, but also determination. "What are you telling me? That Davey and his family did not have our own good fortune and so had to turn to us for help? Surely there's nothing wrong with that?" Except that it meant her cousin's birthright was no longer truly his own. He would inherit only the smaller part of the plantation and be in debt, quite possibly forever, to her father. Unless...

"William, what are you saying?"

"Nothing," he assured her quickly, touching her pale cheek. "At least, nothing to alarm you quite this much. I only thought that you should know the true state of affairs." He took a deep breath and went on. "Davey is a very capable young man. If he can learn from his father's mistakes, he may do well."

"What mistakes?"

"Jeremy refused to recognize the changes brought about by the war. He thought that life would go on as before. But, of course, that was impossible. You remember how Father used to work, out in the fields, as hard as any darkie?"

Elizabeth nodded slowly. "Yes, and I remember that we were still in dire straits when Grandfather Mackenzie died and left the money to rebuild Calvert Oaks."

"You're right, we had some very good fortune. But only because Father made the best possible use of every penny of that money. He poured it back into the land, whereas Jeremy, whenever he did get a little ahead, promptly frittered it away on the comforts he'd known in the past."

"I think you're judging him very harshly."

William shook his head. "I'm not judging him at all; I'm simply stating a fact. Father is an excellent manager; Jeremy is not. As a result, Quail Run was in very serious trouble a few years back. The taxes couldn't be paid, and Durand was on the verge of buying the property for a pittance."

"Yes . . . I remember that." Though she had managed to put it out of her mind until that moment.

"The carpetbaggers are like carrion crows feeding on the carcass of the South. They won't be satisfied until the bones are picked clean."

His bitterness startled her, all the more so because he rarely displayed any negative emotion. For the first time, she realized that his concerns reached beyond Calvert Oaks, to a land that was still in large measure twisted and warped by violence.

"William...I'm glad that father was able to prevent Quail Run from being sold. But what has that to do with Davey and me?"

"Everything, I'm afraid. You must understand that life there will not be comfortable, or even secure, for many years yet. After Jeremy, Davey will have a constant battle to stay afloat. He may not succeed."

"With me to help him, he will."

"With you, or with your dowry?" He was being harsh, and he hated it, but he had no choice. She had to confront the truth.

The quick, angry sheen of moisture that sprang to her eyes was blinked away. "Is that what you think? That Davey cares for me only because of my money?"

"Actually, I don't think that's even occurred to him." She would have spoken if he hadn't held up a hand. "But it will. And it will affect whatever relationship you might have for all time. Were you to marry him, you would never know for sure how much he cared for you and how much he cared for what you can do for Quail Run. Moreover, you would have none of the comforts Father has worked so hard to give us all. And," he went on relentlessly, "there is yet another consideration. You and Davey are first cousins. There are many who believe that is too close a blood tie to allow for marriage."

"Your mother was our father's first cousin," she reminded him, biting out the words between clenched teeth. Rarely had she felt such anger; that it should be directed against William astounded her. Yet he had hurt her badly, and, instinctively, she needed to strike out at him. "Are you saying there's something wrong with you because of their closeness?"

"No," he said imperturbably. "I was lucky, but others haven't been so fortunate. Do you really want to take that risk?"

"Yes!" She all but shouted the word, startling Happenstance, who as usual was at her heels. "I love Davey, and I don't care about comforts. As for the money, let him have it. He'll put it to good use, and our children will benefit from it. Our *perfectly normal* children, because I don't believe for a moment that there could be anything wrong with them."

Before she finished, the tears were flowing down her cheeks. The reality William had forced her to confront was so at odds with the future she had imagined that he might as well have driven a knife through her heart. Yet she refused to acknowledge that the wound might be mortal. It was her life, after all, and she saw no reason why she should not decide for herself how it was to be lived.

"I'm sorry," he said gently, truly more regretful than she would ever know. "But you cannot marry Davey. Father would never permit it."

"I wouldn't need his permission. Not in a few more years. We could run away together...elope...."

Her brother's gaze was full of sympathy. "And lose everything in the process, including Quail Run? Can you really see Davey doing that?"

The misery of it was that she could not. Forced to choose between her and even part ownership of his family's land, she had no doubt what his choice would be.

"It's so unfair," she whispered, her throat painfully tight.

William put an arm around her shoulders, drawing her against his broad chest. "I'm afraid that's the way life is, Bethie. We all have to suffer disappointments."

"And I'm afraid I won't be able to bear this one," she murmured, her voice muffled against his shirt.

He put both his arms around her, offering what small comfort he could, knowing it would not be enough. Over her bright head, he stared out toward the horizon, confronting what would have to be done.

ELIZABETH THOUGHT very seriously that she hated Boston. Never had she imagined a place so cold and gray, so unrelentingly damp and remorselessly somber. Oh, it could be pleasant enough in spring and summer, and the brief fiery burst of autumn was diverting. But winter slogged on forever, beating down her spirit and making her long for the warmth of home.

Not that Aunt Mari hadn't done her best to make her feel at home there. Since her arrival the year before, she had been treated with the greatest consideration and gentleness, introduced to a multitude of new acquaintances, included in every appropriate social event and made to feel as much a part of the life of the city as she could possibly hope to be.

Except that she wasn't really, and was beginning to give up hope of ever feeling like anything but a stranger condemned to live in an alien place where she would never truly belong.

Oddly enough, it wasn't Davey that she missed. She thought of him from time to time, but with no more than nostalgic fondness. If he was the great passion of her life, she reflected ruefully, she was singularly lacking in emotion.

It bothered her that William and her father had been right about that. They had both said, in the days right before she was sent away, that time and distance would put her feelings into better perspective and make her realize that what she had hoped for would truly not have been to her good. In

their certainty, they had appeared unbearably callous,
though deep inside she knew that wasn't the case. Certainly
the frequent letters she had from both of them reflected their
great affection and continuing concern.

Still, only her mother had seemed to understand what
leaving cost her. Elizabeth had forgotten her burgeoning
adult status enough to weep in Sarah's arms. Held close like
a small child, she had sobbed out her anger and her fear. "I
know," her mother had murmured as she rocked her. "I
know how hard it is. But trust us, Bethie. We love you, and
we only want what is best for you."

A year later, from the perspective she had been promised, she could believe that. But was Boston truly best?
Surely not. Rising from the window seat where she had been
dreaming away the gray afternoon, she cast a last look at the
sleet beating against the panes and went in search of some
more cheerful pastime.

Aunt Mari would be back from the office soon. They
would have a cup of tea together and talk over the day.
Elizabeth loved her adopted aunt, feeling toward her as she
would have toward a cross between a mother and a sister.
For Mari, who lacked children of her own, Elizabeth's
coming had been a godsend. Busy as she was with the Mackenzie businesses, she never failed to spend time each day
with Elizabeth and encourage her in her new life.

Which, Elizabeth was the first to admit, was not easy.
Though her grades at Miss Carter's School for Young Ladies were respectable enough, she had no sense of fitting in
there. The other girls were all from various parts of New
England or New York. They talked differently, dressed differently and, it seemed to her, even thought differently from
anything she had known before.

Worse yet, they came to the school already possessing a
body of education she could not hope to equal. Granted,
they had no idea when crops were planted or how they were
harvested, how to care for land and keep it fertile, what to

do with cattle and horses, and all the other myriad details she had absorbed almost with the air of Calvert Oaks. On the other hand, they were far more widely read than she, could speak French, paint or at least draw, and were well versed about the emerging role of women in the changing world.

Much of what she heard, Elizabeth privately agreed with: that women were not merely ornaments, but were in fact the backbone of the family, the transmitters of culture, the upholders of civilization. That to be a wife and mother was the noblest of tasks, and that women were therefore deserving of at least as much respect as any man.

What bothered her—and what kept her silent when such discussions were going on—was the bloodlessness of it all. Her fellow students spoke of running a household, but she would wager that none of them connected that with butchering hogs or spinning wool or any of the other tasks she had seen her mother do, and been taught to do herself. They spoke of having children yet none of them seemed to have any idea of how that came about.

She, at least, knew better, having had the whole process sensibly explained by her mother. She knew that it was bloody and painful, and could be dangerous to both mother and child. But the suffering and risk were redeemed by the love of husband and wife, and by the miracle of the new life they had created together. She even understood, though dimly, that such love was not merely ethereal but was accompanied by passion. She had felt the stirring of pleasure within her on the few times she and Davey had kissed, and she sensed in that something about the mystery of what happened between a man and a woman that both excited and frightened her.

These cool Northern girls with their twangy, nasal voices and their resolute opinions about everything under the sun distressed her. She could never be like them, did not in fact want to be. But that condemned her to being forever a stranger in their midst.

In the drawing room, she sat down beneath a portrait of her grandfather and with a resigned sigh took up her needlework. That was yet another of her failings. Her mother had taught her to make simple dresses and shirts, and with those she had no difficulty. But a smooth satin stitch seemed beyond her reach, and French knots utterly defeated her. Still she persevered for half an hour or so in the hope that she would at least have something decent to show long-suffering Miss Jacobs the next day.

Happenstance laid his head on her knee and whimpered softly. She put down the square of linen and scratched him behind his ears. "You don't like it here any better than I do, do you, poor boy? But don't worry, tomorrow it may clear and we'll be able to go for a run in the park."

The dog, who had been presented as an English springer spaniel but who seemed to have a touch of coonhound in his makeup, emitted a resigned sigh. His cold nose pressed into the palm of her hand as he sought to express his sympathy in the only way he could.

"Whether it clears or not," Elizabeth told him, "we'll go visit Princess. Poor thing, she hates this weather worse than we do." Her chestnut mare, which she had been allowed to bring with her, was cared for in the stables behind the Commonwealth Avenue house. She was doing well enough, but Elizabeth did not deceive herself; the horse longed for green Virginia pastures every bit as much as she herself did.

The front door opened, and there was the sound of murmured voices. Elizabeth rose quickly, dropped her sorry needlework in the bag at her feet and went to greet her aunt, only to discover that it was not Mari who had arrived. The tall, thin man speaking with the servant was familiar to her, but it took her a moment to place him. When she did, she instinctively drew back a step.

Her hesitation drew his notice. He broke off arguing with the footman, who had been reluctant to admit him, and turned his attention to Elizabeth.

"Well, well," Gideon said. "Sarah's brat again. You do keep turning up."

"It's all right, Wilson," Elizabeth said, recalling herself. She was not the child he had so disconcerted at their only previous meeting. Rather she was a young lady, schooled in proper behavior and, she told herself, able to deal with the situation. With a reassuring nod she dismissed the footman and turned to her uncle. "I presume you wish to see Aunt Mari."

Gideon smiled slowly, but there was no humor in the black eyes that glowed with an unholy light. "Don't call her that. She's no relation to you." He tossed his top hat onto the hall table without bothering to shake the rain from it first and began unbuttoning his long ulster.

Fearing that water would spot the table, Elizabeth removed the hat and put it away in a nearby closet. She was then perforce compelled to do the same with his coat, all the while wondering if she was making a mistake admitting him to the house. Mari had said little about her continued battles with Josiah's eldest son, but Elizabeth knew that Gideon had bitterly contested her grandfather's will, and that not even his final defeat in court had stopped him from pursuing the return of the property he considered rightfully his own.

When she closed the closet door again and turned back to him, she found Gideon staring at her from beneath drawn brows. The intensity of his gaze made her want to look away, but she resisted the impulse and forced herself to face him squarely. He did not miss the hint of defiance in her stance as he demanded, "How long have you been living here?"

"About a year. Aunt Mari isn't in at the moment, but she's expected back shortly. Did she know you planned to call?"

Instead of answering her directly, Gideon said, "I'll wait in the parlor. You can keep me company."

There were few things Elizabeth wanted to do less, but good manners demanded that she not leave a guest alone. Briefly she considered refusing on the grounds that her uncle could hardly be considered a welcome visitor, but not even that lessened her social obligation. Reluctantly she followed him as he strode into the parlor and made directly for the cart of cordials and liquors.

Without asking her leave, he poured himself a stiff measure of whiskey and downed it in a single gulp, then refilled the glass before making himself comfortable on the settee. With a narrow smile, he patted the cushion beside him. "Don't stand on formality, dear niece."

Elizabeth ignored the gesture and instead lowered herself stiffly into a chair across from him. She was feeling more ill at ease by the moment and hoped that Mari would return soon.

"So," Gideon said at length when it became obvious that she was finding the task of social chitchat beyond her, "you've been here all this time and I had no idea."

Since she could think of no reason why he should have been aware of her presence, Elizabeth merely shrugged and maintained her silence. After several moments, Gideon said, "You've grown up."

That was stating the obvious and hardly seemed to require comment, but she had ignored the bonds of courtesy as far as she could. "Aunt Mari has been very good to me."

By that she meant that Mari's influence had helped her to mature, but Gideon chose to interpret it differently. "I'm sure she has," he said with a sneer. "Mari would do anything to thwart me."

Elizabeth could not imagine what possible connection there could be between Mari's kindness to her and the problems with Gideon. Her perplexity must have been obvious, for her uncle said, "Mari has no heirs of her own, you know."

"She certainly has family."

"You mean yourself and your dear mother, I presume?"

Elizabeth nodded. "And my father and brother, as well as you, of course. You are...family...aren't you?"

He laughed softly and leaned back against the couch, looking at her over the rim of the whiskey glass. "Most assuredly, which is an excellent reason for you and I to become better acquainted."

Elizabeth could not greet that prospect with any enthusiasm, which must have shown on her face, for Gideon stood up suddenly and crossed the small distance between them. Standing before her, he held out the hand that did not grasp the whiskey glass and cupped her chin. Instinctively, she tried to twist away, but his grip tightened, and she was forced to hold still or risk making a scene.

"You are quite beautiful," he murmured. "Very like your mother when she was your age."

Elizabeth kept silent, her hands clasped in her lap as she struggled against the impulse to wrench herself free. He was, after all, her uncle, and he really wasn't doing anything improper. Yet his touch made her oddly apprehensive.

"Did you know," he went on, "that I rarely saw Sarah in the years before she was married? We were kept apart."

"I don't understand...."

"I was sent away to school, and even when I came home on holidays we were never alone." Almost to himself, he added, "That was Mari's doing. Father would never have thought of it on his own."

The vitriol with which he invested her aunt's name jolted Elizabeth. She was beginning to suspect that she had made a serious mistake by admitting Gideon, but she had no idea what to do about it.

"The fire is dying," she murmured finally through stiff lips. "I'll call the footman...."

"Never mind," Gideon said, abruptly letting her go. He emptied his glass again and turned his attention to the cart. As he was pouring another stiff measure of whiskey, Elizabeth seized the opportunity to stand up. Behind his back she hurried over to the door. He turned in time to see her opening it. "I'll just go and see if there's any sign of Aunt Mari."

"There's no need—"

"I won't be a moment." Ignoring his scowl, and making no mention of the fact that she had no intention of returning, Elizabeth stepped into the corridor. She closed the door behind her with a sigh of relief, as though she had just escaped from something she did not understand but knew she was not capable of dealing with. She wasn't, but she had no doubt that Mari was, and it was with great relief that a short time later she saw her aunt's carriage coming up the cobblestone street.

From the bay window of her bedroom, she watched Mari alight and climb the front steps to the house. Observing her aunt's slight figure, she wondered if she shouldn't hurry down and warn her of Gideon's presence. But she knew the footman would do that, and besides, she didn't want to become any more involved than she already was. Instead she chose a book at random from the dozens kept in her room and curled up on the window seat.

The book failed to hold her attention, which kept wandering to whatever was going on below in the parlor. When the front door opened she leaned forward slightly, enough to catch sight of her uncle, his ulster flying open around him, stomping out of the house. He snapped at his carriage driver and jerked open the door himself before glancing back over his shoulder. For a moment Elizabeth thought he had caught sight of her. She drew back quickly, concealing herself behind the white lace curtains. Not until she heard the carriage rattle away did she release her breath and begin to relax slightly.

She waited a discreet amount of time, long enough so as not to appear too eager, before returning to the parlor. Aunt Mari was there, looking remarkably unruffled. Only an observer as keen as Elizabeth could detect the slight flush on her cheeks that was a certain indication of anger.

Without a word, Elizabeth stepped over to the fire and poked at it until the flames shot higher and a warm glow began to dispel the chill that had seeped into the room. Then she went over to the cart and poured a generous measure of sherry into a crystal goblet.

There were advantages to living in a female-run household. Surely her schoolmates, living with fathers and brothers, were never permitted to pour alcoholic beverages, let alone have the occasional sip. Actually, she preferred whiskey to sherry, though she had only tasted it once and that surreptitiously. It had made her throat burn, and she was in no hurry to try it again, especially since she had seen her uncle drink it, but she had decided that she preferred fieriness to sweetness.

"Is everything all right?" she asked as she sat down across from Mari after handing her the glass. Happenstance had crept into the parlor. He settled himself between them with his head on his crossed paws and pretended to go to sleep, though a twitching ear revealed that he was listening to every word.

Mari took a sip of the sherry before answering. "Gideon was here."

Elizabeth nodded. "I told the footman to admit him. I hope you don't mind?"

"It wouldn't have made any difference if you had tried to keep him out. He is quite...determined."

"Did he come about anything in particular?"

Mari sighed and set her glass down. Wearily, she rubbed the back of her neck with a pale hand. "He wants to buy the mills from me."

"You aren't going to sell?"

"No, of course not. But Gideon isn't prepared to take no for an answer. He claims to have the support of the other mill owners in wanting me out."

Elizabeth could well believe that. Mari had earned the enmity of the other owners by insisting on paying her workers more generously and allowing them to work fewer hours. Despite dire warnings that she would destroy discipline in her mills, she had persevered. The fact that production had risen steadily had only further angered the men who continued to oppose her.

"He can't force you to sell, can he, no matter how much support he has?"

"No, of course not," Mari assured her with a wan smile. "But," she added softly, "he can make things difficult for me."

Elizabeth wanted to ask what she meant, but Mari was clearly unwilling to pursue the subject. Instead, she wasted no time changing it. "I had a note from Emmeline Parkinson today. She intends to present her daughter in a few months and wondered what plans were being made for you."

Emmeline Parkinson was the mother of one of the more officious young ladies at Miss Carter's. Elizabeth had been forced to listen for weeks to the glorious plans for dear Josephine's coming out. She was thoroughly bored with the subject, so much so that the very extent of that boredom was enough to divert her from thoughts of her uncle.

"Personally, I think nothing is more tiresome," she said.

Mari raised her eyebrows. "Oh, do you? How unfortunate, because I was so looking forward to introducing you to society."

Elizabeth's stomach plummeted. Nothing she knew about Boston society suggested that she would be the least bit welcome. "Oh, but surely there's no need?"

"On the contrary. You have been here a year now, and you will be seventeen shortly. It's time for you to begin to do the things a young lady does."

Elizabeth envisioned her sorry embroidery and shook her head. "I don't really think I'll be any good at them."

Mari surveyed her gently. With her caramel-blond hair, her strong but feminine features and her slender figure, Elizabeth had no idea of her own attractiveness. Nor did she have a clue as to how her soft Southern voice, her lilting laughter or her innately sensual manner affected men. But Mari was well aware, and she thought it best for her to be surrounded by the full panoply of propriety before any misconceptions could arise.

"We'll visit the dressmaker tomorrow," she said.

"But your work . . ." Elizabeth said in a last-ditch bid to avoid what was rapidly appearing to be inevitable.

"I can afford to skip a day. Besides," Mari added with a flash of the young girl she had once been, "it will be fun."

FUN? ELIZABETH COULD THINK of a lot of words to describe tromping through endless back rooms looking at bolt after bolt of material, standing still for hours while being stuck with pins and shuffling through page after page of fashion illustrations, all while trying to pretend at least a minimum of interest. "Fun" was not one of her choices.

Mari, however, seemed to be truly enjoying herself. Elizabeth watched wearily as she examined yet another length of silk, stroking it between her thumb and forefinger to judge the quality as she frowned over the color. "This shade of blue is lovely, but it isn't quite right. We need something to match Elizabeth's eyes, closer to periwinkle, with a touch of gray."

"Of course, *madame*," the modiste said as she removed the deficient fabric and swiftly glanced around for another. "Ah, here is the very thing. For a ball gown, I think, with bisque lace to emphasize the young lady's charming coloring."

"Hmmm...possibly. Put that aside and we'll consider it."

Elizabeth surreptitiously wiggled her toes in her boots and glanced at the clock on a nearby mantel. It was well into midafternoon, and they had eaten nothing except the endless cups of tea and tiny sandwiches served by the dressmakers. That might be enough for Mari, but for herself, she needed something more substantial. Her hearty appetite contrasted sharply with her slenderness. In public she tried to restrain it, since it wasn't considered ladylike, but at any moment she feared her stomach would grumble and disgrace her.

"What do you think of this, dear?" Mari asked, holding up a length of rose brocade that might be suitable for an underskirt.

"It's very nice. Uh, Aunt Mari, don't you think we've seen enough? After all, I know Father is being very generous, but I'd hate to bankrupt him."

Mari and the modiste exchanged a surprised glance. "Why, dear," Mari said, "we've barely begun. There are still riding habits, walking dresses, undergarments, shoes, hats and all manner of other delightful things to arrange for. Believe me, the sum your father sent is more than adequate to cover them all."

"Oh...how nice." Despite her best efforts, she could not avoid a glum look.

Mari laughed softly. "Don't worry, this part will be over eventually, and then you won't have to go through anything like it until you buy your trousseau."

Without thinking, Elizabeth said, "If I were to get married quickly enough, couldn't I use the same clothes?"

Mari's eyebrows rose. "Do you have plans for an early marriage?"

"No," Elizabeth admitted. At least, not any longer.

"Just as well. You should enjoy several years of freedom before you even consider marrying."

Elizabeth restrained herself from pointing out that to her freedom meant running barefoot across the meadows of Calvert Oaks, riding her mare astride with her legs flashing in the sun or spending a day deep in one of her favorite books. It did not mean walking in lockstep with proper Boston society, where a young lady could draw censure for simply laughing too loudly.

She felt small-minded and ungrateful not to be more appreciative of all that Mari was doing for her. Yet she couldn't help but wish that if she had to be presented to society, it might have been at Calvert Oaks, where at least she could fit in and feel welcome.

The round of festivities that began at Christmas offered the new crop of eligible young ladies a first chance to see and be seen. These would be followed by coming-out balls throughout the following spring, and in the summer everyone who counted would adjourn to the "cottages" at Newport or to Europe.

At Miss Carter's, there was talk of little else. A few of the girls tried to pretend disinterest, but they tended to be the plainest and least gifted in the social graces. For the rest, there was restrained excitement mingling with the cool confidence that was their birthright. They knew who they were and what was expected of them. Elizabeth wished that she could say the same.

For a while, she considered trying to remake herself in the image of a proper New England girl. She had a good ear and a talent for mimicry; with relatively little effort she imagined she could learn their dry, hard-edged accent. It would be harder to remember to keep her hands in her lap when she spoke, but she could manage. What she would not be able to do was hide her emotions beneath a cloak of ice-tinged civility. When she was happy, she showed it in her glowing blue eyes and radiant smile. When she was not, try though she might, there was no concealing what was missing.

Drake Bennington spotted it right away. He had been watching her for several minutes, wondering who the lovely but apparently bored young lady was. He hadn't seen her before at any of the parties his family frequented, and she wasn't one of the friends his sisters brought home. Yet she had to be someone, because she was there, in the Benningtons' ballroom, appropriately dressed in a gown of rose velvet and white lace, her gleaming hair gathered in ringlets at the nape of her neck, and a dance card dangling from her wrist.

A circle of young men stood around her, vying for her attention, which she gave politely, if without enthusiasm. Drake grinned, certain of his own ability to change that. For the first time, the party he was attending under protest took on a certain appeal.

The ability to turn an unpleasant duty into an enjoyable interlude was characteristic of him. At twenty-one, he was newly graduated from Harvard, where his education had been nicely rounded off in ways his fastidious mother would no doubt find shocking.

In addition, he was amply endowed with the confidence of one who has known only privilege from the cradle. His long-limbed, smoothly muscled body had an athlete's grace. His features were aquiline, with the stamp of British aristocracy his ancestors had acquired as they had everything else: by purchase. In return for ready influxes of cash, certain noble but impecunious houses had yielded up titled brides in whose wombs the Bennington seed underwent refinement. What emerged lacked the raw edges of the original, but none of the energy or determination that had built a vast mercantile empire first on slaves and later on armaments.

Drake was hardly unintelligent; he recognized that he had been born into a life most men would kill to possess. Yet that did not prevent him from being chronically dissatisfied. The problem had started in childhood when, among the masses of toys, games and pets purchased for his amusement, he could never seem to find anything he really wanted to play with. Later on, at school, he had discovered other pleasures in the back street houses of Cambridge, yet they too eventually palled. What he wanted was adventure, the more exotic the better, before yielding himself to the future planned out for him by his deceased father and enforced by his iron-willed mother.

The girl, whoever she was, looked as though she might provide at least a pleasant diversion. With a decisive stride, he crossed the room and smoothly shouldered his way to her side.

"Good evening," he said pleasantly, giving her a smile he knew never failed to reassure virgins and old ladies.

Elizabeth looked into gentle brown eyes fringed by lashes that would have done a girl proud. She took note of thick blond hair, rugged yet noble features, and broad shoulders covered by an elegantly tailored evening coat. Her awareness of the young men surrounding her, who by comparison with this newest arrival seemed no more than boys, vanished abruptly.

"Good evening," she said softly.

His smile broadened and changed in some way that made it decidedly less benign. "You're Southern. How delightful. I don't believe I've ever met a belle before."

He held out his hand, and, instinctively, she put hers in it. Bowing low, he said, "I'm Drake Bennington. We should have been properly introduced, and we still can be, if you insist. Shall I fetch someone to do it?"

Laughing, Elizabeth shook her head. She forgot how bored she had been and instead concentrated on the pleasure of this new acquaintance. "Do you always think to

observe the formalities after the fact, Mr. Bennington?'' she
teased.

''Yes,'' he said with ingenuous candor. ''As any of these
louts can tell you.'' His glance encompassed the half dozen
young men, who stirred self-consciously beneath his gaze.
Still holding on to her hand, which felt very small in his, he
said, ''Isn't that so, chaps?''

They nodded glumly. In certain ways they were his peers,
being products of the same closed society that had spawned
him. But they had grown up in households ruled by living
fathers who remembered clearly their own youth, and they
had therefore not had the opportunity to slip the reins as
Drake had. His reputation on the playing fields—where he
was known not to be overscrupulous about how he won so
long as he did so—was as intimidating as what was said
about him in connection with certain brothels and gam-
bling dens. They were not his match, and they knew it.

The cluster around them faded away, leaving Elizabeth
and Drake standing alone. Neither spoke. Between them,
the air vibrated with sensation. Elizabeth felt oddly dizzy,
though not unpleasantly so. The world had narrowed down
to his eyes, his smile, his hand holding hers.

''You haven't told me your name,'' he said softly.

''Elizabeth . . . Elizabeth Calvert.''

He didn't recognize it. Perhaps she was a poor relation
being magnanimously brought into society, in which case an
affair might be possible. Otherwise . . .

''How is it we haven't met before?'' he asked.

''I haven't been to many parties. This is among the first.
I'm being presented, you see.''

His teeth flashed whitely in the glow of the chandeliers
lighting the large room. ''You make it sound like a sorry
fate.''

''I thought it was.'' Guilelessly, she added, ''Until now.''

Drake sucked in his breath. The look she was giving him,
combining as it did a woman's sensuality with a young girl's

innocence, made his body harden. Oh, yes, whoever she was, he intended to get to know Miss Elizabeth Calvert a great deal better.

The orchestra struck up a waltz. He bowed again. "May I...?"

"Oh...I'm afraid I've already promised this dance." She fumbled for her dance card, unable to remember the name of the young man who had pleaded with her for the first waltz.

Drake forestalled the motion. "Never mind. I'll explain it to him later."

Elizabeth wasn't sure that was done. Certainly in Virginia it would have been frowned upon, perhaps even worse. Young Southern gentlemen were quite capable of coming to blows over such a thing. But here in the North everything was different. "All right..."

They danced well together, as though they had done so many times before. Drake's hand was strong on her waist; his other, holding hers, squeezed her fingers lightly. He was sufficiently taller for her to feel protected by his size and strength. For Elizabeth, there was no awareness of the stares they were drawing, but Drake was fully conscious of them and savored every one. So they did not approve of her, this beautiful creature in his arms. So much the better. He all but laughed to himself as he thought of the amusement she could afford him.

When the dance was ended, he led her to the refreshment table, keeping a proprietary hand on her arm. They sipped punch as he drew her out to speak of her life in Virginia, quickly realizing that although she had been a year in Boston, she was still homesick.

"You miss your family, don't you?" he asked with deliberate gentleness.

She nodded, warmed by his apparent concern. "Aunt Mari is very good to me, but I still don't feel as though I belong here."

She was right, he thought, she didn't. And thank God for that. He was sick to death of the proper Boston girls every ambitious mother thrust at him. In Elizabeth, he sensed the heat of sultry Southern nights and the languid sensuality of what might have been a different world. Yet she looked so demure and uncertain, like an unawakened nymph waiting to be brought fully to life.

At the thought of the rewards that would be his in return for igniting her passions, his body stirred again. He had to be grateful for the relatively loose cut of his evening trousers that prevented her innocence from being abruptly dented. It was all he could do to restrain a smile of pure anticipation as he considered what it would be like to take her virginity. He had never had an inexperienced woman before, had always considered them more trouble than they were worth. But he was rapidly revising that opinion.

"This Aunt Mari you mentioned," he said. "Is she here this evening?"

"Oh, yes, but she had a bit of a headache when we arrived and went to lie down for a few minutes." Elizabeth scanned the assembled guests. "Wait a moment, there she is."

Drake followed the direction of her gaze and a long sigh escaped him. Mari Mackenzie. He had not met her before, but he knew a great deal about her—how she had inherited her husband's estate, defeated her stepson's challenge to the will and taken the reins of a business empire few men could adequately run. He disapproved of her on principle, but he was also far too astute not to realize that she would make a formidable enemy.

So an affair was out of the question. He tucked Elizabeth's arm in the crook of his and let his eyes run over her assessingly. As a bedmate, he doubted she would have any peer—after proper training—but childbirth might be difficult for her. He gave his duty to sire the next generation of

Benningtons no more consideration than any other of the endless series of obligations that had been recited to him since childhood. In this, as in all else, he would follow his own inclination.

_____ *Chapter Five*

FOR ALL HIS DETERMINATION, Drake's courtship of Elizabeth proceeded so slowly as to keep him perpetually in a state between frustration and rage. For the first time in his life, he wanted something that did not fall readily into his hands. Mari saw to that. She took one look at him when he was introduced to her the night of the Benningtons' ball and correctly read what was in his mind. It was her dearest wish to see Elizabeth well married, and she had to admit that the heir to the Bennington fortune would be a marvelous catch. But only once his arrogance was tempered with a sufficient dose of humility.

"Elizabeth is so young," she said to him one afternoon when he had come to call, only to find that the intended target of his attentions was away visiting friends of Mari's in the countryside. "I worry about her being too much in society before she is truly ready for it."

"She will be eighteen in a few months," Drake pointed out as he accepted a glass of sherry. He put it down on the table before him without tasting it, promising himself a good stiff whiskey at the earliest possible opportunity. In the meantime, he thought it wise to keep as clear a head as possible. Glancing at his hostess, he marveled at her apparent serenity. Rumors were rampant that Gideon Mackenzie was cooking up some scheme to ruin her. They must surely have reached her ears, yet she appeared completely impervious to them. She might truly have had nothing more on her mind than the well-being of her young charge.

Mari smiled at him serenely. "Growing up as she did, at Calvert Oaks, Elizabeth has always been completely protected. I consider it my duty to shield her as thoroughly as her father and brother would do."

"How admirable," Drake muttered. Outside the dull Boston winter was giving way grudgingly to spring. Through the open parlor window he could smell damp earth and the tang of salt air. His blood stirred. He needed some hard physical activity to distract and exhaust him, at least enough so that he could sleep through a night without dreaming of Elizabeth.

It was ridiculous how she haunted him. He had to continually remind himself that she was only an unfledged girl. Frequent visits to the better brothels Boston tried to pretend didn't exist helped to some degree. But it seemed that barely was his desire assuaged then it revived more fiercely than ever.

Uncomfortably, he adjusted himself in his chair and tried to follow what Mari was saying. "I had a letter only yesterday from Elizabeth's mother. You will recall my mentioning that Sarah and I are the dearest of friends. I've been so pleased to be able to tell her that Elizabeth is happier now in school. Several of the other girls have at last made a genuine effort to welcome her."

Drake nodded absently. He knew perfectly well why that was. His constant attentions to Elizabeth had made her, if not acceptable, at least desirable to the society they both frequented. With unconscious arrogance, he considered that was only appropriate.

"She will be finished there soon," he reminded Mari, as much as himself. Being besotted with a schoolgirl, however lovely, was more than a bit embarrassing.

"Actually, she's been talking about staying on for another year, to perfect her French. She's gotten quite good at it."

Drake's head shot up. This was the first he had heard of any extended education for Elizabeth. Next thing she would be talking about going on to some damned women's college. "If it's French she wants," he said, "the place to learn it is in France."

"Oh, I agree," Mari said, "but I'm afraid I could never get her father to agree to let her take a trip there. He thinks Boston is quite far enough." In fact, she had never broached the subject to Philip, but forgave herself the small lie as being in a good cause.

Drake leaned back in his chair. One long leg was casually crossed over the other. His trousers were perfectly creased, and his Windsor tie was impeccably knotted. He looked young, virile and supremely confident. "Not even," he said smoothly, "on a honeymoon?"

If he had expected to elicit surprise, he was disappointed. Mari merely shrugged and offered him a small plate of sandwiches, which he graciously declined. "Well, as to that, I couldn't say. It would depend, of course, on the man."

"Of course. Mrs. Mackenzie, I believe the time has come for us to be frank with each other."

"That would be best, Mr. Bennington."

"It is my intention to ask Elizabeth to become my wife. I have waited this long only so that she could have her own coming-out party first."

"How thoughtful of you," Mari said. "I'm sure when she realizes your care, she will very much appreciate it."

"But will she accept my suit?"

Mari raised a delicately arched eyebrow. "Surely you do not doubt it?"

Drake considered pretending that he did and beseeching her assistance, but he had the decided impression that she was too wise to fall for any such subterfuge. "No," he admitted. "I believe she will agree."

"Elizabeth is very...taken with you."

As well she might be, after his meticulous siege. Never had he taken such trouble with a woman. From the beginning, he had lured her with constant attention, gentle consideration and—understanding the usefulness of material expressions—small but well-chosen gifts, such as a bouquet of rare lilies in a season when there should have been none. When she marveled at how he had managed it, he said negligently that they were brought by fast ship from Florida. A book of her favorite poems assembled only for her and privately printed at his behest followed, to still the fear he sensed in her that he did not approve of her growing interest in learning, never mind that he didn't. There was also a small Persian kitten so beguiling that it won even the disreputable Happenstance's heart; around its neck was a diamond-studded collar to make her think of the jewels he would give her once she was truly his.

All of a young girl's dreams, so far as he could divine them, he sought to satisfy in her. To a very large extent, he succeeded. Elizabeth existed in a haze of happiness. At school, her grades were markedly improved, and she had been admitted to the magic circle of young ladies who were the leaders in achievement and style. At home, as she now thought of Mari's house, she won the indulgent smiles of guests and servants alike, who saw in her wholehearted delight in life their own vanished youth. And with Drake, she was cosseted, indulged, enticed by the promise of a future that made her tremble with eagerness.

He felt the excitement in her and wanted nothing so much as to carry it to its natural conclusion. As he might well have done already, except that they were rarely alone and then never for more than a few moments. He had no doubt that was due to Mari's careful surveillance and wondered how much longer she intended to continue it.

"Do I take it," he asked, "that since you have expressed no objection to my intentions you approve of them?"

Mari demurred with a wave of her hand. "It isn't my approval you need, but Philip Calvert's."

Drake had known that all along and wasn't distressed by it. He had no qualms about his ability to impress a simple cotton planter, who would no doubt be overwhelmed by the Bennington wealth and position. "I suppose," he said reluctantly, "that I should plan a trip to Virginia." It would be tedious, but he could manage it by swift train in no more than a few days.

"You needn't bother." Mari folded her hands in her lap and gave him another of her tranquil smiles. "I haven't told Elizabeth yet, because it is to be a surprise, but her parents are coming north for her ball. They will be here next week."

IN HIS MORE TOLERANT MOMENTS, Drake was willing to concede that perhaps it was no bad thing to be taken aback by one's intended father-in-law. Certainly Philip Calvert presented a challenge he had not anticipated but to which he told himself he was more than able to rally. Never mind that the older man, while behaving toward him with perfect cordiality, also made it quite clear that he didn't trust him the proverbial inch. Never mind that Elizabeth's father was tougher, smarter and more determined than Drake could possibly have foreseen. Especially never mind that Philip seemed to know precisely what it was that attracted Drake to his daughter, and was not particularly pleased by it. Drake would win him over in the end. Any alternative was unthinkable.

Sarah Calvert, on the other hand, was the epitome of feminine loveliness and grace. She accepted Drake graciously, engaged him in courteous conversation, which had the surprising ability to draw him out more than he intended, and altogether charmed him with the vision she presented of what Elizabeth was likely to become. If she was an example of what happened to Northern women when they went South, he couldn't help but conclude that the journey should be mandatory.

Even Drake's mother, the formidable Abigail Bennington, was reluctantly impressed by the Calverts. When her son first broached the subject of a reception for them, she had been adamantly opposed. It was bad enough that he seemed to be spending all his time with that upstart little Southern girl, but now he wanted to entertain her parents as well. That could only mean that his thoughts were tending in a dangerous direction, which Abigail meant to promptly quash. She had not lavished her attention on her only son these twelve years since her husband's death only to see him make a marriage that was other than glorious.

She thought at first that it would take relatively little to distract him: the promise of a new racehorse, or a European tour, perhaps. Except that neither worked any better than the other blandishments she trotted out.

"I'm sorry, Mother," he said with a perfect lack of regret, "but I truly think it best for you to get to know the Calverts. All of them, including Elizabeth."

"Such a charming girl," Abigail murmured. She smoothed a strand of iron-gray hair, which had somehow had the effrontery to escape from her chignon, and poured them both another cup of tea from the silver service on the table in front of her. "She reminds me of that adorable little dancer Freddy Ambruster was so taken with several years back."

"If that's supposed to be funny, Mother, I'm not amused. Elizabeth's background may be different from ours, but I assure you that she has been quite properly brought up."

To say the least. The previous evening, at a small dinner party given by Mari, Drake had been distracted by the enticing curve of Elizabeth's breasts above the modestly cut gown she wore. At least, he had been until out of the corner of his eye he noted Philip Calvert looking at him with an expression that could only be described as threatening. A short time later, after the ladies had left them to their port, her father had mentioned seemingly in passing that they were culling the calves in the Calverts' developing cattle herd to decide which should be castrated. Drake had gotten the message.

"I'm sure she's a perfect lady," Abigail said, considering whether or not she should call a servant to lower the shades over her sitting room windows. She was rapidly developing a rather nasty headache, but she doubted any of the usual remedies would be effective. She worried a corner of the linen napkin laid over her gray silk dress and suppressed a sigh of irritation.

"I saw Esme Davenport the other day. Such a lovely girl, and such an excellent family."

"We were discussing a reception for the Calverts."

Abigail regarded her son through her lorgnette. He was looking very handsome, with his sun-bronzed skin and healthy, outdoor ruggedness. No one seeing him could guess at the dissipations he favored. Oh, she knew about them, all right. Had even on occasion tried to stem them, but to no avail.

"Sometimes," she said with a chill in her voice, "you remind me so much of your father."

Drake did not make the mistake of thinking that was a compliment. He knew from the portrait of his father that dominated the front hall that there was a definite resemblance between them, a resemblance that he had come to suspect was more than physical. From hints he had picked up over the years, he had concluded that his parents' marriage had been based strictly on business interests. They had shared a bed long enough to beget five children, but he did not imagine it had been done with any pleasure. On the other hand, several of the madams of the brothels he favored remembered his father quite fondly, and showed him special favors because of it.

"I rather think," he said with a smile, "that were Father still alive, he would approve entirely of Elizabeth." In fact, he added silently, he might be hard-pressed to keep him from trying to take her for himself.

His mother's thin mouth pursed into a hard line of disapproval as the shaft hit home. He could not help but admire her regal dignity when she said, "Of course it shall be as you wish, Drake. You are, after all, head of the family."

If only nominally. At twenty-one, he had come into a substantial trust fund, which at least freed him from her purse strings, but Abigail Bennington still wielded enormous influence. She was a power throughout Boston and far beyond, anywhere there was even a pretense of proper society. If she really chose to voice her disapproval of Elizabeth, there would be no gainsaying her.

"Please, Mother," he said soothingly, "don't take this so badly. After all, wouldn't you like to see me settle down?"

"With a proper wife, certainly."

"Then you should be delighted by Elizabeth."

Abigail very much doubted it, yet she had to admit that her first glimpse of the girl hadn't been what she had expected. To begin with, there was nothing blowsy or overdone about her, as she had expected of a Southern female. She looked demure, even shy, which led Abigail to conclude that perhaps she could be easily led.

"Tell me all about yourself, dear," she said when she and Elizabeth were formally introduced the day before the ball. They were sitting in the parlor of the Benningtons' Beacon Hill house, surrounded by the assorted plunder of some six avaricious generations. Several Rembrandt drawings and a Constable oil graced the walls. Rare Ming dynasty jade sculptures were displayed on a Louis Quinze inlaid marble table. The rug beneath Abigail's trimly shod feet was Persian and dated from the sixteenth century. The porcelain cup she handed her guest, so fine as to be all but transparent, was Meissen.

"I'm afraid there isn't much to tell," Elizabeth said softly. She had been alarmed to receive the invitation to take tea with Drake's mother and now, having met her, saw that her concern was more than justified. The experience was not unlike sitting down for a little chat with a sharp-beaked carrion bird.

"I grew up at Calvert Oaks," she said when the silence from her hostess threatened to drag out, "and lived there until a year and a half ago, when I came to Boston. Since then I've been attending Miss Carter's academy."

"I understand you did quite well there."

"Not at first," Elizabeth said candidly. "It was a big change for me, but I came to enjoy it."

"What a shame, then, that you have finished your course of study."

Elizabeth had in fact graduated two days before. She had an ornate scroll on her dressing table to certify to that fact. Yet she did not feel any sense of completion. Rather she had the sense of having barely scraped the surface of all that she wanted to learn. The possibility of going back for another year was still strong in her mind, but she did not mention it, suspecting that Abigail would leap at the suggestion be-cause it precluded other possibilities.

"Drake has been very kind to me," she murmured over her teacup. "He's introduced me to a good many people and gone out of his way to make me feel at home here."

Abigail swallowed a sarcastic retort about her son's mag-nanimity. She did not believe for a moment that Elizabeth could be as naive as she appeared. "My son is a very deter-mined young man."

"I imagine he must be, to be worthy of his position."

So she wasn't completely oblivious to what it meant to be a Bennington. But then, Abigail hadn't presumed anything else. "I suppose this is all very strange to you," she said. At Elizabeth's quizzical look, she elaborated. "The parties, the big houses, such lovely clothes." The girl was well dressed, she had to give her that. Undoubtedly Mari Mackenzie's influence, and her largesse.

Rather to Abigail's surprise, a faint smile curved her young guest's lips. "Oh, we have parties in Virginia, though admittedly they aren't as grand as before the war. And while the houses I've seen here are quite nice, none is as large as Calvert Oaks. My family was very fortunate, you know. The house itself wasn't looted or burned by the Yankees. All the beautiful furniture brought from France and England at the turn of the century survived, and even through the hardest times we held on to the silver and the paintings. Why, we even have my great-grandmother's wedding china."

"How nice..." Abigail took a quick sip of her tea and regretted having put so much lemon in it. She coughed, waved aside Elizabeth's offer of assistance and after a moment managed to catch her breath. "I have never been to the South, but I had understood that it was quite devastated by the war."

"There was a tremendous amount of damage," Elizabeth acknowledged. "And then, of course, having to suddenly get along without slaves was a problem." Her smile deepened as she reminisced. "Why, I remember when I was a little girl, my father used to work all day in the fields clearing stubble and planting seed himself to bring in a crop. We needed the cash to pay taxes, otherwise we would have lost our land."

"How... enterprising of him."

"Grandfather Mackenzie's legacy helped tremendously, but even before then the plantation was getting back on its feet. Father has been able to invest in a number of other enterprises, as well as completely restore the horse breeding operation and bring in cattle."

"I hadn't realized that your mother had inherited—"

"A quite substantial sum. Put to very good use."

Abigail's thoughts reeled. She had been so certain that Elizabeth Calvert was no more than a fortune hunter that she hadn't bothered to have her family's financial background researched. Clearly that was an oversight that would have to be promptly corrected.

"I'm so glad that we had this chance to chat, dear," she said as she set down her teacup. "And I'm so looking forward to your ball tomorrow. You'll look lovely, I'm sure."

"Thank you," Elizabeth said serenely as she rose. She made her farewells and was ushered to her waiting carriage. Not until she was safely inside did she allow herself a long, slow smile. Abigail Bennington was not so indomitable after all. If nothing else, she promised to make life interesting.

HEADY WITH NEWFOUND confidence, Elizabeth woke early on the morning of her coming-out ball. She lay in bed, staring up at the lace canopy, and thinking about the wonderful twists her life was taking. It seemed a century ago that she had wept at having to leave Davey and Calvert Oaks. Surely it had been another lifetime when she had despaired of ever being pretty. And at least decades had passed since she had thought that she would never feel at home in Boston.

Not that she wouldn't always miss Virginia, but she accepted that life moved on, and in the most delightful ways. Her thoughts drifted to Drake. Sometimes she had a hard time believing that he was real, so perfectly did he epitomize her romantic daydreams. Handsome, dashing, strong, with a streak of rebelliousness that matched her own. Clearly they were meant to be together. She still had some niggling little doubt that he fully appreciated how perfectly they suited one another, but innate optimism kept her from worrying overmuch.

As a special treat, she had breakfast in bed, lying back among the pillows as the maid, Polly, brought her a tray laden with oatmeal, hash browns, fried eggs and ham.

"I can't possibly eat all that," Elizabeth protested.

"You'd better try," the rawboned country girl told her. "You're going to need your strength."

Within a few hours, Elizabeth understood what she meant. At midmorning, the hairdresser arrived, with a manicurist and masseuse in tow. The dapper little French gentleman surveyed Elizabeth as she sat self-consciously in her dressing gown, having emerged soft and rosy from a long bath. After looking her up and down slowly, he made a small moue of concern. "Well, I suppose there is something we can do."

"Now don't be naughty, Felix," Mari instructed, giving Elizabeth a reassuring smile. "You know perfectly well that she's lovely. All you have to do is gild the lily."

He drew himself up to his full five feet in height and sighed dramatically. "Would that it were so simple, *madame*. But the *mademoiselle*, lovely as she is, is a girl, and tonight, I presume, she wishes to appear as a woman."

"Or very close to," Mari agreed. "You must be subtle, of course, but then, I have always considered that your greatest strength."

Mollified, the little man bowed and began to lay out the apparatus of his trade. "It is a matter of possibilities," he muttered to himself. "A vision of what is emerging from the chrysalis." Flinging his arms wide, he announced, "You must be a butterfly, *mademoiselle*, no more a caterpillar."

It seemed that there was a great deal to be done before the cocoon could be ripped away. To begin with, she was told to remove her dressing gown and lie down on her bed, before which a modesty screen had been placed. A large Swedish lady pummeled her until she felt reduced to jelly. When she at last rose from the bed, her legs had apparently liquified, and she could barely hold her head up.

Monsieur Felix allowed her a few minutes to recover, and even permitted a cup of herbal tea, while lecturing her on the damage coffee and cocoa could do to her complexion. That done, the manicurist attacked. In her early childhood, Elizabeth had been briefly guilty of biting her nails. She had gotten over the habit, but had never taken as good care of them as she supposed she should have. In addition, she frequently forgot to wear gloves and to cream her hands each night before retiring.

The manicurist rolled her eyes as she examined what she had to work with. Monsieur Felix looked over her shoulder and tut-tutted. "This will not do, *mademoiselle*," he said. "You have the hands of a small—and, may I say, badly behaved—boy."

Elizabeth managed to look properly contrite, though inside she was blazing. What did it matter what her hands looked like, or how soft her skin was or how pliable her body was? She was still the same person she had always been, and that should be what was important. Except that she knew it wasn't. Men cared about such things, including men like Drake, and therefore she had to care, too.

When her nails were buffed to a soft pink and her hands glowed from copious applications of rose cream, Monsieur Felix at last took over. First he directed her hair to be washed and rinsed with lemon, then dried with a length of silk. That done, he sat her in front of the dressing table, stood back and observed her critically.

"You have too much hair."

"Surely it should be long?"

"*Bien sûr*, but not so . . . wild. Look here, you see these ends?"

"What about them?"

"They are split." From his tone, the magnitude of the offense could not have been greater. Elizabeth hung her head in shame. Sensing her capitulation, he said, "They must be cut."

Before she could respond, he set on her, snipping here, there, everywhere. A flurry of caramel-colored locks fell to the floor, where Polly had prudently laid an old sheet. Elizabeth kept her eyes tightly closed. She had the sudden, awful fear that Monsieur Felix was part of some terrible plot to embarrass her in front of all of Boston. He had already said that she had the hands of a boy; now he would give her the hair of one, too.

She smelled something dry and hot, and opened her eyes just enough to see the curling iron being applied with what looked like purely vindictive abandon. It seemed to go on forever, her hair being pulled this way and that way, Monsieur Felix muttering to himself all the while, the hot iron sizzling away, until at last there was stillness.

"Well," the Frenchman said after a long-drawn-out moment, "aren't you going to look?"

She did so gingerly, only to find herself staring into the mirror at a girl who looked somehow familiar, yet wasn't. Could that truly be herself? That fey-looking creature with the lightly tumbled curls softening the line of her forehead and the rest of her hair caught up in swirling twists that exposed the vulnerability of her throat? She looked...elegant, feminine, beautiful.

"It's...wonderful," she said breathlessly.

"Of course it is," Monsieur Felix acknowledged as he began to pack away his implements. "It is my creation, is it not?"

"But will it...last?"

"Through this evening, *certainement*, if you don't go tumbling around like a hoyden. Then tonight you brush it out, one hundred strokes, you understand? And tomorrow it can be done again."

"Every day? This has to be done every day?"

He frowned at her in the mirror. "What did you imagine, *mademoiselle*? Beauty has its price." Lightly he fingered one of the curls on her forehead. "But now that the cut is right, it will not take so long. Your maid can do it for you in no more than half an hour or so. Once a month I will come to keep all as it should be."

Half an hour each morning to be yanked, twisted and curled. Then there was also the ritual with the bath and with her nails and hands. Not to mention the massage, which she devoutly hoped she wouldn't be expected to endure too often. Truly, as Monsieur Felix said, beauty had its price. She could only hope that it would turn out to be a fair one.

DRAKE WHISTLED TO HIMSELF as he slipped into the evening coat held for him by his valet. Much of his good humor was related to the conversation he'd had earlier that day with his mother. It wasn't very often that Abigail Bennington had to admit that she had been wrong, and in fact she hadn't gone quite that far. But the discovery that the Calverts were, if not as rich as the Benningtons, quite well off had set her back a pace. She had taken refuge in grimly suggesting that any Southern gentleman who managed to come through the war in such good financial shape couldn't be overly scrupulous, a tendency his daughter might well have inherited.

Drake had put a swift end to that line of reasoning. "If you're right, Mother, then Elizabeth is all the better suited to become a Bennington, since we've never been overloaded with scruples, either."

"Really, Drake, the things you say."

"Only the truth, Mother."

"Mark my words, there is more to that girl than you want to see."

"Will there be anything else, sir?" the valet asked, interrupting his train of thought.

Still smiling, Drake shook his head. "Don't bother waiting up, Fitzhugh. I expect to be rather late."

"Very good, sir."

Drake winked, picked up a small velvet box from his dressing table and tossed it casually into the air as he strode from the room. The spring evening was warm and fragrant. He had opted to forgo a carriage and stroll the comfortable distance to Commonwealth Avenue. It would give him time to think over what he intended to do that night, and decide the best way to carry it out.

Anticipation added buoyancy to his step as he approached the Mackenzie house. It was awash with activity as carriages jockeyed for position out front, sumptuously dressed ladies and gentlemen descended to climb the stone steps to the entrance and hangers-on gaped at the display. Through the high French windows illuminated by gaslight, music drifted. Several friends greeted him, and in their company he entered the hall where Elizabeth would be waiting in the receiving line with her aunt and her parents.

Drake was in the midst of exchanging a jest with a former schoolmate when he caught sight of her. He broke off in midsyllable and stared. From the first time he had seen her at the Christmas ball, he had known she was lovely. But the vision before him was vastly more than that.

She appeared to exist in a shimmering column of light radiating from the top of her golden hair—something had been done to that that he could not quite grasp—to the bottoms of her feet hidden by the skirt of her gown. In between was perfection, not the girlish loveliness he was growing accustomed to, but the radiant beauty of a woman warmed from within by barely banked fires.

Distantly he could note the superficial details of her appearance and understand how they affected him. Her gown was of the newer, more form-fitting style that emphasized the delightfully ripe curve of her breasts, her slender waist made all the tinier by corseting, and the correspondingly fuller swell of her hips was further emphasized by a bustle. Her shoulders and arms were bare, her skin gleaming alabaster in the light. Around her white throat she wore a diamond-studded band of dark blue velvet that matched her dress. Her narrow skirt ended in a long train whose weight pulled the fabric more tautly against her body, further hinting at its delights.

But all that, exquisite as it was, counted for nothing when compared to the gleam of anticipation in her glowing eyes or the fullness of her moist, ripe mouth. She looked like a woman on the verge of discovering her own sensuality. Drake took a deep, shuddering breath. For an irrational moment, he was jealous of every other man seeing her like this. He wanted to sweep her up in his arms, carry her away and imprint himself on her with a fierceness that could never be overcome.

Except that he was in Boston, where such things simply weren't done. Especially not to young ladies surrounded by the full protection of loving families.

"Good evening, sir," he said as he bowed to Philip Calvert.

The older man inclined his head. "Nice to see you here, Drake."

"It certainly is," Sarah said, holding out her hand to him. "I trust your mother will be along shortly?"

"She's coming with friends, but shouldn't be long."

He greeted Mari, took note of the satisfied gleam in her eyes as they rested on his flushed face, and was at last free to speak to Elizabeth. Her hand lay lightly in his. He bent, intending to bestow no more than a proper kiss, when some instinct bade him otherwise. Holding her eyes, he turned her hand over and gently touched his mouth to her palm. The small but evocative gesture was done within an instant, and he was confident no one else had noticed, but he had the satisfaction of hearing her faint gasp and seeing the rush of color in her cheeks.

"You're quite beautiful," he told her, having regained some small measure of his equanimity.

"Thank you."

"You will save the waltzes for me."

"What, all of them?"

He nodded, kissed her hand again, properly this time, and vanished into the crowd without waiting for her reply to what had not, after all, been a question.

IN POINT OF FACT, Elizabeth did not save all her waltzes for Drake. She danced the first one with her father. Many a man lacking two good arms would not have been able to hold a partner gracefully, but Philip had no such problem. Father and daughter moved as one across the dance floor, empty except for themselves. From the sidelines, guests and family watched admiringly. Drake found it impossible to take his eyes from Elizabeth. He watched her smile up at Philip, her eyes alight with pleasure, and silently vowed that one day she would look at him like that.

But when he did at last hold her in his arms, she looked at him with wariness, as though remembering his unorthodox greeting and uncertain of whether or not he had been mocking her. Always before when they had danced together he'd had no difficulty keeping up the usual light stream of banter that passed for properly social conversation. But this time was different. He could think of a great deal to say to her; unfortunately, none of it was appropriate for the middle of a dance floor, where they were being observed by all and sundry.

Off to one side, he could see Philip and Sarah Calvert, keeping a careful eye on the proceedings. At the opposite end of the room, his mother was holding court. She appeared to be in rapt conversation with a portly old judge, but he did not doubt that she was taking careful note of everything that passed between him and Elizabeth.

What they needed, he decided, was privacy. But to achieve it in such a mass of people would require all his ingenuity.

Was he angry at her? Elizabeth wondered. He looked so grim, and he'd barely said a word to her since the dance began. And now he kept glancing over toward the French doors leading to the gardens, as though seeking some escape.

If he didn't want her company, there were plenty of other gentlemen who did. That had been made abundantly clear to her as her dance card was filled in record time, though she, fool that she was, had left all but the first waltz for Drake. If he was going to continue to behave like a glum stick-in-the-mud, she would suggest that he needn't feel obliged to dance them with her.

She was about to do so when the music stopped and, amid the applause that followed its end, he leaned forward and whispered, "Meet me in the gardens in half an hour."

"I most certainly will not." The idea of trying to make an assignation with her as practically all the world looked on!

Without moving from the center of the dance floor, he glared down at her. "What do you mean, you won't?"

"I should think the words are perfectly clear. This is my party; I have certain responsibilities."

"Oh, for God's sake."

"Don't blaspheme."

"And don't you tell me you're going to be that sort of wife."

"What sort of... w-wife?"

"Now will you meet me in the garden?" he demanded.

She nodded, wide-eyed. "I suppose I can manage it."

She was going to be trouble, he thought with an anticipatory grin as he waited for her amid the rosebushes and cherry trees. Well-brought-up Boston girls did not have spats of temper in the middle of dance floors. They were far more likely to show displeasure through the coldness his mother had always used as her primary weapon, and that he despised. How much better to have a spitfire for a wife; how much more satisfying the taming of her.

At school, one of the very few pieces of literature he had enjoyed had been *The Taming of the Shrew*. He had rather fancied himself playing Petruchio to some hot-blooded vixen's Katherina, and now it seemed that he would have the chance.

A rustle of silk alerted him to her presence. He turned in time to see her come cautiously down the stairs from the terrace, pause and look around. He had purposefully positioned himself in the shadows so that he could not be seen, and when he called to her, she jumped.

"Elizabeth, over here."

Picking up her skirts, she hesitated a moment longer before stepping lightly across the lawn to his side. "I can't stay long," she said, "or I'll be missed."

He took her arm and led her farther into the shelter of an ancient willow tree whose drooping branches effectively screened them from the world. In a world of dark, moist green and the soft night sounds of hidden creatures, they might have been the only man and woman alive.

"Don't worry," he said as he felt her back tense beneath his lightly stroking hand. "If someone does notice that you've slipped out, you'll be forgiven."

"How can you be so sure?" It was difficult to make out her expression in the dimness, but he heard the challenge in her words.

"Are you suggesting your family doesn't approve of me?" he asked teasingly.

She turned her head away. "I'm suggesting you're very sure of yourself."

"Yes . . . I suppose I am. It's the way I've been raised."

"Have Benningtons always gotten what they want?"

His brows drew together. "I've rarely thought about it, but I suppose we have."

A cool breeze brushed past, making her shiver. He seized the excuse to draw her closer into his arms. Lightly his lips brushed her fragrant hair as he said, "I can't see you with some callow boy who didn't know his own mind."

Neither could Elizabeth, though she was loath to admit it. Pressed against the warmth of his broad chest, she shivered again for a quite different reason. Although she had suspected, even hoped, what their relationship was leading up to, now that the moment seemed upon her, she was stricken with doubts.

She was, after all, still very young, and though she had expected to be married before now—to Davey on her sixteenth birthday had been her fantasy—this was very different. With him, she would have been continuing in the familiar way of life that she understood and accepted. Drake was in many ways still a stranger, one who fascinated her, to be sure, but with hidden dangers she could sense but not define.

"Your mother doesn't like me," she murmured, grasping at any excuse that might afford some delay.

"Nonsense, she's tremendously impressed by you." His hand slipped beneath her chin, gently raising her head. "Besides, it doesn't matter what she thinks of you, or what anyone else thinks, for that matter. I want you to be my wife."

There, he had said it. A rush of relief flowed through him. The great hurdle was past, and he could see nothing but smooth sailing ahead. Of course, they would have to wait several months. She would want a trousseau, and there would be innumerable parties given for them. And then he supposed the wedding would take place in Virginia, after yet another round of feting. But that was all right; it would be great fun, and in the meantime he could undoubtedly persuade her to allow at least a little light lovemaking. The urges that would arouse could easily be satisfied at the brothels where he was always welcome, and would have the added advantage of getting her nicely primed for the wedding night.

He wondered if she would conceive immediately, and had mixed feelings about that, having no idea how sexually available she would be while pregnant. He rather thought that it would be nice to have her to himself for a while before allowing for any intrusions.

Having more or less planned out the coming months, he had lost sight of one small detail: Elizabeth had not yet said yes. But she was vividly aware of that, and of the fact that he was not waiting with bated breath for her answer. Begin as you mean to go on, Mammy Augusta had always told her. It was just as well that they get a few things straight from the outset.

"I'm flattered by your proposal," she said, "but I'm not at all certain that I can accept it."

"What . . . ?"

"We haven't known each other very long, and I am rather young."

"For heaven's sake, Elizabeth. What game are you playing at?"

"Game?" She stepped a short distance away from him, and the motion brought the scent of her jasmine perfume to his nostrils. They quivered as, instinctively, his hands tightened on her arms. "It's hardly a game," she said, "to make a decision that will affect the entire future course of both our lives."

Technically, she was right, he supposed, though he had never thought of marriage in those precise terms. But then, it was different for a woman, who would be expected to live through her husband, and who would have none of the other outlets available to him.

Yet he persisted in believing that she was merely toying with him, playing the age-old female game of hard to get. He was willing to go along, up to a point.

"How can you expect me to wait," he asked as he drew her back into his embrace, "when I can't think of anything except you? You're unlike any other woman I've ever met. I can't imagine asking anyone else to be my wife."

All very pleasant to hear, and Elizabeth would have been less than human if she hadn't warmed to his flattery. Yet she remained unconvinced. A stubbornly rational part of her mind stood apart, observing the charming scene with skepticism.

She didn't doubt that Drake desired her, or that he found her fascinating when compared to the stuffy Bostonian girls of his acquaintance. But that did not add up to the kind of all-encompassing, eternal love she saw between her mother and her father. Wistfully, she wondered if she wasn't aiming too high when she sought to emulate their special relationship, yet she couldn't imagine settling for less.

"Elizabeth," Drake murmured, his warm lips nuzzling her throat, "trust me. We're perfect together. I'll give you everything you could ever want." At that moment, he truly meant what he said, but his understanding of her potential desires was more limited than he could possibly have guessed. He envisioned dazzling her with his lovemaking, swathing her in furs and adorning her with jewels. She would live surrounded by wealth and power, wanting for nothing. What more could any woman possibly ask?

Despite her best efforts, Elizabeth was not immune to his caresses. They ignited a fire in her blood that burned away rational thought. A brief spurt of fear darted through her as she wondered, as she had several other times in Drake's arms, whether there might be something wrong with her. Surely it was wanton to respond so unbridledly to a man's touch. She remembered how she had enjoyed Davey's kisses, shy as they were. Drake's were anything but. When she tilted her head back to look at him, his mouth came down on hers with hungry intent.

Before, when he had kissed her, Drake had been careful to keep at least a part of his passion in check so as not to frighten her. But now, driven by the challenge she had issued, he refused to hold back. His lips parted hers, and an instant later she felt the insistent sweep of his tongue.

Elizabeth gasped and tried to pull away. No one had ever touched her like that. Her immediate reaction was shock and distaste, but that gave way almost instantly to a far different response. Heat curled in her belly. Her breasts ached, and she could feel her nipples hardening. Deeply embarrassed, entranced and frightened all at once, she put her hands on his arms and struggled to break free.

Drake refused to let her go. He sensed the battle being waged between his determination and her innocence, and he had no doubt which would win. Moreover, he was certain she would be glad in the end. She was the furthest thing from a cold woman, and he'd be damned if he would let her pretend otherwise.

"Give in to it," he murmured when he briefly broke off the kiss. "Let me show you at least a little of how it will be between us."

That reference to "a little" reassured Elizabeth enough to undermine her resolve. She allowed herself to relax against him as his fingers stroked the blue velvet ribbon around her throat.

Drake touched the pretty bauble, thinking that it was almost like a collar. How enticing she would look wearing it and nothing else in his bed. A moment later, he regretted the image as his body hardened even further and a groan threatened to burst from him.

Damned if he would wait months for them to be wed. He'd be a wreck long before then. The whole process would have to be speeded up. He had Europe in mind for a honeymoon, and it would be perfect in the summer.

"Say yes," he demanded as his hands wandered down her back to encounter the swell of her bustle and train. He clenched the fragile material as, heedlessly, he ground her against him. His lips caressed the swell of her breasts, bare above her décolletage, his tongue stroking the shadowed hollow between them.

Liquid fire darted through Elizabeth. Instinctively, she arched closer to Drake. What had always before been a shadowy possibility safely ensconced in some future time was suddenly vividly immediate. For the first time she was forced to acknowledge what it would mean to lie with a man, this man. To be entered, penetrated, possessed was a frightening prospect, yet it beckoned irresistibly to a primitive part of herself that would not be denied.

That way spelled terrible danger, yet with Drake she could be safe. He offered the refuge of honorable marriage, to a wealthy man no less. She had seen the jealousy in the eyes of other young women, and some not so young, when they looked at her with Drake. She would be a fool to turn down anyone so eminently eligible. And for what? A nebulous dream of a love she told herself would come anyway?

"Are you sure?" she whispered in one final effort not to make it too easy for him.

He gripped her slender waist between his hands and looked at her with such fierceness that she wondered how she could ever have feared that he took her for granted. "Absolutely. You must agree to be my wife, otherwise I'll keep you here forever."

Elizabeth's laugh was soft, throaty, triumphant. "Oh, I couldn't let you do that. What a scandal it would cause. Best that we marry instead."

He caught his breath and moved instantly to consolidate his victory. "When?"

"Well, let's see, there's so much to be done...."

"Four weeks."

"Oh, no! That isn't nearly enough time." She managed to sound appalled, though she was secretly pleased to have his desires so precisely match her own.

"Not a day longer," he insisted, smiling as he sensed she was not going to fight. "Or I won't be responsible for my actions."

She looked up at him through her long, thick lashes. "Oh...in that case..."

He didn't wait to hear anything more but sealed their pledge in a way that had her privately wishing that the coming month was already over with.

PHILIP WAS LESS SANGUINE when he learned of his daughter and Drake's plans. Though his prospective son-in-law tried to phrase his proposal of marriage as a request dependent on parental approval, he was less than successful. Philip had no doubt that the confident young man seated across from him considered their interview little more than a formality.

Drake had a great deal going for him, he thought objectively as he studied him from beneath hooded lids. Young, handsome, personable, and then, of course, there was the matter of his wealth. Philip had been in Boston only a few days, and had seen his daughter and Drake together only once, when he began to make inquiries about the Benningtons. What he learned satisfied him that Elizabeth would be more than amply taken care of, at least materially. The question was whether this young man who was so blessed by fortune would be able to satisfy her in other ways.

Philip was a practical man; natural inclination and the events of a demanding life had made him so. Some of his inquiries had had to do with matters more personal than money. What he had learned did not precisely distress him so much as give him pause.

Prior to his marriages—first to poor, doomed Daphne and then to the woman he loved more than his own life— Philip had been no stranger to the pleasures of the flesh. He had enjoyed all the amusements that a wealthy Southern gentlemen took as his right. But he had also used the occasions of his visits to some of the finest brothels in Virginia and elsewhere to perfect his own skill as a lover. Beating down a natural fatherly disinclination to think of his daughter in such a context, he wondered if Drake had done the same.

Observing the glowing tip of his cheroot, he said, "You understand, Mr. Bennington, that I would never force my daughter to marry. She is perfectly welcome to return home with us to Virginia and to remain there as long as she likes." He could say this sincerely since, having seen her after the absence of more than a year, he was confident she had put Davey firmly in the past.

"Please, call me Drake. As to any suggestion that Elizabeth should marry without being fully enthusiastic at the prospect, that is naturally out of the question. However, I have reason to believe that I am . . . acceptable to her."

Drake's attempts at modesty were becoming more amusing by the moment. Dryly, Philip said, "I'm sure you do."

This wasn't going as Drake had envisioned. He had expected Philip to jump at the prospect of his daughter making so excellent a marriage. Instead he seemed cagey, even a shade reluctant.

"I can assure you," he told the older man stiffly, "that I have the highest opinion of Elizabeth and will do everything in my power to make her happy."

Philip took a long puff on his cheroot, sent the smoke billowing toward the ceiling and asked, "Are you in love with her?"

Drake flinched, though he managed to conceal the action by shifting in his chair. He hadn't expected Philip to be so blunt. Proper Bostonian fathers did not speak of such matters. But then, he was dealing with a Southerner, a former rebel, and a man who gave every evidence of being less than concerned by conventions.

"I . . . uh . . . hold her in the highest esteem."

"So you have already said, but do you love her?"

"I . . . that is to say . . . yes, of course I do."

Philip smiled inwardly. Sarah had warned him that Drake would be embarrassed to speak of his feelings, and that was proving to be the case. Beneath his healthy tan, the young man's face had reddened.

More kindly, Philip said, "I don't mean to make you uncomfortable, but Elizabeth is my only daughter, and her happiness is my chief concern."

That, at least, was acceptable. Drake relaxed fractionally and even managed a sympathetic smile. "Of course, sir. I wouldn't expect anything less."

"Good, then you'll understand that should anything happen to dim that happiness, I would be most displeased."

That was putting it on the line, Drake thought. For all that Philip Calvert had the uncanny ability to make him feel uncomfortable, a sensation he had rarely experienced in his privileged life, Drake couldn't help but have a niggling liking for him. The Southerner was a definite improvement over the careful gentlemen of Boston, who made a religion of never permitting a flicker of emotion to show through their rigid facades. Drake had never felt able to equal their imperturbability, whether real or assumed, and had always felt at a disadvantage around them as a result. But with Philip he could see that a man—a strong, successful one, at that—could let his feelings show without appearing weak, could in fact use them as a form of intimidation.

Not, of course, that it worked with him. He wasn't in the least afraid of Elizabeth's father, though he had to admit he had every intention of staying on the good side of him.

"I assure you, sir," he said, "that if Elizabeth and I are blessed with a daughter, I will undoubtedly be equally concerned with her happiness."

The cheroot clenched between his teeth, Philip smiled. There would be a certain justice in Drake having a daughter, preferably more than one. Then he would be a good deal less blithe about dealings between men and women.

"Very well," Philip said. "You have my permission to wed Elizabeth."

Drake jumped up, heartily glad to have the interview at an end and his objective attained. He thrust out his hand. Philip rose more slowly. They looked each other straight in the eye as they shook.

"Take care of her," Philip said.

Drake knew a final warning when he heard it. He nodded swiftly. "Count on it, sir."

WITHIN THE WEEK, preparations for the wedding were under way. To Drake's surprise and relief, Sarah Calvert did not even raise an eyebrow when she heard how speedily they wished to be married. She merely indicated that a prompt return to Virginia would be wise in order to facilitate the preparations. But first, there was Abigail Bennington's reception to get through. As it now appeared that it would be one of the very few opportunities for Boston to fete the new couple, everyone who was anyone expected to be invited to attend. From an initial guest list of two hundred, the event swiftly doubled and then went beyond.

Abigail took the news of her son and Elizabeth's engagement with her usual stiff-lipped demeanor. If she was surprised at its hastiness, she made no comment, not even to those Boston matrons who considered themselves her closest friends and who wasted no time staging a decorous but determined siege in her front parlor, an assault waged with visiting cards, knowing smiles and sympathetic nods.

Abigail bore it all stoically. She allowed that Elizabeth was "unusual"—a Boston word for highly suspect—but that she was also undeniably lovely and very well brought up. As the matriarch of the Benningtons, she could say that they were delighted to be united with the Calverts, such an old Virginia family, with their roots in the British aristocracy.

Whether or not that was true, she privately had no idea, but she was also quite confident that no one would dream of contradicting her. More than a few Boston families—having left England virtually one step ahead of the hangman—had barely clambered ashore in the New World before they began claiming noble lineage.

Sarah sat through these encounters with restrained smiles and careful eyes. For herself, she was amused by Abigail and her friends, but when she considered that Elizabeth would have to deal with these women, presumably for the rest of her life, she found the situation less humorous. She worried about how her proud, outspoken daughter would fare in an environment where innuendo reigned and even the worst back stabbing was done with the best of taste.

Her attempts to discuss the matter with Elizabeth had not been notably successful. As mother and daughter, they had always been close, but the separation of eighteen months had inevitably had an effect. Lacking the intimacy of day-to-day contact, they had fallen back on a kind of cautious politeness. Added to that was Sarah's vivid awareness of the changes taking place in her daughter. Elizabeth seemed to be in a headlong race to leave her girlhood behind and assume the privileges of womanhood. Sarah could understand that, since she had once felt much the same way herself, but she couldn't help but wonder if her daughter had any true awareness of the responsibilities that went along with her soon-to-be status.

During their brief conversations, Elizabeth had blithely dismissed such concern with comments along the lines of, "Oh, of course I'll be a good wife to Drake, Mother. We understand each other perfectly."

In the face of such wholehearted confidence, Sarah was stymied. On the one hand, she felt she should caution her daughter that what she was experiencing during courtship had virtually nothing to do with marriage. Not that she expected Drake to suddenly turn into an ogre the moment the vows were said, but there was a world of difference between the romantic suitor and the established husband. Only a very few men, happily Philip included, ever thought to woo their wives once their possession was assured.

Yet she couldn't bring herself to say or do anything that might dim Elizabeth's happiness. She was living at the heart of a brightly burning flame, and for an incandescent moment her mother wanted her to be utterly without doubts or fears. To restrain herself from expressing her concerns was her gift to her child, one that might never be recognized or appreciated, but came from the purest maternal love. Besides, she told herself when her worry became too great, Elizabeth was in all likelihood right about her ability to be a good wife to Drake. She was intelligent, sensible, resilient and strong, the characteristics a woman most needed in order to cope with whatever vagaries fate might toss her way.

But fate seemed to have nothing in mind except to make the new couple's path as smooth as possible. On the eve of Abigail's reception for them, gifts were already pouring in from all the great families of New England, as well as those who hoped to be taken for such. It appeared that Elizabeth's greatest problem after marriage would be finding a place to store them all, and that was taken care of when a dowager living in Louisburg Square only a stone's throw from the Bennington residence had the kindness to die and her heirs wasted no time putting her house on the market.

Drake promptly bought it, and the dowager's renowned collection of antiques, for the stunning sum of five hundred thousand dollars, an amount large enough to give even those fully aware of the Bennington fortune pause. Barely had the contract been signed than surveyors checking out a seemingly played-out mine in California that Drake had won in a card game discovered an overlooked vein of pure gold that promised to produce at least enough to pay for ten such houses.

Drake accepted this embarrassment of riches without surprise. Lady Fortune had smiled on him since the day of his birth, if not before. He was fully confident that she would continue to do so.

As he stood in the receiving line in his mother's house, greeting the hundreds of guests who had come to hear the announcement of their engagement, he gazed proudly at Elizabeth. She was radiant in a gown of lavender satin, the diamond and sapphire necklace he had given her scant hours before gleaming at her throat. Their eyes met, and she smiled with pure, unbridled happiness, which he was certain foretold a perfectly agreeable future.

Chapter Seven

CALVERT OAKS HAD NOT SEEN such frenetic activity since Philip's first marriage, his second having been celebrated far more modestly on the eve of war. Even with the extra servants who had been hired, Sarah was hard-pressed to make sure that everything that needed to be done was indeed accomplished on time. Food had to be prepared, flowers arranged for, liquor procured, furniture moved, the morning room decorated as a chapel, extra seating obtained, gifts acknowledged and so on, until the list seemed endless. To make matters more complicated, old Rameses, who had been butler at Calvert Oaks for longer than anyone could remember, chose that time to pass on to his reward. The middle-aged nephew he had long since trained to take his place promptly did so, but the old man's presence was still missed.

In one respect, at least, Sarah's task as mother of the bride was made easier; Elizabeth vetoed the idea of a trousseau, pointing out that she already had more than adequate a wardrobe, much of which would suit her perfectly well in her new state as a wife. Upon examination by her skeptical mother and Aunt Mari, this proved to be correct. Mari in particular was taken aback to discover how many of the dresses and gowns that had somehow slipped by her were surprisingly mature, almost as though, despite her disclaimer, Elizabeth had known all along what was to happen to her.

That left the matter of the wedding gown, and here again Elizabeth took them by surprise. "When I was a little girl," she said, their first night back at Calvert Oaks as they sat around the dining room table discussing what needed to be done, "I used to sneak up to the attic and stare at Momma's wedding gown. I never had the nerve to take it out of the trunk, but I did peek beneath the cambric wrapped around it enough to see how lovely it is. Before we think of arranging for something new, do you think I might try it on?"

Sarah was deeply touched by the thought of her daughter wearing the gown that had graced a day that still shone golden in her memories. Philip was also pleased; Elizabeth's preference denoted a reassuring sense of tradition and continuity that he thought would serve her well.

The following morning the gown was taken with great ceremony from its storage place by Mammy Augusta and carried down to Elizabeth's room. She stood in her chemise and petticoats in front of a full-length mirror, her unbound hair streaming over her shoulders and her eyes shining with excitement. They glowed even brighter when her gaze fell on the dress.

"Oh, Momma, it's beautiful."

Sarah had to agree. From a perspective accustomed to the newer styles, her wedding gown was undeniably old-fashioned, yet she could not think that a detriment. There was a romanticism about the white satin, aged now to an ivory patina, that perfectly suited Elizabeth.

"It took three seamstresses from Richmond a fortnight to make this," she said as together she and Augusta carefully held the dress for Elizabeth to step into it.

"Ah 'members how yo hated dose fittin's, missy," Augusta said with a laugh. "Yo fidgeted so much ah thought we was neber goin' to be done."

"I don't blame you," Elizabeth said as she stared in the mirror. "It must have seemed to go on forever." She ran a hand delightedly over the fragile pleated flounces and lace-trimmed ruffles. "At least you didn't have to help sew these on." She fingered one of the vast quantity of seed pearls that embroidered the boned bodice and trailed down the leg-of-mutton sleeves. Almost reverently, she said, "It is lovely." Her delighted smile faded slightly as she looked at herself more carefully. "But somehow..."

"It doesn't look quite right," Sarah said. "I was wondering when you would notice." She and Augusta exchanged a conspiratorial smile. In the aftermath of her husband's death, Augusta's own burden of years had caught up with her, but she was still enjoying the occasion.

"The skirt," Elizabeth said. "It doesn't fall right, and it's so heavy. I don't see how I'll be able to move."

"Dat's what hoops is fo'," Augusta said.

"Hoops?"

"I'm afraid so," Sarah said with a laugh. "We must still have a set around somewhere, don't we, Augusta?"

"Shur do, missy." She hurried from the room and returned a short time later, struggling with an ungainly contraption of metal rods and strings.

Elizabeth stared at them askance. "But I've never worn hoops. How will I ever learn to manage them?"

"The same way we all did," her mother said with a reminiscent smile. "Practice."

And more practice. Elizabeth spent the next hour or so alternately laughing and fuming at herself. No sooner did she think that she had gotten the hang of them than she did something foolish, such as trying to sit down, and discovered how far she still had to go.

"Not lahk dat, missy," Augusta instructed, hands on her broad hips and wrinkled face alight with amusement. "Yo gots to float, honey, lahk a bird."

"Some bird," Elizabeth muttered. "I feel as though my wings had been clipped."

Indeed, between the ungainly hoops and the tight corseting needed to fit even her slender waist into the gown's minuscule opening, she could hardly breathe, let alone do anything as energetic as walking.

"Try it more slowly," Sarah urged, struggling to hold back her laughter. She was remembering her own initiation into the sisterhood of the hoop, and her conviction that she would disgrace herself at any moment. "You're doing fine, but really, sweetheart, are you sure you want to wear them?"

"Without them, I can't wear the dress."

"Perhaps it could be restyled," Sarah ventured, without great conviction. Certainly something could be done to the gown, but in the process it would lose all that made it so special.

"Absolutely not," Elizabeth said with an emphatic shake of her head. "I'll master these darn things if it's the last thing I do."

Augusta and Sarah exchanged a glance. Both were wondering why it was so important to the young girl to wear the outmoded gown. Certainly it was a lovely gesture of affection and respect to her parents, but, having encountered difficulties, she could be excused for changing her mind.

Elizabeth sensed their concern and laughed softly. "It seems strange, doesn't it? But you see, it's very important for me to look like a Southern belle, or at least like the image Yankees still have of what such a creature is supposed to look like."

"Why?" Sarah asked.

"So they'll be reminded of who we were, and of how we've survived against all odds."

Sarah did not know what to say. Her daughter's vehemence both surprised and worried her. She understood pride, having a full measure of it herself, but what Elizabeth was experiencing seemed to go far beyond that. She appeared determined to make a point with her future family in a way that would not be forgotten. Whatever happened afterward, memories of the wedding day would linger.

Leaving her daughter and Mammy Augusta to discuss whatever minor alterations were necessary, she went downstairs. Mari was in the entrance hall, accepting a telegram from a dust-splattered rider. She turned with it in her hand and a rueful smile on her lips.

"For you...again. I believe it's from Mrs. Bennington."

Sarah stifled a sigh. The groom, his family and friends were arriving the following day for a week-long round of parties that would culminate in the wedding itself. They were coming by private railroad car and had been preceded by half a dozen telegrams received over the past few days in which Abigail made certain helpful "suggestions."

"I suppose," she murmured, "that it really is useful to know that Drake prefers Earl Grey tea, dislikes biscuits and does not care for starched bed sheets." She perused the latest message, her cheeks flushing slightly. "But I really don't think I need instruction in the seating arrangements for the reception dinner or the selection of appropriate flowers for the church."

Mari gave her a sympathetic smile. "Abigail is not the most tactful of women."

"Tactful? I fear she is going to be the worst sort of mother-in-law: interfering, bossy and oblivious to the strains created by her own behavior. Elizabeth will have her work cut out for her once she is settled in Boston. Perhaps it's just as well that she intends to make her mark right from the outset."

"The gown?" Mari asked. "She's going to wear it?"

Sarah nodded, smiling. "Complete with hoops. Our Yankee guests will think they've gone back in time to a very different South."

"Do them good. Besides, everyone here will be delighted."

"I hope so," Sarah said, her eyes clouding as she remembered the conversation she had had the day before with her stepson. William was not at all pleased by Elizabeth's pending marriage. As was his way, he'd said little about it, but his very silence expressed his concern, if not his displeasure. Considering how important his opinion was to his sister, Sarah could only hope that he would change his mind before the young girl became aware of his feelings.

LEAVING THE STABLES where he had gone to check on a newborn colt, William paused to wipe the sweat from his forehead and look up at the sky. The fields needed rain, but there wasn't a cloud in sight. He was hot, tired, thirsty and not in the best of moods. The mare had labored hard throughout the night, with him beside her all the way. When she at last brought forth her spindly-legged offspring, it looked as though the effort might not be worthwhile. The tiny baby had refused to breathe until William forcibly cleaned out his mouth and blew air into him. He had remained in the stall until just before dawn to reassure the mother and keep an eye on her son. When he had finally been convinced that they would be all right, he didn't bother going into the house to catch a few hours' rest, but fell asleep in the straw, only to toss and turn without relief.

He told himself that he was a fool to be concerned about Elizabeth. She was radiantly happy, and both Philip and Sarah were convinced that the marriage would be good for her. Perhaps once Drake arrived and he had a chance to look him over, he'd think so, too. But in the meantime, all he could see was that his little sister seemed bent on rushing into a decision he thought her far too young and impulsive to make wisely.

"Damn it," he muttered under his breath, kicking a clod of earth with the toe of his dusty boot. Instantly the soil crumbled and wafted into the air on the grudging breeze. He had far more immediate things to worry about than Elizabeth; the drooping crops in the fields, for instance. They hadn't lost a crop since he took over that part of the plantation from his father three years before, but it looked now as though they might be on the verge of doing so.

A passing groom glanced at him worriedly. William managed a faint smile to let the man know that everything was all right. He pulled his sweat-soaked shirt away from his skin and sighed deeply. He was doing no one any good in his present state, least of all himself. Through the span of oak trees beyond the barns, he caught a glimpse of the river running cool and sparkling in the sun. Making up his mind in an instant, he started toward it.

Ten minutes later, floating naked in a secluded creek that branched off from the James and wound its lazy way through the plantation, he sighed again, this time with sheer pleasure. In a life devoted to the endless round of tasks needed to keep Calvert Oaks running smoothly, there were few moments purely for himself. He luxuriated in the stillness of the surrounding glen as much as he did in the sensual lapping of the water against his skin.

Until the snapping of a twig brought him abruptly alert. Standing up in the water so that it came to just below his navel, he looked around swiftly. His eyes fell on a small, slender figure perched elflike on the trunk of a fallen tree.

"Oh," he said, "it's you."

The figure, dressed in roughly woven pants and a shirt, and barefoot, plucked a piece of straw from its mouth and grinned. "There are crabs in there, you know. They're liable to bite something you might think is vital."

William laughed and tossed his head back, sending droplets of water dancing in the still air. "I'll risk it. How about you?"

Slanted eyebrows arched in pretended surprise. "You suggesting I should go swimming in my natural state?"

"Wouldn't be the first time."

After a moment, narrow shoulders shrugged. "True enough." A slim if grimy hand went to the buttons of his visitor's shirt. William watched as they were undone and the fabric fell open to reveal smooth skin tanned an all-over gold and small, high breasts crowned by dusky nipples. He smiled wryly as he felt his body harden beneath the water.

The trousers dropped to the ground, revealing slim legs separated by a tangle of ebony hair the same hue as the silken strands surrounding a face that would have suited a solemn pixie. With unconscious grace, the girl stepped into the water, submerged for a moment, then surfaced laughing.

"Come on," she said with a grin. "I'll race you to the other side."

Before he could respond, she had darted away, a golden streak beneath the blue water. He followed swiftly but could not catch her. She was resting against the opposite bank by the time he reached it.

"I swear you've got webbed feet," he grumbled.

She poked one above the water and studied it. "Nope, don't think so."

"Then you're part mermaid." He reached out a hand, seized her slim ankle and tumbled her back into the water. They wrestled teasingly for a few brief seconds before the nature of their contact changed and he claimed her mouth with hungry intent.

"I need you, Sunbird. Come lie with me."

Her dark eyes already slumberous with passion, she allowed him to lead her from the water. A spreading oak tree gave them shelter from the sun; velvet-soft moss was their bed. They came together swiftly, both too eager to wait. He was her first lover, and in the six months they had been meeting in such a way, he had taught her much about both her own body and his. They had reached the happy state of knowing how best to please each other without falling into the trap of tedium.

When they were done, they lay side by side, Sunbird's head on his chest. His fingers tangled in the shoulder-length ebony hair flowing over them both. Tenderly he stroked her as their breathing steadied.

"You are," he said with gentle mockery, "too much woman for me...almost."

She propped herself up on an elbow and gazed down at him. "Care to try for two out of three?"

"Only if I don't mind not being able to walk back to the house. Speaking of which, when are you going to come to supper?"

She stiffened and rolled away from him, lying on her back and staring up through the web of branches. "Must we talk about that again?"

"Not if you don't want to. All you have to do is agree to accept my invitation and I'll drop the subject."

"How magnanimous of you." She sat up, wrapping her slender arms around her legs, and laid her head on her knees. "Do you really believe your parents would welcome Charles Durand's bastard daughter at their table?" Before he could reply, she laughed harshly. "I can just see me sitting down in my breeches and shirt, not knowing which fork to use and not particularly caring, either."

He studied the proud, stiff line of her back as he wound a hand through her hair, tethering her to him. "It doesn't have to be like that."

She glanced at him over her shoulder. "Doesn't it? I know what they say about me around here. Bastard...half-breed. Probably worse. And they aren't wrong."

His grip tightened, hurting her, though she refused to give any sign of it. "What the hell does that mean?"

"Isn't it obvious? I meet you like this, lie with you, and make no secret of enjoying it. I'm hardly the stuff ladies are made of, William, so let's stop pretending otherwise."

"Ladies bore me to tears."

"Including your mother and sister?"

He leaned closer, brushing his lips over her shoulder. "They're different."

"As your wife will be."

His teeth grazed her lightly. "You exasperate me. If I had wanted a paragon of propriety as a wife, I would have married years ago. God knows I've had the—" He broke off, abruptly aware of boasting.

To his relief, Sunbird laughed. Her dark moods could come upon her quickly, but they fled even faster. Since he understood their source, he was more than willing to tolerate them.

"You've been chased by every girl for fifty miles around," she said with a grin. "If not farther. Oh, I've seen them being trotted out by their hopeful mommas and poppas, all gewgawed up in their fancy gowns. And you know something? Some of them looked pretty darn good. What was the name of that little blonde from Richmond?"

"I forget."

"Really?" She twined her fingers in the thick hair of his chest and tugged hard.

"*Ouch!* All right, I remember. Joanne something-or-other. She had buck teeth."

"She did not. She was absolutely gorgeous, just like that redhead from Washington."

A reminiscent smile flitted across William's face. "Oh, yes...Susan."

"What was wrong with her?"

"Nothing an ice bath wouldn't have fixed, or a good hard—"

"Spare me. My point is that there are plenty of girls for you to choose from, any one of which is more likely to win your family's approval than I am."

"Are you so sure of that?"

"Sure that the Calverts wouldn't welcome a half-Cherokee daughter-in-law who happens to be the spawn of a man they think ought to be run out of the neighborhood on a rail? I'd say it's a fair bet."

"You're nothing at all like your father, as you well know. That's why he and that god-awful wife of his ignore you. And so far as being half-Cherokee goes, it wouldn't be the first time a bit of mixed blood has entered the Calvert fold."

"Not on the right side of the sheets."

He shrugged, dismissing that as unimportant. "None of this matters. I want to marry you, and I think you feel the same way about me. If you don't want to meet my parents first, we'll elope."

Her tawny eyes darkened. "And then what?"

"Come back here and settle down, of course. You know Father has virtually turned Calvert Oaks over to me to run."

"Because he trusts you. But how much longer do you think he'd do that if you made an inappropriate marriage?"

"My father is wiser, and fairer, than you're giving him credit for." He slid an arm around her waist, his hand cupping her small breast as he rubbed her nipple slowly. "Don't you want to marry me?"

"I want..." She gasped softly. "What we have now. That's enough."

He buried his face in the nape of her neck, breathing in the sweet, sun-warmed fragrance of her. "Not for me."

His hand caressed her more insistently. When she tried to slap it away, he moved suddenly, turning her under him and pinning her to the ground. His face was dark and set above her. "All right, if a good rutting's all you want, spread your legs."

"Stop it, William."

"You said that was enough. I'm ready...." His hand dived between the thighs she was trying to keep tightly clenched. "So are you. What's the problem?"

"I don't want you like this. Let me go."

"You said it yourself, almost. That you're nothing but a whore. So why should you care how we do it?"

"Damn you." She was not so much afraid as angry and hurt. He was deliberately turning her words against her, trying to make her seem foolish when all she was trying to do was to protect him. "I swear, if you don't let me up, I'll..."

"You'll what?" She was strong, especially for a woman, but he was far more so. With slight effort, he contained her struggles and held her helpless under him.

Or so he thought, until her knee moved swiftly and with near lethal effect. Pain crashed through him, even though he had managed to jerk away at the last moment to avoid the worst of her blow. She was up in an instant, while he was still trying to draw a breath. Swiftly she dived back into the water and swam to where they had left their clothes. He didn't try to follow her, knowing that he needed some time to recover. But he watched with a wry smile as she dressed and, without a backward glance, vanished into the forest.

ELIZABETH WAS SITTING on the veranda when William returned to the house. It was getting on toward dusk; he had waited by the river until he was certain that no sign of the afternoon's activities remained. Which was just as well, since his sister's sharp eyes missed little.

"You look tired," she said as she hurried down the steps to take his arm. "I've seen the new colt. He's beautiful. What are you going to name him? Are you hungry? Cook baked today; there's a wonderful peach pie."

"I haven't decided yet. Yes. Sounds good."

Elizabeth sighed and fell into step beside him as they headed for the kitchen, which was set apart from the rest of the house but connected by a covered walkway. "I wonder if I'll ever be able to talk to Drake like that and have him understand?"

Something in her tone drew him up short. He looked at her from the corner of his eyes, noting that she appeared pale and rather drawn. "I thought you believed that the two of you were made for each other."

"Oh, we are," she assured him. "Don't pay any attention to me. Drake and all the rest of them are due here in the morning, and I'm just having last-minute jitters."

"Not exactly last minute. The wedding isn't for a week yet; there's still plenty of time for you to change your mind."

"Well, I'm not about to. Drake is the perfect husband for me."

"I can't wait to meet this wonder." At her quick look of concern, he relented slightly. "Sorry, sis. I'm just playing the protective older brother."

"That's all right, but you really shouldn't be worried about me. I'm terribly fortunate, although," she added, "don't ever let Drake even suspect I feel that way."

He stepped aside to let her precede him into the kitchen. "Bad strategy, huh?"

"The worst." As he drew a pitcher of milk up from the deep basin of cool water where it was kept chilled, she removed the linen cloth covering the freshly baked pie and cut them each a generous slice. They sat down at the rough wooden table and ate in silence for several minutes before Elizabeth leaned back with a sigh of pure contentment. "I'm out of my mind to be eating this, what with the dress I have to fit into. You wouldn't believe how tiny Momma's wedding gown is. The waist, at least. I'm sure I won't be able to breathe."

"Then have it let out." Even after growing up in a household with a lovely mother and sister, he couldn't begin to imagine why women were willing to suffer so much for fashion. To him, no one could be more beautiful than Sunbird, and he never saw her in anything but boy's clothes, or none at all.

"What are you smiling about?" Elizabeth asked, puzzled by the look that had suddenly flashed across his face.

He finished his pie and got up for another slice. "Nothing. I'm just glad you're happy, and I hope you always will be."

"That's nice, but I really want you to like Drake, too." She met his eyes as he returned to the table. "It's important to me."

"I know it is, and I'll try." He could promise nothing more, at least not until he had met the man himself.

"Did you know we're going to Europe for our honeymoon? London, Rome, Paris. I can't wait."

"Sounds exciting. You'll have to write and tell us what all those places are like."

"I may be too busy," she said with a laugh. At his startled look, she explained, "Drake wants me to buy all sorts of clothes over there so that when we get back to Boston, I'll set the fashion."

"How do you feel about it?" The Elizabeth he remembered had always liked pretty clothes, but not the effort it took to be fitted for them.

She shrugged and finished the last bite of her pie. "I guess it's important for the new Mrs. Bennington to look the part."

"Yes...clothes can make a difference." He was thinking about what Sunbird had said, that she couldn't see herself sitting down to supper with his parents in her trousers and shirt. If her father paid her the least attention, if her stepmother weren't so spiteful, someone would have taken her in hand and at least helped her to look like a young lady was expected to. But no one ever had, and he found himself wanting to remedy the deficiency.

"You've shopped in Richmond," he said. "Are the dressmakers there any good?"

"Certainly. They use pattern books from Paris and even have a lot of the same materials. Why do you ask?"

"No reason."

Elizabeth did not press any further, knowing from long experience that her brother said only what he chose to. But when she left him a few minutes later, she was smiling. His sudden interest in female fripperies could mean only one thing, so far as she was concerned. Happy as she was, she wanted the whole world to be the same. She could only hope that whatever young woman William had at last focused his attention on was worthy of him. Woe betide her if she wasn't; her brother wasn't the only protective sibling in the Calvert family.

THINKING ABOUT HER BROTHER and his as yet hypothetical marriage prospects helped to distract Elizabeth as she waited out the remaining hours until Drake arrived. Sleep proved elusive that night, and she rose to find with dismay that there were shadows beneath her eyes. Never having paid much attention to such things before, she was at a loss how to deal with them. Her mother prescribed cold compresses and chamomile tea, both of which had a soothing effect.

Nonetheless, she was dressed and sitting on the veranda long before the faintest sign of dust showed on the road beyond the high stone walls. Mammy Augusta clucked over her, having failed to persuade her to eat any breakfast and concerned that she would wilt in the unseasonable heat.

"Such a furnace fo' spring," the old black woman muttered as she handed Elizabeth a fan and urged her to use it. "Lord only know when de rains come."

"Not until after the wedding. I want a bright, sunny day."

Augusta smiled at her. Despite her age, her teeth were still good and her eyes bright. "Sure yo do, honey. An' ah jus' bet yos gets it."

Elizabeth breathed in deeply, savoring the dry, pungent scent of the air fragrant with the familiar scents of earth and growing things. "I'm going to miss this place," she said softly.

"Ain't yo been missin' it up in Boston?"

"Of course, but that was different. I always thought in the back of my mind that I'd be coming home."

"Yo know, honey, yo always can."

Elizabeth shook her head. "No, not after I'm married. Then I'll have a new home and a new life."

"We neber do know what's gonna happen to us on de way through life. Yo jus' 'member dis place always be here fo' yo."

Elizabeth heard what Augusta was saying but paid it little mind. So far as she was concerned, once her vows were said, Calvert Oaks would be a closed part of her life. If she was to succeed at the future, it had to be.

And the future was coming down the road, in a flurry of dust with the clatter of horses' hooves and the jangle of carriage wheels.

Elizabeth jumped up, her eyes straining. "They're here! Oh, Augusta, run inside and tell Momma and Pappa."

The old black woman rose sedately. "Calm down now, girl. Doesn't do to let a man know how glad yo is to see him."

That was wisdom Elizabeth could recognize. She took a deep breath to steady herself and carefully smoothed the skirt of her muslin day dress. "Do I look all right, Mammy?"

"Jus' fine. Dat Yankee de luckiest man in de world. Best he 'member it, too."

He seemed inclined to when he alighted from the carriage before it rolled to a complete stop, took the steps to the veranda two at a time and scooped her into his arms. "Lord but you are a sight for sore eyes," he said as he grinned down at her, his blond hair ruffled and his collar slightly askew. "Don't expect me to let you out of my sight ever again, because I won't do it."

Elizabeth was delighted by his enthusiastic greeting, but even more so by the look of distaste on his mother's face as

Abigail descended from the carriage. Her expression said it all: this was not Boston, and her son was already showing the unfortunate influence of being away from his proper place. Still, she managed a frosty smile as she greeted Sarah and Philip, who had hurried out to meet their guests.

"Such a lovely home," she said, glancing up at the white-columned plantation house. "Exactly as I imagined the better class must live down here."

Sarah suppressed a smile. "Please come in out of the heat." She turned to the butler who had taken Rameses' place. "Foster, would you bring some lemonade to the side parlor? There should be a breeze there," she explained to Abigail as she led her inside. "Or at least what passes for one this spring."

"Yes, it is rather warm." Actually, Abigail thought it unbelievably hot and was wondering why anyone would choose to live in such a hellhole. But it wouldn't do to say that, or to show any sign of distress. Never mind that her heavy travel dress was sticking to her most uncomfortably, or that she could actually feel perspiration trickling down her forehead beneath her broad-brimmed hat.

Behind Abigail came her four daughters, Drake's sisters—Lucinda, Charlotte, Georgina and Henrietta—ranging in age from fifteen to twenty and enough alike that after several months' acquaintance with the quartet, Elizabeth still had trouble telling them apart. All had their mother's brown hair and small eyes, they were similarly outfitted in dark traveling dresses, and though they could on occasion be nice enough, at the moment they were affecting the same expression of resigned suffering coupled with disdain.

The phrase "to look down one's nose" had not had precise meaning for Elizabeth until she met the ladies Bennington. Only then did she realize that was exactly what they did when they were in the presence of anything they could not understand or accept.

Despite their earlier attempts at friendliness—more for Drake's sake than hers—she apparently qualified on both counts, as did her parents and her home. With newfound confidence, she could take a perverse delight in watching them struggle to appear polite as they glanced around the beautifully appointed parlor, all light and air and muted colors, in sharp contrast to the dark oppressiveness of the Beacon Hill house.

Having contrived to arrange themselves with some small degree of comfort on the Hepplewhite sofas, they deigned to sip lemonade while Drake cheerfully accepted Philip's offer of a mint julep. He perched at ease on the arm of the chair where Elizabeth had seated herself, her bright yellow dress spread out like the petals of a flower and her fragrance wafting to him with each breath she took.

"Beautiful place," Drake said. "No wonder Elizabeth is so proud of it." He gazed down at her fondly.

"You must see the stables," Philip said, "and of course go riding."

"I'd like that," he agreed enthusiastically.

"Best make it early in the morning," William advised from the doorway. He had been alerted to the guests' arrival and had left his work in the fields to join them. Though he nodded politely to the women, who gazed back at his work-stained form in frank surprise, his attention was riveted on Drake.

The man his sister intended to marry looked fit and strong enough, but his negligent pose annoyed William, perhaps because it bespoke an unseemly degree of confidence. Surely he should have been at least slightly nervous at being confronted for the first time by his bride's family on their own territory?

Yet it would have been hard to imagine a young man more at ease than Drake. As William was introduced, Drake rose with a ready smile and offered his hand. "At last. Elizabeth has spoken of you so often that I feel as though we've already met.''

William murmured something appropriate, noting as he did so that, unlike his mother and sisters, Drake at least didn't seem put off by the evidence of honest labor.

"How are the fields?" Philip asked as he gestured to Foster to pour William a drink.

"Not good. We've begun bringing water from the river to irrigate, but it may be too little too late."

"At least it's early in the year," Philip said. "If worse comes to worst, we have time to plant again and at least bring in one crop."

William agreed with that, though he did not relish the prospect of what would be for him a personal defeat. If he could have, he would have willed rain from the sky.

"If you wouldn't mind," Drake said with surprising diffidence, "when we ride tomorrow, could I get a look at the fields? I've never been anywhere that people actually grow things, and I'm curious as to how it's done."

William looked at him skeptically. "It's a dusty, wearying business. You might be wise to give it a miss."

Drake saw the assessment in William's eyes as he took in the elegant cut of Drake's traveling suit, but though he would have reacted with instant anger had any man in Boston dared to regard him so disparagingly, in this instance he found himself prepared to tolerate it. And not only for the sake of Elizabeth, who was glancing at him anxiously. His request to visit the fields had been genuine. From the moment he set foot on Calvert Oaks property, he had found it oddly fascinating. The roll of the land, the breadth of the sky, the sense of space and purpose, all excited him in a way he had never known.

"I'll take the risk of a little discomfort," Drake said with a smile.

"And I'll go with you," Elizabeth added swiftly. She had no idea why he was suddenly so interested in something so outside his experience, but she was proud of Calvert Oaks and wanted to be there when he saw it. Moreover, she didn't quite trust her brother not to make the excursion a shade more difficult that it absolutely had to be.

THE SUN HAD BARELY RISEN before the trio left the stables. William was mounted on Wind Dancer, a son of King's Ransom, who had at last gone to his reward and was buried in a field behind the house. Elizabeth rode a cousin of Princess, who romped like a foal. Drake had been given a roan with the innocuous name of Rufus, who spent the first five minutes or so trying to unseat him. To William's surprise and Elizabeth's pride, Drake handled him with easy patience, and the horse eventually settled down.

As they rode, Drake asked questions that were both intelligent and evidence of genuine interest. He wanted to know how many acres were planted and with what crops, how many men labored in the fields, when the seed was sown and when the harvesting took place, as well as all that happened in between.

At first William answered him in as few words as possible, but after a while his enthusiasm caught and the two men began to converse without barriers. Elizabeth listened in contented silence. She was blissfully happy riding with two of the three men she loved most in the world beside her and the powerful motion of the horse carrying her across the land that a secret part of her would always regard as home.

William drew rein near a copse of oak trees and pointed in the direction of the river. "In the last weeks of the war, when the Yankees were marching on Richmond, a band of them came through there. We'd had word of their coming and managed to hide most of what food we had left, as well as the household valuables. Father had also insisted that Mother take Elizabeth and the female slaves who had remained and hide in the woods."

"What happened?" Drake asked.

"When the Yankees realized there was nothing for them here, they went on a rampage. They dynamited the mill and were about to fire the house and fields when a sudden storm hit. I don't know whether it was the lightning and thunder, which were fierce, or the chill of the rain, but something cooled their rage. They left as suddenly as they had come."

He didn't mention that forever after, one of the most vivid memories of his life was the sight of his father standing tall and proud on the veranda of Calvert Oaks, a rifle in his only arm, making it clear to the Yankees that while they could certainly kill him, he wouldn't die alone.

Drake rested his hand on the pommel of his saddle and looked around slowly. For the first time he found himself thinking about the armaments his family had sold during the war. It had been an extremely profitable enterprise for them, not least because they did business with both sides. He had always known that, but had never before truly understood what it meant in terms of sheer human suffering. An unaccustomed sense of shame moved through him. Quietly, he said, "You were lucky."

"Very, but I've always thought that beyond the accident of birth, men make their own luck."

"First they must know what they want," Drake said.

William shrugged. "For the Calverts, that's always been easy. The land comes first. Everything else follows."

Drake pondered that as they continued on their way. Observing William, seeing how the other man's confidence stemmed not merely from inborn privilege but from his own efforts, he felt a tremendous lack in his own life. It did not frighten him, because side by side with it was the belief that any deficiency could be remedied; it was only a question of how. Perhaps he had all unknowingly taken the first step when he asked Elizabeth to be his wife, rather than plighting himself to one of the young ladies who would have been his mother's choice.

They paused at midmorning on a ridge overlooking the plantation and helped themselves generously from the picnic basket Mammy Augusta had packed. When the last of the ham-filled biscuits and honey were gone, they lay back and slept for a little while.

Drake woke first, pleased to discover that while Elizabeth had fallen asleep a decorous distance from him, in the interval she had moved nearer until her head rested on his chest and her arm lay lightly over his waist. She had taken off her bonnet before lying down, affording him uninterrupted access to her silken hair. He stroked it tenderly as he looked forward to the time when they would again lie side by side, but alone.

That pleasant image was still occupying his thoughts when he happened to glance up and discover a slender figure in breeches and a shirt observing them. Seeing that it had been spotted, it stiffened like a startled fawn and might have run away, had not William chosen that moment to stir.

He woke up slowly, aware only that he had been dreaming of Sunbird and that now she seemed to be there before him, except there was no smile of welcome on her face. After an instant, he realized why and stood up, holding out a reassuring hand to her.

"Sunbird, come meet Elizabeth and Drake."

So William knew the fey creature, Drake thought. He was less surprised by that than by the discovery that it was female, *decidedly* female, despite the inappropriate garb. Elizabeth had also awakened by then and stared curiously at the young woman who came toward them with unconscious grace. She had grown up hearing about Charles Durand's half-breed daughter, but this was the first time she had seen her. What surprised her most was her beauty and the innate air of dignity that cloaked her.

In a moment Elizabeth had something more to be surprised about. William took Sunbird's hand, put an arm around her shoulders and spoke to her softly. The stance of their bodies, close together and with an aura of harmony, told Elizabeth a great deal. She breathed in sharply, doubting what she was seeing, yet unable to interpret it any other way.

Her brother and Sunbird? It didn't seem possible. William had his pick of the finest young ladies in the state. Had he adroitly sidestepped them one and all, only to fall into the web of a golden-skinned wood nymph who was the daughter of a man their father despised?

The two girls regarded each other warily. Elizabeth had risen and was standing stiffly, trying to quell the anxiety building in her. Sunbird sensed it and had to fight the impulse to turn and flee. She had always known what would happen if she met any member of William's family; perhaps it was just as well that now he would have to face it, too.

"How...uh...nice to meet you," Elizabeth said.

Sunbird inclined her head slightly. She looked from William's sister to the young man at her side, seeing them both as part of a world in which she would never belong. Yet that did not mean she had to be overwhelmed by them. "I understand you are to be married," she said, her voice soft and controlled. "Congratulations."

"Thank you," Drake interjected, stepping smoothly into the tense silence. He had always taken for granted his ability to be at ease in any social situation, but this one hardly lent itself to casual chitchat. Elizabeth was frowning with worry, William was scowling and Sunbird looked as though—for all her dignity—she would like nothing better than a good cry.

"Why don't you sit down and join us?" Drake suggested hurriedly. "There's lemonade, if you're thirsty."

Sunbird hesitated, but after a moment she shrugged and folded herself gracefully onto the ground, sitting cross-legged with her hands resting on her knees. Drake plopped down beside her, and after a moment Elizabeth and William followed suit.

With an inward sigh, Drake realized that it would be up to him to keep some semblance of a friendly conversation going. "We've been taking a look at the plantation," he said. "Very impressive. There's nothing like this in Boston."

Appreciative of his effort, though she couldn't imagine why he was bothering, Sunbird stirred herself to respond. "Is that where you come from?"

Drake nodded. He told her a bit about the city, in light, amusing terms that actually wrung a smile from her. All the while he was thinking that, different as she was, she was also quite lovely. No wonder William was infatuated with her.

He was also rapidly becoming angry. It was fine that Drake was apparently a friendly fellow, but he didn't have to smile at Sunbird quite so warmly, or look at her quite so appreciatively. She was, after all, his, and the sooner that was made clear, the better.

"Sunbird will be accompanying me to your wedding," he announced. "It's past time for her to meet Mother and Father."

"I haven't agreed . . ." Sunbird began.

"She will?" Elizabeth exclaimed.

"Splendid idea," Drake said.

Sunbird sent William a look that combined anger and hurt. Elizabeth had no difficulty deciphering it, nor did she mistake her brother's expression of near desperate determination. This was no simple flirtation for him. He actually cared about Sunbird, and that meant Elizabeth had to care, too.

The instinctive generosity of her nature compelled her to ask, "Don't you want to go with him?"

Sunbird lowered her eyes. "It wouldn't be appropriate." She sat motionless on the grass, but Elizabeth could sense the turmoil within her and was moved by it.

"Isn't that for William to decide? After all, it's his home and family."

"That's what I've been telling her." He was surprised by his sister's attitude, but grateful for it. If there was any chance of convincing Sunbird, he would not hesitate to seize it.

"Of course," Elizabeth said, "there's very little time to have a dress made."

"And how unfortunate that my wardrobe should be, shall we say, lacking," Sunbird murmured.

"Yours may be, but mine isn't." Elizabeth looked at her assessingly. "We're almost the same size. Any alterations could be quickly done. There's a rose silk gown I got in Boston but haven't worn yet that would be perfect on you."

"I couldn't possibly," Sunbird said, even as the first twinges of temptation stirred in her. To be dressed as a lady, to appear before William's family and friends as their equal, to make him proud of her, that was almost more than she dared to dream of.

"Why not?" Elizabeth asked with deceptive mildness. "I don't see any problem, unless, of course, you simply don't care enough about William to be bothered."

Sunbird's head shot up. Her deep brown eyes glinted with golden flecks. "That's not true."

"Then you'll do it."

"I . . ." She looked at William in the vain hope that he would understand and relent, but he was smiling broadly.

"It's an excellent idea," he said. "Thank you, Elizabeth, for thinking of it."

His sister nodded and got to her feet. "It's settled. You'll ride back with us, and we'll get started right away." She was already warming to the task. It would be a pleasure to do something for William that he could not do for himself, and the challenge of taking Sunbird in hand would distract her from her own prewedding jitters.

In a last-ditch, but halfhearted bid to escape, Sunbird said, "I don't have a horse with me. I walked."

William threw back his head and laughed. "Wind Dancer can carry us both, I promise."

As Drake was lifting Elizabeth into her saddle, he leaned close and whispered, "It's very nice, what you're doing."

Pleased, she nonetheless tried to make light of it. "Someone has to. For heaven's sake, look at her."

"She has a great deal of pride," he warned.

Elizabeth nodded; she had already figured that out. "And stubbornness." A smile of anticipation lit her eyes. "Both of which will serve William right. He's had things his own way far too long."

It occurred to Drake that the same might be said of himself, and that Elizabeth was well aware of it. A slight feeling of unease moved through him as he wondered if he might not be taking too much for granted. But the thought faded as quickly as it had come, and he turned his mind to more pleasant pursuits.

SARAH'S NATURAL EQUANIMITY was slightly dented by the appearance of Sunbird on her doorstep, but she recovered quickly and welcomed the girl with her characteristic warmth. Like her daughter, she had quickly grasped the undercurrents flowing between William and Charles Durand's daughter, and while this was not quite how she had envisioned her son finally falling in love, she was glad enough that it had happened not to be worried about the precise circumstances.

Whether or not Philip would feel the same way remained to be discovered, though she had to admit to being glad that he was not at home that afternoon—having been called away to Richmond on business—and that there was accordingly some time to transform Sunbird into a more accepted vision of a potential daughter-in-law.

Drake diplomatically prevented his mother and sisters from noticing what was going on by claiming a desperate need for a little good music and luring them into providing it. At his most charitable, he thought his sisters' efforts on the spinet and harp to be only slightly less misguided than their attempts to sing. But he suffered both patiently, knowing the cause to be good.

Upstairs in Elizabeth's bedroom, she and her mother wasted no time going to work. They matter-of-factly ordered a thoroughly embarrassed Sunbird out of her shirt and breeches, popped her into a lacy camisole and petticoat and slipped on the rose silk dress, which, true to Elizabeth's prediction, was perfect for her. That was followed by an ivory bisque gown that Elizabeth had suddenly decided she didn't want, and which also happened to look as though it had been made for Sunbird.

When the few needed alterations had been noted and the garments taken away by Mammy Augusta, they wrapped their hapless victim in a dressing gown, sat her down in front of a mirror and went to work on her hair. Everything was happening so quickly that Sunbird had no chance to notice how she looked. She only knew that the Calvert women were not at all as she had imagined, and that she was feeling curiously at home among them.

She even thoroughly enjoyed her first experience soaking in a hot, scented bath, and had to admit that having her nails buffed wasn't anywhere near as bad as she would have expected. It helped that Elizabeth kept up a stream of amusing banter, telling her all about Monsieur Felix in Boston and the terrible things he had done to her.

"I didn't even dare watch," she said as she perched on the side of her bed, observing Sunbird with silent satisfaction. "You're much braver."

"I don't feel very brave," Sunbird admitted. "This is all so new to me."

"You'll get used to it. Wait until tonight; I'll bet you actually have fun."

"Tonight? What happens then?"

"Oh, there's a little reception for Drake and me at Quail Run. That's why you needed the ivory gown as well."

"But William hasn't said anything about . . ."

"He hates that kind of thing. However . . ." She gave a purely feminine smile. "When he sees you, I think he'll suddenly decide that he wants to attend."

In fact, William's first thought was along very different lines. By the time he returned from the fields, where he had gone in the hope of working off nervous energy, the women were seated decorously in the parlor taking tea. Sunbird had been introduced to Abigail and her daughters simply as the daughter of a neighbor. When they felt compelled to comment on her unusual first name, Sarah merely smiled and said, "An old Virginia tradition. So evocative, don't you think?"

When William entered the room, having for a change thought to bathe and don fresh clothes before presenting himself, he stopped on the threshold and stared at the lovely young woman seated on the couch. Sunbird still looked like herself—to his relief—but she also looked different, as though a hidden part of her nature had at last been released. Her ebony hair had been simply arranged off her face and cascaded below her shoulders. Her ivory gown emphasized the golden warmth of her skin, and her eyes, when they met his, sparkled with pleasure rather than the tension he had expected to see.

"Come and join us, William," Sarah instructed, as though the sight of him openmouthed and befuddled was an everyday event. "We'll be leaving for Quail Run shortly."

"Quail . . ." he repeated, hardly aware of what he said.

"The reception for Drake and Elizabeth. Naturally, Sunbird will be accompanying us."

"N-naturally. I'll have a whiskey, Foster, a large one."

The butler handed him a glass and with it a smile. William took the first and missed the second, oblivious to nuances. He rarely drank, but on this particular evening he was prepared to make an exception. Certainly when a man's world turned upside down, he needed all the help he could get to right it.

Sunbird smiled at him serenely as he took the seat next to her, but inside she was feeling anything but. Kind as Sarah and Elizabeth had been, what really mattered was William's reaction, and it seemed to be decidedly contradictory. He appeared both taken and taken aback by her appearance.

Nervousness made her stomach quiver, though she gave no sign of it. From earliest childhood, she had schooled herself to hide her feelings and find safety behind a wall of reserve. Pride alone demanded that she present a confident face to the world.

Observing her, Elizabeth felt a spurt of admiration. She had been through a similar experience, though hardly to the same degree, and knew how difficult it was. To be plunged into an alien world and cope as well as Sunbird was doing required rare strength of character. Added to what was already a rapidly accumulating list of her virtues, that put Elizabeth firmly on her side.

When they were leaving a short time later for Quail Run, she gave Sunbird a quick, reassuring smile. It was returned a little wanly, but with unmistakable determination.

At first the reception for the engaged couple went well. Over the years, the old plantation house had gradually been restored to some semblance of its former grandeur through cash provided by Philip and under the judicious handling of his sister, Kitty. Less and less authority rested in the hands of her husband, Jeremy, who had never come to terms with the changes brought by the war and who remained a bewildered and embittered man. In his de facto absence, Davey struggled to hold the family together while dealing with his own frustrations.

Elizabeth had been apprehensive about encountering him again after a separation of almost two years. Their last meeting, on the eve of her departure for Boston, had been awkward and painful for them both. Since then so much had changed, at least for her, that she could hardly recapture, even in memory, the feelings for him that had once seemed so intense.

She held on to Drake's arm more tightly than usual as they entered the house to be greeted by her aunt and uncle. In Philip's absence—he was delayed getting back from Richmond—William made the introductions. Drake, his mother and sisters were warmly welcomed, but Sunbird was received with barely concealed shock. Within minutes, heads were tilted close together as guests whispered the astonishing news to one another. Sunbird bore the scrutiny bravely, though her hand on William's arm trembled slightly. He covered it with his own as he guided her into the ballroom.

To her great relief, neither her father nor stepmother were present. She did not doubt that it was Philip Calvert's antipathy toward them, coupled with the occasion for the party, that made their exclusion possible, and she prayed that when Philip himself arrived and encountered her, there would not be an unpleasant scene.

Meanwhile, Elizabeth was uttering a silent prayer of her own. Welcoming though his parents might be, Davey was anything but. He greeted her stiffly and barely acknowledged Drake, who looked him over in an instant and saw the lay of the land.

"The boy fancies you," he said in a voice loud enough to be overheard as they walked away from the receiving line. Behind them, Davey stiffened. His fists clenched at his sides as he turned red.

"Please," Elizabeth murmured, "I don't want a scene. There is enough tension with Sunbird here."

Much as he enjoyed hearing Elizabeth entreat him for anything, so rare an occurrence was it, Drake was not altogether mollified. Since his decision to marry her, he was no longer satisfied by merely the outward appearance of possession, and doubted that he would be, even when that became a reality in their marriage bed. What he wanted ran deeper and was much less decipherable. He needed the world, and particularly every other man in it, to know that she belonged to him in a way that went far beyond mere social dictates and conventions. Already he had begun to suspect that he would never again be truly content until he was absolutely sure of her. Yet how he might ever be able to achieve that he could not imagine.

Davey was too clear a reminder that there was a part of her life he had not shared in, and that would, if given the chance, happily continue to exclude him.

Drake allowed himself to be cajoled into a better mood, but his attention never wavered far from Elizabeth's cousin as they chatted with the other guests and danced the first waltz together. He was constantly aware of the looks the younger man was sending her, a combination of desire and anger that made his own temper difficult to control.

Elizabeth tried to pretend that nothing was wrong, but she was increasingly aware of the uneasiness running through the ballroom. Only the most oblivious could have been unaware of the tension between Davey and Drake. When added to the titillation of Sunbird's appearance at William's side, it was enough to make the room vibrate with strained anticipation.

The mood was not eased by Philip's arrival. He came in smiling, apologizing for having been delayed, put his arm around Sarah and kissed her lightly. Immediately, his smile faded as he sensed that something was wrong.

"What is it?" he murmured softly.

She shook her head. "Nothing. Everything is fine. It's a lovely party."

He did not believe her. Long years of intimacy had finely tuned him to her every mood. Something was distressing her. He intended finding out what it was.

But first his eye was drawn to William, standing beside a strikingly lovely girl who, oddly enough, had gone pale at the sight of him. "Who's that with William?" he asked, taking in the protective way his son held her arm and the almost palpable aura of tenderness between them.

Instead of answering directly, Sarah said, "She's exquisite; come and meet her."

Philip needed no further urging. His great love for his wife and his complete fidelity to her did not prevent him from enjoying the presence of another beautiful woman. But more than that, he was consumed with curiosity to meet the lady who had prompted such unaccustomed feelings in his son.

He bowed over her hand as she offered it to him, noting absently that her fingers trembled slightly in his. Beside her, William said quietly, "Father, I would like to present Sunbird Durand."

Philip's eyebrows rose, though he did not release her hand. Slowly he looked into her face, seeing the trepidation there, but also the courage and strength.

He despised her father. To his mind, Charles Durand was the worst kind of opportunist, eager to benefit from the destruction of others and, indeed, to hurry that destruction along by any method he could. Only by the grace of his own hard work and the legacy from Josiah Mackenzie had he avoided falling prey to the man's machinations. Others—his brother-in-law included—had not been so fortunate. Durand still owned more than a hundred acres that had once belonged to Quail Run, and he had rejected Philip's best efforts to recover them.

He could cheerfully have seen the carpetbagger in hell, but looking at the man's daughter, he realized the injustice of presuming her equally at fault. Life had taught him to make swift judgments. He knew what he saw when he looked at her, and even though he cautioned himself that he might be wrong, he suspected that he was not. Moreover, he paid his son the compliment of trusting him. William was the farthest thing from anyone's fool, and he was sufficiently well acquainted with women to be unlikely to be drawn to one of them without good reason.

The smile he gave Sunbird made her all but sag in relief even as she smiled wryly to herself, realizing from whence William got his charm. "My dear," Philip said, "how nice to meet you. I hope you will save me a dance."

"I'll be happy to," she told him smoothly, "provided you don't mind risking your toes. You see, I've never been taught to dance."

Both men laughed, but their regard was admiring. William especially was delighted by her frank response. "That's a deficiency I intend to promptly remedy," he assured his father as he led her away.

So that matter was smoothly settled, to the disappointment of the guests. But that left Drake and Elizabeth, and Davey. An unlikely triangle, to be sure, since the men could not in any way be considered equals, but perhaps all the more dangerous because of that.

Disregarding his mother's silent pleas, Davey had taken up a position on the edge of the dance floor, refusing to lead any of the young ladies out and turning aside all attempts at conversation. His brooding stare was locked on Elizabeth as he thought back over the long, painful months since they had last been together.

He had loved her, though she had been gone before he realized it, torn from him by her father and brother, the same men he had to look to for whatever tenuous security his future held. Hatred seeped through him. He saw the ruin of his own father, the ruin their home would have become without Philip Calvert's largesse, and told himself that none of it was Jeremy's fault. The war had done it, and only men such as Philip and William Calvert had survived intact.

Their prosperity made a mockery of everyone else's suffering. They had turned their backs on the old South, looked away from its most deeply held beliefs and traditions and plunged themselves into the new era without regret. In his mind they were traitors.

Lately he had been meeting with other men like himself, who were determined to restore the South to its former glory. Men who did not shrink from the need for violence, but who were not so foolish as to expose themselves to their enemies before the time was ripe. Men who believed as he did in the undying superiority of their race, and who would tolerate no one who threatened it.

Like the Calverts. It was well known that Philip had been no friend of slavery, opposing it as a young man and going so far as to forbid the slave catchers to hunt their prey on his land. There were other stories, too, only whispered about now, that Philip had a mulatto half brother named Marcus who had hidden runaways, and that instead of killing him for it, as any right-minded man would have done, Philip had saved his life. Marcus was rumored to be living in New Mexico on land deeded to him by his and Philip's father, the late James Calvert.

Davey sneered as he thought of Sunbird. Clearly the newer generation of Calverts had no more respect for the purity of their blood than the older. She was a beautiful woman, there was no doubt of that, but even a damned carpetbagger like Charles Durand had enough sense not to pretend that she could ever be a lady. Her appearance at the party was an affront to every white woman present.

Davey was not alone in that opinion. His sister, Melinda, was frowning as she came up to him. "I just spoke to

Mother," she said, "and she doesn't seem to think there's anything to be done about it."

He didn't have to ask what Melinda meant. Brother and sister had an often uneasy relationship, but one based nonetheless firmly on shared resentments. "It's bad enough that we have to entertain a Yankee," Melinda went on, "but to have that half-breed in our house..."

"Thank the Calverts. What they want, they get, regardless of anyone's sensibilities."

Melinda's features, which would have been pretty were it not for their perpetual stamp of dissatisfaction, lit with malice. She twirled a blond ringlet around her finger. "Why, Davey, I thought dear Elizabeth could do no wrong in your eyes."

He hunched his shoulders and looked away from her. "We might yet have been married, now that she is older. If she had come back still insisting, her parents would have been less inclined to oppose her."

"Except that she didn't. She consoled herself in Boston and came back with the Yankee." Melinda did not add that she was eaten up with jealousy that her erstwhile friend had snared so rich and handsome a husband. It seemed the height of unfairness that one who already had so much should receive even more.

Davey's hands clenched at his sides. The music had stopped and the two couples—Elizabeth and Drake, Sunbird and William—were laughing together. Their happiness festered inside him. It was not to be borne.

THE PARTY ENDED shortly after midnight. Sunbird regretfully turned down an invitation from Sarah to spend the night at Calvert Oaks, but bowed to William's insistence that he escort her home. She was confident that her absence would not have been noticed, since she rarely saw her father and went out of her way to avoid her stepmother.

"Thank you for lending me the gown," she said to Elizabeth as the others were leaving the carriage in front of Calvert Oaks. "I will clean and return it to you tomorrow."

"Nonsense, now that it's been altered for you, you must keep it." Sunbird would have protested, but Elizabeth was having none of it. "You'll be doing me a favor. My closets are full to bursting, and Drake expects me to buy yet more clothes." She gave him an indulgent glance, not missing the look of warm approval in his eyes.

"But I really shouldn't . . ." Sunbird began. She was embarrassed by such generosity even as she longed to accept it.

"You must never turn aside a gift," William told her, his arm around her waist. "It's very impolite."

Laughing, she relented. "Oh, well, in that case . . ."

When the others had gone inside, he looked down at her and smiled. "I was so proud of you. No other woman was as lovely."

"How very unfair to your sister and mother, both of whom are remarkably beautiful."

"True," he admitted. "But you . . ." Rather than try to express in words what he was feeling, he bent his head and kissed her tenderly. For a moment they clung together, her hands on his shoulders, his stroking her back, their bodies drawn taut with passion, until they became aware of the carriage driver watching them discreetly.

William took a deep breath and let it out slowly before he trusted himself to speak. "You can go to bed now, Jim. I'll see Miss Durand home."

The man nodded, jumped down from the rig and vanished into the darkness. William lifted Sunbird into the seat, settled himself beside her and took the reins. "I hope you won't mind," he said, "if I get you home very slowly."

A full moon veiled by misty clouds hung over the river. The low hum of cicadas and tree frogs made the night air vibrate. It was warm, though not unpleasantly so. Sunbird was more than content to rest against William's shoulder, listening to the drowsy clip-clop of the horse's hooves as they made their way along the dirt road.

"Do you know," he asked softly, "the only thing wrong about tonight?"

She shook her head without raising it.

"That I'm taking you home instead of to bed."

Against his shoulder, she smiled. "I agree."

"Then don't you think we ought to do something about that?"

Briefly she thought back to the objections she had raised before; they seemed singularly unimportant now. His family not only accepted her, they made her feel welcomed. No one could have been kinder than Elizabeth and Sarah, and even Philip was not at all aloof. She remembered how concerned she had been and felt foolish. But deep inside a small note of caution lingered.

"After Elizabeth's wedding," she said. "Let's talk about it then."

That wasn't what William had wanted to hear, but he supposed he should be satisfied with it. She had come a long way in a very short time. The rest, he told himself, would happen soon enough.

The happiness that enveloped them both was so startling in contrast to their natural reserve that they were dazed by it. Neither had much awareness of where they were going or why. The reins hung loosely in William's hands, and the horse was left to find its own way down the road as they shared another hot, lingering kiss.

Barely had they paused to breathe than the horse stopped, its head up and its ears pricked. Long moments passed before either noticed. "Something's spooked him," Sunbird murmured lazily. She no longer cared if she ever got home, so content was she to be with William.

"Perhaps there's a mare in a field nearby," he said, though with a note of doubt. If there had been, the horse would more likely have broken into a canter, not stopped. Grasping the reins more firmly, he slapped them against the animal's back, only to get no response. "What the hell...?"

"Wait," Sunbird said, holding out a hand to stop him when he would have gotten down to see to the horse. "I hear something."

So did William, though he wasn't sure what it was. The hair on the nape of his neck pricked, and instinctively he slid a hand along his right thigh, only to mutter a low curse when he remembered that he was not wearing a gun. On his trips through the fields he never went without a pistol, not so much because he expected trouble as because of habits ingrained during the long years of violence. Briefly he wondered if there might be a weapon in the carriage, but he gave up that thought when he realized how long it had been since such a precaution had been considered necessary.

Sunbird's ears strained against the night sounds. Like William, she was instinctively wary, though she could not have said why. Somehow the darkness was no longer comforting; it had become a threat. "Voices," she whispered. "Several men, on horseback."

William nodded. His face was grim as he considered what to do. The men were not far away, and it wouldn't be long before they realized they were not alone. Try though he did, he could come up with no legitimate reason for a party of riders to be abroad at night. Travelers would have put up at an inn or house. Any poor blacks who happened to be on the road would have camped out. Only men whose intent did not bear scrutiny would seek the shelter of darkness.

Rumors he had heard recently flitted through his mind. The anger and bitterness that had festered since the war seemed to be taking on a new form. Men were no longer content merely to rant against the harshness of Reconstruction; they wanted to do something about it. He sympathized with that, since he thought the North had shown its vanquished enemy unnecessary vindictiveness. But there was a remedy for such things in the steady recovery of the Southern economy, the reasoned compromise of democracy, the acceptance that the past was gone forever.

It did not lie in secret violence, in torture and intimidation, in the growth of a mystique of white supremacy decked in the robes of a warped faith and a perverted heritage.

If he had been alone, he would not have hesitated to go forward—with caution—and try to discover exactly which of his neighbors were meeting clandestinely in the woods. But with Sunbird, he could not take such a risk. The sooner he got her safely away, the sooner he could come back.

"Let's go," he whispered, pulling on the reins to turn the horse. This time the animal obeyed, apparently as eager as they to put an end to the encounter.

The horsemen were coming closer. William cursed again under his breath. Sunbird felt his tension and touched his arm gently. She was afraid, but more than that, she was aware of how desperately he wanted to keep her safe. Knowing the world as she did, she understood that he might not be able to do so, but the mere fact that her welfare mattered to him warmed her from inside and gave her the courage to face what she feared was coming.

"They've heard us," she said. "They've speeded up. We won't be able to get away."

He knew that she was right, though he fought to deny it. The best course of action was for them to stop where they were, allow themselves to be overtaken and simply brazen it out. He told himself that the premonition of danger growing in him was misplaced. Whatever the men were up to, they would certainly have the sense not to threaten a neighbor.

And perhaps they would not have, if they hadn't been drunk. Davey swayed in his saddle as he hoisted the jug of bourbon and took another long swallow, part of which ran down his chin onto his stained shirt. He had started drinking at the party, when the sight of Drake and Elizabeth so happy together became too much for him. The other men undoubtedly had other reasons for their own excesses, but it all boiled down to the same thing: resentment and the need to fuel their courage to do something about it.

They had met in the woods to talk over the plans they had for a black sharecropper who was trying to buy the land he worked. The man had money, because he was also an able smith, a skill he had learned in slavery. He was hiring himself out to local farmers at a price the white smiths were unwilling to match.

"Damn nigger," the man beside Davey muttered as they urged their horses along. "I say we burn him out. Only thing they understand."

"Tha' an' a length of rope," Davey agreed, passing the jug. He blinked owlishly, struggling to stay upright. The sound he had heard a moment before reached him again—wheels turning and the jangle of harness. "Wha's tha'?"

The other men—eight of them in all—broke off their mutterings to listen. "Sounds like a carriage," one of them ventured.

"Somebody goin' home late."

"Maybe from the party."

They hesitated, not sure if they wanted to encounter anyone they knew.

Davey smiled slowly. For all his befuddlement, he knew where they were, midway along the road from Calvert Oaks and the river along the route anyone traveling to the old Devereaux place would have to follow.

"'Pears William's playin' the gentlemen, seein' that half-breed home," he said.

"Damn fine-lookin' woman, even if she is half squaw."

"You see that skin and those—"

"She's a whore," Davey said. "Everybody knows she runs around half-naked in the woods. Calvert must be givin' it to her good."

"Can't hardly blame the man."

"'Course not, that's the right use for her." Davey's lip curled upward. "But takin' her to a respectable party, that's another thing. Insult to every white woman there."

"Calverts go their own way."

"Sure do have the devil's luck."

"Richer than ever now. Got everything back they had before the War and then some."

"Doesn't seem right."

"It isn't," Davey said. His head seemed to be clearing as the righteousness of his anger burned away the alcohol-induced haze. The thoughts he'd had earlier were returning with a vengeance. The more he considered it, the more it was evident that the Calverts were at the root of everything that was wrong in the South. No wonder Elizabeth preferred to marry a Yankee; how could she do otherwise, when she'd been raised in a nest of traitors?

"Come on," he whispered, opening his saddlebag and pulling out the white hood that was becoming the badge of men like himself. "Let's show Calvert how mixed bloods should be treated."

A short way down the road, William turned to Sunbird. "Stay in the carriage and keep down."

She looked at him and shook her head. "No, I will not hide."

"*For God's sake,* don't be crazy. This is no time for bullheaded courage."

"I know who those men are, William. Any sign of fear will only make them worse."

"I can talk my way around them," he insisted. "They don't have to know you're here."

"They will know, or at least suspect enough to search, and if they find me cowering, there will be no holding them back."

William feared that would be the case no matter what they did. The mere thought of not being able to protect her brought a surge of bitter bile to the back of his throat.

He choked it down as, out of the darkness, the men approached. At the sight of their white hoods, an exclamation of disgust broke from him. "What's this?" he demanded. "Brave warriors of the old South afraid to be recognized?"

Behind his mask, Davey flushed. "Don't try to mock us, Calvert. We stand for something you can't begin to understand."

"Oh, I understand it all right." The stench of bourbon had reached him on the night air. His contempt mounted, and with it, caution fled. "Couldn't you drink enough courage to get up the nerve to show your faces?"

"Shut up," one of the other masked figures demanded.

"High and mighty Calverts. Nothin' but nigger lovers."

"Not just niggers, any kind of dark meat."

The men laughed, lustful eyes on Sunbird, who sat unmoving, her hands folded in her lap and her gaze far removed from the ugly scene before her. Inside she was terrified, but she refused to show any sign of it. Her loutish father had taught her little, and certainly never with good intent, but there was one lesson he had inadvertently driven home: small, fearful men would seize any opportunity to play the bully with someone weaker.

"You've had your say," William told the men through gritted teeth. "Now let us pass."

"Not so fast," Davey said. "Something happened tonight that shouldn't have. We want to make sure this squaw learns her place."

William had no doubt what they intended; he had known from the first that the men would resort to violence, and what form it would take. If he'd had a gun, he would have used it at that moment and damn the consequences. But instead he had to fall back on his wits, as buried as they were beneath red waves of rage.

"All right, boys," he said softly. "You've had your fun, but enough's enough. You know as well as I do that whatever you think of this *lady*—" he emphasized the word deliberately "—come tomorrow you'll still be living here, right close at hand and, despite those fancy hoods, not all that hard to identify." His voice hardened. "Shaw...Ellison...Harris..." One by one, he ticked off their names. "And of course, Cousin Davey. I'm willing to bet that none of you wants to be looking over your shoulder from now on, wondering exactly when you're going to die. Or how."

The men shifted nervously. They hadn't thought it possible to be recognized. In their inebriated state, his ability to put names to each of them seemed almost supernatural.

Sensing their fears, Davey said, "Don't be fools. He recognized the horses; that's how he did it. Besides, it doesn't matter. We can fix it so he won't be telling anyone what happens here."

But that was more than the men had bargained for. The murder of blacks was acceptable, as was the rape of any woman they felt had dared to step beyond her proper place. But to kill a white man of power and wealth, whose kin would take fearful vengeance, was more than their drunken courage could permit.

One by one they drew rein, turning their horses away from the carriage.

"Uh . . . Davey, maybe we better just forget it."

"No sense stirrin' up trouble."

"We've got bigger fish to fry, anyway."

"What the hell are you talking about?" Davey demanded, turning in his saddle to look from one to the other so abruptly that he came close to unseating himself. "You're gonna turn tail and run?"

"No call to put it that way. Just a little prudence is all."

"Man doesn't want to bite off more than he can chew."

"Listen to them, Davey," William drawled. "They've got more sense than you, but then, most men do."

"*Damn it!* I won't let you do this!" On the sharp edge of his scream, Davey raised his arm. Metal glinted in the moonlight. The sword his father had carried through the War, and that he had appropriated for his midnight sojourns, hissed through the air.

He had drawn it with no clear intent except to strike out at the man who was the epitome of everything he longed to be but was not. Elizabeth's adored brother, who had conspired to send her away, to give her to another man, to rob both him and Quail Run of their only chance to recapture the glorious past. But the blow went astray, and it was not William but Sunbird who flinched beneath cold steel, and whose blood ran red in the waning night.

DRAKE WAS STILL AWAKE when the carriage returned to Calvert Oaks. He was standing by the window, unable to sleep and wryly aware that the problem was of his own making. Had he not coaxed Elizabeth out onto the back veranda and kissed and caressed her until they were both hot with need, he would undoubtedly be peacefully asleep. Instead, he was considering the merits of going downstairs for one of Philip's cheroots and a glass of whiskey when the sound of galloping hooves drew him up short. He was surprised to see the old carriage horse tearing up the gravel drive, William standing in the seat behind him, egging him on for all he was worth.

It might have been that his soon-to-be brother-in-law was merely indulging himself in a little lighthearted sport, albeit at an inappropriate hour, but Drake didn't think so. He was out the door of his room and down the stairs before the carriage screeched to a halt in front of the house.

"What in hell...?" Drake exclaimed as he saw William lifting a crumpled bundle from the seat beside him. "Sunbird...?"

"Wake my mother," William said without preliminaries. "Tell her we need bandages right away to stop the bleeding, and someone must go for a doctor."

"What happened?"

"Later." He took the steps two at a time up to the second floor landing and, without hesitation, carried Sunbird into his room.

Drake almost followed, only to realize that he could do nothing. Instead he ran down the corridor and knocked loudly on the door of his host and hostess's room. It was opened almost instantly by a shirtless Philip, who was in the midst of fastening his trousers.

"We heard the carriage. What happened?"

"Sunbird is hurt, but I don't know how."

Sarah, her chestnut hair hanging in disarray around her shoulders, tightened the belt of the robe she had just pulled on. "There must have been an accident."

With Drake and Philip on her heels, she hurried to her son's room in time to see him gently placing his burden on the bed. Sunbird's head had fallen back, and her skin beneath the golden tan was unnaturally pale. Over the bodice of the ivory gown a dark red stain was spreading.

Sarah put a hand to her mouth to stifle her immediate exclamation. Quickly she seized a clean towel beside the washbasin and held it to the seeping wound. "Philip, you know where the medicine kit is."

He nodded and returned in an instant with it. Meanwhile, Sarah had ripped away the fabric around Sunbird's shoulder, exposing an ugly gash. She stared at it in disbelief. "No accident did this. It's a sword wound."

Standing at the door, Elizabeth gasped. She had heard the disturbance in the corridor and gone to investigate. The sight of Sunbird lying unconscious on the bed stunned her. She had seen injuries before—they were inevitable around the plantation—but never had she witnessed the effects of violence directed against one so helpless and vulnerable.

"Who...?" she breathed, staring at her brother.

His eyes remained locked on Sunbird, all his attention directed toward willing that the slow rise and fall of her breathing continue. Yet he heard the question and answered it through gritted teeth. "Davey."

"No." Elizabeth shook her head in frantic denial. It was inconceivable that someone they knew, someone who was actually related to them, could have done such a thing. It had to be a stranger, a robber perhaps, who could be hunted down and punished with impunity.

"Are you sure?" Philip was asking his son quietly. He understood only too well the implications of William's accusation. A glance at his wife's white face told him that she did, too.

"I wish I weren't," William said hoarsely. "But it was him all right, and the rest of those bastards who think they can dress up in sheets and terrorize the neighborhood. I recognized all of them."

"Men we know?" his father asked.

"Men who have been in this house, and who are planning to come again." He looked from Elizabeth to Drake and back again. "For the wedding."

Philip sighed deeply. "We'll discuss this later," he said. "In the meantime, let Sarah do what she can. Elizabeth, help her. I'm going for the doctor." He strode out of the room, only to encounter Abigail and her daughters in the hallway, clutching their wrappers to their breasts and staring wide-eyed at what was going on.

"Mr. Calvert," Abigail began in her best Boston Brahmin tone, "I really must inquire as to what has happened. My daughters are young ladies, impressionable, and—"

"Not now," Philip said and went on his way without pause.

Behind him, Abigail sniffed. "Well, I never..."

"Go back to bed, Mother," Drake said, drawing her firmly away. "There's nothing for you to do here, and besides, everything is under control."

As her daughters twittered around her, Abigail dug in her heels and refused to budge. "I thought that...young person, Sunbird, had been taken home. Now I find her in William's bedroom. Really, Drake, I must tell you that this is not proper. Your sisters cannot be exposed to this sort of thing."

"Then take them back to their rooms, Mother." Deliberately, he shut the door, cutting off her view.

"You might take this more seriously."

"I do, but not for the reasons you wish." It surprised Drake that he truly meant what he said. He was deeply angered by what had happened to Sunbird and knew that in William's place he would seek to exact heavy retribution. In a lifetime in which he could not remember ever being more than mildly annoyed at someone, the intensity of such emotion was a novelty.

He relished it as he ushered his mother and sisters away, then returned to ask if he could do anything to help. Elizabeth—distracted and clearly worried, but working as competently as her mother—got him to take William away. Her brother protested at first, but finally allowed himself to be persuaded.

Downstairs in the library, Drake poured him a stiff measure of whiskey and made sure that he drank it. Augusta had been awakened by all the comings and goings. Upon learning of what had happened, she hurried upstairs. Foster, shaking his grizzled head under a nightcap, went to wake the kitchen maids and set them to boiling water.

William sat slumped in a wing chair, his long legs stretched out in front of him and his face expressionless. He might have had nothing more on his mind than the next day's amusements, but Drake was not fooled. He sensed a barely leashed rage that both excited and shocked him.

Unable at length to bear the extended silence, he asked, "What are you going to do?"

"Kill him."

The words, uttered so calmly in the quiet room, did not register immediately. "Surely you don't mean . . . ?"

"I mean exactly what I said."

Drake got up, poured himself the drink he hadn't thought he wanted and finished it in a single swallow. He had never felt quite so far from Boston. "Wouldn't it be better to contact the authorities?"

William moved slightly, enough to reveal a sudden flash of amusement. "What do you imagine they would do?"

"Arrest him, bring him to trial."

"Let me explain something to you. Since the end of the War, the 'authorities' here have been a bunch of bloodsucking carpetbaggers inflicted on us for the sole purpose of assuring that the South never rises again. They would relish this situation, seeing it as a way to humiliate one of the few families that has been able to stand against them. On the other hand, even those well-meaning individuals who want to rebuild the South without violence, would still feel compelled to sympathize with Davey, or at least to minimize his crime. Neither side would make him pay as he deserves.'' '

''With his life?''

William rose slowly and went over to the window, where he stood looking out at the gray light seeping out of the east. The day already promised to be hot and cloudless, but for once he was not thinking of the crops. His voice was muffled as he said, ''I love Sunbird, and I intend to make her my wife. If you were in my place and it was Elizabeth who had been attacked, what would you do?''

Everything proper, upright and Bostonian in Drake demanded that he take the high road and forswear any tendency toward personal violence. It was what the lower classes engaged in, what people like himself paid others in positions of authority to do for them. But what if he were in William's place, without the protection of the establishment? ''I . . . see your point.''

''Good, then you will understand that I don't want to involve anyone else who is tied to this place and would be unable to escape the repercussions of whatever happens. Therefore, I would like you to be my second.''

''Your sec—?'' By God, the man was talking about a duel. Pistols at forty paces, or was it to be swords? A strange, almost giddy feeling descended on Drake. He felt as though he had been wrenched not only out of his established world, but even out of his own time, plummeted back into an era that was supposed to be dead and gone but in fact was anything but.

And yet the fascination of it... What could be better than two men facing each other on the field of honor? The most elemental struggle, where only individual will and determination could carry the day. His Anglo-Saxon blood, honed by centuries of adherence to the rule of the strongest, leaped at the thought. Gravely, he said, "It would be my privilege."

IT WAS SWORDS, in the field high above Calvert Oaks, at dawn two days later.

Dressed in a morning coat and properly creased trousers, Drake had made the solemn journey to Quail Run to deliver the challenge. He was greeted by Kitty, who clearly knew nothing of what had happened, and by Jeremy, who equally clearly had his suspicions. Only with reluctance did they accede to his request for a private meeting with their son.

Davey was on the back veranda, brooding over a mint julep. He looked up as Drake approached but did not rise. His clothes were wrinkled, his jaw blurred by a day's growth of whiskers. With the glass, he gestured to the chair beside him.

"Sit down, old fellow. Have a drink."

"No, thank you," Drake said stiffly. "What I have to say won't take long."

"'Magine not. Surprised it's you, though. Wouldn't have thought to involve a Yankee."

"William and I are shortly to be brothers-in-law."

Davey looked up at him narrowly. "Sure of that, are you?"

Actually, Drake wasn't. It hadn't escaped his attention that the outcome of a duel to the death might go either way. But he preferred to believe that William's skill would far outstrip that of the begrimed, bourbon-sodden fool in front of him.

"I gather," he said, "that I don't have to explain matters to you."

Davey shrugged. "William and I may not have much in common, but we both understand the rules." His voice cracked slightly, and he looked away. For all his bravado, he was far more concerned than he cared to admit. Throughout the sleepless night he had agonized over his own actions, wondering how he could have been so incredibly foolish. Being drunk explained some of it, but not all. It was almost as though he really wanted his life to end.

Drawing himself up, he said, "Of course, the choice of weapons is mine."

Drake nodded. William had not had to explain the etiquette of dueling to him, foreign though the activity was to the North. He had read about it often enough in novels and understood how the thing was done.

"William is the best shot in the country," Davey said calmly. "I've seen him bring down a wolf on the run from a hundred yards away."

"I didn't realize there were still wolves here."

"Aren't. It was several years ago. We were hunting in the western part of the state." He tried to smile, but grimaced instead. "A family holiday."

"At any rate," he went on after a moment, "I'd be crazy to choose pistols, so swords it will have to be. Actually," he added as he rose and stretched languidly, "I'm not half bad with a sword."

"I shall relay your decision. As to the time and place, if you will name your second..."

"No need. There's only one place to do this unobserved, and hallowed tradition insists it be at dawn." He grinned weakly and held out a hand to Drake. "Tomorrow, then?"

Drake nodded. He could not fathom the other man's mood, but decided that it was best not to try. Instead he took his leave as quickly as he could, grateful that he didn't encounter Davey's parents again on the way out.

By tacit agreement, neither William nor Drake made any mention of the latter's visit to Quail Run. In the flurry of the doctor's arrival and his pronouncement that Sunbird's injury, while serious, did not endanger her life, no one had noticed that he slipped away briefly. A message had been sent to Charles Durand, who might be supposed to be concerned about his daughter's absence, but as yet no response had been received. Sarah was just as glad about that, since she had no intention of allowing the girl out of her sight.

"Of course you will stay here to recuperate," she said as she and Elizabeth sat in the sunny guest room to which Sunbird had been taken. She lay on the bed, her ebony hair spreading over the pillows, looking fragile and lovely in a white lace nightdress. Only the slight pallor of her skin and the bandage wrapped around her shoulder showed the ordeal she had been through.

"I'm more grateful for your hospitality than I can say," she murmured, "but I do think it would be better if I left." Though she dreaded doing so, she was convinced that to stay where she was would only provoke further trouble. Certainly the brief and unsatisfying meeting she had had with William had indicated that was a strong possibility. He had been very gentle with her, but also closemouthed, giving away none of his feelings. Had he ranted and raved, she would have felt far safer. As it was, she suspected what he was bottling up inside himself, and how it would finally erupt.

"We won't discuss that now," Sarah said, holding the girl's hand. Elizabeth sat on the other side of the bed. She met her mother's eyes and nodded.

"You must concentrate on getting well."

"Yes, of course, but with the wedding and all, you don't need any disruptions."

"We hardly consider you as such, dear," Sarah said. She patted her hand again and stood up. "Now you get some rest. I'll be back in an hour or so to check on you."

Sunbird was tempted to argue further, but lacked both the strength and the will. In a lifetime in which she had never known the slightest cosseting, being cared for was a novelty not to be lightly turned aside. With a sigh, she nestled down in the pillows and was asleep before Sarah and Elizabeth left the room.

"A lovely girl," Sarah said when they stood in the corridor. "I can see why William is so taken with her."

"And she with him," Elizabeth added. "They're perfect for each other. But when I think of what happened..." Her fists clenched at her sides. It was all she could do not to go storming over to Quail Run and tell Davey what she thought of him. To think that she had ever wanted to marry so despicable an excuse for a man.

"Temper, dear," Sarah said as she took note of the dangerous flush staining her daughter's cheeks. "Besides, that part of it does not concern us."

"Of course it does. Davey can't possibly be allowed to get away..."

Sarah put a hand on her daughter's arm, cautioning her to silence. They were passing Abigail's bedroom, to which she had retired immediately after breakfast complaining of a migraine. Sarah did not doubt for a moment that she had her ear figuratively, if not literally, pressed to the wall to pick up any tidbit of information.

"There are some things better left to the men," Sarah said when they were safely past. "This is one of them."

Elizabeth started to argue, then thought better of it and cast her mother a quick, perceptive glance. "I've never heard you say anything like that before."

"It usually isn't necessary to speak of it, but the fact remains that there are times when a woman's presence is not welcome."

Elizabeth had a hard time accepting that, even though she knew it was true. She didn't want to think about the implications of what her mother had said, and she marveled at

Sarah's ability to accept them so calmly. Surely she knew what would be in William's mind.

"You could have a word with Father," she ventured.

"He already knows, I'm sure."

"And will do nothing?"

Sarah smiled at her gently. "I wouldn't go that far."

Elizabeth let her breath out slowly. "At least Drake isn't involved." And how perverse of her to wish differently. Why couldn't she be clearer in her thinking? Drake represented everything she should want—security, position, privilege, even passion. Yet she longed for something more, for the true sense of intimacy she saw between her parents, and between William and Sunbird. Surely it would come with time. She should not presume that because Drake had been raised with different values and expectations, he was somehow weaker than her father or brother.

When she encountered him again, on the veranda, she sought for some reassurance that her fears were misplaced, but did not find it. Drake was unaccountably aloof. He inquired after Sunbird's progress, but upon learning that she was recovering, made no further comment. Her own attempts at conversation drew only monosyllabic replies that did not encourage her to continue.

Abigail joined them, her presence an added damper. There was no mistaking the hostile glance she spared Elizabeth, nor its cause. She was clearly upset by the goings-on in the house, summing up her dismay in a single succinct phrase: "Such things would never happen in Boston."

When Drake made no reply to that, Elizabeth began to wonder if he felt the same way and, further, if he were having second thoughts about tying himself to a family in which such things clearly did occur. That possibility so depressed her that she was silent through dinner and retired early to her room without making any further attempt to communicate with him.

The next day she rose early, having fought a futile effort to remain in bed and avoid seeing what she knew must be happening. The predawn light found her at the window of her bedroom, watching the front entrance of the house. Her expectations were unhappily confirmed when William emerged, formally dressed in morning clothes and with a sword buckled around his lean hips. That was no surprise, but Drake's presence at his side most certainly was.

They got into the carriage driven by Foster and disappeared down the gravel drive before she could collect her thoughts. Hastily, she threw off her wrapper, pulled on a dress, took a brief swipe at her hair with a brush and hurried from the room. She was down the stairs, through the entrance hall and almost to the door when her father called to her.

"Come in here, Elizabeth," he said from the library.

She paused, her hand on the knob, reluctant to stop, yet conditioned to obey him. Slowly, she turned back. Philip was standing by the window, looking out at the drive, and had apparently seen her in the large gilt mirror that dominated the near wall. When she entered the room, he smiled gently.

"Sit down. Foster brought in a pot of coffee before he left. Would you like some?" He gestured to the silver service on a small inlaid table.

She nodded and stood aside to let him pour; though normally that task would have been hers, it was beyond her at the moment. It was all she could do to hold on to the cup once it was handed to her.

"William . . . ?" she began, after taking a quick sip in the futile hope of steadying herself.

Philip sighed and settled himself back in his chair. He had been up all night and was very tired, though nothing in his impeccable grooming revealed that. He and his son had talked until midnight, when it had become apparent to him that William was not to be dissuaded. After that there was nothing more to be done except let him go, and then somehow get through the hours that followed.

"He is very angry," Philip said slowly, "as I'm sure we can all understand. But I persist in believing that he will not do anything... irredeemable."

Elizabeth shivered at the thought. Unlike Drake, she did not need to have the reality of the situation spelled out for her. Southern men still met at dawn with weapons drawn for only one reason: to kill.

"If Davey should die..." she began, though the words all but choked her.

"It will have very sad consequences for our family."

She could only marvel at her father's calmness even as he admitted the seriousness of what they were facing. Davey was, after all, his nephew, the son of his beloved sister. Surely, whatever he had done, his death would be an occasion for genuine grief.

"I can't understand it," she said slowly. "The Davey I knew wouldn't have been capable of something like this." She still could not envision him attacking Sunbird, though William had been so certain in his charge.

"People change," her father said. "They grow embittered by circumstance and are prone to make poor choices."

"You sound so... philosophical about it."

Philip considered that, remembering how he had left his wife only a short time before, after she had finally fallen asleep on his arm, worn out by anguish over William and numbed by the brandy he'd managed to make her drink. It was his hope that she would remain asleep until the deed was done.

Quietly, he said, "I have seen a great deal of violence in my lifetime."

Her eyes fell to his empty sleeve. "I would have thought that war was less... personal."

He laughed shortly and shook his head. "A common misconception. No, I assure you, it is quite personal. There is some similar quality between the giving of life and the taking of it that I cannot pretend to understand, though I acknowledge its existence.''

He intended to say no more, believing that it would be both futile and cruel to try to explain to his young daughter how it was between men locked in mortal struggle. She was still, thank God, too innocent to be aware of such things, and he hoped that her life would allow her to remain so.

The fact that Drake had gone with William was something he took as a good omen for his daughter's future well-being. Though he had admitted it to no one, he had had his doubts about his future son-in-law. Not enough, obviously, to discourage him from agreeing to the marriage, but sufficient to cause him some concern.

In certain ways, Drake reminded him too much of his younger self. He, too, had been born into a life of immense privilege that had fostered a certain callow arrogance. But unlike Drake, he had been tested in the harsh caldron of a changing world. Tragic though the experience had been, it had also served him well.

The father in him shied away from the thought of his son-in-law, and therefore in all likelihood his daughter, ever becoming caught up in such turmoil. But as a man blessed by a mature love that was the cornerstone of his life, he could also regret that the product of that love might never know the joys of such intimacy.

William, born in quite different circumstances, was well on the way to such a relationship with Sunbird. Philip was impressed by the young woman and had already made up his mind to do everything necessary to help her, whatever the outcome of the duel. Because he was a man who never shied away from unpleasant truths, he forced himself to confront the possibility that William, not Davey, would perish.

Elizabeth's pale, strained face told him that was also very much on her mind. He reached over and took her hand. Together father and daughter waited as the sun rose over a land that, for all the blood already shed on it, seemed ever ready to soak up more.

THREE MEN STOOD on the ridge overlooking Calvert Oaks. William and Davey faced each other from the scant distance of a few feet. Drake was off to the side, incongruously holding both coats and observing the scene with growing apprehension.

"Is there any particular reason," William inquired, "why you failed to bring a second?"

Davey shrugged. He was slightly shorter than William, and paler. His physique was less well developed, but nonetheless gave off its own impression of strength. "As I told Drake, it seemed superfluous."

"Perhaps, but two witnesses are better than one."

"Concerned about what people will say about you afterward, cousin?"

Davey's drawling tone grated on William's nerves. The other man seemed determined to deny the seriousness of what they were about to undertake, which raised uneasy questions about how well prepared he might be. William had no compunction about confronting a foe as capable as himself; he felt a good deal less sanguine about one whose motives were swiftly slipping beyond his grasp.

"A doctor, then," William went on. "You might have thought to bring one."

"It didn't occur to me," Davey claimed. "After all, we are embarked on an enterprise that, strictly speaking, is illegal. I didn't think it right to involve anyone else."

That was so specious an argument that William was frankly dumbfounded by it. Granted, duels were against the law and were consequently no longer as common as they had been only a few short decades before, but they still occurred, and more than a few doctors had taken part in them, at least to the extent of standing by in case of need.

There was a willful self-destructiveness about Davey's lack of preparation that disturbed William. Yet it was not enough to turn him from his purpose. Had it been, the mere thought of Sunbird lying bleeding in his arms would have hardened his resolve.

"You are a drunkard and a fool," he told his cousin. "Through you lies the South's destruction, not its salvation."

"I disagree," Davey said calmly. As an afterthought, he added, "Though I will admit that, had I to do it over again, I wouldn't have bothered with the girl."

"Are you attempting to say that you are sorry?"

Davey bared his teeth in a parody of a smile. "And give you a way out of what you have begun? I wouldn't dream of it." In a swift, easy motion he drew his sword from its scabbard. "*En garde*, cousin. We are here for a purpose, and I intend to see it fulfilled."

William had no choice but to draw his own weapon and take up the position to defend himself. The twin naked lengths of steel, cast by the same swordmaker and carried by their fathers in the same war, glinted in the relentless sun.

Duels should not be fought on such bright and shining days, William thought as the first clash of sword on sword rang out between them. They should be done in darkness and gloom, appropriate to the emotions that provoked them.

Then there was no time to think of anything as the two men grunted and strained in a deadly pas de deux, bodies taut with the force of their struggle, skin streaked with sweat. Davey was good; that was confirmed for William in the first few minutes. Swordplay was one thing his cousin had taken the trouble to thoroughly learn. He had the feint and parry down well, the thrust and withdraw, the careful balance between defense and attack.

But he lacked the instinct of a true killer. That was a disconcerting revelation in light of the purpose of the duel. It raised doubts in William's mind as to whether or not Davey had ever really intended to harm Sunbird, and that in turn was all it took to undermine his concentration just enough to give Davey the upper hand.

Drake watched in growing dismay as the tide of the struggle turned. Now it was William on the defense, Davey on the attack. They moved back and forth across the clearing, trampling the grass beneath their boots. At one point William began to slip, and Drake's heart lurched. He watched as, with an effort, William regained his balance and fought on.

That brush with disaster blew the mists from William's mind. He drove on, pressing Davey more and more insistently. Both men were breathing in labored gasps, their sword arms aching. For Davey the pain was like a wall of fire hurtling at him, a source of agony and fear. For William it was simply a tiresome reality to be ignored. He pushed it to a corner of his mind and let it howl, oblivious to its effects.

His blade nicked Davey's sword arm above the elbow, enough to cut through flesh, not sufficient to sever muscle or sinew. Yet the drawing of first blood gave him an advantage. He thought again of Sunbird's blood and pressed on.

There were two ways to fight a duel: the slow, insidious playing with an opponent that meant a long struggle and a painful death, or the swift going for a mortal wound that could kill instantly. William was well versed in both, though this was the first time he had fought as anything other than practice. He knew where the body was most vulnerable, which wounds meant immediate death, which killed more gradually, and which meant only incapacitation with the hope of survival. His knowledge was not new; it had been passed down from the days of the gladiators, when the battlefield was an arena and the purpose of the struggle was no more than decadent amusement.

With grim purpose, he had intended to kill, but in adherence to his own honor, he had meant for it to be swift. That was still possible, for Davey was weakening quickly. For just an instant his sword lowered, giving William a clear chance to end the contest. When he hesitated for a split second, the chance disappeared, only to occur again a few minutes later.

Like William, Drake had been trained in the finer points of swordplay, and he saw the opportunities that the other man let pass. Much as he wanted to believe that they were the inevitable result of Davey's weakening, a horrible suspicion was growing in his mind. An execution was something he could bear to witness, if he had to. A suicide was a different matter altogether.

He fought the impulse to call out, knowing what such a distraction could cost both men. But it was needless anyway, because William had already sensed what was happening. He drew back a fraction, waiting to see if Davey would have the sense to concentrate on defending himself. When he did not, but instead let his guard drop further, his worst fears were confirmed.

Provocatively, he tested how far Davey meant to go, and in the process nicked his cousin's arm again, this time more seriously. The flow of blood that resulted was bad enough to assure him that within a few minutes the arm would be numb.

Davey realized that as well, and his face set with grim desperation. "Stop playing," he bit out. "End it."

"So anxious to die, cousin?" William inquired.

Davey did not answer directly, but his eyes told the truth. They were bleakly resigned, the eyes of a tired old man who welcomes death.

To William, they were an obscenity. Everything young and strong in him welled up against the idea of deliberately seeking extinction. So revolted was he that he might have killed Davey then and there, had not a flicker of compassion intervened.

Though he could not begin to understand the level of self-hatred that would drive a man to engineer his own death, he could recognize it. The white-hot flow of his own anger abated in the face of this even more deadly rage. He could not, would not, allow himself to be used as the instrument of his cousin's self-destruction.

Davey sensed the shift in his attack and was infuriated by it. "Damn you," he snarled. "You were eager enough. What's holding you back now?"

"You are," William said, his mouth drawn in a hard line. "I · on't accept this burden."

"Accept it or die yourself," Davey said, and to prove his words he lunged at William with a sudden thrust that came perilously close to being deadly.

Kill or be killed. The terms were clearly set, yet William still rebelled against them. Which left him only one way to save them both.

Drake saw the blow coming and knew what it meant. He watched, caught between fascination and revulsion, as William's sword slashed downward. Davey, too, realized what was happening, but too late. He had no chance to move before the muscles of his shoulder were severed, arm and sword left to dangle uselessly at his side.

For a moment he swayed on his feet, overcome by pain and the refusal to believe what had happened. Then slowly he crumpled, hitting the ground with a low thud that he did not hear.

IN THE AFTERMATH of the duel, Elizabeth told herself that she should be grateful for the austerity of a wedding all but devoid of guests. How much better to gather around her the comfort of her family, a bulwark against her mother-in-law's anger and the strangeness of her own newly married state.

The Calverts had always clung together in the face of adversity. They had no patience with false friendship offered only in acknowledgment of their influence, and shunned the fumblings of their neighbors, who could not decide on their own whether or not it would still be appropriate to attend the festivities. To spare them that conundrum, Philip simply let it be known that the wedding would be private. The response was a general sigh of relief, followed by the avid murmurings of gossip as the events on the hillside were chewed over with relish.

Davey had lived; that much, at least, everyone agreed on. He could even be seen taking the air on the veranda at Quail Run, his right arm and shoulder heavily bandaged, his face gaunt. To the numerous visitors who found some excuse to call, he was frustratingly taciturn. But then, Davey had no need to say anything. He had proved himself to be the epitome of the Southern gentleman, first by fighting the duel, and secondly by refusing to name William to the authorities.

"It's so unfair," Elizabeth said to Drake as they stood side by side after the ceremony, receiving the congratulations of her family, if not his. "Davey holds court at Quail Run while we're ostracized. Not," she added quickly, "that I care what people think. I'm glad we decided on a small affair rather than tolerate their stares and whispers."

Drake, who was simply glad to have the business done with, smiled benignly. He had no real sense of her annoyance, having no comprehension of how she had envisioned her wedding day. Instead of the proud reassertion of her Southern heritage that it should have been, it was almost a hole-in-the-wall affair at which she felt like an overdressed participant.

"What an...unusual gown," Abigail said at the first possible opportunity. It was one of the few comments she deigned to address to her daughter-in-law, or, for that matter, to anyone, but she could not resist following it up. "Wasn't there time to have something new made?"

"I preferred to wear my mother's dress," Elizabeth said stiffly. "It is my hope that it will become a tradition and that perhaps someday my own daughter will wear it."

Abigail's only response to that was a barely raised eyebrow. She had already made up her mind that the mistake upon which her only son had just embarked would have to be rectified. How, exactly, she did not know, since there was no possibility of divorce, but neither could there be any question of the marriage continuing indefinitely. She could only trust to Drake's good judgment, or, more appropriately, to his selfishness, that there would be no children before repairs could be made.

Now she frowned as she observed the young couple chatting with William and Sunbird. What kind of family would welcome such a girl, particularly when her relationship with the young man was all too clear? They must think her a naive old woman not to see the passion that flowed between the two. She need not have experienced it in her life, and indeed was infinitely grateful that she had not, in order to recognize it.

The fastidious distaste she felt whenever she remembered the cruder aspects of marriage for once brightened her mood. Drake, dear boy that he was, looked little better than a young stallion frothing at the sight of a mare. But then, all men were like that, even those who pretended to accept the restraining hand of propriety. They were all brothers under the skin, uncivilized, animalistic, ruled by their anatomy. Elizabeth, that supercilious little chit, would soon discover what that meant.

Drake smiled down at his wife again and wondered how soon they could decently depart. Among the advantages he had discovered to so small a wedding was that everything moved along much more rapidly. After the ceremony itself, there would be a family dinner, which, he reasoned, could not last longer than a few hours. With his mother and sisters sulking, it might be over even sooner.

Several days before, he had arranged for a paddle wheeler to be awaiting them on the river. It would carry them to Portsmouth, where they would take ship for Europe and their honeymoon. The thought of being alone with Elizabeth in their cabin prompted him to lean closer and ask, "You are all packed, aren't you, darling?"

She nodded but did not look at him. A sudden feeling of dread was threatening to overtake her when she considered how soon she would be leaving the home of her childhood, and what that departure would mean. Fine time to think of that, the more caustic part of her mind said. No one has ever made a secret to you of what marriage entails.

And she had wanted it, not only the outer form and privileges, but the private, secret part that went on behind closed doors. When Drake held and caressed her, she longed for him to go further. Or at least she *had.* Faced with the imminent realization of her fantasies, she wanted nothing so much as to flee.

Instead she accepted his arm and decorously walked in with him to dinner. Mammy Augusta had outdone herself.

The long mahogany table covered in white lace and decorated with white roses from the garden fairly groaned under the weight of a succulent pink ham studded with cloves, golden biscuits dripping honey, pickled snap beans and corn relish, fluffy mounds of rice, crisp fried chicken dripping gravy. On a separate table off to one side the multitiered wedding cake decorated with spun sugar roses held pride of place. Beside it in silver buckets bottles of champagne chilled.

"To my beloved daughter," Philip said when the first bottle had been opened. "May this day always be as treasured a memory for her as it will be for us." He had intended to say that he hoped she would always be as happy as she was just then, but the look in her eyes as they settled at the table stopped him. Her apprehension, particularly in light of Drake's blithe confidence, was worrisome. He could only hope that his new son-in-law had the sensitivity to understand his young wife's fears.

The long-ingrained habit of protecting her was difficult to give up, but he knew that he had no choice except to relinquish that task to Drake. That rankled even as he accepted it with the same forbearance he had learned to bring to all of life's inevitable twists and turns.

For Sarah it was at once easier and more difficult to accept the change in Elizabeth's status. She loved her fiercely, would always do so, but having made the same transition herself, she knew that it need not be painful or saddening. Need not, but could be. She cast a swift look at Drake, seeing in his easy manner the same source of concern her husband had felt.

Everything was so simple for him. Life fell into his hands like the proverbial ripe plum. Even now, faced with the obvious discontent of his mother and sisters, he simply ignored them and went on enjoying himself. She could only hope that he would not be so oblivious to Elizabeth.

William was thinking much the same thing. He looked at Sunbird, remembered that his own initiation of her had been less gentle than it might have been, and thought that at least Drake would not have the excuse of underestimating his bride's innocence. Whether or not he would cherish it as he should was something that had to be settled between the two of them.

The flow of champagne around the table did little to ease the tension that half the small party tried valiantly to elude, the other half to exploit. Taking their cue from their mother, Drake's sisters sat stiffly proud and silent. They made a show of picking at their food, as though seeking in vain for something edible. Their wine remained untouched. Abigail sighed once, deeply, but was frustrated when that failed to draw any notice.

When she tried again, more loudly, Drake relented enough to ask, "Something wrong, Mother?"

She waved a hand weakly in innocent denial. "Oh, no, I was just thinking of your dear father and how much he would have enjoyed being here today."

With the single statement, uttered in sepulchral tones, she managed to inject the mood of a Boston wake into the skeletal festivities. Thus vindicated, she sat back and at last began to enjoy herself.

For all her concerns about what the next few hours would bring, Elizabeth was relieved when the meal at last ended. She stood with Drake to cut the cake and even managed to smile brightly, but behind the false joviality there were only weariness and something dangerously close to resignation.

She had chosen her own course, as much as any woman could, and she would live with it. But already it seemed that the carefree girl she had been was disappearing into the distant past, and she was left with some new creature she did not know or particularly like.

So much for what was supposed to be the happiest day of her life. Upstairs in what would soon be her bedroom no longer, she suffered herself to be undressed by her mother and Mammy Augusta.

"We'll clean the gown and pack it away," Sarah said, determinedly matter-of-fact. "It will be sent to you wherever you wish."

"Perhaps it should remain here," Elizabeth ventured. Free of the punishing corset, she stretched and took a deep breath. "Sunbird may wish to wear it."

"William has already told us that they intend to be married quietly in Richmond," Sarah said.

"Are quiet weddings to become a Calvert family tradition, then?" Elizabeth asked.

The two older women exchanged a worried glance before Sarah put her arm around her daughter's shoulders. "I know you're disappointed, darling, but believe me, the wedding is only a tiny part of all that follows."

Elizabeth ducked her head, embarrassed by her own weakness. "I know . . . but it was the part I understood."

"The rest will come. You'll see." It sounded so inadequate, but what, after all, was she to say? The gulf between innocence and knowledge was too wide to be breached by mere words.

"Pay no attention to me." Elizabeth smiled wanly. "It's only bridal jitters."

"It will be all right," Sarah said, struck again by her own inability to influence the situation. The best she could do was bolster her daughter's sense of self-confidence, which heaven knew Abigail had done her best to undermine all day.

"You looked lovely in the gown," she said after she had held the lilac traveling suit for Elizabeth to step into, "but this is absolutely breathtaking."

Elizabeth did look remarkably beautiful in the trim outfit tailored to her slender figure. Her hair was swept back in a simple chignon, revealing the diamond earrings that were her parents' wedding gift, and the paleness of her skin made her blue-gray eyes look larger than ever. She was femininity and grace personified, a woman to be admired, even held in awe, and most certainly cherished.

Drake thought the same when he saw her. As she descended the curving marble stairs to the entrance hall, he was waiting at their foot. The luggage had gone on ahead, and he was impatient to follow. His long fingers ran around the rim of the hat he held between both hands, and he glanced at the grandfather clock every few seconds.

Beside him, Philip took another puff on his cheroot and resisted the impulse to suggest they stay the night. When he saw Elizabeth, he almost reconsidered and insisted they remain. Only by dint of biting down hard on the cigar did he prevent the words from leaving his mouth.

"You look...exquisite," Drake said as he moved quickly to claim her. There was a faintly dazed look in his eyes, and he stumbled over his words. "Ravishing" was a more exact description of her appearance, but that evoked images he did not care to entertain in front of her parents.

"Thank you," Elizabeth murmured, lowering her eyes. The warmth of his hand holding hers and the nearness of his body, exuding heat, blocked out her thoughts. Her numbness made her better able to deal with the final farewells, carefully couched in the language of a very temporary separation.

"Perhaps we'll see you for Christmas," Philip suggested as they stepped out onto the veranda.

"Sure," Drake said, ready to agree to anything at that moment. Behind him, his mother glared, but he remained happily oblivious even to her presence. In truth, he could see nothing but Elizabeth. In the wedding dress, she had been a lovely bride, *his* bride. But now she was transformed into something far more, his wife. The woman he would possess with the full weight and authority of law, who would belong to him in a way more thorough and absolute than anyone else ever could.

"Have a good voyage," Sarah said, skipping lightly over the threat of tears. "And write."

"Yes, of course," Elizabeth said. "I'll tell you all about the Paris fashions."

There was time for a quick round of embraces, and then Drake was urging her into the carriage. Suddenly she couldn't see very well, and she was glad for the support of his arm. The world was becoming blurred, familiar objects misting over. She blinked and, when that didn't help, gave up.

The driver's whip cracked in the air, and the horses lurched forward. The carriage rolled down the gravel road, bordered on either side by ancient oaks. In the oaks' cool green shadows, Drake put his arm around her and smiled tolerantly.

"There's no need to cry, sweetheart." In the face of her need, he felt deliciously strong and in control. She leaned against him, small and vulnerable. His heart swelled at the thought of how dependent she was on him now, and would be forever. "We'll come back," he promised. "Perhaps at Christmas."

She nodded, though she barely heard him. Behind her lay all that she knew and held dear; ahead lay...what? Natural fear of the unknown made her tremble, but the Calvert courage stiffened her spine. She drew a deep breath, let it out slowly and sat up.

"I'm sorry, Drake. I had no intention of turning weepy."

He frowned, hardly able to tell her that he rather liked her that way. The sudden resurgence of her self-control threw him, until he remembered how soon and how thoroughly he would overcome it. "No need to apologize, my dear," he assured her. "You're entitled to a bit of upset today."

Perhaps, but there was no sign of any such emotion by the time they reached the dock where the paddle wheeler awaited them. The *Dixie Princess* usually plowed a regular course from Richmond to Portsmouth and back again, carrying several hundred passengers each time. But only the captain was in evidence as Drake alighted from the coach and handed Elizabeth down.

Stiffly formal in a navy-blue uniform trimmed with gold, Captain Jonah Danvers stepped forward to greet them. He inclined his silver head gravely. "Good afternoon, sir, madam. May I be among the first to offer my congratulations?"

"Thank you," Drake said, taking Elizabeth's arm. She was looking around, a bit puzzled, wondering why there was no sign of the other passengers on deck. Surely they would have gathered to comment on the unscheduled stop and determine the reason for it. Yet the gleaming mahogany decks were empty, and no one stood at the polished brass railings.

"Your luggage has already been taken on board, sir," the captain was saying. "If you would be so good as to follow me..."

They did, along the plank gangway that had been carefully lashed into place. Once on board, Elizabeth was even more forcibly struck by the silence and the odd air of vacancy.

"Is something wrong, Mrs. Bennington?"

"What? Oh, no..." It was the first time anyone had called her by her new name, and she was momentarily taken aback by it. The captain was, of course, trying to be cordial, if not more than that. There was a labored respectfulness about him that she supposed she would have to get used to, seeing who Drake was. At least it made him easier to question. "I was just wondering where the other passengers are."

Captain Danvers shot a puzzled look at Drake, who merely shrugged and left the explanations to him. "There aren't any, ma'am. Your husband took the entire boat."

A fleeting image of all those rows of empty cabins darted through Elizabeth's mind. Rather unsettling, as though she had wandered into an abandoned house. Which was a foolish way to think of it. Drake was simply being romantic and typically extravagant; she should be delighted.

Yet the thought of being so completely alone with him distressed her. With a start, she realized that she had unconsciously been counting on having other people nearby, not because she was so silly as to believe that she might need help, but simply for the restraining influence any measure of society always imposed.

Except that on this voyage down the James there would be only the hired crew, who would undoubtedly count for no more in Drake's eyes than the all but invisible servants who flitted through every corner of his life.

Their stateroom was, predictably enough, the largest and most luxurious on the vessel. Two teak-paneled cabins had been put together to provide a sitting room furnished with overstuffed sofas and tasseled lamps, adjacent to a bedroom that boasted, to Elizabeth's wide-eyed surprise, an immense brass bed.

Her maid had already been and gone, hanging those clothes she would need for the trip in the oak armoire. Drake's valet had done the same, so that his suits and her gowns now shared the space in casual intimacy. Through an open door, she could see into the large private bath, complete with a claw-footed tub. Beside it was a marble dressing table, where her toilet articles lay next to his.

He had followed her into the stateroom and shut the door behind them. She heard the click of the lock before she turned to look at him. When she did, she instantly regretted it. Any hope of a reprieve, however temporary, vanished. The taut set of his features spoke of a hunger she did not understand or, at that moment, share. And the impatient strength of his body as he strode toward her warned that what she might not be able to give freely would nonetheless be taken.

"THERE'S NO NEED to be nervous, darling," Drake said as he walked toward her. "After all, we are man and wife now."

Elizabeth looked away from him. She straightened a vase on a nearby table and stared sightlessly at the painting hanging above it. "Yes, of course." Her voice sounded hollow, even to her own ears, but Drake appeared not to notice.

"It's only natural that I should want to be alone with you," he said.

Natural, but unwelcome nonetheless. She needed time to recover from the events of the past few days, which had seen her family threatened by forces she was still reluctant to acknowledge. She had been a naturally cheery child and was instinctively an optimist. Her experience so far had largely confirmed the conviction that everything worked out for the best. Given the chance, she would rebound quickly, but to do so she needed a small amount of patience and understanding.

Drake was feeling neither. He had already waited what for him was an extraordinary length of time. Never before had he been forced to postpone his own gratification to such an extent. He had accepted the need because there had been no alternative, but that didn't prevent him from resenting it.

His eyes narrowed as he studied her pale, averted face. "You do know what I want?"

She nodded even as she thought what a crude way that was to put it. If he had wanted to find out how well-informed she was about the wedding night, he could have found a gentler way to ask. But such consideration seemed to be slipping away from him. To her dismay, she sensed that he was growing more tense and determined by the moment.

"I thought," she murmured, "that we would wait until tonight, after supper."

Drake relaxed slightly and even smiled. So that was it. She thought lovemaking could only take place in the dark. It would be his pleasure to teach her otherwise.

"Why should we, sweetheart?" he asked, taking her hand and drawing her toward the bedroom. Accustomed as he was to experienced women, he was pleased by her innocence. It put him firmly in control, where he intended to remain.

"No one will disturb us," he promised as he slid his hands up to her shoulders. Beneath her traveling suit, her bones felt very delicate. Above the high collar fringed with lace he could see a pulse beating in her throat. Her lower lip trembled slightly.

Her eyes focused on the large bed hung with diaphanous gauze curtains, its feather pillows plumped and its covers already turned down. "My maid," she breathed. "I'll need her assistance."

"Nonsense. I'm more than capable of helping you."

"A bath..."

"Later we'll bathe together."

The idea shocked her, but it was also exciting in a primitive way that both repelled and enticed her. She had realized some time ago that Drake appealed to a side of her nature she knew very little about. Love was something she was perfectly at home with, because she had had the great good fortune of growing up in a family where it flourished. But passion was another matter entirely. That was something she had been as rigorously protected from as any other young lady her age. Drake was poised to rip the veil from her eyes and reveal the mystery that drew her as a moth to a flame.

He sensed her wavering and took it as a confirmation that all she really needed was a firm hand. Her family clearly adored her and had perhaps given her a bit too much rein. Now that she was his wife, she would have to learn to do without that. In return, she would be more than amply compensated with a life any woman would envy.

Complacent in his certainty that what he was doing was right, he put a hand under her chin, tilted her head back and kissed her thoroughly. There was nothing gentle or coaxing about his touch; he was driven only by the need to release some small measure of his own pent-up desire.

Elizabeth gasped when he thrust his tongue into her mouth. He had kissed her like that before, but not so roughly or impetuously. She stiffened and tried to pull back, only to discover that his hands had slipped to her hips and were holding her firmly against him. Heat darkened her cheeks as she felt his arousal.

"Drake," she protested as she wrenched her head to the side. Her mouth was wet, and she could taste him on her tongue. Anger bubbled up in her. Her wedding had not been what she had expected, and now it seemed that her wedding night wouldn't be, either. There was only so much she could be expected to tolerate. "You're too rough."

He raised an eyebrow, but looked singularly unperturbed. "You think so? You've been too sheltered to know what it's like between a man and a woman." Large fingers touched the tiny pearl buttons holding her jacket closed and began matter-of-factly to undo them. "Don't expect me to be a polite, diffident lover, Elizabeth. I want you too much for that."

Big though his hands were, they were hardly clumsy. He had made short work of half the buttons before she recovered enough to try to slap him away. When he persisted, she tried to compromise. "Let me do it myself."

"All right," he agreed, stepping back a pace. "Go ahead."

She started to turn around to give herself some small measure of privacy, but he would not permit it. "I want to watch you."

Again she felt the conflicting sensations of annoyance and excitement. Confused, she took refuge in sarcasm. "Is that what proper Boston ladies do?"

He shook his head, the lines on either side of his mouth deepening with his smile. "I didn't marry a proper Boston lady."

She was beginning to understand. The passion she sensed as an alien presence within herself was perfectly recognizable to Drake. It was at least part of what had drawn him to her. Dimly, she sensed something of what she must represent to him, a uniting of two types of woman he had previously known only as completely separate.

In public, she did not doubt that he expected her to appear as the quintessential lady, above reproach. But alone, as they were now, he wanted something altogether different. Something that, to her growing surprise, she realized she was tempted to be.

Slowly, not taking her eyes from him, she finished unbuttoning the jacket and slipped it off. Beneath she wore a soft white silk blouse appliquéd with delicate flowers. The fringe of lace he had seen was its high-necked collar. Long sleeves reached to her wrists, where a shower of matching lace half covered her hands. Tiny seed pearls ran down the front of the blouse to disappear beneath the tightly cinched waist of her bustled skirt.

Casually, as though she did this every day of the week, she hung the jacket on the back of a nearby chair and stood before him her hands primly folded. "I believe it's your turn."

Drake's eyes widened at her boldness, but he managed to conceal his surprise and, with more haste than grace, stripped off his jacket. Going her one better, he also removed the waistcoat he wore beneath it and tossed both negligently onto the couch.

Elizabeth's gaze drifted over his broad chest, concealed only by a starched linen shirt tucked into form-fitting trousers. He stood with his hands on his hips, feet planted slightly apart, and regarded her impatiently. "Go on."

"I can't...the blouse buttons in the back."

"Turn around."

She obeyed, though her legs were trembling and she feared they might give way. The fine silk caught, and Drake cursed under his breath. He yanked a button off, and it fell to the carpeted floor, where it lay white and gleaming.

"Sorry..." he muttered.

"I-it doesn't matter."

At last the blouse fell open. He pulled it out of the waistband and began easing it off her shoulders. The bareness of her back above a lacy camisole was revealed to him. He could see the delicate ridge of her spine and her shoulder blades, lightly covered by pale skin from which rose the scent of lavender.

Lightly he brushed his lips against the nape of her neck, feeling the shiver that ran through her. Her arms were almost impossibly smooth. The blouse slipped down them easily, to land on the floor beside the errant button.

Instinctively, Elizabeth bent to pick it up, but Drake stopped her. Looking over her shoulder, he could see the rise of her breasts partly bared above the camisole. The sheer fabric could not conceal the darker circles of her nipples, nor hide their hardness.

"Beautiful," he murmured, and with that single word the last of his patience fled. He all but wrenched open the back of her skirt and pushed it below her hips. She half turned her head, as though to object, only to be stopped by another hard, demanding kiss that robbed her mind of whatever she had intended to say.

She was barely aware when he sat her on the edge of the bed and pulled off her small kidskin shoes. Her stockings followed, along with a froth of petticoats, until she was left only in her pantaloons, corset and camisole.

"Stand up," he ordered as he jerked his shirt off. She had barely obeyed when he seized both her hands and spread them over his bare, heated skin. She gasped, but made no effort to pull away. The feel of him fascinated her. She was seized by the sudden desire to touch him all over, to learn every inch of his body as thoroughly as she sensed he intended to learn hers.

But she was not quite ready for that and could only stand motionless while he traced the hard, whalebone corset that extended from just below her breasts down over her waist and belly to end above her thighs. As corsets went, it was lighter than many and undeniably more comfortable than the one she had had to wear to fit into her wedding gown. But it was also a barrier between them that drove their fevered senses to even greater heights.

Drake fumbled with the laces, only to discover that they were double-knotted at the end, a little surprise from Mammy Augusta, who had suspected who would be undoing them. "Damn," he murmured under his breath. "These things should be outlawed."

"Many women think so, too," Elizabeth murmured. His impatience was no longer quite so frightening. She was beginning to feel more confident and to relish the fact that she could arouse him so. Then his fingers tightened on the laces and, without apparent effort, snapped them in two.

The stark expedience of that act, and the ruined garment that resulted, stunned her. She was not yet so accustomed to having things that she could view their destruction with equanimity.

"It will have to be repaired," she murmured.

"Forget it," he said, tossing the offending garment away. "You don't need a corset, and I don't want to be bothered by one."

Did that mean he intended to undress her regularly? Elizabeth almost asked, but stopped herself, suspecting that she didn't want to know the answer. Besides, there were other things to think about, such as the groan of pleasure that escaped him as he cupped her breasts and squeezed them lightly.

No one else had ever touched her there, and all he had ever done before was brush his fingers over her when she was decorously covered by several layers of clothing. This was altogether different. His thumbs rubbing over her nipples made her ache, while the rhythmic kneading of his hands sent tremors racing through her. The soft silk camisole felt suddenly unbearably heavy against her skin. She wanted to be free of it, and of everything else that separated them.

No silk could compete with the smoothness of her skin, Drake thought as he slipped the narrow straps from her shoulders and bared her to the waist. Her nipples were dark pink and tilted upward. He bent his head and grazed one with his teeth before fastening his mouth on it and suckling her voraciously.

Elizabeth cried out. She could not suppress the sound any more than she could banish the rush of flame that tore through her. Only his arm wrapped tightly around her waist kept her from falling. As it was, she felt as though she were sinking into an abyss of pleasure from which there could be no return.

Sheer survival instinct compelled her to try to pull back, but Drake was implacable. He stilled her struggles without even being more than dimly aware of them and pursued her relentlessly. The camisole bunched around her waist. He jerked it up and over her head. His hands tangled in her hair, pulling out the pins one by one until the caramel-hued skeins fell over her shoulders. Slowly, with artful concentration, he arranged them over her naked breasts, letting the taut nipples show between them.

Leaving her like that, he sat down, yanked off his boots and undid his trousers, but did not remove them. Elizabeth swayed before him. Instinctively, she raised her hands to shield herself, but at a sharp command from him, she let them drop again.

He beckoned her to him until she stood between his parted legs. Inch by inch, he pulled down the pantaloons, revealing the curve of her hips, the smoothness of her belly, the golden shadow of hair between her thighs. She was shaking uncontrollably before he finished. Her hands grasped his shoulders, nails digging into the smooth, hot skin that felt like rough velvet. When his mouth brushed her beneath her navel, she moaned. But it was the darting thrust of his tongue into the cleft of her womanhood that caused her knees to buckle.

With an easy movement, he caught her up and strode over to the bed. Lying there on her back, gazing up at him with widely dilated eyes, Elizabeth watched as he removed his last garments and stood before her proudly naked, unabashedly aroused. She stared fixedly at his maleness, the long, thick organ thrusting away from the nest of hair at his groin. It moved spasmodically beneath her gaze, as though possessed of a life of its own.

The sudden remembrance that he intended to penetrate her with that jerked her out of her sensual haze and made her stiffen. She half sat up, as though poised for flight.

Instantly he was on the bed beside her, pressing her back against the mattress. "It's all right, sweetheart. Whatever pain you feel this first time will be quickly gone."

Reason, what little she had left, told her he was right. Hadn't her own mother assured her that the experience was beautiful? Besides, women's bodies were made to accommodate the birthing of babies and therefore could presumably adapt to a great deal.

She repeated that to herself almost frantically as he lowered himself onto her. His weight was considerable, even though he took much of it on his powerful arms. The heat of his body enveloped her, as much an intrusion as his very presence. She felt the roughness of his skin against her breasts and trembled.

Drake was watching her carefully. He was relieved by her acceptance and pleasantly surprised by her responsiveness. Comments he had heard from married friends indicated that virgin brides were more often stiff-necked martyrs to the animal lusts of their husbands. If, in the back of his Boston-born-and-bred mind, he was a bit taken aback by her sensuality, he recognized that niggling doubt for the foolishness it was and thrust it firmly aside.

How right he had been not to marry a cold New England girl, he thought as he ran a hand possessively down the smooth length of her. Her skin glowed with a porcelain sheen that seemed to possess its own inner light. Behind her right hip near the curve of her buttock he was delighted to find a small brown mole. He touched the tip of his tongue to it, wondering what other pleasures he had yet to discover.

Elizabeth lay very still beneath him. She had passed through several stages of emotion from resentment to anticipation to the first stirrings of fear. Now all that was blanked out by shock. No one had ever handled her so intimately. She felt invaded before he had even entered her. Even more, she was struck by his clear assumption that he had the right to do whatever he wished, an assumption society would only approve.

But it was her body that he was touching, almost examining, so thoroughly. Her breasts he was suckling at, her legs he was parting. When he touched her between her thighs, she had to stifle a cry of protest. Physically she was aroused, his expertise had seen to that. But emotionally she remained aloof and faintly repelled.

Perhaps it didn't matter. Certainly Drake seemed unaware of her reluctance. He was murmuring to her softly, praising her beauty. His voice was thick and slightly slurred, and as his control began to deteriorate, the words he used shocked her even further.

The thought flitted through her mind that this must be what it was like to be one of those women she wasn't supposed to know about. She tried to shove it aside, telling herself that she was completely wrong. Drake was her husband; they were joined together by both man and God. Moreover, she could hardly object that he wasn't being gentle with her. Nothing he had done hurt, except in some vulnerable inner core of her being.

That changed when he began to penetrate her. Then there was pain, but to her relief it was brief and far from intolerable. He seemed to understand that to prolong it would be cruel, and he thrust hard and deep to open her quickly. After that it was easier, even though it seemed to go on for a long time. She was acutely aware of his ragged breathing and of the dampness of his skin against hers. From beneath her lashes, she looked at him, seeing his handsome face pulled taut, head thrown back.

Then something warm and wet filled her, Drake groaned deeply, and it was over.

Or at least that part was. Afterward, he held her close and gently stroked her back. That felt good, as, she had to admit, did the knowledge that she had given him pleasure. Certainly he seemed well satisfied, if slightly rueful.

"It will get better for you," he murmured sleepily. "I promise."

She had no idea what he meant. It was enough that the experience was over and that, in retrospect, it hadn't been bad at all. Dimly she remembered what her mother had said and felt troubled, wondering if she had missed something.

But the sensation lingered only for an instant. Then she, too, tumbled into sleep to the rhythm of the paddle wheeler carrying them steadily downriver.

SUPPER WAS BROUGHT to their stateroom by two white-jacketed waiters who wheeled in a trolley laid with fine china and crystal. A Lalique vase held a single perfect rose. Champagne chilled in a silver ice bucket. Delectable aromas wafted from the chafing dishes set out on the sideboard.

"That will do," Drake said when everything was ready. "We'll serve ourselves."

The two men nodded and saw themselves out. They had been in the room perhaps five minutes, and in the way of good servants everywhere had never once made eye contact with the tall, golden-haired man in the burgundy silk dressing gown who gave them their instructions. Nor would they make any comment about the newlyweds once they were gone. Each had worked some ten years on various riverboats and in that time had seen far too much of human variety, not to mention depravity, to find anything of interest in a married couple.

Elizabeth did not share their sangfroid. She had remained secluded in the bedroom until the men were safely gone, only emerging when Drake called to her. That was partly because of how she was dressed—or, rather, not dressed—but she would not have faced the men in full church-going regalia.

"You look lovely," Drake said, and meant it. He'd had some trouble convincing her to wear the peignoir, though it was modest enough by the standards of some he had seen. But then, one hardly expected one's wife to dress in the same manner as the bawdy house girls. Still, the thin white silk was sheer enough to more than hint at the beauty of the body he had so lately enjoyed, and that he looked forward to possessing again in the not-too-distant future.

If she had not been his wife, and so lately a virgin, he would already have taken her again. But he prided himself on his restraint, believing that his patience with her would reap dividends later.

"Sit down," he said gesturing to one of the velvet wing chairs pulled up beside the table. As she crossed the room toward him, he noted her self-consciousness and hid a smile. She had nothing to be embarrassed about. Besides being beautiful, her every movement was graceful. She held herself erectly, her back straight. Her hips swayed slightly as she moved. He thought of them moving under him and was glad of the dressing gown that hid his sudden arousal.

"To us," he said, touching his glass to hers. She looked at him for a moment as though she didn't quite understand, then managed a smile and took a sip of the crisp, cool wine. It slid more easily than she would have thought down her clenched throat. The next sip was even easier, and she finished half the glass before she realized she had done so.

Drake refilled it and settled back in his chair. He was enjoying simply looking at her. Her honey-hued hair lay over her shoulders. She had tried to brush the tangles from it, but there was still an aura of disarray he found very appealing. Her cheeks were lightly flushed, and the eyes that had such difficulty looking at him directly were heavy-lidded with remembered passion.

The gown he had insisted she wear left her shoulders bare and hugged the curve of her breasts. He was very tempted to reach across the table and touch her, but resisted, knowing that banked fires tended to burn all the more brightly when they were finally fed.

"Are you hungry?" he asked.

Elizabeth shook her head. Though her stomach was empty, she couldn't imagine swallowing a bite. Not even the crab cakes she normally loved could appeal to her, nor the consommé, succulent slices of rare roast beef, small parsleyed potatoes, braised carrots and fresh baked rolls, which formed what would be considered a fairly simple if perfectly prepared meal. She did manage to nibble on a few strawberries and even to accept one from between Drake's fingers after he had swirled it in champagne.

She laughed then, feeling daring, not stopping to think that it was the wine that gave her courage. He had been refilling her glass steadily without her noticing, and now she felt pleasantly removed from the tensions that rippled through her.

The opposite was true for Drake. With each passing moment, his arousal became more intense. He had done greater justice to the meal than Elizabeth, but might have been eating sawdust for all the attention he paid. Only one thought occupied his mind: to get her back to bed as expeditiously as possible.

Meanwhile, he occupied himself in talking to her, telling her of the things they would do once they reached Europe. He had been there three years before on his grand tour and had fond memories of the place. Letters had already gone ahead alerting friends of their arrival, and he had no doubt that he and Elizabeth would be liberally feted. She would enjoy that, as he would enjoy introducing her to aristocratic society.

Elizabeth listened to him, nodding occasionally, but without really taking in anything he was saying. It was enough to focus on the deep timbre of his voice, his low chuckle, the smile that made him look almost ingenuous.

"They all call him Bertie," he was explaining, speaking of the Prince of Wales, into whose gilded circle they could expect to be received. "Not to his face, of course. Formalities are almost ridiculously observed."

"What do you mean?" Elizabeth asked, rousing herself from her languor to at least pretend interest.

"Only that the...proprieties aren't quite what they are in Boston." Drake frowned as he said that, remembering that the sexual liberties of the British upper class that had so amused him three years before must now be seen in a somewhat different light. According to the complex, hidden creed of the Marlborough House set—the lords and ladies who flocked to the prince's side—affairs were perfectly acceptable so long as the couple was discreet. Any married woman was considered fair game, provided she had already done her duty by her husband and borne him at least one heir.

Remembering that last part reassured him. Married Elizabeth was, and undoubtedly desirable, but as a bride yet to produce progeny she should be considered off-limits. Should be, but not necessarily would be. The fact that she was an American and merely passing through, as it were, might tempt certain gentlemen to stretch the rules a bit.

Which merely meant that he would have to make it clear that any such interference was not to be tolerated. His eyes hardened as he considered how he would feel if any other man touched her. Perhaps because he had only just taken her virginity, he was feeling unaccustomedly possessive about her. It was just as well that the mores of Queen Victoria's randy son had not reached Boston.

Abruptly Drake stood up and held out his hand. "Come."

Confused, by the wine as much as by his sudden shift in mood, Elizabeth shook her head. "Where...?"

"Back to bed. It's growing late."

It was a specious explanation, hinting as it did that sleep was the objective. Elizabeth was not misled. She saw the light in his eyes and knew what he intended. Part of her rebelled, as she had before. But this time her resistance was undermined by the desire to experience more fully what she had so far only glimpsed.

His fingers were warm as they curled around hers. The strength of his body—and his will—drew her upward. She went with him almost docilely, though the rapid beating of her heart indicated that she was anything but a passive participant.

That night, as the *Dixie Princess* rode at anchor on the slow-moving tide and cicadas hummed along the river-banks, Elizabeth discovered more about passion and the married state. She learned that what she had thought was shocking intimacy was only the prelude to far greater intrusions on her person, and she began to realize how much Drake expected of her. She also began to sense, if only dimly, something of the power that lay hidden within herself, a secret, female power whose existence she had never really suspected before.

When at last he slumped asleep beside her, exhausted by his exertions, she lay propped on her elbow studying him. The masculine mystery and mystique that had surrounded him were gone. The unknown male no longer had the power to awe her. If anything, she was awed now by what she felt within herself, not him.

Rain began to drum against the tin roof of the state-room. She listened to it for a time before she remembered why it was important. At Calvert Oaks the parched fields would be turning richly dark and moist. The drooping cotton and tobacco plants would be soaking up the life-giving wetness, their stalks and leaves gathering strength. In the workers' quarters as well as in the big house, people would wake, listen to the rain and know relief. Come morning, there would be laughter in the fields.

She would not be there to share it. Listening to the rain, she felt the moisture on her cheeks but did not brush it aside. Instead she let it flow silently in her own tribute to the land, and to the past.

After a time, she lay back against the pillows beside her husband and slept heavily and without dreams.

_____ *Wife*

LONDON WAS NOT what Elizabeth had expected. She had thought to encounter another, grander version of Boston, and there was something of that in the bustle of what everyone persisted in calling the City, as though everything surrounding that single rather small section of the capital was of lesser consequence. Perhaps the title had been earned because it was there that the great business of the empire was done, the stock exchange and banks flourished, and somber-faced men in tails and top hats hurried about their daily affairs.

But there was also so much more that she could not have anticipated. To begin with, the pace of social activity was so hectic as to make Boston seem by comparison as slumberous as any Southern backwater. Barely had they settled into their suite of rooms at the Carlton Hotel than a steady stream of invitations swept them into the whirl. It was the height of the spring season, which extended from just after Easter to the Ascot races at the end of June. All the great families were in town, and delicious gossip ran rampant along Rotten Row and in the elegant town houses of Berkeley Square.

The prince was finished with Miss Langtry; the Jersey Lily had, after a tumultuous few years in the royal bed, at last begun to bore him. He was approaching forty and was looking for a quieter arrangement, which did not prevent him from enjoying a brief fling with the fabulous Sarah Bernhardt.

His long-suffering princess, the beautiful if exasperating Alexandra, was rumored to be pregnant again, though no one who was truly knowledgeable believed it. Bertie's strongest partisans, those of the Marlborough House set who stood most firmly for him against the thin-lipped displeasure of his royal mother, believed that he had deserted Alexandra's bed to spare her the danger of further child-bearing and that his infidelities were merely the natural outcome of such husbandly consideration.

Certainly they set an example few were loath to follow, as Elizabeth swiftly learned. Her tutor in the labyrinthine world of Edwardian morals was a doe-eyed lady of some twenty-four years, one Cornelia Marie Cardingham, marchioness of Luxtable, wife of Charles David Cardingham, marquess of the same and Drake's great good friend from his grand tour days. The Cardinghams wasted no time taking the newly married couple in hand, and Cornelia in particular set out to make Elizabeth a social success.

"You're absolutely lovely, of course," she said one afternoon shortly after the Benningtons' arrival as the two ladies sat at tea in Cornelia's parlor. "But unfortunately that isn't enough. You must be seen to shine."

"I'm not sure I want to," Elizabeth said in her soft Southern voice. "It sounds rather exhausting."

Cornelia frowned. She had enjoyed a great success during her first season some six years before. Her soulful eyes, transparent skin and Grecian features put her on a par with the best of the professional beauties whose photographs were snapped up by the eager masses. Thanks to careful coaching by her mother and aunt, both of whom had been considered among the incomparables of their day, she knew how to transform a certain natural shyness into the pose of mysterious inaccessibility to which gentlemen of her class were so susceptible. Before the end of her debut season, she had received a dozen proposals of marriage. Deciding among them had been relatively easy, since she understood exactly what sort of life she wanted to live and what it would take to achieve that.

Ever since, Cornelia had been tantalized by the possibility of repeating her success, if only vicariously. In her American guest, she saw the chance. Granted, Elizabeth was no untouched young girl fresh to the marriage mart, but that was an advantage, not a liability. She could enjoy the greater freedom of a married woman while remaining aloof and untouchable by virtue of her lack of progeny.

That was a tempting combination, in Cornelia's view, though she was glad enough to no longer be in such limbo herself. Her nursery was well stocked with two sons and a daughter, leaving her to pursue other interests. That she hadn't done so thus far was only because she continued to find her husband unaccountably attractive, a social faux pas she did her best to conceal.

"Don't be foolish," she told her guest firmly. "You'll adore all the fuss; besides, Drake will be so proud of you."

As she had expected, the sally struck home. Cornelia sensed a certain insecurity in Elizabeth, a rather touching desire to please her husband while also asserting her own importance. There was no better way for a woman to do so than to be the cynosure of approving eyes.

"You're an exotic," Cornelia went on as she leaned forward slightly to freshen their tea. Neither woman had touched the trays of delicate cucumber and watercress sandwiches, or the finger slivers of ginger cake laid out for their enjoyment. As tightly corseted as they were, it was all they could do to sip a few drops of reviving liquid.

Elizabeth had been briefly tempted to stop wearing the torturous contraptions, given Drake's dislike of them and his conviction that they were unnecessary anyway. But she quickly discovered that, given the present styles, such a decision was not practical. Fashion above all, had to be served, if only because her husband expected her to be as admired in public as she was accessible in bed.

"Not only are you American," Cornelia was saying, "but you're from the South. We see so few Southerners that they fascinate us, a legacy of that nasty war, I suppose."

Elizabeth restrained a smile. She wasn't quite sure how she felt about being an object of curiosity, however admired, but she did want Drake's approval. It troubled her how increasingly vital that was becoming to her. He was like a boy set loose in London again, all eager enthusiasm and vivacity. He and Charles had gone off to the latter's club, where Drake was undoubtedly busy renewing old acquaintances and accepting invitations.

Not that she minded. Whatever niggling wish she had not to share him was at odds with her equal need to be diverted from an intimacy that still threatened to overwhelm her. They had had two days to themselves while traveling down the James, which for her, at least, had been quite enough solitude. Beginning with the ocean voyage, she had been relieved to see him draw the eager friendship of both men and women, who were attracted as much by his own personality as by his illustrious name.

Made uncharacteristically shy by her newly minted state, Elizabeth had hung back at first, but no more. She was determined to be as significant in her own way as he was in his, even if that meant she had to "shine."

"All right," she said. "Perhaps it would be fun. But how do we begin?"

Cornelia wasted no time telling her. The strategy for such a campaign had been bred into her at the tenderest age. She knew every feint and parry that would bring a woman into the limelight.

"To start with," she explained, "you must go to all the right parties. That's no problem, since you're being invited everywhere. But there must be no slips, no little gaucheries."

"I don't see how I can avoid them," Elizabeth protested. "First, I'm a stranger here, and second, I already sense that nothing is quite what it seems on the surface."

Cornelia laughed and clapped her hands. "Bravo! I was right to think you intelligent. Our set is like a giant petit four, wreathed in pretty icing and containing numerous layers, some sweet, some tart. There are even a few hard nuts on which it is possible to crack a tooth. To avoid that, you must have some history."

Which she proceeded to provide, regaling Elizabeth through the damp afternoon with tales of old scandals that had the advantage of being fresh to the newcomer's increasingly reddened ears.

"The queen," Cornelia said with a reverent hush, "does not approve of Bertie, not at all. She thinks him weak and frivolous and persists in treating him like a naughty six-year-old, rather than the man he has become. She allows him no involvement with the workings of government, which is really a shame, since he has a first-class mind and would be a great help to her."

"Why is she like that?" Elizabeth asked. "It seems very shortsighted, since presumably he will be king someday?"

Cornelia glanced toward the door, which was discreetly closed, then whispered, "No one knows for sure, but some say she blames him for her dear Albert's death. You know, she's never recovered from that and still persists in wearing mourning nearly twenty years later, even though it makes her look so dumpy."

"How awful!" Elizabeth exclaimed. "What could the prince possibly have done to be blamed for his own father's death?"

"He was involved with an actress, Nellie Clark was her name, hardly unusual for the young man of twenty that he was then. But the prince consort was the most puritanical sort. He was absolutely horrified, even went all the way to Cambridge, where Bertie was, to have it out with him. He caught a cold on the way, which developed into typhoid and killed him. The queen never recovered; to this day she believes that it was the scandal that caused her widowhood.''

To Elizabeth, raised in a society where it was tacitly understood that young men would take their pleasures, the story was all but incomprehensible, yet she had to believe it. Even to a novice such as she, it was clear that a deep schism existed in the highest reaches of British society, with what were in effect two courts, one surrounding the dour, rigid queen, and the other drawn to her ebullient son.

''How sad for the prince,'' she murmured. ''He must have been left feeling that he had lost both father and mother.''

''Don't spare him too much sympathy,'' Cornelia advised. ''Bertie has a staunchly practical turn of mind and is remarkably resilient. He knows perfectly well he wasn't responsible for Albert's death, but the rift with his mother has enabled him to go his own way to a degree that might otherwise have been impossible.''

And she went on to describe in lavish detail the prince's *affaires d'amour* with such illustrious ladies as the Princesse de Sagan who, for years, had kept him company on his annual cures at various Continental spas; Lady Georgiana Dudley, who greatly preferred him to her middle-aged and some said rather peculiar husband; as well as Lily Langtry and Sarah Bernhardt.

He was quite simply a man who enjoyed women, and Cornelia was certain that he would welcome Elizabeth even though he would regard her as off-limits.

''Of course,'' she explained, ''the prince sets the style others follow.''

''You mean . . . his aren't the only affairs?''

''Precisely. One of the greatest challenges facing any hostess is the house party. Bedroom assignments can be a positive nightmare, since no one wants to go wandering through too many miles of chilly corridors at night, yet it would hardly be proper to have husbands and lovers encountering each other at every turn."

"No," Elizabeth murmured, working hard to hide her shock, "it wouldn't."

So much for any thought of similarities between Boston and London. The former seemed positively provincial in its straitlaced morality, so different from the sophisticated tolerance here in what was truly the center of the civilized world.

"Not," Cornelia added, "that there aren't rules." She went on to explain them, to Elizabeth's great relief, since she had no desire to be the target of any gentleman's amorous intentions other than her husband. Which raised the uncomfortable question of Drake's position in all this. Presumably there was the usual double standard governing the behavior of men, leaving them free to do pretty much as they wished, while women were restricted, at the very least, by severe discretion. But surely Drake had no intention of...

Her thoughts had not gone beyond that uncomfortable point when there was a flurry at the parlor door and both husband and host entered, each looking well pleased with himself.

"Tiresome day," Charles said as he bent to kiss his wife lightly on the cheek. He was a tall, slender young man with a rather round face, a full mouth partly concealed by a mustache, and deep-set gray eyes that Elizabeth found both wise and kind. "Couldn't go riding in all this rain. Still had a good enough time at White's. Saw Harty-tarty get into a fine tussle with some explorer chap just back from Africa."

"Harty-tarty?" Elizabeth murmured, casting Drake a puzzled glance. She thought he was looking exceptionally good that morning, despite what had been a rather late night. They had started out at the theater and gone on to several parties. She had told her maid not to wait up, and Drake had insisted on helping her undress, though he had been far from sober. She had thought the intricate stays and laces of her clothing would defeat him, but, on the contrary, he made short work of them and she was quickly tumbled across the bed. A soft smile touched her lips as she remembered the lovemaking that followed.

Their eyes met in a glance redolent of things to come. Her cheeks warmed, and she looked hastily away.

"Lord Hartington," Charles explained, "eighth duke of Devonshire and a ripping good sort. Thought he'd make PM a few months back when the Liberals came in, but Gladstone put the quash on that. Wouldn't serve with him, you see. Told Her Majesty he wasn't anything but a young pup gotten above himself. Ridiculous, what?"

"Poor Louisa," Cornelia said with an exaggerated sigh. "She must be so frustrated."

"Louisa, duchess of Manchester," Drake explained. "Harty-tarty's mistress lo these many years and an extremely ambitious woman."

"Say what you will about Louisa," Charles said, "but she is true to her friends. Who else has stuck with the Churchills? When Bertie broke with them and announced he'd enter no house where they were received, she told him she'd invite whomever she liked. He had to back down, with her, at least, though God only knows when Randy and poor Jennie will be back in society, if ever."

Elizabeth wasn't sure she was up to hearing about yet another scandal, but she listened patiently as the rift between the Churchills and the prince was explained. It seemed to have something to do with a particularly nasty divorce case several years before, during which the intemperate Mr. Churchill had foolishly tried to help out a friend by bringing pressure to bear against the Prince of Wales. For this purpose, he had unwisely approached the princess.

Not even Elizabeth, stranger though she was to this peculiar society, had to be told that it was the height of bad taste to carry tales to the prince's wife. The results had been predictable, with the Churchills effectively banished from the Marlborough House set. The lovely, vivacious Jennie was left to content herself with her husband and infant son, Winnie, while hoping they would eventually be forgiven.

"I am beginning to think," Elizabeth said some time later when she and Drake had left the Cardinghams and were returning to their hotel to dress for dinner, "that I'm going to need some sort of scorecard in order to keep everyone straight. Just trying to remember who has been or presently is involved with whom is mind breaking."

"Think of it as a game of musical chairs," Drake suggested. He had almost said musical beds but stopped himself in time, not wanting to give his young bride the impression that he viewed such matters frivolously.

During his previous visit, he had been first astounded then delighted by the laissez-faire attitude toward sexual dalliance. He had also enjoyed the favors of several ladies who had been taken with the big handsome American, and in their beds he had learned a great deal. The temptation to indulge again was definitely present, but he virtuously thrust it aside. After all, he was a newly married man with an undeniably desirable wife. It was both foolish and unnecessary to go hunting for pleasures that were already at his fingertips.

His instincts about Elizabeth had been right from the start: she was warm, passionate, willing, everything a man could possibly want. Under his expert tutelage, she was rapidly acquiring skills that would have made her the most talented of mistresses. Since that first night on the river steamer, when he felt he effectively established their relative positions of dominance and compliance, he had been careful not to push her too hard. The result was that she had actually begun to initiate some of the refinements of their lovemaking with a combination of shyness and seductiveness he found entrancing.

Simply thinking about that made him want to take her to bed again, but there was no time. They were due at a supper party in little more than an hour. As though to emphasize that, Elizabeth's maid was waiting for them at the door of their suite. She hid a flash of impatience as she nodded to her mistress.

"Best you're back, ma'am. There's a great deal to be done."

Elizabeth nodded absently. She had hired Deborah Taylor herself after the maid who set out with her from Calvert Oaks was taken ill and had to be dispatched back without ever leaving Virginia. Deborah, a British girl in her mid-twenties, had been stranded by the sudden death of her former employer, probably from the same summer fever that had sickened Elizabeth's maid, and had been delighted to find not only a position but a way home. She had told Elizabeth frankly that she was not at all sure she wanted to return to America, but had promised that in the event she did not, she would see to it that an adequate replacement was found.

Deborah—or, more correctly, Taylor, which she had lost no time explaining was the proper mode of address—was a plain-faced, no-nonsense girl who took her profession of ladies' maid with a seriousness Drake could not comprehend, since it seemed more appropriate to a religious calling. He knew only that since she had joined their little group, Elizabeth had looked even lovelier than ever and life seemed to run more smoothly. Therefore, he approved of Taylor and was inclined to be tolerant of her stiff-lipped tyranny.

"My fault, Taylor," he said as he shot the girl a smile. "I kept her gabbing at the Cardinghams'."

"Don't concern yourself, sir. *Madame*'s bath is already run and her clothes laid out. If you would excuse us…" She arched an eyebrow as though to remind him that his presence in his wife's bedroom was really not quite proper at such an hour, and, furthermore, that his valet was every bit as anxious to get him in hand.

Drake would have liked to linger. He thought the sight of Elizabeth in her bath was one he would enjoy, but it certainly would not get them to supper on time. With a long-suffering sigh, he departed through the connecting door to make his own preparations.

Taylor wasted no time getting her mistress out of her day dress, which she hung away carefully in the black walnut cupboard. She would iron it while the Benningtons were at supper, inspecting it at the same time for any rips, stains or loose buttons. She had already noted that *madame* had a tendency not to be as careful with her clothes as she might have been. Several hems had been caught on heels and torn, a pretty bit of lace had been damaged by the sharp edge of a ring and an ostrich plume in a riding hat had been crushed.

Like it or not, she simply had to face the fact that her employer was not as concerned about her appearance as she would have wished. Elizabeth accepted Taylor's ministrations patiently, and even thanked her for them, but it was clear that she considered the need for such care to be overdone and even foolish. Left to herself, Elizabeth would be just as happy going about uncorseted and plainly dressed.

Taylor suppressed a shiver at the thought. Her professional reputation rested on the appearance of the lady she served. Much of her willingness to accept the position with the Benningtons had stemmed from a shrewd assessment of both Elizabeth's beauty and Drake's willingness to indulge her. She, too, wanted her young American charge to shine, and she was determined that nothing would get in the way of achieving that.

Stripped down to her shift, Elizabeth obediently stepped behind the modesty screen, where she removed the remainder of her clothes and slid into the tin hip bath placed before the fire. A soft sigh escaped her. Sometimes she felt that the only chance she truly had to relax these days was in the bath. At no other time, not even when she was in her husband's arms, did a certain alertness and caution leave her. The reason was not hard to come by. She was very much aware of being out of her element, both as a stranger in a foreign land and as a newly minted bride. At every moment, in every situation, she was inclined to tread warily.

Taylor had scented the water with patchouli, a perfume Elizabeth did not particularly care for. She preferred the lighter, more floral aromas, but had not yet found the nerve to tell the maid that, and doubted now that she ever would, since only the previous night Drake had murmured how entrancing he found the perfume clinging to her skin.

Though they had separate rooms, he visited her bed every night, often not leaving until after dawn, and then only grumblingly. He teasingly threatened to let Taylor find him there when she came with her mistress's morning tea, though Elizabeth knew perfectly well that he would not do so. Even a man as exuberant as Drake understood the importance of always maintaining decorum in front of the servants.

She leaned her head back against the curved head of the tub and let her eyes close. Though it was May, she was glad of the fire that took the chill from the large, high-ceilinged room. Her years in Boston had apparently not changed her thin Southern blood, which responded to the slightest lowering of temperature with shivering dislike.

Lazily, eyes still closed, she found her sponge and slowly trickled water over her shoulders and breasts. On the other side of the screen, she could hear Taylor moving about, getting out the brushes and combs for her hair, opening and closing the wardrobe door. The maid was always busy, as was every other servant with whom Elizabeth came in contact. It made her feel rather guilty to think how hard they worked.

In Boston it had been different. In opposition to more common practices, Aunt Mari insisted on shorter working hours and more holidays for her staff, undoubtedly because of her own early exposure to relentless hard work. And at Calvert Oaks, everyone worked. It would no more occur to her mother to sit by idly when something needed to be done than it would occur to her to fly.

Elizabeth was having a difficult time coming to terms with the fact that she wasn't supposed to do *anything*. Wherever she turned, whatever she attempted to set her hand to, there was someone already there to do it for her. The only reason she was even allowed to bath herself, she suspected, was because of the prevailing code of modesty handed down by the black-garbed queen and often carried to absurd lengths.

She smiled to herself as she remembered the shocked looks she had caused the other day at yet another interminable tea when she had solicitously suggested that the shortness of breath suffered by the older woman to whom she was talking might be caused by too tight lacing. Apparently the blatantly obvious fact that women wore corsets was not to be mentioned, even in exclusively female company.

Elizabeth's smile faded as she considered how tightly Taylor would insist on lacing her. The one time she had dared to suggest that quite so much constriction was not really necessary, the maid had told her bluntly that she would not look like a proper lady unless she complied, and besides, the clothes she was planning to buy in Paris wouldn't fit properly without the firmest corseting. All of which meant that she was about to attend yet another sumptuous, multicourse banquet that she would not be able to eat.

A discreet throat-clearing from behind the screen recalled Elizabeth to more immediate matters. She sat up, lathered herself efficiently and reached for the can of hot water kept warming by the fires. After pouring it in carefully so as not to overfill the tub, she rinsed herself, then stood up. Several thick white towels had been left draped over a nearby chair. She wrapped one of them around herself and used another to finish patting herself dry. When she had discarded the towels and covered herself in a blue silk dressing gown, she stepped out from behind the screen.

Taylor wasted no time getting to work on her hair. It had been washed that morning and had been trimmed only the week before, so no major effort had to be made. Nonetheless there was much fiddling with brushes, curling irons and so on before the maid was satisfied.

"That style suits you, *madame*," she declared as she stood back to survey her work. "Lovely, it is."

There, at least, they were in agreement. The soft curls that framed Elizabeth's face drew attention to her eyes and cheekbones. The rest of her hair was swept up in a loose chignon that revealed the slender line of her throat. She looked both beautiful and sophisticated, not at all like the somewhat overwhelmed young girl she still sometimes felt herself to be.

Half an hour later, when she stood fully dressed before the mirror, there was even less to be seen of that secret part of herself. Much as she was looking forward to Paris, she could not believe that anything she acquired there could rival the gown she now wore. Made exclusively of black velvet, with none of the elaborate touches she was accustomed to, it was startling in both its simplicity and sensuality. The rich material perfectly set off her alabaster skin. Small puff sleeves left her shoulders bare. The bodice was daringly low cut, exposing the swell of her breasts, which were thrust into even more than usual prominence by her corset. Her waist had been whittled down to a perfect eighteen inches and looked so small that she thought it appeared about to snap in two. Certainly her ribs felt that way when she injudiciously attempted to take a too deep breath and all but choked on it.

It was no wonder that she looked so pale, Elizabeth thought, when she could hardly breathe. Only the upper part of her lungs still functioned; she had to inhale and exhale shallowly, which meant she was constantly breathless, her voice little more than a whisper and all her movements restricted by an artificial languor she deeply resented. Yet such were the dictates of fashion, and such was her own insecurity that she did not feel equipped to contest them, at least not yet.

Drake entered the room as she stood before the mirror. He paused with his hand still on the doorknob and stared at her. Their eyes met in the glass, and she saw the look of blatant male approval in his. A soft blush touched her cheeks.

"Thank you, Taylor," she murmured. "That will be all."

The maid nodded and left the room with a rustle of starched skirts. Her own highly critical perusal of her mistress had left her more than satisfied. She could only hope that "Sir" wouldn't insist on rumpling her before they left.

Drake was tempted, but resisted. He was beginning to appreciate the advantages of delayed gratification. For the next few hours he would enjoy looking at her and seeing other men do the same, knowing all the while that when they returned to this room he would be the one to possess the beauty others could only yearn after.

As a stamp of that privileged possession, he took from the inside pocket of his evening jacket a flat rectangular box. "I thought these might be appropriate," he said as he shut the door connecting their rooms and walked toward her.

Elizabeth recognized the name of the Mayfair jeweler stamped on the box. At the time of their marriage, Drake had given her several lovely pieces that had been in his family for generations. She cherished them, but nothing had prepared her for the almost blinding radiance she saw when she opened the box.

"Oh, Drake," she murmured. "They're lovely."

"I thought so," he agreed, lifting the necklace set with dozens of diamonds, none smaller than four carats and the largest an oval-shaped marvel the size of a robin's egg.

A frisson of shock ran through her as she stared in the mirror. The necklace glittered against her pale skin with barbaric splendor, the largest stone lying cold and gleaming between her breasts. Drake's fingers were strong and warm on the nape of her neck as he fastened the clasp, then reached back into the box for the two remaining pieces.

"It's just as well that you had your ears pierced," he said.

She nodded silently as he attached the earrings. They matched the necklace, with similar pendulous stones to weigh down her earlobes. When she turned slightly, the light they caught was torn into a thousand shards and thrown back at her like liquid fire.

Drake's hands moved down over her bared shoulders and across the swell of her breasts to linger at her tiny waist before lightly crushing the fabric over her hips. His touch encountered the hard, unyielding corset, the barrier of propriety always imposed between man and woman, but that he, at least, had the right to strip away.

He was smiling, still thinking of that, as they left the suite.

THE PARTY TO WHICH Elizabeth and Drake had been invited that evening was being given by Lord and Lady Brooke, more commonly known to their intimates as Brookie and Daisy. They were, so Cornelia said, a storybook couple, she the beautiful heiress to a great fortune, he the stalwart young heir to a great name, and hardly penurious himself. They had married after a whirlwind courtship during Daisy's debut season the previous year and, most delicious of all, after she had turned down a proposal from no less than Prince Leopold, the queen's delicate, hemophiliac son.

"They would never have suited," Cornelia explained as the foursome entered the reception hall of Lord and Lady Brooke's London house. A baroque masterpiece of marble and gilt, it rose three stories to a domed cupola painted to resemble the sky at the moment of creation. Gloriously garbed angels and cherubs were portrayed in exultant celebration. Somber-faced lesser deities, perhaps sensing their imminent eclipse by a greater god, stared out from plaster medallions. Fluted columns soared majestically to frame a staircase that would not have looked out of place at Versailles. A small sigh escaped Elizabeth as she contemplated the dizzying edifice, a proclamation of position and privilege virtually beyond her comprehension.

"Leopold is so fragile," Cornelia was saying, "his health so precarious, and Daisy wants nothing more than to be able to ride to hounds every day. She wouldn't even be in town if it weren't for the season.''

Elizabeth nodded absently, her eyes scanning the glittering assemblage filling the hall and extending into the vast expanse of the ballroom. Most of the guests were young, in keeping with the youth of their host and hostess, and they shone with inborn confidence and grace. If only a handful of the women could be considered classically beautiful, all were memorable. They vied with one another like so many hothouse flowers, each one more gloriously dressed and bejeweled than the last.

Beside them the men looked relatively somber in their dark cutaways and trousers, but they had an aura of power and arrogance that stamped them unmistakably as masters of the earth, if only in their own estimation.

The reception hall and the ballroom beyond were no more than the proper setting for such beings. It was rumored that Lord and Lady Brooke were slipping into the fast Marlborough House set surrounding the prince, and Elizabeth could well believe it, not only because they were a handsome, engaging couple, who welcomed her and Drake with more than simple courtesy, but more tellingly, because of the man at their side.

Since arriving in London, she had caught several glimpses of His Royal Highness, Albert Edward, Prince of Wales, but this was the first time she was actually to be presented to him. Her heart pounded as she swept into the low curtsy she had practiced with Cornelia. It had been her great fear that she would lose her balance and topple over ignominiously, but that did not occur. When she rose, greatly relieved, it was to see that the portly, genial man with the pointed brown beard and gleaming gray eyes was smiling at her.

''Welcome, Mrs. Bennington,'' he said in a voice raspy from cigars and overshadowed by the slight German accent that invariably took people by surprise, at least those who did not understand how little removed the royal family was from its Germanic origins. "I'm always delighted to meet Americans. A fresh breeze from the West is invariably welcome."

Something about him, his unexpected warmth perhaps, made the tension of the moment evaporate for her. She returned his smile brilliantly. "That's very tolerant of you, sir, considering how rudely we once blew."

He looked startled for a moment, then laughed. "More than once. This poor old empire has been shaken on several occasions by the behavior of our impetuous offspring, but we still count ourselves proud parents." He leaned forward slightly, his eyes just brushing the curve of her breasts beneath the glittering diamonds. "Sit next to me at supper, my dear. We'll discuss this further."

Elizabeth could only nod obediently, aware of Daisy Brooke making a frantic gesture to a servant. The seating arrangements were undoubtedly already in place, the result of careful thought and much effort. Now they would have to be undone to make room for her beside the prince. But, of course, no such effort was too great if it pleased H.R.H.

She, on the other hand, was far more concerned with Drake's reaction. He and the prince exchanged a few courteous words before the reception line moved on. Moments later they were in the ballroom and Cornelia was drawing her to one side, whispering ecstatically, "Marvelous, absolutely marvelous. You've scored a coup already. Nothing could be better."

Elizabeth cast a nervous glance at her husband, who seemed relaxed enough but whose expression was impenetrable. She moistened her lips with the tip of her tongue. "I thought you said..."

"What?" Cornelia asked.

"That...there were rules."

Her friend looked startled for a moment, then had the grace to flush. "Is that what you thought? That he might...approach you?"

"It flitted through my mind." She was embarrassed by the admission, since it seemed to suggest that she thought a great deal of herself, but Cornelia merely nodded wisely.

"If you were older," she explained, "and had a full nursery, it might be different. But, as I told you, a purely practical desire to avoid scandals puts you safely off-limits. However," she added, her eyes gleaming, "that doesn't mean you can't enjoy an innocent flirtation with Bertie that will absolutely guarantee your social success."

"I suppose Drake understands all this," Elizabeth said, looking again at her husband, who was deep in conversation with several gentlemen. He caught her eye and smiled, but made no effort to return to her side.

"Of course he does," Cornelia said. "After all, my dear, it was men who invented the rules. They understand them perfectly and play the game better than we can ever hope to."

The merest hint of bitterness in her young friend's voice was enough to distract Elizabeth. Charles and Cornelia gave every indication of enjoying a happy marriage, yet there was still a faint sadness about Cornelia that suggested all was not quite as she would have wished. Elizabeth found herself wondering if her friend indulged in what she called "the game." Somehow she doubted it. The potential was certainly there, for Cornelia was a lovely woman, but Elizabeth sensed that she was trapped in a web of her own emotions, complicated by a morality not quite in step with such sophisticated pursuits.

In other words, she wasn't all that different from Elizabeth herself. But would Drake see things the same way Charles did?

The mere thought of her husband with another woman sent a stab of jealousy through her so profound that for a moment she found it impossible to breathe. What little color there had been in her cheeks vanished, her eyes glittered, and her usually full mouth drew back in a tight line.

"Is something wrong?" Cornelia asked. Louisa Manchester was sweeping down on them, accompanied by several other of the grandes dames. Word of the prince's interest in Elizabeth had already spread. This was hardly the time for her to be looking so perturbed.

"No," Elizabeth said recovering herself. "It's just a bit warm in here...."

Cornelia nodded. In fact the ballroom was rather chilly, but there was no point in mentioning that, any more than there was in revealing unsuitable emotions.

True to her hopes, her protégée carried off the hours that followed with grace and charm. Even the crustiest of nabobs looked down their slender noses and decided that they liked what they saw. H.R.H.'s approval helped a great deal, of course, but by the end of the evening Cornelia was convinced that Elizabeth had been accepted on her own merit.

Elizabeth herself was less confident. She had smiled until her jaws hurt, chitchatted until her brain felt numb, and done her best to ignore the speculative looks of the men, who regarded her rather like a tasty morsel they had to regretfully pass up.

What she did not do was see much of Drake. They were seated too far apart at dinner to exchange even a word, and they did not dance together, it apparently not being the done thing. Instead Elizabeth was partnered by a succession of dukes, baronets and honorables, who ran the gamut from predatory to gauche. Her diamonds and the breasts they ornamented were silently admired in what she had to consider equal measure, her feet were stepped on until her toes throbbed and her silk slippers threatened to shred, and all the while a headache of massive proportions was building behind her bright smile and guarded eyes.

At last, with infinite relief, she said good-night to her host and hostess, and to Charles and Cornelia. "You were marvelous," her friend murmured as they touched cheeks. "A clear triumph. Tomorrow you'll be 'at home' with me, and the next day we'll make calls. You'll have to set aside several hours to sift through the invitations and decide which you'll attend, and we'll have to look over your wardrobe again. Then there's the—"

"Please," Elizabeth murmured, "let's go into this tomorrow. I'm rather tired...."

"Of course, how thoughtless of me. Drake, do take good care of her and see to it that she rests. We're going to be so busy." With a gay tilt to her head, Cornelia vanished into her carriage, followed by Charles, who paused long enough to exchange an indulgent, man-to-man look with Drake.

"I hope," Drake murmured as soon as their friends had departed, "that you have some small amount of strength left." Before she could answer, he ushered her into their carriage and settled beside her, his arm around her shoulders. The fur-lined cape she wore over her velvet gown was tied at the throat and gapped open slightly below. She felt more than saw his eyes settle on the paleness of her skin, against which the diamonds glittered coldly.

"Lovely," he murmured as he touched a finger between the furred edges and gently eased the cloak farther apart. The carriage was picking up speed, rocking them slightly so that they pressed close together on the leather seat. The soft shadowy glow of gaslights alternated with patches of darkness, revealing and concealing.

The memory of how he had looked as he put the diamonds on her brushed against her fatigue as a careless hand might touch a bruise. "Drake... I really am tired."

He bent forward, his mouth nuzzling her throat. "Hmm... you'll feel better soon."

"It's very late...." She feared that her reluctance, even so tentatively expressed, might anger him, but instead he seemed oblivious to it. His arms slipped around her, and he drew her closer, bending her back slightly to give him greater access to the scented swell of her breasts.

That position might suit him, but it was acutely uncomfortable for her. The whalebone stays of her corset dug into her, and she found it all but impossible to breathe.

"Drake," she said more urgently, pressing a hand against his chest, "let me up."

Either he did not hear her over the clip-clop of the horses' hooves and the creak of the carriage wheels, or he again chose to ignore her. His long, warm fingers slipped beneath the neckline of her velvet bodice, easing the fabric down the fraction necessary to bare her nipples.

Shocked that he would do such a thing in the absence of complete privacy, she tried again to push him away. "Don't..."

"Why not?" he murmured without raising his head. His fingers caressed what they had revealed, setting off an ache inside her that was all too familiar. She felt herself responding to him and resented it deeply. How dare he approach her in such a way, as though she had no feelings of her own?

"I told you," she said more firmly. "I'm tired. Tomorrow we can..."

He looked up then, his eyes suddenly narrowed. "Are you refusing me?"

She swallowed against the sudden tightness of her throat. "No, of course not, it's just that tomorrow I won't be so tired and..."

"Tomorrow you'll be gadding about with Cornelia again. Perhaps you prefer to save your strength for the besotted swains who will undoubtedly be dancing attendance on you."

"I don't know what you're talking about!"

"Don't you?" He let go of her abruptly, so that she slumped back against the carriage seat. The force with which he turned away suggested disgust, if not outright dismissal.

With some difficulty she straightened up and stared at him. Seen in profile against the shifting backdrop of the gaslights, his features were harshly drawn. The hollow beneath his cheekbone was darkly shadowed. As she watched, an angry pulse sprang to life within it.

"Drake . . . I didn't mean . . ."

"Let it go."

"You're angry."

He turned slightly, enough to look at her. "Don't flatter yourself. A reluctant woman is hardly worth getting angry about. At worst, she's merely boring."

Elizabeth drew her breath in sharply. The impulse to effect a swift reconciliation vanished in the white heat of anger. "I am not 'a woman.' I'm your wife."

"I don't appear to be the one who's forgotten that."

"You think that means I should do whatever you wish, no matter what my own feelings."

He frowned slightly, genuinely surprised that she should raise such a point in apparent argument, as though it were open to dispute. "Of course. I'm your husband."

"But I'm still a human being! Marrying you didn't transform me into an object . . . some sort of vessel for your desires."

"Vessel for my . . ." He shook his head ruefully. "Please, my dear, you're becoming overwrought, not to mention melodramatic. You're my wife. So far as I am concerned that says it all." He laid his head back against the seat and closed his eyes, signaling that the conversation was at an end.

Elizabeth was not so readily satisfied. Far from it. Her mind seethed with arguments and charges. Tempted though she was to voice them, she held off, sensing that Drake's dismissive attitude was merely a pose beneath which lurked an emotion she did not truly want to confront.

They completed the trip back to the hotel in silence and remained silent as they rode up in one of the newly installed wrought-iron lifts. For once, Elizabeth was sorry she had told Taylor not to wait up. She would have welcomed some intermediary between her and Drake, if only for a short time.

But far from appearing inclined to linger, her husband crossed directly to the door connecting their rooms, opened it and paused only long enough to bid her a frosty "good night" before disappearing from sight.

But not from thought. Long after she had recovered enough from her surprise to discover that his abrupt departure left her with no way out of her stays, she fumed at his high-handedness. It required half an hour to summon assistance and send the footman to wake Taylor, who was asleep in one of the top floor rooms reserved for servants. A further half hour was spent enduring the maid's silent ministrations, knowing all the while that Taylor was aware that Drake had abandoned her.

Only then was she finally free to crawl into bed, where she lay staring up at the ceiling, feeling more alone than she ever had in her life.

DRAKE HAD LEFT the hotel by the time Elizabeth awakened the following morning. He had left no message about where he had gone, nor did he mention when he would return. She spent the day with Cornelia, attempting to find some solace in her newfound popularity. If her husband did not care for her company, a great many other gentlemen did. A steady stream of them passed through Cornelia's parlor.

Each obeyed the proprieties scrupulously, even going so far as to retain his hat and cane rather than give it to the footman, an act that would suggest he expected to be welcome and invited to stay. Such delicate courtesy was at odds with the frankly admiring stares Elizabeth received and the faint but discernible air of flirtatious mischief that hung over each encounter. She was left wondering how much more palpable the hint of seduction would have been had she possessed, as Cornelia put it, the requisite full nursery.

Cornelia did possess that chief requirement for dalliance; Elizabeth had met her children and thought them adorable. So did their mother who spent rather more than the fashionable amount of time with them. It did not escape Elizabeth's notice that her friend all but sighed in relief when the last of the callers departed and she was at last free to indulge herself, at least in the brief time left before it would be necessary to dress for the evening.

"Would you mind," she asked Elizabeth, "if I had the children down for a few minutes?"

"Of course not. I'd love to see them again."

Cornelia hurried over to pull the bell cord. The footman who responded was quickly dispatched to the nursery with a message for Nanny. Afterward the ladies spent a delightful if furtive hour playing with the children. Elizabeth found their company far more stimulating and rewarding than that of most of the adults she had met. She returned to her hotel reluctantly, not in the least because she feared a confrontation with Drake.

As it happened, she needn't have worried. There was no sign of him as she dressed. He still had not appeared when Charles and Cornelia arrived to pick them up, as had been arranged. But he had been heard from. Charles mentioned casually that he had spent part of the afternoon at the club with Drake, who would be joining them later.

Cornelia gave Elizabeth a long, thoughtful look in which there was a disturbing measure of sympathy, but she said nothing. Nor did anyone at the supper party seem to take it amiss when she arrived without Drake. More than a few of the other ladies were similarly unaccompanied, except by friends.

"It's quite the fashion for husbands and wives to arrive separately," Cornelia assured her when they had retired briefly to freshen themselves. "In fact, many couples make a point of never attending the same functions."

"How enlightened," Elizabeth murmured as she gazed absently at her reflection in a full-length mirror. She was dressed in sapphire silk that evening and wore Drake's diamonds. By any standard, she knew that she looked lovely, and she tried to take comfort in that. But the knowledge that her husband was not on hand to appreciate her dulled her senses. She drifted through the evening, her eyes shuttered and her smile brittle.

They were about to sit down to supper when Drake finally arrived. He greeted their host and hostess, who were not at all put out by his late appearance, and he exchanged a few words with Charles, who, as usual, was not at Cornelia's side. To Elizabeth he said nothing. So far as she could make out, he wasn't aware that she was in the room.

Pride came to her rescue. It enabled her to hold her head high and deny the tears that threatened to spill from eyes that suddenly burned. At least she had the comfort of knowing that in this society, where husbands and wives lived such separate lives, no one took Drake's behavior amiss or, more important, pitied her for it. Cornelia's restrained sympathy was all she could bear; anything more would have been intolerable.

Part of her wanted to believe that he really wasn't doing anything wrong because there was no intent on his part to hurt her. He was simply behaving as the people all around them behaved. It was a classic case of "when in Rome..." Except that they weren't Romans, or, more to the point, British aristocrats. Like it or not, they had been raised to follow a very different and far more traditional code of morality. Drake might want to pretend otherwise, but she did not. He knew what he was doing, he fully understood the effect it would have on her, and he had deliberately chosen to make his anger and his contempt clear, if only to her.

All because she had dared to refuse him. The injustice of that sparked an anger that dulled her pain and brought a dangerous flush to her cheeks. She had known from the beginning that he was an arrogant man; his upbringing guaranteed that. But she had also believed him to be fair. Apparently she had been wrong.

So complete was her absorption in Drake and his behavior that she hardly noticed the man seated at her right, until he called himself to her attention and, in a low, matter-of-fact voice, said, "It won't do any good, you know. There is absolutely no possibility of my allowing so beautiful a woman to remain oblivious to me."

Startled, Elizabeth turned slightly. The man next to her was young, about twenty-five, and well built, with a muscular slimness his evening clothes did not disguise. He was as dark as Drake was light, with thick black hair, a carefully tended black mustache and swarthy skin. His complexion was startling, given the relative paleness of everyone else. She guessed that he had spent a great deal of time under a tropical sun and was immediately curious to know more.

"I'm sorry," she said. "It was rude of me to be so preoccupied. I'm Elizabeth Bennington, by the way."

He smiled and inclined his head. "I know. When I saw that we were to be seated together, I inquired about you. You're a Virginian, aren't you?"

"I was, but I suppose I'm a Bostonian now." At his inquiring look, she added, "My husband is from Boston."

"Ah, yes, the Bennington millions. They're on my list."

Elizabeth must have looked startled, for he laughed out loud. "Forgive me, I usually enjoy being deliberately provocative, but for some reason, in your case I feel an urge to behave better. I'm Jack Tyler. If you haven't already been warned about me, be assured that you soon will be."

"And why," Elizabeth asked after she had regained her composure, "would that be necessary?"

"Oh, I'm a reprobate of the first water. Born of perfectly good stock, could have done the decent thing as a second son and gone into the army or the church, but you see, I was born with a perfectly awful itch. More than a few months in one place and I have to move on. Been most everywhere and always looking for somewhere new."

"You're the explorer," Elizabeth said. Dimly, she remembered Charles mentioning an argument at his club between Harty and someone just back from Africa. Afterward Cornelia had said it was likely Jack Tyler, society's favorite wild man, who could always be counted on to do the improbable with élan.

"You're very well spoken of," she added as the waiters came around to begin pouring the first wine. "Your exploits are legendary."

"Nicely put. I should tell you I'm highly susceptible to flattery."

Instead of pursuing that, Elizabeth said, "Tell me why the Benningtons interest you."

Before he could reply, their host and hostess took their place at either end of the table, which stretched almost the entire length of the dining room and was large enough to seat some sixty guests. Four matching candelabras of beaten gold were placed at evenly spaced intervals. In between, bouquets of rare lilies were arranged in silver bowls. Behind every two chairs stood a footman in a velvet cutaway and pantaloons. Over all drifted the stern eye of the butler, who orchestrated the entire event so unobtrusively as to make it appear effortless.

The guests rose to make the traditional toast to Her Majesty the Queen, then settled back down amid a welter of conversation. Jack Tyler took another swallow of his wine, draining his glass, and allowed a footman to speedily refill it.

"They don't," he said as the first course was placed in front of them.

In the tumult of supper starting, Elizabeth had momentarily lost her train of thought. But she regained it quickly and frowned. "I thought you said..."

"About being on my list. That's true enough, only it's their money that interests me, not the Benningtons themselves. Present company excepted, of course."

His dark brown gaze was a shade too familiar for Elizabeth's taste, yet she couldn't find it in herself to be offended. The fact that Jack Tyler clearly appreciated her as a woman soothed the hurt inflicted by Drake. It did not by any means banish it entirely, but it gave her a weapon, however small, that she was very tempted to use in her own defense.

Leaning forward slightly, she said, "How fascinating. Does being so candid ever get you into trouble?"

"Invariably," Tyler said, his eyes drifting briefly to the white swell of her breasts. "Which is one reason I stay on the move."

"Why do you want their money?"

"Not theirs, necessarily. Anyone's will do. I find that millionaires are excellent sources of opportunity for ne'er-do-well explorers trying to finance their expeditions."

Elizabeth nodded thoughtfully. She had drunk almost none of her wine, yet she was suddenly feeling rather giddy, as though the danger of flirting with such a man knocked her pleasantly off balance. Which was precisely where she wanted to be. "Undoubtedly the best use for their ill-gotten gains."

His eyebrows rose in wary surprise. "Ill-gotten? That's the first time I've heard a rich man's wife even suggest that he didn't absolutely deserve everything he possessed, except possibly herself."

Elizabeth glanced down at her consommé, on top of which floated paper-thin slices of truffles. It was undoubtedly excellent, but she had no desire to even taste it. The reminder, however inadvertent, of her difficulties with Drake robbed her of appetite.

Instead, she summoned the brightest smile she could manage and turned it deliberately on Tyler. "Tell me about this new adventure you're planning."

He was silent for a moment studying her as she imagined he might some rare specimen he encountered in the course of his wanderings. With a slight shrug, he apparently came to some acceptable conclusion about her and set himself to satisfy her curiosity.

"I'm going to find the source of the Blue Nile. You may know that Livingstone pinpointed Lake Victoria as the source of the White Nile, but I'm convinced the Blue Nile's origins remain to be found. I tried last year and came damn close, but the country is rough and the natives less than friendly. It will take another go to get it right."

"I see," Elizabeth murmured. He spoke so straightforwardly that he might have been discussing a trip to his tailor's instead of a journey into what remained one of the earth's most mysterious and dangerous places. Such simplicity of purpose impressed her deeply. He seemed to possess the quintessential ingredient of a true hero: a lack of conceit about his own heroism.

"How marvelous it must be," she said, "to go off wherever you wish, to throw aside all the usual restraints and test yourself against the greatest challenges. What I don't understand is how you can bear to come back."

"Don't you know that women like you are supposed to be secretly offended by men like me? At the very least, you're supposed to express well-bred disapproval of our refusal to accept the restrictions of so-called civilization."

Elizabeth glanced down the table to where Drake was deep in conversation with a lady whose décolletage was as daring as the gleam in her eyes. Drake looked up for a moment, caught her gaze and turned away. "In my experience," she said to Jack Tyler, "civilization isn't all it's cracked up to be."

As ABRUPTLY AS IT HAD STOPPED, Elizabeth's intimate life with her husband resumed. Two weeks after their argument, Drake returned to her bed. She did not comment on that, nor did she withhold herself. If he wanted to believe that she had learned her lesson, fine. As it happened, he was right, though she suspected that the lesson was not what he had intended.

Elizabeth was learning about independence. It surprised her that she needed to. She had never thought of herself as particularly dependent, but with hindsight she realized that the privileged position of a dearly loved daughter and sister had given her a false sense of security. With Drake, she recognized intuitively that she had to become self-sufficient or risk becoming like so many women she saw, all sense of her own worth dependent on her husband's approval, his to bestow or deny as he chose.

The task she set herself was no easy one, and it was further complicated by her feelings for Drake. She desperately wanted to be close to him, to share her most intimate thoughts and needs. But he showed no similar yearning, and she understood that to open herself to him without reciprocation would be to put a weapon in his hands that he would not hesitate to use.

She was beginning to understand that beneath his pleasant manner and sophisticated charm her husband possessed a streak of ruthlessness greater than any she had previously encountered. Certainly her father and brother were strong-willed men, but they were also men who looked beyond themselves, who put others first, and who were no strangers to the arts of compromise and conciliation.

So far as she could tell, Drake viewed the world strictly from the perspective of his own desires. As long as she made herself agreeable to him, he was everything she was supposed to want in a husband: tender, protective, generous. But should she cross him in any way, he withdrew coldly and deliberately, denying her even the satisfaction of an honest argument.

It might have been easier if there had been someone for her to talk the problem over with, but that was not the case. Much as she liked Cornelia, she could not bring herself to confide in her. The matter was too personal for such short acquaintance. Their conversations revolved around parties and gowns, conquests and flirtations.

Occasionally they spoke of Cornelia's children, but always with the sense of women straying from their proper spheres of influence. What went on in the nursery was strictly the province of Nanny, a tight-lipped, starch-souled paragon who plainly terrified Cornelia. Yet each day she dared the woman's disapproval to spend some time with her offspring. As she shared many of those encounters, Elizabeth promised herself that when her own children arrived, she would deal with matters very differently.

In the meantime, there were other things to think of. Thanks to H.R.H.'s clear approval and her own charms, Elizabeth was the toast of fashionable London. She went everywhere, met everyone and did her best to believe that she was having a wonderful time. The ruse seemed to work; certainly all who knew her were convinced that she couldn't have been happier. All except Jack Tyler, who dismissed her supposed contentment with blunt disdain.

"Don't tell me you're enjoying this," he said one afternoon when they were riding together along Rotten Row. "You're far too intelligent to waste your life in idleness."

Elizabeth shot him a sharp glance from beneath the peaked rim of her black velvet riding hat. She had taken particular pains with her appearance that morning, in a futile attempt to rouse Drake's curiosity about where she might be going. In the daylight hours, he seemed sublimely oblivious to anything she said or did. The fact that he offered no objection to her being so often in another man's company annoyed her intensely, though she did her best to hide it. And catching herself stooping to such childish bids for his attention did nothing to improve her mood. Worse yet, the effort had been useless, since he hadn't even been on hand to see her before she left with Tyler.

A tart edge sharpened her tongue as she said, "I would hardly describe myself as idle."

"Because you go to a lot of parties and come riding with me? It's mental idleness I'm talking about. Mental and emotional. You're taking the line of least resistance, pet. In the end, it won't get you anywhere you want to be."

"Has anyone ever told you," she inquired pleasantly, "that you're insufferable?"

He flashed her a grin, his weathered features taking on the mien of a mischievous boy, one gifted—or cursed—with ageless wisdom. "No more than once or twice a day. It's my stock-in-trade."

"I think you only do it to be perverse. You like to provoke people, then stand back and watch the results."

"You've just reminded me of why men are afraid of intelligent women. They strike too close to home."

Elizabeth laughed and dug her heels into the side of her mare. The day was warm, but not unpleasantly so. She was wearing a new riding habit in a form-fitting style that only the shapeliest of women could carry off. For once she had resisted Taylor's efforts to lace her tightly, insisting that she had to be able to breathe in order to ride. The simple physical comfort that she had once been foolish enough to take for granted endowed her with a rare sense of well-being. She enjoyed the verbal jousting with the man at her side even as she was conscious of treading a dangerous line between flirtation and something more.

He was aware of it, too. With his usual bluntness, he had even alluded to it. "You're far too beautiful," he had told her the day before as they shared a private moment in the midst of an otherwise crowded garden party. "I've always made it a point to steer clear of too much beauty. It dulls a man's common sense and leaves him open to all sorts of foolishness."

"Then by all means don't let me detain you," Elizabeth had said cordially, then almost laughed at his quick frown. Tyler was undoubtedly different from other men in many ways, far freer in his thinking, for example. But he was also like them in several important respects, chief among them the preservation of his fragile male ego.

"Speaking of home," Elizabeth said as she returned to the matter at hand, "I must be getting back."

"It's early yet."

"Madame Bernard is coming for a fitting." The French seamstress was the current reigning favorite among ladies having any pretension to fashion. Elizabeth had been fortunate to secure her services for several essential additions to her wardrobe. "We'll be going to Cowes next week," she reminded him. "I need the gowns by then."

"London will be emptying out," he muttered. "So much the better. It's a ghastly place when society is in residence."

"I thought you also planned to depart soon." They were cantering out of Hyde Park toward the mews that housed the stables where both their horses were kept.

"Actually, I had thought to already be on my way, but I've been detained."

"By what?"

He shot her a glance that had the desired effect of causing her to blush. An unwritten rule of their friendship was that candor stopped at the door of genuine emotion. They never spoke of their true feelings for each other, Elizabeth because she wasn't sure what hers were, Tyler because he knew nothing would be so certain to set her in flight.

Silently he damned Drake Bennington to hell. The man had everything in the world except the sense to appreciate his own good fortune. Not for a moment did Tyler envy him his wealth; for all that his own need for money was constant, he had no real difficulty securing it, nor did he regret that he would never possess the kind of power and position Drake had.

What galled him was that the arrogant American had somehow managed to acquire the woman Tyler wanted for himself. Worse yet, she gave every sign of being loyal to her difficult, unappreciative husband. She was willing enough to engage in mild flirtation, but beyond that he had not dared go. For once in his life he appeared to face a challenge he could not overcome. That was unacceptable to him on the most deeply rooted level.

"Actually," he said as he helped her dismount in front of the stables, "I may be going to Cowes myself."

Elizabeth glanced up at him. They were standing very close together. Tyler's hands were still on her waist. He should have removed them the moment her feet touched the ground. That he had not told her more than she wanted to know.

"I thought," she said as she moved away, accompanied by the soft swishing of her skirt, "that you found yachting unutterably boring."

"Did I say that? How tiresome of me. What could be more pleasant than a day on the water, racing the wind, sails slapping overhead, that sort of thing?"

His chagrined expression was so at odds with his determinedly cheery words that Elizabeth couldn't help but laugh. She was still doing so when an odd look flitted across his face. He reached for her arm and drew her into the shadows near the stable doors.

"Elizabeth...you..." Whatever he had meant to say, he apparently thought better of it. Instead he lowered his head and, to her astonishment, touched his lips to hers.

For an instant Elizabeth was too surprised to respond. She stood stock-still as he deepened the kiss. It was only when he groaned and drew her closer into his embrace that she at last reacted.

Jerking her head back, she thrust both her hands against his chest and pushed hard. "Stop it! Let me go."

Tyler appeared not to hear her. His hand grasped the back of her head as he used his considerable strength to hold her in place. "So beautiful..." Despite the dim light, she could see the fire burning in his eyes and had no difficulty recognizing it. His arousal frightened her more than his strength. Without thinking, she lifted her booted foot and stomped down hard on his instep.

Tyler reacted instinctively, dropping his hands and moving back sharply. "What the...?"

Elizabeth took advantage of her sudden freedom to dart away from the stable door, back into the sunshine of the mews. She was breathing hard and shaking all over. Her heart pounded painfully and her stomach churned. With startling clarity, she realized that she felt exactly as she had when she was six years old and stuck her hand too close to a fire. Then she had been surprised and frightened; now she was also ashamed.

"Tyler...I'm sorry..." He had stepped out from behind the door and was regarding her warily. At her apology, he came forward to look at her more clearly.

"Wouldn't you say I should be the one to apologize?"

Elizabeth shrugged, not meeting his eyes. "If you like, but it was also my fault."

He ran a hand wearily through his hair. "Don't do this. You should be playing the outraged goddess who has caught some mere mortal trying to climb up her pedestal. I can deal with that, quite easily. But honesty...that's another matter entirely.''

They faced each other across the expanse of several feet, both oblivious to any curious looks that might come their way. Elizabeth knew a brief, tantalizing flash of regret. If only she were free...

She pushed that thought aside as quickly as it arose. On the crest of a deep, steadying breath, she said, "Don't you expect honesty in women?''

"Never," Tyler said bluntly. "Most of you are completely incapable of it, and not," he added quickly, "because of any inborn deficiency. Honesty is a luxury paid for in the currency of power, which women lack.''

Elizabeth shook her head. "I don't see it that way. Honesty is a necessity, not a luxury.''

"The truth at all costs?'' he inquired with a derisive lift of his eyebrows. "Are you sure that's what you want?''

She raised her head, her eyes at last meeting his. So softly that he had to strain to hear her, she said, "The truth is that I value you as a friend.''

Tyler tore his gaze from hers with a near-painful wrench. He stared off into space, fighting to control himself. For a man who had faced down wild animals, unfriendly natives and every manner of natural disaster, he felt singularly ill-equipped to deal with the present situation. But then, he had never been in love before.

"I don't want to be your friend," he said through gritted teeth. "I want to be your lover.''

The words were barely out, the challenge hardly issued, before he regretted them. She looked so saddened and alone, standing there before him with the breeze making her wide skirt ripple and stirring the wonderful confection of her hair beneath the impertinent little hat. Absurdly he wanted to protect her when every particle of common sense he possessed told him that he was the one in need of protection.

He made a quick, dismissive gesture. "Forget what I said, and what I did. This isn't a good day for me."

"I'm sorry..."

"Don't start that again. You have nothing to be sorry about." Briskly, he took her arm, managing somehow to keep his touch impersonal, and set off down the street. "Did you enjoy the ride?"

"It was lovely. Tyler..."

"I suppose you'll be at Lady Montgomery's supper this evening?"

"I had planned to attend, but..."

"Save a dance for me."

The words echoed through her mind, reminding her of the night Drake had tried to preempt all her waltzes. "My husband may be there."

"What a remarkable coincidence. He doesn't usually turn up where you are." Actually, that wasn't quite true. Lately he had noticed that Bennington had been much more in attendance on his wife.

"We've had some problems," Elizabeth acknowledged quietly. "But one way or another, we have to get them under control."

Despite the sharp pain that gripped his chest, Tyler managed a wan smile. "Do you imagine, lovely child, that life is so simple?"

"I'm not a child, and no, I imagine nothing of the sort."

"How awful of me to sound avuncular. I assure you, I feel anything but."

"Perhaps," she murmured, "this isn't the time to speak of feelings." They were almost back at her hotel. She viewed the elegant stone edifice in the near distance with regret. The afternoon stretched out before her. After the fittings, Cornelia expected her for lunch; then they were due to pay calls. She would spend several hours listening to polite social chatter before returning to dress for supper and more of the same.

Her spirit stirred in restless rebellion. It was a magnificent day, the sky azure, the light golden, the air warmly caressing. On such days at Calvert Oaks she had always contrived to be outside, usually roaming freely over the fields. A soft smile played over her features as she considered that though what she had said to Tyler was true, she was no longer a child, neither was she so very far removed from one. Part of her would have liked nothing better than to throw all prudence to the winds and cajole him into spending the day with her. They could get the horses back, ride out to Epping Forest, lunch at a pub, do all the things that ladies and gentlemen not overly concerned with social censure did. All the things.

A low, regretful sigh escaped her. They had stopped in front of the hotel. Tyler turned to her, his brow furrowed. "What's wrong?"

"I was thinking that it should be possible to take a holiday from oneself every so often."

"And be who instead?"

"Someone without responsibilities, loyalties, commitments."

"I have spent my life avoiding those very things," he said, "with a large measure of success. I used to think that their absence meant freedom, but lately I've realized that isn't the case."

"What does, then?"

"The very opposite, I fear. The ability to make commitments, construct loyalties, accept responsibilities, lies at the heart of being free. To do all that and ultimately find happiness in doing so must be the greatest achievement of any life."

She blinked, against the sunlight, she told herself. "Dear Tyler, you are in danger of becoming conventional."

He shook his head. "Sadly not. The means for such a transformation are undoubtedly at hand, yet they remain tantalizingly out of reach."

"You should be glad of that," she murmured. "Whatever you may think at the moment, you have far more freedom than most people will ever know. Lose that and you lose yourself."

"Suppose I thought the price ridiculously cheap?"

Her mouth moved in a wistful smile, the provocativeness of which she could not begin to guess. "I would accuse you of being a romantic."

He leaned his head back to laugh at the gleaming sky helmeting the city, and at the tiny humans who stood beneath it and imagined themselves of such significance. "I suspect I always have been."

They remained where they were, facing each other for several long moments. Around them the city moved on its oblivious way, granting them the brief, deceptive gift of anonymity. At length, Elizabeth offered her hand and Tyler took it. He held her eyes as he pressed a gentle kiss into her palm.

A long, shuddering breath broke from her. Against his impropriety she could protect herself, but not against his tenderness. With the suddenness of a woman who knows that the danger she faces is as much within herself as without, she turned and hurried into the hotel.

Tyler stood on the sidewalk and watched her go. His hands were clenched at his sides, his lean body pulled taut with need. The starkness of his desire was stamped clearly on his face.

Clearly at least to the man who stood at the window several stories above. Drake had not moved so much as a muscle as he watched his wife and the explorer. To the outward observer, he was merely perusing a mildly interesting street scene. Only the darkling glint of his eyes betrayed otherwise.

ELIZABETH ENTERED the suite lost in her own thoughts. She was deeply regretful at leaving Tyler, yet convinced that she had had no choice. It would have been the height of foolishness, not to mention cruelty, to encourage him. Yet the temptation had been there, and that alone was enough to concern her.

However lax the morals to which she had been exposed over the past few weeks, however genuine her concern about her marriage, the fact remained that she did not want to be unfaithful to her husband. Once she would have dismissed as absurd the mere thought that she might do such a thing. But now she could no longer take her own behavior for granted. She had seen how very easy it was to want something she knew full well she could not have. Not if she was to be true not only to Drake, but, even more important, to herself.

That problem of being true to the self she felt she was only beginning to get to know preoccupied her as she removed her hat and gloves and left them on the inlaid table near the door. There was no sign of Taylor, but she knew she had only to pull the bell to summon her. Then the complex, seemingly endless ritual of dressing and undressing would begin again. Sometimes she felt like an actress in an immense, never-ending play, her sole role being to effect an inordinate number of costume changes.

The idea made her smile, and she looked almost happy when she glanced up and saw the man studying her. "Drake..."

"Having a pleasant day, my dear?" He stood with his back to the window, a cigar clasped between his teeth and his feet planted slightly apart. He had discarded his jacket, and his shirt was partially unbuttoned. Like Elizabeth, he had been riding, but unlike her, he had gone alone, seeking not a polite canter but a hard, punishing gallop. His boots were splattered with mud, as were the snugly fitted trousers that clung to his long, muscular legs.

"I didn't expect to find you here," she said, hoping she didn't sound as flustered as she felt. Drake was never around during the day. He left her bed before dawn, dressed and breakfasted alone, and was gone before she began to stir. She did not see him again until evening, at the earliest. More often than not, they merely passed on their ways to separate social occasions. Yet since he had resumed his husbandly prerogatives, he had not let a night pass without exercising them. Darkness found them entwined together in the only form of communication they seemed to have.

Certainly words were not working very well. Drake frowned at hers. He removed the cigar from between his teeth and crossed the room to stand before her. His hand beneath her chin held her still for his scrutiny. She smelled the pungent aroma of his tobacco mingling with the scents of leather, horses and sweat. Her eyes fastened on his chest, partially exposed by his open shirt. Tendrils of hair clung damply to bronzed skin.

From between stiff lips, she murmured, "You need a bath."

He smiled coldly. "Do I offend your ladylike sensibilities? How unfortunate."

She tried to pull away, but his hold on her tightened, and she wisely subsided. "Imagine, then," he went on, his voice low and steady, as though nothing were amiss, "how offensive I find it knowing that my wife has been kissing another man."

Her eyes flew wide open, meeting the icy mockery in his. "How did you . . . ?"

"It shows, my sweet. If you're going to indulge in dalliance, you should forgo the lip rouge, or at least remember to replace it."

Abruptly he let her go. She touched a shaky hand to her lips as though to blot out the evidence he had so unerringly discerned. In the back of her mind, she wondered if Tyler had simply failed to notice her dishevelment, or if he had deliberately chosen not to mention it. Either way, she felt betrayed. "It was nothing . . . a misunderstanding."

He had turned away and was stubbing out the cigar in a crystal dish she suspected wasn't intended for that purpose, not that she or anyone else was likely to point that out to him. Elizabeth stared at his broad back, wondering what he intended to do.

"Is that what they're calling it now?" he inquired, still in the same pleasant tone. Before she could answer, he went on. "Did you enjoy it? Tyler's quite infatuated with you. That alone should make him an agreeable lover."

"He isn't," she whispered, hardly able to breathe. The room was closing in around her. She felt sick and wanted only to escape, even though she knew that was impossible. They had been coming to this moment for a long time, perhaps since the instant of their marriage, which had been founded on such a lack of understanding. The man she faced might as well have been a stranger, yet he held inordinate power over her, and she did not doubt that he intended to use it.

"What a shame," Drake said, deliberately misinterpreting her. "All those years in the jungle must have shortchanged his education."

"I meant that he isn't my lover." She spoke through a severely constricted throat. Her husband had returned his attention to her; his hands were on the lapels of her riding habit. Instead of attempting to undo it, he merely gripped both sides of the velvet jacket and ripped them apart. Buttons flew in all directions even as she gasped and tried to pull the fabric back together. "Stop it! What do you think you're doing?"

"Undressing you," he said coolly. Before she could even attempt to stop him, her ivory lace blouse was rent by the same harsh treatment. Beneath it she wore a corselet of moiré silk, above which her breasts gleamed white and full. "Does he at least make a tolerable ladies' maid?"

"You're insane," Elizabeth whispered. "All Tyler did was kiss me. I admit that was bad enough, but what you're thinking..."

"That he had you," Drake said. "That he touched you as I have, plunged inside you. Do you have any idea how that makes me feel?"

"It didn't happen."

"So you say. I prefer to judge for myself."

She shut her eyes against the sting of tears as he lifted her into his arms and strode into her bedroom. She almost wished he had taken her into his instead. Over the weeks that she had used the room, it had acquired an undeniably feminine ambience that his mere presence under such circumstances was sufficient to violate.

When he laid her on the bed, she made no attempt to escape but remained motionless as he pulled off her boots, following them quickly with her skirt and petticoats. Vaguely she was aware of the sounds of him undressing, and knew when he returned to her side. A muted curse broke from him when he encountered the knotted lacings of her corselet. For less than an instant, he tried to undo them; then his patience broke, and he simply wrapped the ties around his hands and jerked.

Distantly she felt the coolness of air on her nakedness and realized that the rest of her garments were gone. The heat of his body engulfed her as his weight pressed her down onto the mattress. His mouth was against her throat, murmuring words she did not care to understand. She remained motionless, concentrating all her energies on escaping in the only way she knew how.

Drake felt the stillness in her and correctly interpreted it, yet refused to believe that it could last. He was too skilled a lover and her body was too intimately attuned to his to allow her the victory she sought. Deliberately he set out to compel her response. His tongue stroked repeatedly over each of her nipples before his teeth raked lightly at the aroused flesh. His hands, the palms callused through long hours of holding reins without benefit of gloves, slipped from the narrowness of her waist to the burgeoning fullness of her hips and beyond. He was rewarded by the slightest of tremors, but nothing more.

Such strength of will disturbed him. He did not associate it with women. In his experience, women were simplistic creatures who acted solely from a combination of guile and instinct. Between the stick of familial responsibility and the carrot of sexual satisfaction, they sought to manipulate men to their own ends. Nothing more concerned them, certainly not such complex matters as choosing honor over expediency.

"Stop playing at this," he murmured. "What there is between us is too strong to be denied."

She did not look at him, but continued to stare at the ceiling, as though she were completely alone. Yet she answered readily enough. "Suspicion? Anger? Is that what you're referring to?"

Stung, he rolled away onto his back. "You know it isn't." After a moment, when she did not reply, he felt compelled to add, "I didn't really think you had given yourself to Tyler."

She did not respond at once, but let her silence tell him what she thought of so feeble a concession. They lay side by side, a man and a woman beautiful in the singular contrasts of their nakedness, touching along the length of their bodies, yet held apart by ineluctable tensions that could not be denied.

If Elizabeth had yielded to him then, if she had used his desire to placate and soothe him, he would have graciously forgiven her transgression. But she stubbornly refused to play her preordained role. The tenacious Southern pride bred into her character forbade it.

"If you've changed your mind," she said finally, "I'd like to get dressed."

He swallowed the angry retort that sprang to his lips and instead said, "There's plenty of time before Lady Montgomery's supper."

She hid her surprise that he had known where she intended spending the evening and did not allow herself to wonder if he had planned to join her. "Madame Bernard will be here soon."

"She'll be disappointed when she knocks and there is no response."

The hardness of his voice warned her that his intentions had not changed. She fought the stirrings of an excitement she did not wish to acknowledge. "Cornelia expects me later. We're due to pay calls this afternoon."

"I would rather you stayed here."

She turned slightly, her eyes silvery in the filtered light. "You must have some understanding of the consequences if you force me."

"You're my wife," he reminded her rather unnecessarily. "Force is hardly an issue."

"A moment ago I had the opposite impression."

He touched a hand lightly to her cheek. She tolerated the caress but nothing more. "I was angry."

"And very ready to think the worst of me."

"Of Tyler. He wants you."

Her lids had fallen over the darting light of her eyes, turning them to mere slits that veiled her thoughts. "Do you have every woman you want?"

"I haven't . . . that is . . ." He broke off, embarrassed to admit that, despite no lack of opportunity, he had been faithful to her.

Elizabeth's mouth turned up at one corner, eloquent of her skepticism. That did not ease when he said, "It's different for women."

"So men have always claimed, but I don't quite see how."

"You're more . . . susceptible."

The sound she made, somewhere between a laugh and a snort, was hardly ladylike, but it expressed her derision more than adequately. "The weaker vessel? Of all the myths ever propounded, that is surely the greatest."

Looking at her stretched out on the bed, one leg bent at the knee, her hair spilling over the pillow and her slender arms lying upraised near her head, he could understand what she meant. For all his implied violence, his attempt to master her, she was not afraid. On the contrary, she appeared more than capable of enduring anything he might do and emerging from it stronger than ever. She would turn his physical superiority against him, make him feel ashamed of the weakness that urged him to cruelty, and in the process engineer her own purely feminine victory.

Only one thing might have saved him, if he hadn't truly cared for her. If he had been able to see her merely as an object, a possession—a vessel, as she had said—he could have done anything and walked away immune to guilt. But there was within him a deeply buried streak of gentleness, rarely given expression, yet stubborn in its resilience. Dimly he understood that he had been drawn to her from the beginning at least in part because she offered him the opportunity to exercise that gentleness. Very simply, he wanted her to be happy, and to acknowledge him as the author of that happiness. It was a strange desire for one who had never placed the well-being of any individual above that of his own. Yet he was doing so now, and even daring to acknowledge how much that meant to him.

Gently he touched her, his hand settling on the slight fullness of her belly in a gesture that was at once tender and provocative. He said nothing, not trusting any words that might come to him, but there was in his patient stillness a hint of apology that grew as a bridge between them, spanning the two distant points of their pride.

Elizabeth was silent for what seemed like a very long time. Above her, shadows danced along the ceiling, reminding her of the shadows by the stable door and of the bright light waiting just beyond them. At length she said softly, "It's cold. Let's get under the covers."

SO AT LAST SHE KNEW what he had sought to reveal to her since the beginning of their marriage, and in knowing it she understood something more of herself and him.

Lying back against the pillows, Elizabeth gazed absently at the bedroom windows where lace curtains fluttered softly. Night had fallen. It was hours since Madame Bernard had knocked futilely at their door, and far beyond the time when they should have departed for the Montgomerys' supper. She had no regrets about missing either.

Beside her, Drake slept deeply. A purely feminine smile curved lips swollen from his kisses. The satisfaction she felt went far beyond the merely physical; she was content in both body and mind. Part of her new understanding was an awareness of the frustration he must have felt at her inability to respond to him as completely as he wished. It cast his temporary withdrawal in a more acceptable light, as it did some of her own recent behavior, which had seemed to go against her fundamental character.

The episode with Tyler might have been a century ago, instead of less than a day. She wanted to believe that it had been another person who'd been tempted by him, not herself. But in her great relief that she had not betrayed her marriage, she felt the stirrings of tolerance. She could forgive herself for what had almost happened, even as she could pardon Tyler for what he had tried to do. Now that she had experienced the full effect of passion, she could far more easily comprehend the lengths to which people would go to attain it.

Only one small chink marred her happiness, that was the realization that what she had just known for the first time was something Drake had undoubtedly experienced many times before with other women. Far from being exclusively their own, it was for him simply part of the life of a sophisticated, virile man. Try though she did, she could not delude herself into believing that the passion he gave her in such abundance was the love she sought.

She did not want to think about that and did her best to push it aside, sensing that if she did otherwise it would swiftly grow to overshadow all her contentment. Yet it remained nestled against the most vulnerable of her emotions like a pebble in a shoe, inconsequential until brought to notice by the slightest movement and then potentially crippling in its effect.

With a soft murmur of distress, she turned and nestled against him. The warmth of his body reached out to engulf her. He did not wake, but he did lift an arm and draw her closer. His nearness and his strength comforted her, and it was not very long before she slept, albeit uneasily.

As it turned out, she did not require Madame Bernard's services. By mutual agreement, she and Drake decided to cut short their stay in England, to skip the yachting season at Cowes and go on instead to the Continent. She saw Jack once before leaving, but they exchanged few words. He seemed to know what had happened simply by looking at her, and she could not bear the regret in his eyes. It was with relief that she turned her attention to a late summer spent in the south of France, and the coming of an autumn to be spent journeying on to Rome and Venice.

The social life absorbed them as it had in London, though not quite to the same extent. They managed to make more time for each other, although they were rarely alone together. Drake's presence at Elizabeth's side was a silent but nonetheless effective discouragement to dalliance of any kind. They became the source of titillation to the jaded social circles through which they moved. It was thought amusing, if rather risqué, for a husband and wife to be so involved with each other.

Elizabeth found her position easier but by no means secure. She continued to have the sense of journeying toward a distant goal rather than having arrived at it. Their marriage had taken on the tenor of a truce in which the potential for further conflict was every bit as strong as the hope of peace. Wish to though she did, she could not let down her guard with her husband any more than he could with her. They remained, to a very large extent, strangers to each other, though it was the strangeness of freshness and novelty, not alienation and suspicion.

The glamorous, exciting cities they visited became merely the backdrop for the intimately exotic setting of their marriage. They might have been anywhere, so long as they were together. It was that realization that ultimately sent them back to Boston.

They returned in October, in time to settle into the house in Louisburg Square before the holiday season began. It was their intention to spend Thanksgiving with Drake's family and Christmas with Elizabeth's. The letters she received from Calvert Oaks provoked in her the sweet pain of homesickness even as they were dearly treasured.

William and Sunbird had been quietly married. Neither Charles Durand nor his wife had attended the ceremony, an omission that had added to rather than detracted from the pleasure of the occasion. Nothing further had been heard from the white-hooded men who had attacked the couple, but certain neighbors chose to give the Calverts a wide berth, whether to express their displeasure or out of simple prudence could not be said.

The estrangement between the Hudsons and the Calverts ran deep and dark, though it was by no means absolute.

Expediency dictated that the two families have at least some contact. Since most plantation business had been ceded to the younger generation, William and Davey were inevitably thrown together. They kept their dealings to a minimum, but, even so, they were difficult. After its first swift explosion the clash between them had settled down to smolder. It awaited only the proper tinder to make it erupt again.

None of this, of course, was said directly in the letters to Elizabeth. But with her new awareness of what lay beyond the sheltered borders of her childhood, she could read clearly enough between the lines. She did, and tried not to worry too much about what the future might bring to the place she still loved most in the world.

It was to that future that Elizabeth's thoughts turned more frequently as the fiery blush of autumn turned good gray Boston gaudy. She had suspected before leaving Europe that she was pregnant. Now, as she attempted to gather the fabric of her new life around her, that was confirmed.

The joy she felt reached to the center of her being, transfiguring her and giving her beauty a radiance she had never before possessed. But with that joy came an equal measure of apprehension. So long as she could think only of the child and herself, as two inseparable beings, she was content. But when she cast her mind farther afield and saw the wider perspective, she became afraid.

The lack of tranquillity in her relationship with Drake made the relationship she would have with their child all the more important. With the negative example of Abigail Bennington before her, she was determined that her son or daughter would at least have a good mother. Yet she wasn't absolutely sure what that meant. Her own mother formed the standard by which she measured herself, with the result that she vacillated between being certain of her own maternal abilities and being fraught with doubt.

To comfort herself, she read and reread the letters from Virginia, finding despite the hint of problems a measure of solace available nowhere else. Yet that did not come without a price. William's correspondence, though it rarely spoke of personal matters, was flavored with a deeply rooted happiness in his marriage that Elizabeth could not help but envy. It made her vividly aware of how far she and Drake still had to go to attain anything similar.

From her mother and father's letters, she caught the sense that, having given up one daughter, they were delighted to find themselves with another. Elizabeth's vague stirrings of resentment that the family had so successfully weathered her departure were quashed beneath the innate generosity of her character. She was glad for them, even as she missed them all desperately.

The longing for home that settled over her as her pregnancy made itself known was a surprise. She had expected to experience it immediately upon leaving Calvert Oaks, not realizing that her marriage and honeymoon would be ample distractions to hold it at bay. Not until she attempted to look upon Boston, and more particularly her marriage, as her new home did she understand how far she felt from any true sense of belonging.

Mari tried to help. She accompanied Elizabeth on shopping expeditions for the house in Louisburg Square, saw to it that she met everyone of interest, and included her in all manner of social events. All the while the older woman was aware that her efforts, sincere though they were, could not penetrate the wall of isolation rapidly growing up around her young friend.

For that Abigail Bennington was clearly to blame. Elizabeth's mother-in-law went through the motions of accepting her son's wife even as she waged a silent but deadly war against the marriage that would never have her approval. The knowledge that there was soon to be a child from that marriage only redoubled her efforts. With the wiliness of a general forced to conduct a subterranean campaign, she set out to sow misunderstanding and bad feeling at every opportunity.

"I'm so sorry," she said with a smile one afternoon as she visited with Elizabeth in the parlor at Louisburg Square, "that Drake has to be away so often. But you do understand how much I depend on him."

Elizabeth understood only too well, or at least she thought she did. Her husband, who to the best of her knowledge had never taken more than the most cursory interest in his family's many enterprises, was suddenly involved with them night and day. No sooner did one problem seem to be solved than another reared its head, always brought to his attention by his apologetic mother, who simply could not bring herself to cope alone and who could no longer trust the men who had guided the family's affairs for so long.

"It's quite all right," Elizabeth said stiffly, fighting the wave of nausea that threatened to consume her. Generally, she was ill only in the mornings, but Abigail's presence had a decidedly deleterious effect on her. She closed her eyes briefly, only to find that did not help. The room shifted uneasily around her as she fought to hide her discomposure. "I'm sure Drake will have everything under control soon."

"Such a shame that he had to go to Chicago," Abigail said as she lifted her teacup delicately. Over its rim she observed her daughter-in-law benignly. "And that nasty storm there. I do hope he'll be able to get back in time for Thanksgiving."

"I'm sure he will," Elizabeth said though she was anything but. The weather aside, the situation in Chicago, where the Benningtons had interests in the butchering industry, seemed to fascinate Drake. He had settled the original matter that took him west quickly enough, but was staying on to investigate the possibility of joining forces with a railroad trust. At least, that was what she gathered from his latest letter, brief though it had been. He sounded enthusiastic and happy. Only as an afterthought had he inquired after her health and that of the baby.

"Is everything all right, dear?" Abigail inquired. "You look a bit peaked."

"I'm fine," Elizabeth assured her. It was a point of sheer survival that she never admit to any weakness in her mother-in-law's presence.

Abigail paused delicately in the act of placing a large cream bun on her plate. It was quite warm in the room, because the older woman had insisted that all the windows be closed and a roaring fire be kept going. The air was stifling, made even worse by the cloying scent of carnation perfume with which Abigail habitually doused herself in cooler weather, eschewing as she did frequent baths.

Already that afternoon she had given her opinion of Elizabeth's many bad habits, from continuing to wash her hair every other day despite the imminent danger of consumption that it presented, to her refusal to give up her frequent walks, even though everyone knew such exercise was not good for one in her delicate condition. Worst of all was her daughter-in-law's absurd idea that small, plain meals were best for both her and the baby.

"You really must eat more, dear," she said as she reconsidered the cream bun and offered it instead to Elizabeth. "You're far too thin as it is."

Elizabeth's eyes dilated as she stared at the object being pressed on her. It squatted on the plate, oozing clotted cream of a peculiar shade of bilious yellow from a crack in its side. She gazed at it with the horrified fascination she might have reserved for something that had crawled out from beneath a rock. "I really don't think so...."

"Nonsense, dear. Have this nice bun and a few sips of hot chocolate. You'll feel much better."

In Elizabeth's humble opinion, the only way she could possibly feel better was to die, the sooner the better. She stood up hastily, a hand to her mouth. "If you'll excuse me..."

"Oh, my..." Abigail's hand lashed out, catching Elizabeth's arm and holding her firmly in place. "Not feeling well, dear?"

In another moment, Elizabeth thought desperately, her mother-in-law was going to find out precisely how far from well she really was. With any luck, she would at least have the consolation of ruining the ugly black dress Abigail wore. But she would also have humiliated herself, and that was something her pride would not permit.

With the last of her strength, she wrenched herself away and made a speedy exit. She got no farther than the entrance hall, where a hapless umbrella stand was pressed into unseemly service. Afterward, she felt better, though she made no attempt to return immediately to the parlor. Instead, she went upstairs, where Tilly, the young Irish maid she had hired after Taylor chose not to return to the States, relieved her of the evidence of her discomfort and, clucking gently, fetched her a damp cloth with which to clean her face.

"Don't you be worrying, ma'am," the girl said as she eased Elizabeth down on the window seat opposite the bed. "You'll be feeling better soon. Why, my sister, Kathleen, bless her soul, has nine kiddies, and she's been sick as a dog with every one of them. But it passes, it does, and then you'll feel wonderful."

Elizabeth leaned her head back against the window seat, her eyes closed. She felt exhausted, despite the fact that she had slept some ten hours the night before. Abigail had arrived just as she was thinking about a nap. Her delicate hints to that effect had been met with a deaf ear. But then, they always were. "I really should go back downstairs."

Tilly's normally generous mouth tightened in disapproval. She might be only seventeen and still fresh off the boat, but she had more than her share of common sense.

There was nothing wrong with her eyes, either. She saw quite clearly what her mistress's mother-in-law was up to, and she didn't like it one bit. Tilly deeply appreciated Elizabeth's willingness to trust her with the important job of being her maid. She knew that a dozen more experienced women had also applied for the post, and considered it her great stroke of good fortune to have been chosen. She also happened to like babies, though she was in no hurry to have any of her own, and she didn't care for anything that might threaten the one Elizabeth was carrying.

"You need to rest, ma'am, if you don't mind my saying so. Certain people should understand that."

Elizabeth smiled wanly. "It would be considered very rude for me to fail to reappear."

Tilly sniffed audibly. "Manners is as manners does, I always say. Certain people shouldn't come calling when they know perfectly well a body isn't up to receiving."

Elizabeth opened her eyes a slit and observed her maid. "Mrs. Bennington means well."

The young red-haired maid snorted. Under her breath, she muttered, "And pigs fly."

"What was that, Tilly?"

"Nothing, ma'am. I was only clearing my throat."

"I do that myself from time to time."

"I could go downstairs, ma'am, and tell Mrs. Bennington that you need to rest for a while."

The maid's willingness to brave her mother-in-law touched Elizabeth deeply, but she knew how futile it would be. "She'll take that as an excuse to get Dr. Greeley over here, if she hasn't already sent for him."

Elizabeth did not like the doctor Abigail had insisted she use. Never mind that he took care of all the best families in Boston, there was something about him that rubbed her the wrong way. She dreaded her visits to him, finding the examinations both humiliating and hurtful, and took no comfort from his assurances that when the time came, she would feel no pain.

"Ether," he said. "That's the answer to childbirth. There's no reason for the mother to be concerned at all. You won't know anything is happening."

Elizabeth would have been hard-pressed to explain why she found that so disquieting, since she was no more attracted to the idea of pain than any other normal person. But something in her rebelled against the idea of being oblivious to her own child's birth.

As the baby grew within her, and with it her dislike of Dr. Greeley and everything he represented, she longed for the capable hands of her mother and Mammy Augusta, who between them had helped birth scores of healthy babies. When she saw them at Christmas, she intended to sound them out on this business of ether, and if they reacted as negatively as she expected, it was her intention to find some alternative, no matter what the repercussions.

But for the moment she had her mother-in-law to deal with as best she could. Gathering herself together, she made her way back to the parlor, where she found Abigail finishing the last of the cream buns.

"There you are, dear. I was about to come looking for you."

"I'm sorry I had to leave so precipitately," Elizabeth murmured as she took a seat as far away as she could manage. "But I'm sure you understand."

"Actually," Abigail said, "I was never sick a day with any of my children. But then, I was quite resigned to my fate and simply accepted it as God's will."

"I don't see what that has to do with—"

"Now, my dear, the last thing I want to do is upset you, but you know perfectly well that the only mothers who are ill are those who are not reconciled to their condition. Dr. Greeley must have told you that the surest way to regain your own health is to stop resenting your child."

"Resenting? But I don't..."

"If you didn't," Abigail said firmly, "you wouldn't be ill. You have an extremely strong will, never an asset in a woman, and that is causing you to fight against what is happening to you. It is unnatural, so inevitably you're paying the price."

"I never heard of such a thing," Elizabeth protested. She was too surprised to even be offended by her mother-in-law's claim, though she knew that would come. "Wherever did you get such an outlandish idea?"

Abigail frowned, being by no means accustomed to contradiction, even when it was so richly deserved. "I would hardly call it that. Dr. Greeley has written a learned paper on the subject. The best scientific minds concur. Women who rebel against their predestined circumstances make themselves ill and run the risk of harming their babies."

"Dr. Greeley," Elizabeth said carefully, "has a great many ideas, but not many of them seem to have had the benefit of common sense."

"That is exactly what I mean. A woman who would question the wisdom of so learned a man has unnatural tendencies. I only hope you will get them under control before they overwhelm you."

Having delivered her judgment of the situation, Abigail rose with magisterial dignity and drew on her gloves. "I trust you understand, dear, that I'm only thinking of your welfare, and that of my grandchild. With Drake away, everything is bound to be very difficult for you."

"Actually," Elizabeth said before she could consider the wisdom of it, "I doubt he would be of very much help in this situation."

Abigail's eyes gleamed briefly, but she merely shrugged and made her way to the parlor door in a rustle of black bombazine. "I shall be writing to him later today. Naturally, I will mention that you haven't been feeling well."

"I would prefer that you say nothing of the matter," Elizabeth said as she followed her. "There is no need to concern him."

"On the contrary," Abigail said. "He has every right to know." Her gaze drifted to Elizabeth's still flat stomach. "It is, after all, his child."

There was in those words the faintest note of inquiry, the merest hint of doubt. It was enough to bring a dull flush to Elizabeth's otherwise pale face, but not so much that she could strike back. With an effort she contained herself, though only just. "You will, of course, do whatever you think right."

"Always, my dear," Abigail assured her as a footman opened the front door for her. She smiled the cold, brittle smile of a huntress as she glanced back at her distraught daughter-in-law. "Always."

LATE THAT NIGHT, Elizabeth woke from an uneasy sleep to discover that she was bleeding, only a few drops but they were enough to terrify her. She lay awake, her hands clasped over her belly, frozen by fear and formless guilt. For hours she was afraid to move, even to summon Tilly. When the maid did come at the usual time, she found her mistress curled on her side, holding herself tightly and crying silently.

"Sweet Jesus!" the maid exclaimed as she all but forced Elizabeth to let her see what the matter was. "Is that what's upset you now? Is there pain, then? Bad, in your belly?"

Dimly, Elizabeth shook her head. "Some, but not so bad. It's the blood...."

"This happens," Tilly assured her. "Would it be your time of the month, if it weren't for the babe?"

Fighting down her embarrassment, Elizabeth nodded.

"Sometimes nature doesn't quite get the idea," Tilly assured her as she straightened the bed and made her more comfortable. "Not for the first few months, at least. It doesn't mean anything is wrong. But," she added hastily, "you should still rest. No visitors today."

"Mari is coming...."

"She's all right," Tilly allowed. "But if Mrs. Bennington comes by, I'll tell her you're indisposed. And if she tries to bring that doctor around, I'll tell him you're asleep and left instructions not to be disturbed."

Despite herself, Elizabeth managed a wan smile. "I feel sorry for them if they try to cross you, Tilly."

The little maid grinned and bustled about, opening the curtains to a bright sunny day. "Aye, I'm tough all right, ma'am. You have to be to crawl out of the bogs the way I did. But if you don't mind my saying so, you've got your share of steel. Only don't let this place make you forget it."

"I won't," Elizabeth said, strength flowing back into her even as the night's terrible tension eased. In retrospect, she was amazed at her own fear and could only explain it as having been for the baby rather than herself. The thought of being afraid for someone who was still no more than an unfelt flutter buried deep within her astonished her, and brought home the depth of her love for the child yet to be born. Already it was a person to her, as real and whole as if she held it in her arms. Whenever she thought of it, she was awash with a fierce protectiveness that made her willing, even eager, to take on anything or anyone that might threaten its safety.

Tilly saw the healthy color flow back into her face and smiled. "That's it, ma'am. You rest, and I'll bring you a few biscuits. Later you might like a nice bath."

Elizabeth agreed that would be very nice. She lay back against the pillows, listening to the early-morning sounds filtering up from the street. Beneath the covers, her hands moved lightly over her belly, reaffirming the life that clung there and reasserting her own worthiness to nurture it.

Later in the day, after her stomach had settled down, she wrote a long letter to her mother and a shorter one to Drake.

To Sarah, she expressed some of her concerns and said how much she was looking forward to seeing her family at Christmas. To Drake, she said only that everything was well.

As it happened, he did not receive the letter, being already on his way back from Chicago before it could be delivered. His return, sooner than he had planned, was prompted by a telegram from his mother in which she expressed her conviction that he was needed at home. Surprised, but also touched by her apparent concern for Elizabeth, he dropped what he was doing and took the first train east. In fact, he was glad of the excuse since he missed Elizabeth more than he would have thought possible. It troubled him that she had assumed such importance in his life. The habit of insulating himself from emotion, begun in childhood, gave way only slowly and reluctantly. Inevitably, he resented the cause of new and not always comfortable feelings.

Bad weather delayed the trip, but he arrived back in Boston two days before Thanksgiving and went immediately to Louisburg Square, only to learn that Elizabeth had gone riding and was not expected back for several hours.

"Riding?" he repeated when Tilly told him. "Surely she shouldn't be doing that?"

"She's feeling perfectly well, sir," the maid said. "In fact, she's much better than she has been. She needed to get out and get some exercise."

Drake frowned. He distinctly remembered his mother mentioning that such behavior was not appropriate. Whatever else he might think of her, the fact remained that Abigail had borne five children. She presumably knew a great deal more about the process than his wife, who he felt should be glad of his mother's guidance. Instead Elizabeth had apparently chosen to disregard it, for what reason he could not imagine.

"I'm going after her," he said as he strode back down the front steps. "If she returns while I'm gone, tell her not to leave again."

Tilly was given no opportunity to respond as he reentered the carriage that had brought him from the station and gave brisk instructions to the driver. Half an hour later he was standing at the edge of the salt marshes on the outskirts of the city, where he knew Elizabeth liked to ride. She said the place reminded her of the tidal flats she had visited as a child when her parents took her and William on excursions to the sea. He suspected that the lonely solitude afforded a measure of communion with the loneliness of her own spirit, which he had been unable to assuage. For that reason he had resented her excursions. Now he had even more reason to dislike them.

He paced back and forth anxiously for several minutes before catching sight of her. The horse she rode was not Princess, but an old and gentle mare capable of little more than a sedate canter. At the moment she was plodding amiably along, the reins held slack in Elizabeth's hands, both horse and rider pleasantly absorbed in their own thoughts.

Drake did not see that. It did not occur to him that his wife must have deliberately chosen the safest possible horse, nor that she had curtailed her own natural impulses in order to eliminate any chance of risk. Short of the earth suddenly rearing up beneath her, there was no way she could have been unseated from so steady a perch. She was as safe on the mare's back as she would have been in her own parlor. But all that escaped his notice. He saw only that she was alone, on horseback, behaving in a manner he could only think of as the height of irresponsibility.

Angrily he started toward her. She saw him and smiled, only to have that smile fade as she caught sight of his expression. "Drake..." she said cautiously. "You're back."

"And not a moment too soon, from the look of it," he said, grabbing hold of the mare's bridle. "What in hell do you think you're doing?"

The mare shied nervously. Elizabeth leaned forward, trying to soothe the horse with a gentle hand on her mane. "Me? What are you talking about?"

"You, here, riding. Don't you have any more sense than to do such a stupid thing?" Still holding the horse with one hand, he reached up with the other, took hold of Elizabeth's waist and pulled her from the saddle. Staring down at her, his face dark, he added, "Or maybe you don't care."

Elizabeth shook herself free. She was beyond anger, in a state bordering on disbelief. His sudden appearance, her initial gladness, the abrupt discovery of what he thought her capable of, all combined to stun her. She had thought they were at last beginning to approach some understanding. Now she was forced to realize how wrong she had been.

"How dare you. *How dare you!* Don't you suggest for a moment that I would do anything to harm my child. I have far more care for it than you ever could, and I know far better what is right for us both."

Concerned by her sudden outburst, he attempted to reach for her again. "Elizabeth, I didn't mean . . ."

She took a step back and held up both her hands to ward him off. "Stay away from me. Just stay away."

The intensity of her rage struck him. There was a fine sheen of tears in her eyes, and her mouth trembled. She seemed like a wounded animal, but one still fully capable of turning on her attacker. Belatedly it occurred to him that there were forces at work inside her he could not understand. A sense of his own inadequacy to deal with the situation descended on him and softened his manner.

"Don't be upset," he said. "That isn't good for you, either."

It was the wrong approach. To Elizabeth, he seemed only to be criticizing her further, suggesting yet again that she was not sufficiently mindful of the child. The look of contempt she shot him spoke more eloquently than any words. Turning on her heel, she presented him with a rigid back as she strode stiffly away, leaving him to cope with the mare.

He caught up with her near where the salt flats merged with the sandy road that eventually led back into the city. The carriage waited nearby. Before the driver could jump down from his seat, Elizabeth wrenched open the door and climbed inside. Drake tried to assist her, only to have his hand thrown off. His mouth was drawn in a hard line as he tied the mare behind before joining her. In silence, they rode back to Louisburg Square.

ELIZABETH'S UNBORN CHILD, so dearly loved and so looked forward to, nonetheless continued to be a bone of contention between its parents. If Drake had barely understood his wife before, in her new incarnation of mother-to-be, he comprehended her even less.

Difficulties abounded. His continued desire for her was a source of both concern and embarrassment to him. Vaguely he thought that such sexual yearnings should have ended when he learned of her pregnancy. Not that he felt he should by any means have been neutered, only that his wife was no longer a fitting object for his lust. Yet however much he considered the more than plentiful options, he could not bring himself to act on them. It was Elizabeth he wanted—hurt, prickly, defiant Elizabeth, who drifted through his dreams as stubbornly as she did his days.

The changes in her body fascinated him. He observed them surreptitiously from his privileged position in her bed, which he had, despite his qualms, failed to relinquish. The swelling of her breasts and their heightened sensitivity delighted him, as did the slowly growing roundness of her belly. Through the exercise of considerable restraint, more than he had known he possessed, he managed to resist the temptation to make love to her nightly. But several times each week the need became irresistible, and then he sweetly plundered her body with a fine disregard for any thought of her sanctity.

So far as Elizabeth was concerned, their lovemaking was all that was right between them, yet even that had a darker side. She was appalled by her continued desire for her husband, not because she shared his ideas about pregnancy, but because she was bewildered by the continued harmony of their bodies in the absence of anything similar between their spirits. Yet on those nights when he turned to her, she went into his arms with a sense of profound relief.

Thanksgiving came, bringing with it the obligatory dinner chez Abigail. If Elizabeth had hoped that her mother-in-law's sniping would draw Drake's objections, she was disappointed. He seemed oblivious to the tension between the two women, or perhaps he merely wrote it off as inevitable. Certainly he remained convinced of his mother's good intentions, at least so far as her future grandchild was concerned.

"I hesitate to mention this," Abigail said toward the tail end of the sixteen-course meal, which had begun with consommé and ended with pumpkin pie, in between encompassing a whole shad baked in pastry, a glistening clove-studded ham with dumplings, a stuffed turkey that appeared to have died of obesity, four vegetables cooked to the required limpness, two ices served between other courses to clear the palate, and three relishes all involving cranberries. "But," their hostess continued, "do you really think it's a good idea to make the trip to Virginia for Christmas?"

Since she had addressed the question to the table in general, Elizabeth half expected one of her sisters-in-law to respond. She herself had no desire to do so, sensing as she did that this was yet another salvo in a battle that apparently had no end. The past few weeks had brought home to her the full extent of the problem presented by the woman she had taken to referring to sarcastically, if only in her own mind, as Mother Bennington.

No one could have been less maternal than the black-garbed foe who confronted her from across the table. It had not escaped Elizabeth's notice that her mother-in-law was always dressed in black these days, not unlike Queen Victoria, to whom she bore more than a passing resemblance. No one dared to ask what she was in mourning for, mainly because everyone knew.

"Elizabeth is looking forward to seeing her family again," Drake said at length, when it became obvious that his wife had no intention of replying. He leaned back in his chair and smiled benignly. As the sole male at the table, he assumed a rather lordly position, further catered to by his mother and sisters, who made it clear nothing was too much trouble so long as it pleased him.

Such obsequiousness, made all the worse by Drake's acceptance of it as no more than his due, threatened a return of the sickness Elizabeth had hoped was gone for good. Though she had eaten lightly and drunk only mineral water, she was feeling far from well. The overstuffed dining room crammed full of heavy mahogany furniture and shrouded by thick velvet curtains oppressed her. She longed for the airiness of her own rooms, the first in the Louisburg Square house to reflect her tastes.

"Of course," Abigail said, glancing at her daughter-in-law. "I understand that Elizabeth would want to return home. But she can do that any time. Surely it isn't worth the risk...."

"What risk is there," Elizabeth inquired, "in a perfectly healthy woman taking a trip during which she will be surrounded by every possible comfort?"

"Clearly you enjoy travel more than I do," Abigail said. "I have always found it impossible to be comfortable in public conveyances."

Since that hardly described the private railroad car Elizabeth knew could easily be placed at her disposal, she didn't bother to reply directly. But she was stung to respond when Abigail added, "And then, of course, there is the matter of being away from Dr. Greeley."

"A reason in and of itself to make the trip."

"Why, my dear, I had no idea you still felt that way about the doctor," Abigail said with a note of deep concern. Turning to her son, she went on, "He is, after all, one of the most respected medical men in New England. Every lady of any standing sees him."

Drake nodded, his attention on Elizabeth. "He does have an excellent reputation."

"I don't like him," his wife said, knowing full well what she was provoking, but irked beyond discretion. Her head had begun to pound, and even the loosely laced corset she wore was uncomfortable. She despised the smug looks of her sisters-in-law as much as she did their mother's incessant baiting.

"Don't be concerned," Abigail advised her son soothingly. "It's quite natural for Elizabeth to be out of sorts. The strain of her condition..." She let her words trail off deliberately.

"Has anyone noticed," Elizabeth said, "how often someone in this family fails to complete a sentence? It seems a standard technique to leave thoughts dangling, so much more effective when one is engaged in innuendo."

Drake straightened in his chair and waved aside the waiter, who had been about to refill his wineglass. "Perhaps we should be going."

"But, dear," Abigail protested, "it's so early yet, and I had hoped we could have a nice chat about various matters that require your attention."

"Another time, Mother." He tossed his napkin on the table and rose. Elizabeth studiously avoided his gaze, even when he came to stand beside her and held out his hand. "I think," he said softly, "that you need to rest."

She was tempted to protest, but thought better of it. Nothing would please her more than to escape. Mutely, she allowed him to help her from her chair.

"I'll call on you tomorrow, Mother," Drake said as he tucked Elizabeth's arm through his. "In the meantime, I'm sure you understand."

In fact, the hard line of her mouth made it perfectly clear, at least to Elizabeth, that she did not. Abigail enjoyed few things less than seeing her son being protective of his wife. Only her awareness of the tension reverberating between the couple prevented her from feeling that she had suffered a defeat.

As it was, Elizabeth could hardly claim victory. Not when, upon their arrival back at the house, Drake returned to the subject his mother had raised. "I think we should consider postponing our trip to Calvert Oaks."

They were alone in Elizabeth's bedroom. Tilly had appeared to help her undress, but Drake had sent the maid away again, saying there was no reason for her to interrupt her holiday simply because they had returned early. Despite Elizabeth's protests that she really didn't need to lie down, he was rapidly undoing the back of her ivory lace dress.

"You don't mean it," she said, looking back over her shoulder at him. In the fading afternoon light, the planes and angles of his face were more pronounced than usual. Perhaps it was her imagination, but he seemed to have changed in the past few months, to have grown even more solid and mature. The hint of self-indulgence that had previously softened his features ever so slightly was gone. She sensed that he was coming into himself in a way she could not truly fathom. It had to do with his taking control of the family business, that much she understood. He was testing himself and discovering strengths he hadn't known he possessed. He was also, she suspected, learning that he had some use in the world besides the mere pursuit of his own pleasure.

She was glad for him, even as she wondered when it would dawn on Abigail what she had unleashed. She could almost feel sorry for the older woman, who would inevitably have to realize that the son she had merely intended to manipulate to her own ends was instead staking his claim to manhood in unmistakable terms.

Which meant, of course, that she herself might not have any success in manipulating him either. "Drake," she said as casually as she could manage with his hands moving over her bare back, "I'm really counting on going home for a while."

He paused, staring at the graceful line of her shoulders and the soft vulnerability of her neck touched by tendrils of hair falling from her upswept coiffure. Her skin was flawless and exuded a tantalizing warmth. He had only to bend slightly to press his lips to it.

Instead, he finished unfastening the dress and deliberately slid it down her arms. Instinctively, she caught it before the bodice fell completely away. When she turned to him, the provocative swell of her breasts above the disarranged lace and silk sent a bolt of hunger through him.

"We'll talk about it another time," he said, distracted by the rampant needs of his body.

Elizabeth frowned. Conscious though she was of his nearness and of the impact it was having on her, she did not like being put off in much the same fashion as he had done with his mother. Besides, the trip to Calvert Oaks was far more important to her than he seemed to realize.

"There's nothing much to discuss," she said, shivering slightly as he ran the back of his hand down her bare arm. His other hand was on her waist, drawing her to him.

"Your mother is quite wrong about my not traveling," she went on, despite the all-too-familiar feeling of languor seeping through her. "And as for Dr. Greeley, I've been thinking of changing physicians anyway."

Drake stifled an impatient sigh. He really didn't want to get into the matter just now, but it seemed she was leaving him no choice. He released her and turned away to sit down in the wing chair near the bed. From an inside pocket, he removed a flat silver case and flicked it open, glancing at her as he did so. "Will it disturb you if I smoke?"

Mutely, Elizabeth shook her head. His sudden withdrawal put her at a loss. She was uncomfortably aware of her state of undress and was tempted to put on a robe, but to do so would reveal how ill at ease she felt. He had lit a cigar and taken the first few puffs when it occurred to her that it was ridiculous to be standing in front of him like a supplicant. She sank down abruptly on the edge of the bed and tugged on her dress until she was somewhat more properly covered.

"What's wrong with Dr. Greeley?" Drake asked as wisps of smoke drifted toward the ceiling.

"He . . . makes me uncomfortable."

Drake frowned. Necessary though he knew it to be, he preferred not to think about what was involved in his wife's prenatal care. "Everyone speaks very highly of him."

"Your mother does," Elizabeth corrected. "But I don't think she's necessarily the best judge."

"She means well."

Her raised eyebrows and the sudden tightening of her mouth warned him that she disagreed. Drake glanced up at the ceiling, as though patience might be summoned from such a source. He really didn't care whether Abigail's intentions were benign or not. Time and his own actions would eventually make clear to her that he was no longer a child, vulnerable to her whims. Never again would any woman be permitted to touch his emotions to such an extent that she could use them to control him. The sooner Elizabeth also learned that, the better for them all.

"If you could give me some sensible reason for wanting to change doctors, I might be inclined to agree. But under the circumstances, I think it best that you remain under Dr. Greeley's care." Before she could begin to argue, he raised a hand, forestalling her. "Furthermore, our plans to visit

Calvert Oaks were made before we knew of your pregnancy. That changes everything." More gently, he added, "We can always go next year."

"I want to go now."

Drake took a long draw on his cigar and regarded her narrowly. He reminded himself that she was very young, and that women were, at any age, more akin to children than to men. He wanted to be kind to her, but he also intended to be firm.

"I'm sorry," he said. "That isn't possible."

Elizabeth stared at him. He didn't appear to be at all embarrassed or uncertain about exercising his authority over her. On the contrary, he seemed perfectly comfortable with it. She had never before encountered such a situation. From the time she was capable of understanding, no one had ever simply ordered her to do certain things or not to do others. The reason why behavior was necessary—or forbidden—had always been explained. In that way, her parents had expressed not only their love for her, but also their respect. Drake was showing neither.

"Has it occurred to you," she asked with deceptive softness, "that I may not be inclined to simply obey your orders?"

"Yes, but I prefer to believe that you wouldn't be so foolish as to do anything of which you knew I disapproved. Besides," he went on as he rose and came to stand before her, "I don't imagine you'll strike out for Virginia on your own."

His complacent certainty irked her. She longed to throw off the hand he placed on her bare shoulder and tell him exactly what she thought of his tyranny, but caution kept her silent. There was nothing to be gained by airing her feelings, and too much to be lost.

Later, when she lay with her head on his shoulder, their bodies still entwined together in the aftermath of lovemaking, she tried to be glad of what was right between them instead of dwelling on what remained so clearly wrong. But the fulfillment of her body, complete though it was, could not erase the disquiet in her mind and heart. Somehow she had to reach her husband on a deeper level, to make him see her as more than a beautiful possession. It was for his sake as well as her own that she had to try. Unlike him, she knew what made for a happy marriage, having seen what her parents shared. She wanted the same for herself and Drake.

She fell asleep holding on to the hope that it was still possible for them, but troubled by the conviction that it would come only at a high cost.

THANKSGIVING WAS BARELY OVER before Drake left for New York, where he had business involving the family's shipping line. Traditionally, the Benningtons had confined their shipping activities to the Atlantic run, principally serving England and France; it was Drake's intention to expand into the Orient. The question he faced was whether to try to do so using the present management and facilities, or whether to start an entirely new company devoted to that purpose.

This choice—with its complex financial and political implications—was very much on his mind right before he left, with the consequence that he had relatively little attention to give to Elizabeth. He did not notice that she was more silent than usual, nor that whenever they were together— which was not often—she had taken to watching him carefully, as though by observing him closely enough she might uncover some clue that would help her deal with him. It did occur to him that Mari was a more frequent guest at the Louisburg Square house, and that she seemed concerned about Elizabeth, but he put that down to worry over her pregnancy and thought nothing of it.

In fact, Mari was far less concerned about her young friend's physical well-being than she was about what was happening to her spirit. She found Elizabeth withdrawn and preoccupied. Looking at her as they sat in the parlor on a dreary afternoon early in December, Mari was struck by how much she resembled the unhappy girl who had come to her several years before. She seemed to belong in her present surroundings no more than a lushly blooming orchid would belong encased in ice.

Putting down her needlework, Mari said gently, "Boston isn't at its best at this time of year, is it?"

Elizabeth looked up at her with a faint start. She realized belatedly that silence had stretched out between them for some time. So caught up had she been in her own thoughts that she had ignored her duties as hostess. "I'm sorry," she murmured. "What did you say?"

"Only that Boston isn't very appealing just now. Once winter really sets in, it can be quite picturesque. But between when the leaves fall and the first true snow comes, everything is rather gray."

"Gray... yes, that's a good word for it." Despite herself, Elizabeth smiled. "Also soggy. It seems to have been raining forever."

As though to confirm that, raindrops splattered against the parlor windows. Both women were grateful for the fire that kept the dampness at bay. Mari had come from her offices, where she had spent a difficult morning meeting with a brace of lawyers. Gideon was trying once again to wrest control of the mills from her. After all these years, she would have expected him to give up, but experience had taught her that Josiah's eldest son had at least inherited his father's stubbornness, if nothing else of his character.

"You look tired," Elizabeth said gently. She was not so absorbed in her own problems that she couldn't be aware of someone else's.

"I am," Mari admitted with a reluctant laugh. "It's a shock to me to realize that I'm not as young as I used to be."

"You're hardly ancient. Why, you can run rings around anyone I know." Elizabeth admired Mari as much as she did her own mother, seeing in both women tremendous strength and courage that would be the envy of any man. Thinking of that brought her mind back to Drake and made her frown. "Why do men always insist on underestimating us? They belittle our every accomplishment, while making a great fuss over their own. From the cradle to the grave they try constantly to convince us of our inferiority."

"So do many women," Mari pointed out gently. "You will hear many of our own sex declaim that we are the helpmates of men, put on earth to serve them, and that we can aspire to no higher purpose without losing everything that makes us womanly."

Elizabeth scoffed openly. "Tell that to the women crossing the country in covered wagons, risking death at every turn in order to achieve a better life. For that matter, tell it to my mother, who faced down Yankees and slave catchers alike and held our family together under the worst circumstances. Or tell it to yourself; you run a business empire as well as any man could." She shook her head adamantly. "I'm convinced we can do anything men can do. Not only that, we can do something they can't, give birth. Why," she added, as though the thought had just occurred to her, "when you come right down to it, I'm not sure what we need them for at all."

Mari smiled gently at her young friend, her face composed beneath the soft blond hair that was turning almost imperceptibly to silver. She would always be a beautiful woman, but the accumulation of years had added a degree of wisdom to her features that far surpassed mere beauty. She had seen a great deal of life, both good and bad, and no longer made the mistake of believing that anything was simple.

"I seem to remember," she said softly, "that they have their uses."

The words were innocent enough, but the tone in which they were spoken was laden with innuendo. Mari could, when she chose, be quite frank, enough so that Elizabeth actually blushed.

"I suppose so," she allowed, trying hard not to remember how easily Drake had roused her to passions of all sorts. "But they can also be infuriating."

"I gather that all is not blissful harmony."

"Hardly. Married life isn't turning out to be at all as I expected."

"And what was that?" Mari inquired.

"Harmony," Elizabeth said after a moment's thought. "Of all the words I can think of, that sums it up best. My parents were always in harmony. Even when they disagreed about something, they worked it out smoothly between themselves. Drake and I can't seem to agree on even the simplest things."

"Such as?"

"Oh . . . just everything. It's hard to explain, exactly. We had certain . . . misunderstandings while we were in Europe, and even though they seem to have been settled, more have cropped up. I suppose what it comes down to is that he feels he can order me about, and I'm not eager to be so accommodating."

"Drake's mother is very strong willed, isn't she?" Mari asked.

"Yes, but what has that got to do with it?"

"Only that men with strong willed mothers sometimes seem to fear anything similar in their wives and to be determined to stamp it out at the slightest sign."

"You're not suggesting that Drake compares me to his mother?" Elizabeth asked, horrified by the mere notion. To her way of thinking, she had nothing whatsoever in common with Abigail.

"It's hard to say. My point is only that it couldn't have been very pleasant for him, growing up with such a woman. Strength by itself is neutral; it can be turned to either good or bad purposes. In Abigail's case, I suspect they were bad."

"She is a very bitter woman," Elizabeth acknowledged, "who seems to think only of herself. But how could he imagine that I'm like that?"

"I'm sure he doesn't. What's far more likely is that he lumps all women together and judges them all by the same criteria. It's up to you to teach him differently."

Elizabeth did not relish the prospect. The more she dwelt on her husband, the more she viewed him as an implacable stranger, beyond her ability to influence. "I wonder," she said almost to herself, "if I will ever feel at home here."

"It sounds as though you think that unlikely."

"I didn't at first, but now... Everything is so different, I wonder how I will ever fit in. Or, for that matter, if I want to."

"I take it," Mari said, "that you aren't talking about the obvious differences between Virginia and New England, since you were well aware of them before your marriage."

"Of course I was," Elizabeth agreed, "and they seemed inconsequential. Truth be told, they still do. No amount of difference would trouble me if I could only find something familiar to hold on to in my life with Drake."

"Something of what you saw between your parents?"

Elizabeth nodded. "That's the only standard I have by which to weigh a marriage, and by that criterion, mine is a failure." She turned her head, not wanting Mari to see her tears. She cried so easily these days, undoubtedly because of her pregnancy, or at least so she told herself.

The soft rustle of Mari's skirt was the only sound in the room as the older woman sat down beside Elizabeth and took her hand. They sat together in silence for some time before Elizabeth sniffed and managed a watery smile. "Pay no attention to me. I'm very emotional these days."

"You're going through a difficult time," Mari agreed, "but I don't for a moment think it's because of the baby. Where is Drake, by the way?"

"New York." Briefly Elizabeth explained what little she knew about the business that had taken him there.

"Eventually," Mari said, "he will have to hire men who are accountable to him rather than try to run everything himself."

"He's enjoying it too much to do that."

"The novelty will wear off. A warm, loving home will tempt him away."

"That seems an impossibility at the moment," Elizabeth said.

Mari's hand tightened on hers. "I don't for a moment believe that the daughter of Sarah and Philip Calvert would give up so easily."

"I'm not," Elizabeth insisted. "But I am realistic enough to know that I can't build the sort of marriage I want all by myself. Drake has to want it, also."

"That's true, but it's up to you to show him what he will be missing if he persists on his present course."

"How?" Elizabeth asked.

"I don't know," Mari said. She smiled apologetically. "I'm sorry that I don't have any neat and tidy answers, but this is completely beyond my experience. Josiah and I got along very well, perhaps because we understood and accepted each other long before we were married."

"Whereas Drake and I seem to have been strangers."

"The fact that you can see things from his point of view as well as your own suggests that there is a great deal of hope for you to eventually work things out."

"I wonder," Elizabeth murmured, "how he imagined me to be."

"Beautiful," Mari said, "and a challenge. Drake is too much of a man to resist either. Tell the truth," she said after a moment. "How did you see him?"

Elizabeth laughed, embarrassed. "A knight, if not quite in shining armor. Handsome, strong, everything I could possibly want. Also," she added in a burst of candor, "the fact that he wanted me so much didn't hurt, either."

"Of course not. One would hardly choose an indifferent husband. But relationships, in order to survive, have to mature beyond that early stage when people are seen in idealized roles. Believe it or not, I saw Josiah in similar terms in the beginning. Over the years, I learned to know him as a man and, even more important, as a human being. He was far from perfect, but then, the same is true of myself. Sometimes I think it's our flaws that make us interesting."

"Then I must be fascinating."

Mari laughed. "Drake thinks so, and you feel the same way about him."

"You're right about my feelings, but he seems perfectly content to be away from me."

"I doubt that," Mari said. "Though he may very well find it prudent to put some distance between the two of you just now."

"Do you think I've become so difficult to deal with?" Elizabeth asked.

"As a matter of fact, I do." Mari smiled at the reaction her bluntness drew. Once again, Elizabeth flushed, though this time more with chagrin than embarrassment. "What I mean is that you are demanding things of him he doesn't know how to give. You want him to be open and honest with you, to give you his trust and respect, as well as his desire and protection."

"Is that so much to ask?"

"To a man like Drake it is. Think of it this way. Would you expect a small child to always put others first and never behave selfishly?"

"Of course not," Elizabeth said. "Small children are by nature selfish. They have to be taught to think of others."

"And a man whose only experience with family life involves a philandering father who died when he was very young and a mother who has seen him merely as a means to her own ends has to be taught to love."

That had never occurred to Elizabeth. In her experience, love was simply there. It existed as naturally as the sun that shone over the fields of her childhood. Love was something she had learned to give by first receiving. Unconsciously she had expected her relationship with Drake to follow the same pattern. Now she realized that wasn't going to happen. For once in her life, she had to take the initiative, even though that meant placing her most tender feelings at great risk.

It was impossible for her to know at first glance whether she was even capable of such action, much less how to go about it. As she looked out the window again at the bare, dripping branches set against the somber sky, she shivered. The well of doubt and loneliness inside her was growing more profound with each passing day. It undermined her native strength and made her feel as though she were being buffeted by a strong, cold wind that at any instant could overwhelm her.

She closed her eyes and let herself be swept with longing for the sweet, golden sanctuary of childhood, when everything had seemed so simple and all things were possible. She knew the impression was erroneous; nothing was simple, and everyone faced limitations. But in the life her parents had created, and that she had been fortunate enough to share, there was a moral center that held all else together. That, more than anything, was what she missed.

"I want to go home," she murmured, hardly aware that she spoke. Her hand touched her belly, and she felt the child within her stir.

FOREVER AFTER, Elizabeth was to think of her return to Calvert Oaks as at once the most impulsive action of her life and the most inevitable. Against even the obviously important anniversaries of her marriage and the births of her children, that day stood out as a turning point that shaped all that followed.

She came alone, except for her maid, Tilly, having taken advantage of Drake's absence from Boston to depart unnoticed. Not even Mari knew what she had done, though Elizabeth was certain that she could guess easily enough. Above all, she had said nothing to Abigail, not because she thought her mother-in-law would have tried to prevent her from going, but, on the contrary, because she suspected she would have done everything possible to hasten her departure.

For Drake she left a note saying simply that, having thought it over, she had decided that there was no sensible reason for her to change her plans, and she would therefore be at Calvert Oaks for Christmas. She added, after due consideration, that she hoped he would join her there as originally intended.

Whether he would or not, she had no idea. But the question preoccupied her almost from the moment she left Boston, and it continued to do so throughout the journey south. Aware of her mistress's concerns, Tilly busied herself seeing to her comfort. As an experienced traveler, having journeyed by donkey cart from her family's small farm in Fermoy to the port of Cobh, from there to England and finally all the way to Boston, she felt more than capable of making the necessary arrangements.

Given the suddenness of their departure, there had been no time to arrange for a private railroad car. Tilly had to make do with a double stateroom, set up as a parlor with a daybed, where she slept, and a spacious bedroom with bath for Elizabeth. By mercilessly harrying every employee of the railroad unfortunate enough to cross her path, she saw to it that Elizabeth was as well served as she would have been had she remained at home in Louisburg Square. Most important, she assured that her mistress's privacy was scrupulously observed.

In this she was backed up by Happenstance, who accompanied them on the journey. Princess had perforce been left behind under the care of the devoted stablehand who had been exercising her for Elizabeth ever since she stopped riding the mare herself. With the dog for company and Tilly to see to her needs, Elizabeth did not set foot outside her stateroom from the time she boarded the train in Boston until it pulled into the Richmond station.

Her father was waiting for her. She had sent him a telegram as they passed through New York, advising him of her impending arrival. But not until she saw him standing on the platform did she allow herself to think what his reaction might be.

Philip was frowning. Around him harried travelers and heavily laden porters swirled and shoved, but he remained oblivious to their presence. All his attention was focused on his daughter as she alighted from the carriage, assisted by an ostentatiously respectful conductor and followed by a stern-faced maid.

"Easy now, ma'am," Tilly said. "Watch your step, and you," she added, addressing the conductor, "clear the way here. Mrs. Bennington can't be getting poked at." Tilly had dropped enough less than subtle hints about her mistress's condition to ensure that the conductor sprang to obey. He waved his arms authoritatively as he strode ahead, his mustache quivering and whistle tooting. Before this curious spectacle, the crowd parted, all except for the tall, golden-haired man who continued to walk purposefully down the platform.

"Here now, sir," the conductor said, having thought to remove the whistle rather than risk swallowing it. "If you'll wait a moment . . ."

Philip ignored him. Indeed, it would be more accurate to say that he was unaware of so feeble an attempt to stop him. He reached his daughter and took her hand, all the while surveying her carefully. Her face was white and strained, there were shadows beneath her eyes, and he thought he spied the glint of tears, though they were swiftly suppressed.

"Father," she murmured as they embraced, "I'm so glad you're here."

"And where," he asked, holding her tenderly, "did you imagine I'd be?"

They parted enough to look at each other again. Elizabeth managed a wan smile. "I wasn't sure you'd gotten my telegram."

Philip didn't believe that, but he was wise enough not to pursue the matter, at least not then. Laying her hand over his arm, he led her through the station to the waiting carriage.

Throughout the drive to Calvert Oaks, he kept her diverted with talk of the plantation. The weather had been good, and the crops were bountiful. New workers were being hired and additional fields acquired. Several foals had been born, and each looked promising. The mill was working to full capacity; William was thinking of expanding it. He and Sunbird were both well, as was Sarah. The only sad note was that Augusta was failing. Since the wedding, she had become progressively weaker, though she assured everyone that she was not in pain.

"She misses Rameses," Philip said as they turned into the gravel drive that led to the big house. On either side of them, the ancient oak trees from which the plantation took its name cast silvered shadows of the winter sun. "Sometimes I even think she misses the old days. She says things have changed too much, but not enough."

"That sounds like Augusta," Elizabeth said. "It also makes sense."

Philip nodded. "Emancipation hasn't been what many of us hoped. On the contrary, a case can be made that it's only led to another form of slavery."

"Yet none of us would choose to turn the clock back, including Augusta."

"Some would," Philip corrected softly. "But they weren't the ones in shackles, or under the whip."

Elizabeth was silent for a moment before she asked, "How are things at Quail Run?"

"About the same."

She sighed, not wanting to think what that meant. A moment later she caught sight of twin brick chimneys silhouetted against the cloudless sky, and thoughts of everything except her homecoming vanished.

"It's as lovely as ever!" she exclaimed as she stepped from the carriage, smiling with her first genuine sign of happiness. Already the bleakness was easing from her eyes, and she looked noticeably more relaxed.

"Calvert Oaks never changes," her father said as he escorted her up the steps to the front doors.

"I was counting on that." The doors flew open, and her mother was there. Elizabeth went into her arms, and Sarah held her for far longer than would have been normal. Over her daughter's head, she exchanged a glance with Philip that spoke volumes.

"We're so glad that you're here," Sarah said when they at last went inside. Tilly had been introduced before bustling upstairs to see to the unpacking. She could be heard directing two of the servants to step carefully with a trunk, while warning another not to crush the hatboxes. At the same time, she was giving instructions for Elizabeth's bath to be readied and reminding her mistress, in an aside that floated down the stairs, that she shouldn't see how long she could be on her feet.

"She seems very... capable," Sarah said, watching her daughter as Elizabeth sat down. She noted the tension that radiated from her and wondered at its cause. "Drake must feel very confident of her to allow you to travel with no other attendant."

Elizabeth took a deep breath. She had decided during the long train ride not to tell her family the truth. It would simply have raised too many questions that she did not feel equipped to deal with. But the habit of candor had been too long bred into her to make deception of even the mildest sort easy. She lowered her eyes to her hands, folded in her lap. "Drake is away on business in New York. He hopes to join me later."

"It must be very important business," her father said, "to keep him from traveling with you."

"It is," Elizabeth assured him, hoping to head off any discussion of Drake's behavior. "He's assuming much more responsibility for the family businesses."

"I see..." Philip said. He was standing by the mantel. His face, which time had honed to a fineness not known among younger men, was set in hard lines. The blue eyes that had seen both the best and the worst the world had to offer shone with a gleam that, had Drake been present, would not have behooved well for him. He could hardly criticize his son-in-law for taking a more active role in business affairs. That was the proper sphere for a man of property and far preferable to the dilettante's existence he had led prior to his marriage. Yet neither did Philip appreciate whatever it was that had led his daughter to lie to him.

That she was lying, he was convinced. The father of two children by two different wives, he did not mistake the slight thickening of her waistline or the unconscious way she held her hands in front of her belly in the instinctive gesture of a woman seeking to protect something precious. Anger welled up in him as he considered her vulnerability and the pride that drove her to try to conceal it.

"We're delighted you were able to come," Sarah said. Even more sensitive than Philip to every nuance of their daughter's welfare, she had formed her own suspicions the moment she set eyes on Elizabeth. Later there would be time to work out whatever had gone wrong, but first she sought to deflect any confrontation between her husband and the child they both loved so dearly. "You'll have to get plenty of rest while you're here and allow us to pamper you."

Elizabeth gave her a grateful smile. "I have to admit that sounds very nice. Besides, Tilly will insist on it."

"About Drake," Philip began, only to break off as he caught his wife's warning look. With an effort, he repressed the urge to ask exactly what his son-in-law had done to cause Elizabeth to behave so uncharacteristically. For the moment it was enough that she was once again under his roof, where he could keep her safe.

"It's just as well he stayed away," Philip said to his wife a short time later as they were changing for supper. Elizabeth was lying down in her room and would be joining them later, as would Sunbird and William, who were due back shortly. Little by little, Sarah was beginning to turn some of the duties of running the big house over to her daughter-in-law, to prepare her for the day when she would be solely responsible for them.

In the aftermath of the annual hog butchering, which had taken place a few days before, Sunbird was supervising the preparation of sausages, bacon and smoked hams. The yearly chore, which Sarah had early on in her marriage learned to loathe, was less onerous than it had once been. Fewer hogs were killed as more of the products they had once supplied were purchased from outside the plantation. While traditional self-sufficiency was thereby lessened, the lot of the plantation mistress was made a bit easier, something both Sarah and Sunbird appreciated, if for no other reason than that it left more time and energy for dealing with their husbands.

"We shouldn't jump to any conclusions," Sarah said as she turned around to allow her husband access to the buttons of her day dress. Her maid could as easily have undone them for her, but Sarah and Philip preferred to be alone whenever possible. Besides, he enjoyed doing such intimate chores for her.

"What else can we think," he asked when the buttons were undone, "except that they've argued? Elizabeth is far too reasonable to go off on her own without cause."

Sarah cast him a sidelong look from beneath her lashes, a look that managed to suggest without quite saying so that he was not the best judge of his daughter's actions. Philip had been besotted with her from infancy and had never lost the habit of believing that she was immune from all human failings. Somehow he had managed to juggle that tendency with the occasional need to impose fatherly discipline, but it had never been easy for him, and since her marriage, he had given up the effort altogether.

Sarah, on the other hand, saw things far more objectively, if only because she, too, was a woman and a wife, and she knew the difficulties inherent in those states.

"The early days of marriage are never easy," she said as she stepped out of the dress. "Problems are bound to crop up."

"Which a good, loving husband is more than capable of dealing with. The idea that she should have felt desperate enough to go off with only a maid is preposterous. I can only conclude that Drake drove her to it." As he spoke, he wrenched off his collar and tossed it on the dresser in a gesture that suggested he would have liked to dispose of his son-in-law as easily. "The damn fool. What the hell could he have been thinking of to let matters reach such a point?"

"Perhaps he doesn't understand how she feels," Sarah suggested. "Men don't always, you know."

The gentle words were a reminder that their own marriage had known its share of difficulties, especially in the early years, when their disparate backgrounds caused them to clash more than once.

"I can hardly claim to have been the perfect husband," Philip said as he removed his shirt, "but you never felt driven to leave me."

"I thought about it."

His hands stilled on the buckle of his belt, and he stared at her. "When?"

"During the war. You were away so much, and when you were here, there were such misunderstandings between us. It occurred to me that I could return to Boston. It would have been difficult, but I could have managed it."

His hands dropped to his sides, his eyes locked with hers. "Yet you stayed."

She folded her petticoat before answering him. "Yes, but my circumstances were different from Elizabeth's. If I had left, I could hardly have expected you to follow me."

"Do you think that's what she expects?"

"I don't know," Sarah admitted. "But the possibility must certainly have occurred to her."

"He'd better think twice before he shows up here."

Sarah smiled to herself and shook her head. "If you were he, would you hesitate?"

"No," Philip admitted as he pulled the shutters closed across one of the bedroom windows. Sarah, dressed now only in a lacy camisole and slip, did the same. "But then," he added, "I would never have been so foolish as to let you get away."

"Drake doesn't realize how spirited Elizabeth can be."

"Who," Philip asked as he reached for his wife, "do you suppose she gets that from?"

"I would say," Sarah murmured as a familiar heat began to steal over her, "that the poor child got a double dose."

Philip laughed deep in his throat. "Perhaps Drake does deserve a bit of sympathy."

"Nonsense, he only needs to appreciate how fortunate he is to have a wife who isn't all milk and whey."

"Dreadful combination," her husband said against the silken smoothness of her throat. "I prefer a much spicier dish."

As he proceeded to demonstrate to their mutual satisfaction.

AFTER WAKING the following morning in the room that had been hers for so many years, Elizabeth lay curled on her side with her eyes closed. For several minutes she played a little game that dated from her childhood: if she concentrated hard enough, when she opened her eyes everything would be exactly as she wished it to be. The sun would be shining, birds would be singing and Drake would be at her side. Not the distant, preoccupied stranger who had left her alone in Boston, but the handsome prince she had imagined she was marrying. A paragon of sensitivity and consideration who would beg her pardon for causing her the slightest unhappiness before vowing to make her life perfect from that moment on.

Barely had the fantasy begun than it sputtered to a halt. She made a feeble attempt to restore it before giving up. Some illusions were too absurd to be indulged, even in dreams. As Mari had said, Drake was a man, not a creation of her own imagination. He had a separate existence from her, just as she did from him. Each had been shaped in ways that might take a lifetime to fully understand.

In the safety of her bed, she could accept what she had not been able to while still in Boston. She and Drake would never see everything exactly the same way, never agree on all matters, perhaps never even cease to surprise and on occasion frustrate each other. But that did not mean that they couldn't have a successful marriage, provided she hadn't ended all hope of that by leaving Boston.

She was glad enough to have that train of thought interrupted by Tilly, who bustled in with a breakfast tray. "You've got to keep your strength up, ma'am," she said as she laid it across Elizabeth's knees. "And don't be tellin' me that your stomach's misbehavin'. If you could eat even a morsel on that nasty train, you can eat anywhere."

"I thought you liked the train," Elizabeth said before she obediently took a sip of coffee liberally laced with thick cream. Fluffy scrambled eggs, a thick slice of bacon and fresh cinnamon buns completed the repast. To her surprise, she found that she was actually hungry.

"I liked it about as well as a person can who's being shaken from head to toe," Tilly said as she went over to the armoire to begin laying out her mistress's clothes. "Give me a ship any day. Better yet, a nice calm donkey. Takes you a while to get places in a donkey cart, that's true, but at least you're all in one piece when you do."

"We'd have a hard time getting back to Boston that way," Elizabeth said, nodding her acceptance of the blue and white silk dress Tilly held up for her approval. It was one that she had recently had let out and it was therefore still comfortable, though she could not expect to get away with such measures for very long. If she stayed more than a short time at Calvert Oaks, she would have to tell her family of her pregnancy, certainly before she had to resort to the sacque dresses designed for expectant ladies.

At least no one would expect her to stay sequestered inside once her pregnancy showed, as would undoubtedly have been the case in Boston. She could go for walks, help her mother and Sunbird and even join in some of the Christmas entertainments. There would be plenty for her to occupy herself with for some time to come.

"Have you any idea when we'll be going back, ma'am?" Tilly asked. She sought to give the impression that the matter was of no particular importance to her, but Elizabeth was not misled. She knew that the maid was far too intelligent not to understand the implications of their departure.

"We've only just arrived," she pointed out. "There's no rush getting back."

Tilly sniffed. "As you say, ma'am."

Elizabeth finished her breakfast and was dressing when there was a knock on the bedroom door. Tilly answered it and stood aside to admit Sunbird, who greeted her sister-in-law with a smile. Despite the hard work of the past few days, the young woman looked radiant. Only a shadow of worry darkened her deep brown eyes, and that lifted as she saw Elizabeth. "You look well rested," she said, perching on the edge of the bed. "Much better than last night."

"I was worn out," Elizabeth admitted. Tilly went back to brushing her mistress's hair, arranging it in a circlet of braids pinned to the back of her head and decorated with silk flowers that matched her dress. Elizabeth glanced at herself in the mirror and was satisfied by what she saw. She thought she looked remarkably self-possessed considering the turmoil going on inside her.

Sunbird, however, was not fooled. She remembered the concerns William had expressed after they retired the previous night. He was deeply worried about his sister, convinced that something had to be done to help her, and frustrated as to what that might be.

So was Sunbird. She was still so new to the family that she was hesitant about interfering in any way. Moreover, she was inclined to believe that Elizabeth should be allowed the privilege of solving her problems for herself. This was so novel an idea where women were concerned that she was reluctant even to mention it, yet she had noticed over dinner that Sarah, too, seemed disinclined to step in.

Accustomed as she was to making her own decisions, if only thanks to the negligence of her father and stepmother, Sunbird, too, had found difficulties in the adjustment to marriage. But in her case these were greatly eased by the love she and William shared, a love she still sometimes could not quite believe in, despite the daily evidence of it.

"You must tell me all about life in Boston," she said as they left Elizabeth's room and went down the curving marble stairs to the main floor. "In your letters, you mentioned that you're furnishing a house."

Relieved to have so impersonal a topic offered to her, Elizabeth described her efforts while they strolled outside and walked in the direction of the stables. Behind them were the pastures, where the new colts gamboled with their mothers. Leaning against the white picket fence, the two women observed them with smiles.

"I miss all this," Elizabeth said after a moment. The care Sunbird had taken not to intrude on her private thoughts had relaxed her enough to make this admission. She trusted the other woman not to seize the opening to pry into feelings she was not ready to reveal.

Her faith was not misplaced. Sunbird merely nodded and said, "It must have been hard to leave such a home."

In a burst of frankness she had not intended, Elizabeth said, "If I had thought about it more carefully, I might not have had the courage to go."

"And that would have been a shame, wouldn't it?"

"I suppose..."

"Elizabeth...I don't want to overstep myself, but if you will allow, there is just one thing I'd like to say."

"What's that?"

"I think Drake and I have something in common that may be hard for you to understand. Neither of us knows very much about love. I'm still learning what it means, and I suspect he is, too.''

''Someone else pointed that out to me recently.''

''But you don't believe it?''

''On the contrary, it makes perfect sense.''

''Then why...?''

''Why am I here without him?''

Sunbird nodded. ''It's two weeks to Christmas. You could have waited in Boston for him to return, or gone to New York with him.''

''That's true, but I happen to like Virginia better than either of those places.''

She looked away as she spoke, staring sightlessly at a colt that leaped high before it raced across the pasture. Its patient mother stood off to one side, watching. When the colt, exhausted, came to her, she nuzzled it gently.

''Of course,'' Sunbird said, ''your private affairs should remain exactly that, private.''

It took Elizabeth a moment to realize that her sister-in-law was politely telling her that she didn't believe her. She could hardly blame her, but neither could she bring herself to tell the truth. The day before, in the aftermath of her trip, she had thought it was simple fatigue that prompted her to dissemble. But now she realized that it was something more: loyalty to Drake and to their marriage kept her silent. That and pride, which made it impossible for her to admit that the venture she had embarked on with such vaunting confidence was turning out to be far more difficult than she could ever have imagined.

It grew even more so as several days passed and no word came from Drake. She was hard-pressed to pretend that this was what she had expected. Tilly, observing her attempts, took to sniffing often and audibly. Moreover, whenever the maid happened to be in the vicinity of Sarah or Philip, she made pointed references to the need for her mistress to rest and eat more. Elizabeth remonstrated with her about it, but to no effect. Tilly had her own ideas about what was right, and nothing could shake her from them.

Elizabeth was, in her own way, just as stubborn. She held her head high and got through each day without faltering. It was only at night, when she lay alone in her room, that her fears overcame her and she wept, silently and, as night followed night, with increasing despair.

Until Drake came.

He arrived when she had been at Calvert Oaks for eight days. Elizabeth was out on the veranda, watching as several of the servants draped the doors with boughs of evergreen and mistletoe. From the nearby kitchen succulent aromas wafted. They had been busy for days making fruitcakes, plum puddings, mincemeat and benne brittle. The latter was a particular favorite of Elizabeth's; she loved the taste of the sesame seeds that were its chief ingredient.

Augusta had even felt well enough to come down to the kitchen for a few hours, but her strength had soon failed her, and she had reluctantly returned to the room under the eaves that she had occupied for more than half a century. Elizabeth meant to visit her there shortly, taking with her a pot of chamomile tea and some biscuits stuffed with ham as she did about that time each day. She had greater success than anyone else in persuading Augusta to eat, and she was thinking about what else she might tempt her with when she happened to glance down the road and see the column of dust that heralded an arriving visitor.

Moments later a hired carriage pulled to a stop and the door opened. Elizabeth stood very still as a tall, somber-faced man stepped out, paid the driver and dismissed him. Only then did Drake look at her.

He stood at the bottom of the steps leading up to the veranda, his single traveling case on the ground beside him. He was hatless in the late-afternoon sun. A slight breeze off the river ruffled the hair that glowed like beaten gold. His eyes were hooded, and there were deep lines etched into his face.

Elizabeth thought that he looked tired. That was her first impression, but hard on it came another: he was angry, more so than she had ever seen him. She could almost feel him struggling to control himself as he climbed the steps to her.

She stood frozen into immobility, torn between the temptation to flee and the equally strong urge to stay and face whatever might be coming. Sheer practicality dictated that she remain where she was, if only because there was no place else to go. In an instant she realized that by withdrawing to the one place where she felt truly safe, she had effectively cut off all other lines of retreat. She was trapped.

Drake knew it. His lips, thin with tension, curled faintly. He inclined his head in a gesture of courtesy as meaningless as it was automatic, then took her arm, turning her toward the door.

"What have you told them?" he demanded without preamble.

She did not have to wonder why he asked. Pride drove him as remorselessly as it did herself. "That you had business in New York."

"And therefore you came on without me?"

Elizabeth nodded. His fingers were digging into her soft flesh, yet she felt no pain. A blessed numbness had settled over her. She was only dimly aware of entering the hall. Alerted by the arrival of the carriage, Philip had left his office, where he had been catching up on correspondence. He stood, cigar in hand, watching them.

"Good afternoon, sir," Drake said without relinquishing his hold on Elizabeth. On the contrary, he drew her closer into what might have looked to the unobservant to be a tender embrace.

Philip was not misled. He frowned, but forbore revealing his thoughts as he studied the pair. "I hope you had a pleasant journey."

"Very agreeable," Drake said, ignoring the fact that his travel-stained trousers and disheveled shirt revealed that he had traveled hard and fast. He had not slept since leaving Boston, but rest was the farthest thing from his mind. A great many matters had to be settled before he would lay down his head at Calvert Oaks.

"If you don't mind, sir," he said, "I'd like to freshen up."

"By all means," Philip said, as rigidly correct as his son-in-law. He waved a hand to the footman passing through the hall. "Have a bath drawn for Mr. Bennington and see that his bags are unpacked."

"Only one bag," Drake said with a faint smile. "I prefer to travel light."

The two men looked at each other as Elizabeth held her breath. She could sense the barely suppressed conflict between the two, even if she could not fully understand it. A long moment passed before Philip said, "I'm sure we can make you comfortable."

"Your hospitality is appreciated."

"But not, I trust, abused."

Silence again as the point sank in. Drake inclined his head, his smile sardonic. "As you say, sir."

Satisfied, if only temporarily, Philip returned to his office. With her husband's arm still firm around her waist, Elizabeth had no choice but to accompany him upstairs. When she balked slightly, he said from between clenched teeth, "I'll carry you if I have to. If anyone sees us, we should look quite romantic."

"Don't bother," she muttered. The thought of being in his arms was more than she could bear. Grimly determined to reveal none of her inner turmoil, she held her back rigidly straight as they climbed the stairs and walked down the hallway to her room.

_____ *Chapter Nineteen*

THE DOOR HAD BARELY CLOSED behind them when Drake dropped his arm from around her and stepped away. Without looking at her, he said, "I've never been a violent man, but you tempt me to it."

Elizabeth inhaled sharply. Threats were hardly the way to win her over. But then, when had Drake ever cared about how she felt? Surely not since their marriage, when he put his stamp of possession on her and presumed that from then on she would do exactly as he expected.

"Go ahead," she said, her voice low and hard. "Isn't that how men always respond when a woman dares to stand up to them? Perhaps it will make you feel better to remind me that you're stronger than I am and that you can hurt me."

Drake looked at her wearily. "No, it won't. But you already know that, or you wouldn't be so bold."

Stubbornly, Elizabeth shook her head. "I don't know anything of the sort. As far as I'm concerned, you're a mystery."

She was surprised when he laughed, humorlessly and with a faint edge of desperation. "How odd, since I could say exactly the same thing about you."

"Me? But that's ridiculous. I—"

He raised a hand, cutting her off. "Let's not argue about which of us is the more incomprehensible. There are far more important matters requiring our attention."

"Such as?"

"Such as why you left Boston and when you intend to return."

"I left because I wanted to spend Christmas here. As to when I return . . . that's up to you."

"Is it? I got the distinct impression that I have virtually nothing to say about where you go or what you do."

A flash of sorrow rippled through her. She regretted making him feel that way. "You don't mean that."

He turned away from her, started to light a cigar, thought better of it and tossed it on the table. "How could you expect me to feel otherwise? I wanted you to stay in Boston for your own welfare and the welfare of our child. That seems a perfectly reasonable request, yet you—"

"It wasn't."

"Wasn't reasonable? Why not? You may like to think that you're impervious to the slightest weakness, but the fact is you need looking after. There's nothing wrong with that."

"I didn't say there was. What I meant was that you didn't ask me to stay in Boston. You simply decided that was the way it was going to be and there was to be no further discussion."

"Are you seriously telling me that you came here because of some failure of tact on my part?"

"It sounds foolish when you put it that way, but—"

"Foolish?" he interrupted. "It sounds positively asinine. Of all the stupid, thoughtless things you could have done . . ."

"If that's your attitude, I don't see any point in our discussing this further."

"Oh, no, that's the mistake I made before, as you just reminded me. This time we talk, whether you want to or not."

Despite herself, Elizabeth smiled. "You can hardly force someone to speak against her will, at least, not if you wish to retain any claim to being a gentleman."

He frowned, frustrated by the truth of her words. "You aren't a child to sulk."

"I'm not a child, period. For some reason, I seem to have to keep pointing that out." She was remembering Jack and his attempts to deny his own feelings by treating her as though she were far more innocent and far less capable than she actually was. Perhaps Drake was doing something similar.

That thought had never occurred to her before. She turned it over for a moment, letting the confidence it inspired seep through her. If Drake did feel driven to protect himself from her, it implied that he was vulnerable in some way. Which, given her own susceptibility to him, put them on a far more equal footing.

"Would you really want to be married to a child?" she asked. "Someone who was both subject and tyrant, who would be completely dependent on you, but who would also rule you by that very dependency? Is that truly what you want?"

"I don't know," Drake admitted slowly. "Put that way, it hardly sounds attractive. But I've always presumed that women were capable of nothing else."

"And I always presumed the opposite: that a wife is supposed to be a true friend and helpmate."

They faced each other across the short distance separating them, aware that a far greater gulf loomed on the emotional landscape. Their contrasting expectations seemed to defy resolution. The patterns of their lives had been set, as was always the case, in childhood. They were caught in them as surely as though they were trapped in a spider's web.

Or at least, Drake was. For Elizabeth, the experience was different. Love did not trap, it freed, and she had always had the benefit of love.

"Drake," she said, gathering her courage, "I need you very much. It's not the kind of dependency you expected from a woman, but it's very real, nonetheless."

Wanting to believe her, but afraid to do so, he said, "If that's the case, why did you come back here?"

When he had asked her that before, she had given him the most superficial answer she could. Now she was driven to greater honesty. "Because I couldn't stand being in Boston. When you were there, it was like living with a stranger. But when you left, I didn't feel any relief. All I felt was loneliness that not even Mari, no matter how much she tried, could ease."

Drake understood such loneliness. He was beginning to realize that it had dogged him all his life. Not until he had met Elizabeth had he allowed himself to feel the need for true intimacy that went far beyond the physical.

With a faint, self-deprecatory smile, he said, "I used to think everything was so simple."

Tentatively, she smiled in return. "There was a time when I felt the same way."

Her honesty was rewarded with his own. "I can't promise to be what you want."

Her smile faded. Implacable realities were never pleasant, but avoiding them only made them worse. That much she had learned. "I can't make *you* that promise, either."

"Many people live without ever achieving what they feel is most necessary to them."

True enough. She had known such people. Counted them, in fact, among her relatives at Quail Run. "But they don't live well. The thought of such an arid existence terrifies me."

He had to admit that it terrified him, too, although not very long ago he had taken it for granted, not thinking it arid at all. He had come to manhood presuming that what satisfactions life did have to offer were external, to be seized as hard-won booty from a grudging world. Now, distantly, he was beginning to sense that there were satisfactions to be won from within himself.

But that thought was as yet too formless to even be called a hope, whereas the fear that he was wrong, that there were

no such possibilities to be found, was immediate and real.
Part of him resented Elizabeth for cutting through the
carefully constructed wall that had shielded his inner self
throughout almost his entire life. She dared him to place
himself at risk and damn the consequences.

He was not ready to do that, but he was prepared to take
a first step toward reconciliation.

"Do I take it," he said, "that you would prefer not to return to Boston until after the baby is born?"

Startled by an option she had not even dared to consider,
Elizabeth nodded. "It's true. I would like the baby to be
born here."

"Because you feel safer?"

He had summed up her feelings at their most elemental,
which suggested that he understood her far better than she
had thought. "Yes," she said slowly, "that's it."

"Then you should stay."

Such an unexpected answer took her aback. It seemed to
suggest that he could do very well without her. "And
you . . . ?"

He hesitated, long enough for her to wish that she hadn't
asked. What did she expect him to say? That he cared for
nothing except her and could not be dragged from her side?
If she believed that, she would be back in the same romantic fantasy she had rejected earlier. His life was elsewhere.
She had to accept that and go on with her own as best she
could.

But when Drake spoke again, he surprised her. "There is
a great deal I have to attend to," he said, "some of it in
Boston and some elsewhere. I do need to see quite a few
people in Washington. . . ." He paused for a moment before
deciding. "I'll stay here through the holidays, then take care
of my business elsewhere before moving on to Washington.
That way I'll be able to visit from time to time, and be here
when the baby is due. All right?"

The very fact that he asked her opinion warmed Elizabeth almost as much as the knowledge that he would not leave her alone. She nodded quickly, before she could think of how important he had become to her. "Yes, I'd like that."

Concerned that he might have given her the wrong impression, he added, "Of course, I'm not sure how often I'll be here."

"I understand."

Oddly enough, she did. Drake was afraid, but that was all right, because so was she. Even fear was better than the emptiness she had glimpsed away from him.

They had come upstairs in the grip of so much tension that its sudden disappearance left them at something of a loss. They stood looking at each other, neither sure of what to say or do next. The problem was solved for them when a servant knocked discreetly at the bedroom door to tell Drake that his bath was ready.

He went almost with a sense of relief, needing some time to himself. Elizabeth lay down on the bed, listening to his faint movements from the room next door. She heard him dismiss the servant, then heard the sound of his boots hitting the floor as he removed them, before the water splashed softly. She closed her eyes, imagining the long, hard length of him naked and at ease. Her own body tightened.

With a sigh, she touched her thickening waist. The impulse to go to him was very strong, but lately she had become uncertain about her attractiveness. The child was making itself felt more each day. Besides her greatly expanded waistline, her breasts were much heavier, and her belly was no longer the small, soft pillow it had been in early pregnancy. It was far larger now, and harder. Occasionally it rippled with the baby's movements.

A tiny smile touched her lips. It was only just beginning to sink in to her that her child would be born at Calvert Oaks. Augusta might not be able to assist, but her mother would be there. There would be none of Dr. Greeley and his dreaded ether. Already she felt safer and more at peace.

When Drake returned to the room, he found her lying on top of the counterpane, curled on her side and fast asleep. For a long time he stood staring down at her, watching the way the light and shadows played across her features. Her lips were slightly parted, and he could see the gentle rise and fall of her breasts as she slept.

Desire stirred within him, but he suppressed it. She needed to rest, as, now that he thought about it, did he. Carefully he stretched out on the bed beside her and drew her into his arms. He held her tenderly, cherishing both her and the life nestled in her womb.

It was a shock to realize how precious they were to him. He had wanted the child from the first, but more as a symbol of his own transition from boy to man rather than for its own sake. That had changed. Now he thought of the child to come as a bond that would forever unite him with Elizabeth. No matter what else might happen between them, there would be something in the world that they had created together.

That thought reassured him. He, too, slept deeply as the old house held them safe, if only for the moment.

TRUE TO HIS WORD, Drake remained at Calvert Oaks for Christmas and New Year's. Elizabeth had feared that he might be champing at the bit to get back to business, but instead he gave every sign of being content to stay.

On Christmas Eve, when the family gathered in the parlor to exchange gifts, Elizabeth at last told them that she was expecting a baby. They didn't pretend to be surprised, but showered both her and Drake with congratulations. Philip ordered several bottles of champagne to be opened, and a toast was drunk to the coming child and its parents.

Afterward the family attended a service at the church where several generations of Calverts had worshiped. It did not occur to Elizabeth that anything might be amiss until she stepped from the carriage, assisted by Drake. Barely had she taken a few steps up the path than she noticed a flaw in the order of things that rang sharply in her mind.

The terraced lawn in front of the church was a traditional meeting place for neighbors. Before any service, greetings were exchanged, news was traded and, on occasion, business was done. That had not changed except that the Calverts were no longer included in the easy camaraderie. The standards, however, for such acceptance appeared to have been loosened, at least enough to include Charles Durand and his wife. They, like the others, made a show of ignoring the Calverts, though Sunbird's overblown stepmother could not resist a sneer in her direction.

Wary looks followed them as they made their way up the path. Philip and Sarah led the way, with William and Sunbird directly behind them. Drake and Elizabeth came last, and that position allowed them to see clearly what was going on.

An avid tension gripped the attentive clusters of men and women who had come to celebrate the birth of their Savior. They leaned forward eagerly as the small party approached a group standing just outside the church.

Jeremy Hudson turned slowly. As a youth, he had been tall and slender, with an engaging shyness and a lack of complication about his personality that had won him many friends. All that had changed. In place of height, his shoulders were stooped and his back bent, as though he were decades older than his true age. His face had the pouches and sags of dissipation; his nose was swollen and streaked with broken blood vessels. The body that had once possessed a young man's grace was bloated and moved only with difficulty.

He was not sober, but then he hadn't been in longer than anyone could remember. Despite the mint leaves his wife had made him chew before leaving for church, an odor of

bourbon clung to him. Still, he wasn't yet falling down
drunk, though he would be before the night was over. At the
moment he was still sober enough to recognize his brother-
in-law.

With a jerk that set him slightly off balance, he attempted to draw himself erect. His jaw worked spasmodically, and the light that entered his bleary eyes suggested
violence.

Kitty laid a hand on his shoulder. She would not meet
Philip's gaze but stood with her mouth set in a hard line,
deliberately looking away from him. Only Davey appeared
to be at ease. He smiled at them, though his gaze never left
Elizabeth. Deliberately he let it wander over her with a di-
rectness that made Drake stiffen.

"Happy holiday, cousin," Davey said, loudly enough for
their avid audience to hear. Unlike his father, he was coldly
sober, but that only made him all the more dangerous. He
inclined his head with mocking courtesy. "Still playing the
lady, I see, and very well. We might almost be fooled if we
didn't know the Calverts better."

Drake took a step forward, only to be intercepted by
William. With quiet urgency he said, "That's what he wants
you to do, so he and his craven friends will have an excuse
to go after you. They're afraid to attack us directly, but
you'd be an acceptable target."

"That hardly concerns me," Drake muttered, pressing
forward to get at the man who watched him with a mixture
of eagerness and fear. In the back of his mind, it occurred
to him that his wife's cousin was not rational, but that
thought was blotted out by the force of his own anger, which
drove him to want to wipe out the insult in the most graphic
way possible.

"Perhaps it doesn't," William said, "but Elizabeth is
concerned. Look at her."

Against his will, Drake dragged his attention away from
Davey. What he saw drew him up sharply. Elizabeth had

gone ashen. Her hands were clasped tightly together, but nothing could still their trembling. In fact, her whole body seemed to shake. She was looking at him with huge eyes gone unnaturally dark, in which he could clearly read both her terror and her pleading.

His anger was swiftly forgotten as tenderness overcame him. Swiftly, he put an arm around her and murmured, "Don't be afraid. He isn't worth that."

"He isn't worth you," she corrected through lips still tight with dread. "Please, forget him."

To his surprise, Drake found that he was able to do so. Concern for Elizabeth outweighed all else. Gently he smiled at her, indicating his acceptance, and was rewarded by a sudden easing of tension that caused her to slump against him slightly.

But by the time they had entered the church and taken their places in the family pew, Elizabeth had recovered enough to be angry herself. She could not bear the thought that those she loved had been subjected to such treatment without her even knowing about it. Drake glanced down at her sympathetically. Softly, so that only she could hear him, he asked, "They said nothing of this in their letters?"

She shook her head. "I was led to believe that everything was fine."

"Clearly it's not."

"Damn Davey and the rest of them."

On that note, the service began. Elizabeth tried to join in, but found that she could barely go through the motions. The joy she had always before felt at such a time eluded her. Her thoughts were dark as the final prayers were said and the bells rung.

They left the church much as they had entered it. Only the minister spoke with them, and he did so cautiously, one eye on the other congregants, whose tight-lipped glances made their disapproval clear. Philip and Sarah appeared oblivious to the coldness of their fellow worshipers, as did William and Sunbird. They conducted themselves as though nothing whatsoever was wrong. Elizabeth could not match their composure. Her face was flushed, and she seethed inwardly throughout the ride back to the house.

Once there, her mother and Sunbird went upstairs to check on Augusta. Elizabeth stayed below, knowing that, fading though she was, the old woman would sense her turmoil and be troubled by it. She took a seat near the fire in the parlor, accepted a small glass of sherry from the butler and listened restively as the men talked business.

Drake was developing a considerable interest in the growing and marketing of cotton. He had recently purchased several mills and, in addition, was a partner in a railroad venture that would ship both raw materials and finished goods throughout the country. He spoke knowledgeably of the problems inherent in reaching remote markets, and Philip and William listened respectfully.

Philip, in particular, liked what he heard. He was unexpectedly impressed by this son-in-law of his, who seemed to have matured in several satisfactory ways since his marriage. Above all, Philip approved of his attentiveness to Elizabeth. As involved as Drake was in their conversation, he looked at her frequently, as though to assure himself of her well-being.

As well he might since Elizabeth was becoming increasingly agitated. Her fingers drummed on the arm of her chair. She had given up trying to listen to the men and was staring into the fire, her brow knit in concentration.

At last Philip said, "What's troubling you, Bethie?"

It had been so long since anyone had called her by that childhood name that she was momentarily taken aback. A quick sheen of tears sprang to her eyes at the cascade of tender memories it evoked. She blinked them back furiously and shook her head.

"I'm not troubled; I'm angry. How can you put up with it?"

No one had to ask what she meant. Philip merely sighed, William looked concerned and Drake touched a gentle hand to her shoulder, as though to calm and restrain her. It didn't work. Instead her agitation increased. "It's despicable! Davey was the one in the wrong. What William did was absolutely right. If anything, he was too easy on him."

"That's the problem," her father said quietly. At her puzzled look, he went on. "They can't forgive William for behaving more honorably than any of them. It's intolerable to them that he is a far better representative of our Southern traditions than any white-hooded coward."

"There's nothing to be concerned about," William interjected. "Given time, the whole matter will be forgotten."

"How can you say that?" Elizabeth demanded. "I'll never forget what it was like at the church. The insult—"

"Don't you see?" William broke in. "None of that matters. By feeling this way, you're making those people far more important than they should be. You're giving them power over you."

Elizabeth had not thought of that. She was still young enough that her reactions were instinctive. Only gradually was she learning to step back a pace and consider whether or not they were valid.

"I'm not . . ." she protested.

"You are," Drake said gently. What William said also gave him pause. He had put into words something Drake had known for years, but had never before really thought about. Since childhood, he had sensed that much of what went on between people had to do with power, who possessed it and who bowed before it. That had certainly been the case with his parents, and it was also true of almost every other relationship to which he had been a party.

Except for his marriage. Not that Elizabeth hadn't made it clear that she refused to be subordinate to him. But she did so within the far larger context of respect for both herself and him, respect that ultimately was the foundation of love.

"Don't let them hurt you," he said as his eyes held hers. "What does it matter what they think of your family? Their opinion is meaningless. All that counts is what we think of each other."

Drake did not notice the pronoun he had used, but Elizabeth did. She was vividly aware that he had said "we" rather than "you." Without even realizing it, he was identifying himself as a Calvert.

Philip also noticed. He exchanged a quick glance with his son before gesturing to the butler to refill their glasses. Sarah and Sunbird returned then, but their minds were still on Augusta, and they did not notice the fading echoes of tension in the room.

Sarah sat down on the couch with a sigh. She had learned long ago to accept the inevitability of death, and to be grateful when it came without great suffering. But letting Augusta go was still difficult for her.

"How is she?" Philip asked as he took his place beside his wife. His fingers pressed hers lightly, imparting warmth and strength.

"She's in no pain," Sarah said, "and she seems genuinely happy. I suppose that's more than we have any right to ask for."

Elizabeth frowned. The incident at the church had pushed Augusta from her mind, if only temporarily. Regretting that, she began to glimpse what William had meant. It was not in her to be manipulated by others, particularly not those who intended only harm.

With an effort, she put her thoughts of Davey and the others aside and listened to what her mother was saying. Sarah had deliberately turned the conversation in a more pleasant direction.

"It's hard to believe," she said, smiling at her husband, "that by this time next year we'll be grandparents."

Philip nodded, his eyes appreciative as they lingered on her. "You hardly look old enough."

Sarah laughed, pleased by his flattery even as she dismissed it. "I wasn't a young girl when Elizabeth was born, and I'm hardly one now. How quickly the time goes by." She spoke without regret, a woman satisfied with how her life was turning out. Listening to her, her daughter wondered if the day would come when she felt the same.

Her mind was drifting over that tantalizing question when she happened to focus on William and Sunbird. The two were sitting close together on the couch, holding hands. Her brother's face was alight with such love and tenderness, returned in full measure by Sunbird, that Elizabeth's throat tightened. She had to swallow painfully, knowing as she did that she and Drake did not look at each other in such an open, unguarded way. They approached each other with the instinctive wariness of well-matched opponents who did not make the mistake of underestimating each other.

"About next year," Sunbird said, just as Elizabeth began to wonder at the sudden shyness that had settled over her, bringing a blush to her cheeks and a faintly bemused smile to her lips.

"About grandchildren..." William said, looking very pleased with himself.

Thoroughly diverted from herself, Elizabeth exclaimed, "You, too?"

Her sister-in-law nodded with an air of wonder, as though she herself could hardly believe it yet.

"But that's marvelous," Sarah said, in her excitement looking very much like the young girl she had said she wasn't. Her eyes danced as she rose to embrace both Elizabeth and Sunbird. "My two daughters," she said, clearly deeply moved. "And so soon..." Her voice broke with happiness, and she turned to Philip, who took her in his arms and embraced her tenderly.

Over her head, he said what they were all thinking. "Compared to this double blessing, nothing else matters. We truly could not be more fortunate."

Elizabeth had to agree. Feeling as she did about her own child, she was delighted for William and Sunbird. But more than that, it was a revelation to her to see how Drake responded.

He thrust out his hand to William with unfeigned enthusiasm. "Congratulations. That's the best news a man can get."

"I was taken aback at first," William admitted, "it being so soon. But it's amazing how quickly the idea grows on you."

The women exchanged amused glances as the men soberly agreed with each other that birth was indeed a miracle. The butler filled champagne glasses, and for the second time in a few short hours, the health of an unborn child was drunk.

"Have you thought about what you'll name him?" Drake asked, still surprising Elizabeth with the degree of his interest.

"Or her," Sunbird chimed in.

Drake looked momentarily taken aback. "Yes, of course, it might be a girl." He glanced at his wife as though the possibility that she, too, could produce a daughter had only just occurred to him.

Elizabeth smiled to conceal a sudden spurt of unease. While she hardly expected him to actually reject a daughter, it was easy to presume that he would be disappointed. The thought that she might go through so much and in the end have her efforts unappreciated troubled her deeply.

The others continued to talk of the coming children as Elizabeth sank more deeply into silence. That did not go unnoticed by her mother, who understood the cause, but was too wise to try to intervene. Instead, after a time, Sarah said, "It seems almost superfluous, but do let's open our presents."

A round table covered with a lacy cloth was piled high with gaily wrapped gifts. As he did each year, Philip took over the task of handing them out, and soon a happy babble of exclamations and laughter filled the room.

Elizabeth had given considerable thought to her gift to Drake. Since she had left Boston so hurriedly, without knowing whether or not he would join her, she had brought nothing with her for him. It had required a special trip into Richmond to secure the magnificently tooled saddle of Spanish leather. She held her breath as it was drawn from beneath the table, where the lace cloth had concealed it, since it had been too big to wrap and put out with the other gifts.

"Now who could this be for?" Philip inquired as he fingered the small card attached to it. He knew the answer perfectly well, but was enjoying drawing out the moment. As a superb horseman in his own right, he approved of his daughter's taste and hoped that her husband had the sense to appreciate the compliment she was paying him by suggesting that he rode well enough to merit such an excellent saddle.

Drake did. After an initial moment of surprise when the gift was revealed as being for him, he took it between his hands, holding it easily despite its weight, and turned it this way and that, admiring every inch of it. "Magnificent," he said. "I've never seen better." Turning to his wife, he added softly, "Thank you, Elizabeth. This will always mean a great deal to me."

She flushed at his praise, though she attempted to brush it aside. "It was an obvious choice, since you do enjoy riding."

Drake's gift to her was far smaller and elaborately wrapped in golden paper, with a sprig of mistletoe someone had laboriously fashioned from fine cloth attached to the ribbons. Elizabeth opened it with a faint sense of reluctance, supposing that she would find some fabulous piece of jewelry inside.

The irony of her attitude did not escape her; the vast majority of women would be thrilled by such a gift. But she regarded it as somehow impersonal, the automatic response of a rich man to a woman who has pleased him. That brought a wry smile to her lips as she undid the wrappings. Since that wasn't the case, perhaps it wasn't jewelry at all.

It was, but not what Elizabeth had expected. Instead of the cold glint of the diamonds she had thought to see, it was the warm glow of gold in the form of a heart-shaped locket that met her eye. She gave a low murmur of appreciation as she lifted it from its velvet-lined box and held it up to admire.

"Drake, it's lovely."

"It's rather more modest than what I would ordinarily have given you," he said, "but, I thought, more appropriate." He leaned down to her, showing her how the locket opened and the spaces within for two small images.

"I thought," he went on, "that we would have a photograph made of the baby, and you could wear it in here."

Elizabeth looked up, meeting his eyes. "There are two spaces."

He shrugged, as though slightly abashed. "We might have another child."

"Or several, in which case I shall quickly run out of room."

"Well, as to that, a locket does have only two sides."

"True, and I really wouldn't like to walk around with one of them empty for some time. No," she said decisively, "I think I shall have to have a photograph of you, as well."

Drake flushed, a phenomenon so extraordinary that it took Elizabeth a moment to be sure of what she was seeing.

"I can't imagine," he murmured, "why you would want such a thing."

She looked directly into his eyes, and her smile deepened. "Why indeed?"

SHORTLY AFTER THE NEW YEAR, Augusta died. She went peacefully in her sleep and was laid to rest beside Rameses in the old slave cemetery. Philip had instituted the practice, never before followed at Calvert Oaks, of erecting stone tablets to mark the graves of slaves and former slaves who once would have had only wooden crosses to show where they lay. There were a few such still standing in the grave-yard, but most had long since disintegrated in the wind and rain. With them had gone the mute voices of men and women who had lived and died in obscurity, denied even the final solace of an enduring memorial.

That was no longer the case, but there was nonetheless a feeling of discomfort among the Calverts as they gathered beside Augusta's grave. They would have liked to bury her in the family cemetery, but she had refused, saying with simple dignity that she preferred to lie beside those whose station in life she had shared.

In the final days of that life, before she slipped into un-consciousness, Elizabeth had visited her often. She had sat beside the old woman's bed, sometimes reading from the Bible, sometimes merely holding her hand. Occasionally, they had talked.

Augusta's high, thin voice had spun out tales of birth and death, love and hate, peace and war. She had talked of people long gone, of events Elizabeth had barely heard about, in a final imparting of wisdom that would carry be-yond the grave.

"Now don' yo be worryin' none 'bout birthin' dat baby," she had counseled toward the end. "Yo Mommy knows jus' wha' t'do. Didn' ol' 'Gusta herself teach her?"

Standing in the graveyard, watching as the first few clumps of earth hit the plain wooden coffin—which Augusta had also insisted on—Elizabeth felt the child stir within her. She put her hand to her belly and, through the layers of muslin and cambric, savored the movement of new life.

"Don' yo shed no tears fo' me," Augusta had told her. "Ah's goin' to a better place dan dis sad ol' earth. Yo jus' raise dat baby up to do right and maybe by an' by de sadness go away."

Elizabeth wanted to believe that it could be so simple, but with Drake's return to Boston, her mood had turned somber. She found it increasingly difficult to get around, even though she was still several months from her confinement. Sunbird, whose baby was due only about a month after her own, was far smaller. When Elizabeth mentioned that to her mother, Sarah said only, "It's different for each woman. Sunbird is taller than you are, and her hips are slightly wider. That's why she seems smaller."

Elizabeth accepted that, for the moment, but when several more weeks passed and the difference between her and her sister-in-law became even more marked, she broached the subject again. "I feel absolutely huge," she said on a day when it was all she could do to rise from her bed. Walking up and down the stairs had become a chore, and as for bending over—that was something she had all but forgotten how to do. Tilly had taken to giving her thoughtful looks, but so far had made no comment, though Elizabeth suspected that her maid was finding such reticence difficult to endure.

Sarah had the same problem. Though she strove to hide it, she was becoming more and more concerned about her daughter. While it was true that Augusta had taught her a tremendous amount about childbirth, and that she had presided at dozens of deliveries, she had never before encountered a situation so near to her own heart, or one that puzzled her so much.

Like it or not, the fact was that Elizabeth was getting huge. Her belly had swelled to such proportions that Philip actually winced when he saw her. Drake was due back shortly, and Sarah had the distinct impression that he would find his welcome, at least from his father-in-law, less than warm. Such hostility was natural, she supposed, but it did not lessen her own concern.

"Tell me," she said as they sat in Elizabeth's bedroom one morning in February, "what you had to eat yesterday."

Dutifully, Elizabeth recited the list. Sarah had gotten her into the habit of paying strict attention to everything that went into her mouth. She forgot nothing, nor did she try to cheat. The list was honest, and it comprised only reasonable amounts of healthy foods.

"I don't understand it," her mother said at length. "If you were eating pastries, perhaps that would account for it. But you're hardly fat. On the contrary, your arms and face are thinner than before."

That, at least, reassured her. Without saying anything to Elizabeth, she had determined that her daughter did not seem to be holding excessive amounts of water, a danger Augusta had warned her about repeatedly. Her complexion was lovely, her hair shone with a special sheen, and she was—though she would not have believed it—quite beautiful, for a lady who appeared on the verge of giving birth to a child who wasn't anywhere near due.

"Would you mind," Sarah asked finally when she had run through her mental list of everything that might be wrong and come up blank, "if I took a look at you?"

Elizabeth shook her head. She was almost desperately glad of her mother's presence, particularly because she trusted her skill far more than that of the Dr. Greeleys of the world.

When Elizabeth had lain down on the bed, Sarah sat beside her and laid a hand gently on her enormous belly. She held it there for some time, her head tilted to one side, as though she were listening intently. Then she went further and actually leaned over, pressing her ear where her hand had been. As Elizabeth watched, puzzled, her mother moved her head over her abdomen, pausing in several places to listen.

Finally she straightened, a faintly bemused smile touching her lips. "I think I know why you're so big."

"Why?" Elizabeth asked, propping herself up on her elbows to look at her mother.

"Now I could be wrong...."

Elizabeth held her breath, girding herself for terrible news, which she would somehow have to cope with.

"I think you're carrying twins."

"T-twins...?"

Sarah nodded and touched her daughter's face with infinite tenderness. "As I said, I might be wrong, but I think I hear a heartbeat in two distinct places. That and your size point to twins."

Her brow knitted as she added, "You must take especially good care of yourself. Twins are liable to come early, and we don't want these two born before they're good-sized."

Elizabeth shook her head vigorously, determined there and then that she wouldn't stir out of bed until the children—children!—had safely arrived. But Sarah assured her that was carrying precautions too far. "You still need some exercise, taken prudently, of course. And fresh air is very important, as well."

She didn't add that it would be as well for Elizabeth not to be closed up in a single room, where she would be bound, despite their best efforts, to quickly run out of distractions.

Then she would dwell far too much on her condition, including what Sarah suspected was still a stormy relationship with Drake. Despite the congeniality between the two of them at Christmas, she had sensed an atmosphere of tension before he left. There was still a lot to be worked out there.

Elizabeth could think of little in the following days other than how Drake would react. She had thought of writing to him, but hated to impart such news in a letter, if only because it would mean missing his reaction. Over and over she played the scene in her mind: he would be astonished at first, even disbelieving, but then, after a few moments, he would be awed, even humbled by the extent of her accomplishment. He would sweep her off her feet. . . .

She laughed and shook her head wryly. Drake was very strong, but it would still be less a matter of sweeping and more a question of hoisting to get her bulk off the ground. Still, with the new upswept hairdo Tilly had contrived for her and the gowns made by her mother's seamstress in Richmond, she had to admit that she didn't look bad at all. Certainly well enough for a walk in the garden, where she could keep an eye out for the coach she hoped to see arriving at any time.

It was, for February, an unusually warm day. There was a tantalizing hint of early spring in the air. She carried her hat in her hand and let the caressing sun brush her face. A sense of well-being flowed through her with each breath she drew. She was enjoying the singularly simple but elusive pleasure of just being alive until a slight disturbance behind the yew hedge lured her from her thoughts.

She glanced toward it with no premonition of what she would see and was abruptly jerked from her reverie. Davey stepped from behind the hedge, dressed in a shirt and breeches, a wide-brimmed felt hat shading his features.

"I'm sorry to startle you," he said as he swept the hat off. He looked abashed, with a tentative smile that seemed to ask her not to be annoyed with him. "I was afraid if I came to the door, I'd be turned away."

"Most likely." With a conscious effort, she loosened the fingers that were clenching the brim of her own hat tightly enough to damage it. "You're not welcome in this house."

"Please, Elizabeth, don't be like that. I can understand why you would be, but just give me a few moments. All right?"

"For what? To insult me again?"

"I can't tell you how sorry I am about that. It's been troubling me ever since it happened. I behaved abominably."

"I hope you don't expect me to disagree?"

He shook his head. "You're perfectly right not to wish to speak with me."

Mollified, however reluctantly, by his apparent penitence, Elizabeth unbent slightly. Davey was, after all, her cousin, and she had once thought they would be more than that. Perhaps it wasn't altogether his fault that he had gone wrong in life. There might even still be a chance that he could be redeemed.

Davey was apparently hoping so, for he said, "You're the only one who can help me, Bethie. There's no one else I can even talk to."

With a sigh, she gestured to a nearby stone bench. "Let's sit down, shall we?"

He hastened to agree, springing forward to offer her his arm. "Yes, of course, you shouldn't be standing."

His reference, however oblique, to her condition brought a flush to her cheeks. Drake might find her bulk off-putting, but at least he would have the consolation of knowing that it was his children she was carrying. Davey had only the evidence of her possession by another man. Yet far from seeming dismayed by it, he appeared to be only concerned.

"Are you all right?" he asked as they sat down on the bench some little distance from the house and sufficiently hidden by the yew hedges as to be out of sight. Though she was willing enough to speak with him, Elizabeth doubted anyone else would approve. She would just as soon that neither Philip nor William knew of his presence.

"I'm fine," she assured him. "But thank you for asking."

"It's only natural for me to do so. We are family, after all."

She nodded slowly. "Yes, we are, but even the closest family can be fractured beyond repair by the sort of thing that's happened to us."

Davey sighed deeply. He sat slightly hunched over, as though the weight of what had gone before was too much for him to bear. His arm hung at his side, looking not so much like a deadweight as like something that simply didn't quite work correctly anymore. "It was all so stupid," he murmured.

"The duel?"

"And what led up to it." His face reddened, and he didn't look at her. "I was drunk, you know."

"Yes, I'd guessed that."

"Otherwise I never would have gone along with such a crazy scheme."

"It wasn't your idea...?" She had somehow thought that the attack on William and Sunbird had been of his initiating, but now that she thought about it, no one had actually said so.

"Of course not," he insisted, appearing genuinely shocked at the notion. "You'll understand that I can't say who suggested it—it's a question of honor—but I *can* assure you that harming Sunbird was the farthest thing from my mind."

"It was my understanding that you were aiming at William."

Davey flushed more deeply. "You're right, though I'm ashamed to admit it."

"Why on earth would you have wanted to hurt him?"

He turned and, for the first time, met her eyes directly. "Don't you know? William was the one who convinced you to go away. If you hadn't, you wouldn't have met Drake and married him. Instead, I might have had a chance with you. That was all I could think of. I know it was insane," he went on hurriedly, "but I truly couldn't help myself. Losing you was simply too much for me."

Elizabeth heard him out with growing astonishment. She'd had no idea that Davey had taken the situation so seriously. They had not, after all, been actually pledged to each other. "It was better," she said softly, "the way things worked out. Surely you realize that."

He nodded at once. "I was never the man for you. Drake is exactly what you need. If only I had accepted that sooner...." His voice trailed off as he slumped once again, the picture of a dejected and remorseful man.

Without pausing to think, Elizabeth laid her hand on his in a gesture of comfort. "There's nothing done that can't be undone. Why don't you talk to Father and William?"

"Because even if they could be convinced to see me, I'd have no idea what to say to them."

"You've explained it all to me quite well."

"That's different. I could always talk to you. No," he said, shaking his head, "I couldn't begin to approach them. But perhaps..."

"Perhaps what?"

"If we could be friends again, then I might feel confident enough to go to them. It's a great deal to ask, I know, but if you could somehow see your way clear to forgiving me...?"

"Of course I can." Elizabeth truly meant that, but she fully realized that others in her family might not feel the same way. "If only you hadn't actually wounded Sunbird...."

"It's perfectly ghastly, isn't it?"

"Still, she's a very nice person. I think she would forgive you, too."

"I would be forever grateful to her," Davey said humbly. "But as to William..."

"And Father."

"It's too much to expect that they would ever put what happened behind them."

"Not necessarily," Elizabeth said, intent on encouraging him. With even the possibility of reuniting the family, she could not let him weaken now. "It's simply a matter of how you ask them."

"I couldn't begin to try."

"Then I must convince you otherwise."

But Davey, sincere as he appeared to be, was hard to persuade. Both that day and the next, when they again met surreptitiously in the corner of the garden, he expressed fear at even the idea of approaching his uncle and cousin.

Still, she was glad enough to have him to distract her as the days passed and Drake did not return. Instead there was a telegram from him—frustrating in its brevity—that said: Delayed in Boston. Letter follows.

Elizabeth presumed rather sourly that his mother had staged some disturbance to keep him at her side, but when the letter arrived she discovered that was not the case. Though he clearly did not want to alarm her, Drake was frank in spelling out the reason for his extended stay.

"Mari did not ask me to intercede," he said, "but her difficulties with Gideon are such that, being her nearest male relative, I felt compelled to offer my assistance. He appears to be at the root of a campaign of harassment against her that runs the gamut from labor problems at her mills and various other concerns to sudden difficulties in shipping her goods. I am doing what I can to put a stop to this, but there are problems, because no one wants to admit what's going on. It appears that my best hope is to tackle Gideon directly."

At any rate, he had continued, he would do his utmost to wrap things up and be back in Virginia shortly. In the meantime, he trusted that she was in good health, and he remained her devoted husband.

The "devoted" raised Elizabeth's eyebrows. It was not a word she would have expected Drake to use. Yet he had done so, and she had to caution herself not to read too much into it. He might have dashed off the letter in a hurry and added the obligatory closing without much thought. Except that she was beginning to realize that he was always cautious in his dealings with other people and unlikely to express any emotion that was not well and truly founded.

That made it a little easier for her to accept his continued absence, though it rankled enough for her to look forward to Davey's secret visits. He came almost every day. Without speaking of it, they fell into the habit of meeting in the same place in the garden at the same time. So far as Sarah was concerned, her daughter had adopted the healthy habit of a regular stroll. Tilly knew better, but then, Tilly knew most things. This time, however, she would not content herself with mere disapproving sniffs.

"I suppose you know best," she said one morning when she was helping Elizabeth to dress. "But I saw some family feuds back home, and I can tell you, I wouldn't have tried to patch them up for all the world. That's thankless work, that is."

"We're not feuding," Elizabeth said, her voice muffled by the apricot silk dress that was being dropped over her head. Not even its ample folds concealed her bulk, but in its elegance it somehow managed to make her look fragile. Although she was conscientious about her diet, the babies were taking a significant toll on her. Whatever slight amount of spare flesh she had had was long gone. Her features were honed to their purest form, her shoulders and arms were delicate, and her legs had more than retained their slenderness.

"If it's not a feud," Tilly said, "then what is it, I'd like to know?"

"There was an incident, a very sad one. You must have heard some talk about it."

In fact, Tilly had heard all the details several times in several different versions. The servants had their own opinions about Mr. Davey, being about equally divided between those who felt he was genuinely bad and those who thought he was merely crazy. They did, however, all agree that he was obsessed with envy of the Calverts and would do anything he could to hurt them.

"All I know," Tilly said, "is that a man who's hurt one woman can hurt another. We've got them back in Ireland sure as they're anywhere. Me mum always said you can't trust them. They'll swear they're sorry and promise never to lift a hand again, but turn around and they'll be right back at the same thing."

"Davey isn't like that," Elizabeth insisted. She was growing impatient with her maid's insistence that her cousin could possibly present any danger to her. But then, Tilly had come from a hard background and was liable to suspect the worst until proved otherwise. Unlike Elizabeth, who was far more inclined to believe the best.

"He's genuinely sorry and wants nothing more than to be forgiven. It's only a matter of convincing him to speak to Father and William."

"If you say so, ma'am." Tilly clearly was no more ready to believe that than she was to believe that she had only to spread her arms in order to fly. But short of standing in the doorway to prevent Elizabeth from going out, there was no way she could stop her visits with Davey. If it did occur to her that simply going to Philip or William would do the job, she put that out of her mind at once. Her loyalty was to Elizabeth, and she would not betray her, not even for her own good.

A week passed, and the weather grew still warmer. Elizabeth took to walking farther from the house. She discovered that if she took things slowly and paused to rest often, she held up quite well. Davey encouraged her in this. He was forever telling her that exercise was important to her well-being. Rather to her surprise, he didn't hold to the traditional view that an expectant woman should stay off her feet. Instead he supported her determination to get about, albeit with prudent regard for the tiny beings growing inside her.

"Look at the darkies," he said one morning when they were walking by the river. "They work up to the last, drop their pickaninnies and are back in the fields before you can say boo. Doesn't do them any harm at all. On the contrary, if you let them lie about, it only leads to complications."

Elizabeth frowned. She was struck by the fact that Davey was speaking of the blacks as though they were still slaves. He might wish they were and even seek to treat them as such, but nothing could erase the great changes that had occurred. A force with tremendous momentum had been set in motion by the War, and though the final results might very well not be seen in their lifetimes, the interim effects still had to be dealt with. Attempting to deny them would only lead to further problems.

Besides that, he seemed, however subtly, to be equating her with his female field hands. She found that off-putting, not so much because of her attitudes, but because she knew Davey could only intend it as an insult. That finally convinced her that he was completely unaware of how his remarks could be interpreted and would be horrified if she pointed it out to him.

Which, of course, she did not. She was far too busy trying to build up his confidence so that he would agree to see her father or brother. That was proving to be a difficult task. To begin with, Davey seemed incapable of believing that she had truly forgiven him, even though she had told him so a dozen times.

"I don't see how you can," he said, after she had been driven yet again to repeat herself. "What I did to William and Sunbird was bad enough, but then, to insult you as I did at the church..."

"It really didn't bother me. I presumed you weren't yourself."

"Drake seemed quite angry."

"He was," Elizabeth admitted, wondering if Davey had any real idea how narrow his escape had been. "He's very protective."

"Is he?"

The note of doubt in Davey's voice brought Elizabeth up short. "Why do you ask?"

He hesitated, as though wrestling with himself. "I shouldn't...I don't have the right...but..." In a rush, he blurted, "Why isn't he here with you now, when you need him most?"

"There are problems in Boston that require his attention."

"I can't imagine anything more important than being with you."

"That's very sweet, but the fact is, not only am I perfectly healthy, but I'm with my family, where I'm continually looked after." That was no exaggeration. Her walks with Davey were a break from what amounted to constant attention. Much as she appreciated all their efforts, she had to admit that it was nice to get away a bit.

"Besides," she went on when Davey seemed inclined to pursue the subject, "Drake will be here shortly."

Her cousin stopped walking abruptly, forcing her to do the same. "You definitely expect him?"

Elizabeth nodded, pardoning herself silently for a small whiff of smugness. If Davey had thought her an unhappy wife, he was bound to be disappointed. She'd had another letter from Drake assuring her that he was doing everything possible to settle the problems between Mari and Gideon. Moreover, Mari herself had written to tell Elizabeth how grateful she was. She had reluctantly admitted to being ill recently and therefore unable to cope as well as she was used to doing. Drake had stepped in at the vital moment and proved an enormous help to her.

Glad though she was of that, Elizabeth was looking forward eagerly to his arrival. Her last communication from him had been a telegram telling her to expect him the following day. He was even passing up several important meetings in Washington to be there.

When she told Davey that, he looked suitably impressed. "I see . . . perhaps I've misjudged him."

"What do you mean?" Elizabeth asked, trying not to bridle at the suggestion that Drake might have done something wrong.

"Only that I didn't realize he was quite so devoted."

There was that word again, only this time it surprised Elizabeth less. She had come to realize that Drake *was* showing his devotion, first by doing his utmost to help Mari, whom he knew she loved, and then by putting his business interests second to his responsibilities as a husband and father.

"Drake has changed," she said, only fully realizing that for the first time. "So have I."

"Yes," Davey agreed, "you have." He was silent for a moment before he said, "Once he's back, we won't be able to meet anymore."

Elizabeth had been thinking the same thing. "Surely you're ready to see Father and William now?"

Davey shook his head. "I don't know...." At her frown, he added, "Don't be angry at me. I'm not like you, able to jump in headfirst. I never had your sort of confidence."

Her annoyance faded as she remembered a shy, gentle boy who had been battered between opposing forces of his family's expectations and the reality of an increasingly difficult situation that made them impossible to fulfill. "There's nothing to be afraid of," she said gently.

"I need more time to think. Only a little," he added quickly as she was about to point out to him that no great amount was left. "Away from here."

"What do you mean?" Surely Davey wasn't thinking of leaving. Running away from the problem was hardly the way to solve it.

To her relief, his intentions appeared far more modest. "Come for a carriage ride with me, like you used to. It will clear my head."

Elizabeth hesitated. Except for a brief trip to Richmond before Christmas, she had not left Calvert Oaks since her arrival. A change of scene would do her good, but she had to consider the welfare of her children.

As though he had read her thoughts, Davey said, "The river road was just repaired. It's as smooth as you could wish, and we'll take Old Ned and Dapples."

At the thought of the two aged nags, Elizabeth laughed. "It will certainly be a slow drive, then."

"You'll come?"

She considered a moment longer before deciding that, after all, there could be no harm.

"WHY, MR. DRAKE," Tilly said as she came down the stairs to the front hall, "you weren't expected until tomorrow."

"I got an earlier train," he explained, setting down his case and taking a quick look around. There was no sign of Elizabeth. He supposed she was upstairs resting.

Sarah had been in her sitting room going over the household accounts when she heard the carriage draw up. She smiled at the sight of her son-in-law. "Drake, how nice that you're early. How was Boston?"

"Difficult," he said with a grimace. He didn't want to think about the problems with Gideon, which he suspected would take a very long time to work out, if they ever did. The man was impossible: obsessed, unscrupulous, capable of the greatest infamy. When he thought of some of the stories he had heard about him, Drake's skin crawled. It was incredible that the lovely woman standing before him was sister to such a creature.

"I'll tell cook to fix something, shall I?" Tilly offered.

"Not for me," Drake said. "I ate earlier. Besides I'd rather see Elizabeth. Where is she?"

Sarah started to answer, presuming that her daughter was walking in the garden, as was her custom at that hour. But a quick, negative movement of Tilly's head stopped her.

"Why, I'm not sure," she said instead. "Tilly?"

The maid looked singularly uncomfortable, but she stood her ground and, in a tone that made her disapproval clear, said, "She's gone for a ride with him."

Sarah and Drake exchanged a quick, perplexed glance. "A ride?" Drake repeated disbelievingly.

"A carriage ride," Tilly clarified.

"With whom?" Sarah asked.

The maid's mouth pursed. "That Mr. Davey."

"Oh, no, that's impossible."

"I'm sorry, ma'am, but it's the truth."

"I don't understand," Drake said. "What earthly reason would she have for getting anywhere near him, much less going off for a carriage ride?"

"They've been talking," Tilly said. "She told me about it. He claims he's sorry for what he did and wants to get back in with the family, but was afraid of what would happen if he tried. She's been trying to convince him that Mr. Philip and Mr. William would forgive him."

Sarah shook her head disbelievingly. "Forgive him? He should be grateful simply to still be alive and leave it at that."

Drake's hands were clenched at his sides. A dark flush stained his lean cheeks as he turned toward the door. "I'm going after her."

Sarah grasped his arm. "Wait. William and Philip are in the fields. I'll send for them. They'll know where he's most likely to have taken her. Otherwise, you're liable to go off in the wrong direction."

Drake knew she was right; he didn't know the area around Calvert Oaks well enough to have much chance of finding Elizabeth. But the need to wait even a few minutes was all but intolerable. He was saddled and waiting in front of the house when the other two men rode up.

"What's this about Bethie?" Philip demanded without dismounting. He and William had been inspecting a new levee built to drain future tobacco fields. The work was progressing well, and they'd been about to move on when the houseman Sarah had sent caught up with them.

"She's gone with Davey," Sarah explained hurriedly. "They're in a carriage. She may be perfectly safe, but..."

Philip didn't wait to hear more. He dug his spurs into the flanks of his mount and sent him galloping hard down the gravel road. Drake and William followed just as quickly. Behind them the sky was turning gray with an approaching storm.

Sarah watched them go, her hands clasped before her and her eyes dark with worry. Sunbird had come out of the house and was standing next to her, equally concerned. Both women wanted to believe that it was possible Davey meant no harm, but neither had any real confidence that was the case. Sunbird thought of the hatred with which he had attacked them that night in the carriage, and shivered. She wrapped her arms around herself and, closing her eyes against the winter sun, said a silent prayer that Elizabeth would escape unharmed.

Beside her, Sarah did the same. All she could think of was her daughter, heavy with a difficult pregnancy and in the hands of a man who might mean her terrible harm. Her whole body clenched as she struggled not to cry out with the outrage of a mother who would suffer any pain rather than have it inflicted on her child. Yet she was helpless to prevent whatever Davey intended. All she could do was wait, and pray.

Elizabeth had come to much the same conclusion. She sat crouched on the dirt floor of the cabin to which Davey had brought her, trying hard to control her fear. It couldn't be good for the babies, but then, neither was anything that had happened in the past few hours.

At first the carriage ride had seemed perfectly normal. Davey had kept up a stream of innocuous conversation as they moved sedately along the river road, drawn by the two plodding old horses. With the sun-warmed air and the steady motion of the carriage, Elizabeth had come close to nodding off, until a cool breeze redolent of a change in the weather had roused her, and she had abruptly realized that they were leaving the road, turning onto a small, rutted lane that ran back toward Quail Run.

"Why are we going this way?" she asked, clinging to the side of the carriage to keep from being roughly tossed around.

He didn't answer, but kept his eyes straight ahead. The hands that grasped the reins were white at the knuckles. The ominous set of his shoulders told Elizabeth more than she wanted to know.

"Davey, why are you doing this?"

"Be quiet," he said, finally driven to respond.

"I don't understand...."

He turned on her, his face red with what could have been either fear or fury, "Shut up! I don't want to hear anything you might say. You've always been able to talk your way around me, get me to do whatever you wanted. It won't work this time. If I have to, I'll gag you."

Elizabeth's lips parted in a shocked reflex, but instantly she clamped them together. Every instinct she possessed told her that Davey was deadly serious and that it would take very little to provoke him into carrying out his threat.

They rode on for perhaps half an hour, going deeper and deeper into the woods surrounding the part of Quail Run that had always been left in its natural state. Above them the sky continued to darken. The wind had shifted, bringing with it leaden clouds. Elizabeth shivered in her thin dress and wrapped her shawl more tightly around herself.

At length they came to a small, ramshackle cabin, where Davey pulled the carriage to a halt. "Get down," he ordered as he jumped to the ground and tied the horses to a nearby tree.

It was utterly beyond Elizabeth to do as he said. She wanted to obey him, if only to avoid further trouble, but the distance to the ground was four feet, with only a small step in between, and while she could easily have managed it in her normal state, in her present condition it might as well have been miles. Briefly she considered making the attempt, but knew that there was no way she could safely ease her bulk down without losing her balance and risking serious injury.

Davey saw her predicament and frowned. He was clearly reluctant to help her, but when he tried to bully her with further threats she simply shook her head. "I can't. Surely you can see that."

"All I can see," he said as he reached out for her, "is that you let that goddamn Yankee have you and you deserve anything you get for it."

Elizabeth shivered as much from the hatefulness of his words as from the rough intent of his hands. He handled her with nearly ostentatious contempt, as though he needed to convince both of them that she was nothing to him. The moment her feet touched the ground he thrust her away from him, so that she fell heavily against the carriage and only with difficulty regained her balance.

"Come on," he said, heading toward the cabin. For a moment Elizabeth considered the possibility of escape. She wondered if she had made a mistake getting down from the carriage, but there had been no way for her to grasp the reins, and without them she could not compel the horses to do her bidding. On foot, she had no hope of eluding Davey. She wouldn't even reach the edge of the clearing before he would catch her.

A dull sense of inevitability threatened to overwhelm her. She fought it down determinedly, letting anger rise in its place, but not to such a point that it would become uncontrollable. She must at all costs keep control of herself. That was her only hope of containing Davey and whatever he intended to do.

"What's the purpose of this?" she asked as they entered the cabin. "You must know that my father and William will come looking for me."

"I'm counting on that."

"W-what do you mean?"

He kicked a corner of the mat that was crumpled in a corner and watched imperviously as a rat scampered out. "The mistake I made last time was in going to them, or to William, at least. I tried to fight honorably, when I should have realized that can't be done when the enemy is a man with no sense of honor, so this time I'm forcing them to come to me."

His words sank into Elizabeth's mind slowly, bringing with them a meaning she could not evade, though she desperately wanted to. They would come into the clearing, with its complete lack of cover, where they would be easy targets for the three rifles propped beside the window. She stared at them and swallowed with great difficulty. "You're mad."

She said the same thing several hours later when her body had grown stiff with waiting and her mind ached from the necessity to keep from screaming at him. She had to think of the babies, had to keep calm, had to find some way out. Except there was none. Davey watched her too carefully, even as he kept one eye on the clearing and the forest beyond.

"Probably," he said with the same lack of expression that had come to frighten her. "I've often thought so. But then, it's a mad world." His smile defied her to try to convince him otherwise.

Yet she had to make the attempt. Ignoring the ache in her belly that had grown worse with the passing hours, she managed to stand up by pressing her shoulders against the rough plank wall and slowly straightening her legs. The effort taxed her breath and made it impossible for her to speak for several moments.

Finally she said, "Your parents... I can't believe they would want this."

"That doesn't matter."

"But it must! You love them." At least she prayed that he did and had not become immune to all emotion other than hate.

The chill sound of his laughter dashed that hope. "Love? I don't have any idea what that means. I did once, but I found out it was only an illusion. Besides," he went on, fingering the stock of one of the rifles, "why should I care about them? My father is a drunkard who spends his few sober moments fantasizing about a past he helped to destroy, and my mother, while she may mean well, is completely incapable of dealing with reality. She has to have her pretty gowns every bit as much as Father has to have his bourbon. Between them they caused my birthright to be sold out from under me before I was old enough to do anything to stop it."

Elizabeth desperately wanted to contradict him, but knew that she could not. He had described the situation all too accurately. She was only surprised that he understood it so well, having believed that he blamed *her* parents for his misfortune, rather than his own.

A moment later she discovered that she had been at least half right after all. "Of course," he said, "nothing my father's done equals the crimes yours has perpetrated. He took advantage of his own brother-in-law's weakness to make himself wealthy. He's a traitor and a thief. I only regret that he'll die quickly."

The enormity of his madness struck Elizabeth. A thousand words to contradict him clamored in her mind, but she could utter none of them. Instead, she had to turn away, bile burning the back of her throat, and lean her head against the wall. Another cramp seized her, making her moan.

"What's wrong?" Davey demanded.

"Nothing." She gasped the word and was unable to stop herself from pressing a hand to herself in a gesture he could not ignore.

"Don't lie to me. It's that brat you're carrying, isn't it? You're not going to have it here, are you?"

Elizabeth shook her head; she sincerely prayed not. "It's too soon."

His gaze spanned the considerable width of her belly. "Doesn't look that way."

"You don't understand. There are two...." She broke off as a brilliant finger of lightning briefly illuminated the cabin. It was followed by a crack of thunder that would have drowned out anything she might have said. In its aftermath, a cold, pelting rain began to fall.

"Please," she whispered over the drumbeat of the rain, "you have to let me go."

He shook his head before she had even finished speaking. "Go ahead, drop the brat here. I wouldn't mind watching you suffer. Besides, it won't make any difference in the end. We'll all be dead."

"A-all...?"

"You don't think I expect to get out alive, do you? Your father and William won't come without help. Somebody'll get me, but it doesn't matter. Before I go, I'll take care of them—and you."

"Oh, God..." She doubled over, holding her belly, as another moan was torn from her. The realization that she was in labor coupled with the knowledge that he did not intend to let her children live came close to driving her to her knees. Only with the greatest effort did she remain upright, fighting the waves of pain that threatened to overcome her reason.

At all costs, she had to hold on and not panic. There was still a chance, however slim. The storm might actually work to her advantage. In the dim light, her father and William would be better able to approach the cabin without being seen. Unless the lightning that flashed with increasing frequency gave away their position.

Which was not to say that they were necessarily any-where nearby. She had to remember that, lest she delude herself with false hope. Her absence must surely have been discovered by now, and Tilly would have revealed whom she had gone with. But Quail Run's property was still extensive, despite parcels having been sold off, and it would take hours, if not days, to search it properly. She wondered if Davey had thought of that, and how long he would wait before turning his wrath on her.

If Davey had not, Philip had. He quickly dismissed the notion that Elizabeth might be in the main house; whatever differences he had with his brother-in-law, and they were ample, he still could not see Jeremy acquiescing in a kid-napping. Nor would Kitty have permitted it. His sister might be very far from the ideal plantation mistress, but she still knew every inch of her domain and would instantly spot anything unusual, which made it unlikely that Elizabeth could be hidden in one of the dependencies near the house. She had to be some distance away.

"He may not be here at all," William said, his voice thick with worry. "He could have headed downriver, perhaps in-tending to catch a steamer. They could be anywhere."

"That's not likely," Philip said with a quick shake of his head. "Any man traveling with a heavily pregnant and un-willing woman would quickly come under suspicion. Whatever story he concocted, he'd run the risk of being stopped at least long enough for us to be summoned."

"Then he has to be nearby," Drake agreed. "But where?" They had stopped at a crossroads, one branch of which ran off toward the river, while the other turned in the opposite direction, going deeper into a copse of trees that thickened out into a forest. It was raining heavily, and a cold wind had sprung up. Winter was returning with a vengeance. The jacket he had donned that morning had quickly been soaked, along with his shirt and breeches, but he was oblivious to any discomfort. His thoughts were focused solely on Elizabeth and whatever might be happening to her.

The possibilities tortured him. He wanted to lash out violently at anyone and anything. Each passing moment made it more and more difficult for him to hold on to his self-control.

"Why are we stopping here?" he demanded. "We're wasting time."

"I'm trying to remember something," Philip explained. He was as anxious as Drake was, perhaps more so, since he had a better idea of his daughter's condition than her husband did. But he understood that to rush haphazardly in any direction would avail them nothing. Reason far more than rage was needed to save Elizabeth.

"There was a small cabin not too far from here," Philip said. "I can remember playing there with Jeremy when we were both boys."

"Is it possible it's still standing?" William asked above the rush of the rain.

Philip nodded. "It was well enough built. If it wasn't deliberately torn down, it should still be there. All I have to do is remember exactly where...." His voice trailed off as he concentrated fully, seeing in his mind's eye the golden days of his boyhood, when life had seemed so uncomplicated. That had been an illusion, of course, but one he could still appreciate. He was grateful that, despite all the upheavals since then, he had been able to give his daughter the same kind of childhood. She was the fruit of his greatest love, and there was nothing he would not do for her.

"We'll find her," he said grimly. "And when we do..."

"He's mine," Drake said, quietly and implacably. Philip looked at him for a long, intent moment before he nodded.

They moved on, taking the road that led into the forest. In the twilight dimness of the storm, they could see little. Nothing moved except the men and their horses. It was as though all other life had gone to ground, hiding from the forces nature had unleashed.

Elizabeth wished that she could do the same. She was caught between forces within and without her, but it was the turmoil of her own body that frightened her the most. More even than her fear of Davey was her terror that the children would come too early. Her mother had said that each day she gained was vital to the twins' survival. Born this long before their time, they would have little chance. Yet the pains remorselessly gripping her with greater and greater frequency made it clear that her womb might too soon give up its precious burden.

"Don't do this," she whispered, uncertain whether she was pleading with her maddened cousin or with God himself. "Please, let them live."

If Davey heard her, he gave no sign. He was staring intently out the single window, struggling to see through the storm. "They're coming," he muttered. "I can feel it."

"It's not too late," she said, raising her voice so that he had to hear her. "You can still let me go."

This time he responded. His hand lashed out and cracked across her cheek, knocking her head into the wall. *"Shut up!"*

Elizabeth bit her lip hard, tasting the iron tang of blood. Her head throbbed, and her face burned. Davey continued to loom over her threateningly for a moment before abruptly jerking himself away. He returned to his vigil at the window, grasping one of the rifles, with the other two ready at his side.

She was staring at them, trying to convince herself that she had a chance of reaching one and firing it before he could react, when the sound of a horse's neighing reached her over the storm. Davey heard it at the same moment and smiled triumphantly.

"I told you they would come."

Denial shrieked in Elizabeth's mind even as she knew he was right. Her father and brother were somewhere nearby, within range of his guns. All he had to do was spot them. She opened her mouth to scream a warning, but he caught the movement and slammed a hand down over her lips and nose, effectively cutting off her air. She struggled frantically as a ringing noise began in her ears and darkness threatened to engulf her. Not until she had gone limp did he let her slide down onto the floor. She was lying there, struggling to recover, as he said, "Try that again and I'll kill you now. A few more minutes either way won't matter to me."

Elizabeth believed him. He was beyond any hope of mercy. Already he seemed to have slipped away from life to stand on the side of death, where he intended to take her and all those she loved. Except, she thought thankfully, for Drake. In the midst of the most terrible darkness, she could be grateful that he was not there. He, at least, would survive, though he would do it never knowing how much he had meant to her.

"Only three of them," Davey murmured. "I thought there would be more."

Three? Elizabeth dared his wrath to peer out the window, seeing through the swirling rain the shapes of three men on horseback at the edge of the woods. Two she recognized at once: her father and William. The third she tried to deny but could not.

Drake. Her heart thrilled to the knowledge of his nearness, even as she was filled with dread. He shouldn't be there. She had been counting on his being safe. He wasn't, and that realization broke the last slim bonds of her self-control. As Davey raised his gun, she threw herself at him—clumsily, because of her bulk, but with considerable effect, for all that. Knocked off balance, he struggled to remain upright and to throw her off. The effort was too much; as she grabbed for his arm, the gun went off with a sharp report that seemed to echo through the clearing and far beyond, into the cloud-strewn heavens.

Drake thought what he heard was thunder. Philip and William believed the same. Seconds passed before all three realized that was not the case. Heedless of their own safety, they hurled their horses forward. Drake reached the cabin first. He flung himself from the saddle and thrust his full weight against the door. It gave so easily that he stumbled and might have fallen had not Philip and William, who were directly behind him, grabbed him and held him upright.

The scene that met their eyes had a certain dreamlike quality. Elizabeth stood by the window, the rifle in her hands. From below her breasts, across her swollen belly and as far down as the hem of her gown there was a blood-red swath that appeared almost to cut her in two.

The blood was Davey's. He lay at her feet, his eyes closed and his features in repose. He might have been asleep, except that half his head was blown away.

Drake reached Elizabeth first. He took the rifle from her and set it against the wall with the others, then wrapped his arms around her and held her close, murmuring to her gently. She made no response, and fear grew in him. Shielding her from the horrible sight at her feet, he gathered her up and carried her to a far corner of the cabin, where Philip hurriedly spread out his cloak. She stirred slightly when she was laid on it, and the eyes that had been staring sightlessly blinked.

"D-Drake?"

"I'm here, my love. It's all over. Don't be afraid." She was so pale that it might have been she instead of her cousin who lay dead. At the thought of that, terror filled him, and he clasped her close again, only to abruptly release her when he felt the sudden tightening of her belly. "Elizabeth . . . ?"

She exhaled on a harsh, long-drawn sigh. "Oh, my love, I'm so sorry. . . ."

Then William was racing for the door, Philip was saying something Drake could not understand, and there were only the night and the storm, seemingly without end.

SUNLIGHT FLOODED the room where the scent of roses lingered. A fresh breeze fluttered the white curtains. Elizabeth stirred and opened her eyes. She looked down the length of her body clear to her toes and smiled. Her hand drifted wonderingly over her nearly flat belly and her smile deepened.

In the chair beside the bed, Drake stirred. He had refused to leave her side, despite Sarah's best efforts to convince him that Elizabeth was all right. His lean jaws were unshaved, and his hair bore the marks of a hand passed through it many times. Elizabeth glanced down at that hand, lying dark against the pale fawn of his breeches, and saw the marks her teeth had made. She grimaced and reached out to touch him lightly.

He was instantly awake, coming alert with the reflexes of a man who has been followed into sleep by his waking cares. His eyes were shadowed with concern as they settled on her. "Elizabeth...?"

"I'm fine," she assured him quickly, then paused for a moment and assessed her true condition. She hurt, but so little, in comparison to the sea of pain she had passed through, that the discomfort was inconsequential. Her stomach growled, and she smiled. "I'm hungry."

He looked at her disbelievingly for a moment, then straightened quickly. "I'll get you something right away."

"Wait a moment. First I want to see them."

"Them . . ." He paused, swept by remembered wonder, and his smile matched her own. "They holler a lot."

Joy flooded her. "They're strong, thank God."

"And your mother." It had been Sarah's skill, passed down from Augusta, that had prevented the twins from coming the night Davey died. As the storm had raged, she had come from Calvert Oaks with herbs that she brewed and gave to Elizabeth to drink. Then she had sat holding her hand and, Drake did not doubt, praying, until slowly but surely the contractions had stopped. Not until the next day had they felt safe in removing Sarah from the cabin, carrying her back home on a litter.

Four weeks later, long after Davey's death had been ruled accidental and he had been buried, Elizabeth's labor began again. This time there was no stopping it, nor had Sarah tried. She recognized that the twins were ready and bent her efforts to helping her daughter bring them into the world. The labor had been long and hard, lasting from one night into the next. But toward the second dawn the first small, slippery morsel of humanity had entered the world.

"A girl," Sarah had exclaimed, holding up the baby for Drake to see. He had remained at Elizabeth's side, wishing desperately that he could take her pain on himself and marveling at the courage with which she bore it. Barely had he begun to comprehend that he had a daughter than he also had to deal with the fact of a son, smaller than the first child, but no less vigorous.

Remembering, he was smiling broadly when Sarah knocked at the bedroom door. She held one of the babies; a widely grinning Tilly had the other. "Little Miss Catherine wants to be fed," the maid announced as she followed Sarah into the room. "Mr. James already had his." Elizabeth had reluctantly accepted her mother's advice and engaged a wet nurse to help feed the children. Tiny as they were, Sarah had predicted that they would have ample appetites. At the first fierce tugging by her daughter at her nipple, Elizabeth realized that she had been right.

She lay back against the pillows, holding the baby close, and gazed down into the small, wrinkled face. There was no sign of incipient beauty there, but Elizabeth needed none. She already adored her daughter, as she did her son. Drake was holding him, watched over by a cautious Tilly, who looked ready to leap the moment he showed the slightest incompetence. Rather to his own surprise, he was proving more than adequate to the task.

Sarah watched them both, a smile playing around her lips. She had been up all night keeping a close eye on the babies and should have felt tired, but instead she was exhilarated. With the dawn, she had at last allowed herself to believe that both her grandchildren were healthy and fit. The miracle of that blessing swept over her. Silently, she beckoned to Tilly, and together they slipped out of the room.

Neither Drake nor Elizabeth noticed that they had gone, but then, they had been barely aware of their presence to start with. The wonder of their children absorbed them completely. Long, timeless moments passed before Drake said softly, "I want them to have everything. All the love, security and happiness I never knew." He frowned. "But I'm not sure I know how to give that to them."

Elizabeth looked at him, holding his son so gently. She remembered the night before, his strength and his tenderness. He knew more than he thought he did, but she was not averse to his learning more.

"I'll show you," she said, and reached out her hand to him.

Sarah

MAURA SEGER

Sarah wanted desperately to escape the clutches of her cruel father.
Philip needed a mother for his son, a mistress for his plantation.
It was a marriage of convenience.
Then it happened. The love they had tried to deny suddenly became a
blissful reality... only to be challenged by life's hardships and brutal
misfortunes.

Available NOW at your favorite retail outlet or send your name, address, zip or postal code along with
a check or money order for $4.70 (includes 75¢ for postage and handling) payable to Worldwide Library to:

In the U.S.	In Canada
Worldwide Library	Worldwide Library
901 Fuhrmann Blvd.	P.O. Box 609
Box 1325	Fort Erie, Ontario
Buffalo, NY 14269-1325	L2A 5X3

Please specify book title with your order.

 WORLDWIDE LIBRARY

SAR-1R

A breathtaking roller coaster of adventure,
passion and danger in the dazzling
Roaring Twenties!

SCANDALOUS SPIRITS

ERIN YORKE

Running from unspeakable danger, she found shelter—and desire—
in the arms of a reckless stranger.

Available in January at your favorite retail outlet. or reserve your copy for December shipping by sending your
name. address. zip or postal code along with a check or money order for $5.25 (include 75¢ for postage and
handling) payable to Worldwide Library to:

In the U.S.	In Canada
Worldwide Library	Worldwide Library
901 Fuhrmann Blvd.	P.O. Box 609
Box 1325	Fort Erie. Ontario
Buffalo. NY 14269-1325	L2A 5X3

Please specify book title with your order.

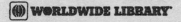 **WORLDWIDE LIBRARY**

SCA-1

**In the spellbinding tradition
of Barbara Taylor Bradford, a novel of
passion, destiny and endless love.**

Season of Loving

Shirley Larson

He possessed everything: wealth, power, privilege—everything except the woman he desired and the son he loved
more than life itself.

Available in February at your favorite retail outlet, or reserve your copy for January shipping
by sending your name, address, zip or postal code, along with a check for $4.70 (includes
75¢ for postage and handling) payable to Worldwide Library to:

In the U.S.	In Canada
Worldwide Library	Worldwide Library
901 Fuhrmann Boulevard	P.O. Box 609
Box 1325	Fort Erie, Ontario
Buffalo, NY 14269-1325	L2A 5X3

Please specify book title with your order.

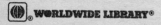 **WORLDWIDE LIBRARY®**

SEA-1